Praise for Em

"... commendably brisk ... superior fantasy"
- Publishers Weekly

Diana Hignutt is a master at the intersection of fantasy and science fiction…slathered in high wattage entertainment…a smelting furnace of fantasy suspense written with a crisp tone loaded with energetic intensity. Ms. Hignutt has upped the ante for writing fantasy/science fiction.

The author blends Druidic mysticism and folklore fantasy, with a liberal sprinkling of the metaphysical to keep her story moving at a break neck pace.
-Midwest Book Review

Empress of Clouds

Book 2 of the Moonsword Trilogy

by

Diana Hignutt

Behler™
PUBLICATIONS
California

Behler Publications
California

Empress of Clouds
A Behler Publications Book

This is a work of fiction. Names, characters, places, and incidents either are the product of the author's imagination or are used fictitiously. Any resemblance to actual persons, living or dead, events, or locales is entirely coincidental.

Cover design by Sun Son – www.sunsondesigns.com

This is a work of fiction. Names, characters, places, and incidents either are the product of the author's imagination or are used fictitiously. Any resemblance to actual persons, living or dead, events, or locales is entirely coincidental.

Library of Congress Cataloging-in-Publication Data is available
Control Number: 2004104974

SECOND EDITION

ISBN 0-9748962-4-1
Published by Behler Publications, LLC
Lake Forest, California
www.behlerpublications.com

Manufactured in the United States of America

For Liz

PART I

THE PRINCESS

Chapter 1

Prince Kelvris of Lorm was afraid. He was not terror-stricken by any means, but he rode in a state of uneasiness that nagged him. *Am I doing the right thing?*

It was a hard, cold December night, and the ground echoed sharply with each fall of his horse's hooves. The north wind whispered its bitter chill through the tall pines and bare oaks surrounding the deserted road—that and the occasional snapping of limbs from gusts or frozen sap were the only sounds he could hear. The icy air stung his lungs when he inhaled. He was shivering, not so much from the cold, for he was well protected by rich furs, but from his trepidation over the thing he was doing and the person he was going to meet. He slowed his horse. Maybe this was a mistake.

Kelvris was twenty-seven years old; he was tall, handsome, witty, ambitious, and, he had to admit, bitter. He liked to think he was doing this for the good of Lorm, for the good of the House of Hemris—that he was making things right and proper again. He was aware there was a certain jealousy at work in his thinking but only to a degree; he could only be so jealous of his cousin. Thoughts of her brought out more of his dwindling resolve to carry out his task. *Tolian has no right to the throne. I am the rightful heir.*

At first, Prince Kelvis was sure he was going to be given what he felt was rightly his. Was his uncle, the King, insane? Did he not know their kingdom would be the joke of the entire civilized world if Tolian ascended to the throne? It boggled Kelvris's mind that the old man would even consider such a thing. The prince would be damned if he would allow a woman to take the Warrior's Throne of Lorm. He assured himself it would only be treason if he were caught. And he was too smart to get caught. He tightened his grip on the reins and kicked his mount to greater speed. *That bastard better be there.*

He had never met his fellow conspirator, but he had heard many of the legends and stories about him. Until last year, he did not even believe he existed. A lot of things had changed during the last year. When the prince got the message from him two months ago, he almost dismissed it as a hoax. There was something in the messenger's eyes, though—the boy was as frightened as anyone he had ever seen. The paper, ink, and handwriting all possessed that otherworldly quality, a vague shimmer of alien nature Kelvris had come to recognize as faerie. The note was brief and to the point. He had long since destroyed it, lest it fall into the wrong hands and incriminate him, but he had burned every word into his mind:

"Good Prince Kelvris,

Hail to thee, who could be Lorm's king, if you have the courage and ambition. Meet me at the Well of Aslor on the first New Moon of December, at midnight, if you would see your country spared the folly of a woman-king. I have a plan that will solve problems for both of us. Come alone. Tell no one.

Your Faithful Servant,

Dowbreth."

Kelvris had a great many questions, of course. Not to mention reservations. Why did the faerie warlord even care who the heir to the Lormian throne was? Why would he suspect Kelvris would be interested in any such schemes of power? It was true enough that Kelvris had made no secret of his unhappiness at the King's announcement to his circle of friends at court, initially at least. Still, it seemed difficult to believe that word had somehow made its way to the realm of the faerie folk. For a while after he received the message, he feared that others closer to the palace might have heard tell of his grumblings. No one seemed to. What did Dowbreth expect to gain? What was his plan? Kelvris hoped murder wouldn't be necessary. He wasn't sure he could do that to his cousin. She had saved the world, after all. For that matter, he wasn't even sure she could be killed. And what about the baby, Relinder? He, too, was now ahead of Kelvris in the line of succession. With Dowbreth's fearsome reputation, the prince was certain whatever plan the Elven chieftain had, it would be thorough and prone to success.

So, it was a mixture of ambition and curiosity that, against his better judgment, brought Prince Kelvris out so late on the night of the first New Moon in December. Around the road, the taller trees became sparse and gave way to a copse of mountain laurel, the leaves of which were curled tightly together like needles in the cold, moonless night. They shivered and rustled in the icy gusts that bit at Kelvris's cheeks. The druids were predicting a harsh winter and the prince was inclined to believe them. How long had he been riding? His best estimate was about two hours. He should be nearing the well soon.

Why would Dowbreth pick the Well of Aslor for their meeting? It was obviously not for Kelvris's convenience that was clear. The long trek on such a night was sure to discourage all but the most stalwart spies. The well was ancient. There were no records or stories of its builders. It was there long before the Lormians settled these lands. Kelvris remembered a story of particular relevance to him that night. He only remembered the fewest details. When the first Lormians came to their country, more a band of warring barbarian tribes than anything else, they fell in love with the wild land and sought to establish themselves there. An Elven lord had laid claim to the land as his own, however, and refused to allow the settlers even passage through his territory. The Lormian warlords agreed that whichever one of them could defeat the Elven lord would be the rightful king of all the tribes. It was told that seventeen of the wild chieftains were slain before Threld, who was the first king of Lorm, bested the fierce faerie warrior at the Well of Aslor.

The Well of Aslor. Kelvris had never ascribed any truth to the old tale, of course. Myth. Legend. Nonsense. Now the story was making the hairs on the back of his neck stand on end.

The mountain laurel gave way to a small field to the right of the road. Kelvris had only been there once before, but he recognized it as the site of the well. He cautiously turned his horse off the road; the loud clop of the horse's hooves was immediately softened and cushioned by the dead grass. He peered into the darkness; he could just discern the outline of the well, now little more than a great pile of rocks and rubble in the midst of the field. There was no one else evident. He was alone as far as he could tell.

Without warning, a rough blow came from behind. He tumbled off his horse and fell to the cold hard ground with a thud. He had hardly time to register what had happened when someone jerked him up by the collar and thrust a lantern towards his face, blinding him.

"Prince Kelvris?"

The voice caught Kelvris off guard. He was familiar with the accent and the otherworldly timbre by now. He had heard other faerie folk since the Battle of Lorm, but this voice was different. It hissed the question with such violence it was as though the thinnest of veils held a torrent of wrath in check, and the voice itself would rip him to shreds if it could. The light from the lantern blinded him. He felt his attacker's impatience like a strange force ready to crush the life out of him if he did not answer. He fought through his fear to force some kind of answer past his trembling lips. "Y-y-yes."

"You are Kelvris of Lorm?" the savage voice asked from within the light.

"I am Prince Kelvris of the House of Hemris, nephew to the king." His voice wavered.

"Then, perhaps, Lorm would be better off with a woman-king," grunted the voice.

Kelvris was pulled to his feet and the light removed from his eyes. He squinted, but he was still blind for a moment or two. "Yes, well, you rather caught me off guard, there, that's all," he said.

He rubbed his eyes. The spots of light across his vision faded. The faerie loomed before him. He was by far the tallest person Kelvris had ever seen. He had to stand at least eight feet high. The prince got only the briefest glimpse of the fellow's face before the lantern was put out. Bright red eyes set deep and narrow. A scar across the nose and cheek. Teeth filed to sharp points. The unearthly pallor of the faerie. Then the blackness of the night again. Kelvris gulped.

"Lord Dowbreth?"

"I am Dowbreth of the Sidhe."

The faerie's voice was audibly calmer. The Lormian sighed. "So we meet at last," Kelvris said, unsure of the exact protocol for the situation.

Silence.

"It certainly is cold out here," the prince pointed out in an awkward attempt at small talk.

Silence, still.

Kelvris felt Dowbreth's stare. It made his skin crawl and his hands shake.

"Look," he said finally, "I received your message. I'm here. Maybe we could attempt to communicate like civilized people and get down to business."

"Do you wish to be king?" the faerie asked.

"I'm here aren't I?" returned Kelvris, attempting to bring a little courage and power to his voice.

"When do the Yule Jarrels begin?" Dowbreth asked.

"The Yule Jarrels? What difference does that make?"

"When?" Dowbreth demanded in a harsh whisper.

"Um, the fourth day before the Solstice," replied Kelvris.

"I shall come to the palace on the third day; you need only do two things for me," said the faerie warrior. "Take this vial and add its contents to the Jarrels wine immediately after I arrive."

Kelvris shook his head in the darkness. "I can't poison everyone," he said. "I can't do that."

"No one will be hurt; the drug causes only sleep. Try it on a dog first if you do not believe me," Dowbreth said.

"All right," said Kelvris, taking the vial. "I can live with that. What else?"

"I will give you a signal, and you will give this bracelet to your cousin. You must be sure to put it on her right away. Stay near her after you have drugged the wine and watch for my signal. If you fail in this, all is lost." Dowbreth slipped the bracelet into the prince's gloved hand.

"That's it?" Kelvris asked. "That's all I have to do? How is that going to make me king?"

"You must trust me, Your Highness. I will do the rest."

"Are you going to kill her?" asked the Lormian.

"No, I need her alive. But she will be no more trouble to you," answered Dowbreth.

Chapter 2

Princess Tolian had few friends at the palace that Yule and she felt the lack of friends acutely. She could understand people's difficulty with her situation, but that didn't ease her hurt and loneliness. She was an awkward presence in the lives of those around her. Many people resented her, and she knew it. In general, the men were discomforted and displeased by her femininity, angered by her acceptance of it, and furious over her status as heir to the throne. Tolian noticed these feelings—expressed most by members of the noblest houses of the court—diminished and blended with curiosity and lust amongst the army and peasant folk. They all respected her power, her strength, and the fact that she had saved them all in the Battle of Lorm last year, though some of the women tended toward some measure of jealously. Tolian suspected their jealousy arose from the fact that she, once a he, had saved them all and now, as a woman, was more powerful than the other women. But she wasn't sure these were the only reasons. Of all the women Tolian had heard express their dislike for her, it was mostly the noble women of the court who tended not to like her at all. She also suspected that many of the men in the court held the same feelings, but dared not be so vocal.

She had some friends at court, but her closest were away for the Yule. Brythia, her beloved wife, was celebrating the Solstice with the Druids in their distant temple stronghold, Hyge Bryth, hidden in the Haunted Mountains. She was upset when Tolian had refused to go with her. It was difficult for them to be apart; the unbreakable spells that had brought them together tore at them painfully across the distance. Tolian had been adamant. To the Druids she was a goddess, and though she was now beginning to come to terms with her womanhood, and she relished her supernatural strength, she could not tolerate the adulation and worship which the nature priests and priestesses felt obliged to bestow upon her. She did not like to be reminded of her differences so dramatically. She did not feel worthy of adoration after the way she had almost let the world down last year in the toppled towers of Keythion—the passing memory of which sent a shiver down her spine. She preferred the bites of loneliness, the ridicule, and quiet ostracizing of the Lormian nobles to the undeserved devotion and praises at the Druidic Solstice celebration. Even as she thought this, she realized it wasn't true; what she wanted was something between loneliness and adoration. *What I want is my old life back.*

Brythia had begged her to come. It was the first time since their marriage that they had been parted. Eventually the druidess realized Tolian would not change her mind, and she relented. Instead, she took along Myrthis, who was the mother of Tolian's son as well as a druidess, and as escort (the King had insisted on one), Delorick, captain of the Royal Guard, thereby leaving Tolian friendless at the palace.

There was another reason Tolian wished to stay in Lorm for Yule but she had kept it to herself. It had to do with the Yule Jarrels, and her father's choice of the Jarrels' Champion.

Tonight Tolian was restless. She found herself empty, yet agitated by the New Moon and filled with a nervous energy to the point of being unable to sleep. She tried to ignore her restlessness as much as possible, but she was the Goddess of the Moon—a truth she couldn't ignore—and so the influence of the New Moon and the nervous energy it stirred in her could not to be discounted.

She paced in her chambers, her silky nightgown streaming behind her. She occasionally cast glances as she passed the mirror and admired her womanly curves, her long brown curly hair, and lovely pouting face. Tonight, though there was something else at work in her agitation, not simply her denial of her divinity but the crux of the matter, which had kept her there.

The Yule Jarrels began in just a few days and her father, the King, had not announced the Jarrels' Champion yet, and that troubled Tolian. She stopped in front of the mirror and sighed. She knew her reflection was the reason the decision had been delayed. It wasn't fair. She was undeniably the greatest warrior in Lorm, in the world. There should be no decision to make.

Before last year, when the Jarrels were cancelled because of the siege, Tolian had been the Jarrels' Champion as a matter of course. Tolian had been a man back then, before the druids and their prophecy, before they transformed him into the physical manifestation of the Moon Goddess to fight the Demon. It seemed like eons ago. She studied her delicate reflection, and tried to remember her old bearded face. She could vaguely remember the young warrior-prince, once the pride of Lorm and undoubted commander of the fiercest army of the West. Everyone in the palace loved him then. Tolian did not mind that type of adoration. It was earned through courage and hard fought battles, not bestowed by magickal transformations. She stared hard at the woman's face in the mirror. This was her destiny, the druids claimed. She remembered her extreme discomfort at first. Thankfully, the dysphoria she felt at first had lessened. Brythia's unquestioning love helped promote acceptance of her new situation. When they were together her gender was almost irrelevant, and they did not allow it to interfere with their lovemaking. She was becoming used to life as a woman as a result. She had stopped fighting herself, for the most part, and attempted to embrace her new life. Was it the deepening of the magick that had transformed her, that helped foster this acceptance? She did not know. Occasionally, she would feel a pang of guilt whenever she caught herself feeling too comfortable with her new form. The guilt came less and less, now, though she was certainly not without regrets. She would have liked to have been a husband to the woman she loved, though in a few ways, she honestly preferred being female. She had come to realize, however, that she did not prefer being treated like one.

King Tolris had been surprisingly understanding about the whole business at first. In his happiness at discovering his "son" was still alive, he had proclaimed her his heir. She was proud and happy to be so honored. There had never before been a female ruler in Lorm. They were a proud and chauvinistic people. She thought it was about time a woman held the reins of power. She knew it was because she had been a man that she was still the heir, despite her femininity. Now, apparently, her father's faith in his own decision was ebbing. There were incredible political factors at work, she knew, but it did not matter to her. She so wanted his trust again, his confidence in her.

She felt as though she would jump out of her skin. She paced about a little longer, shivering slightly as a particularly icy draft found its way through the stonewalls and thick tapestries adorning her and Brythia's chamber. She had to get out of there. She would go berserk if she stayed in that room one more minute. She slipped into a warm robe and went out into the palace corridors.

It was late at night. Most nobles had retired into their chambers for the evening, but the passages were busy with servants at their Yuletide preparations. Some cleaned and scrubbed the stone floors and walls, while others hung seasonal tapestries and garlands of pine and holly. The torches, hung on the walls to illuminate the way, were made with cinnamon and lent a sweet, festive scent to the hallway. She had always loved this time of year. She sighed as the servants whispered behind her as she passed.

There was one person in the palace with some understanding of her circumstances. They were not as close as they could be and Tolian knew it was her own fault. It wasn't easy sometimes to look at him; often it brought back the most frightful memories. But one of her best friends was part of him now. And he did save the world after all. He had also earned the status of favored advisor to the King. She headed straight for his rooms.

She stood outside his door, which was made of heavy oak like all the doors in the palace. She reached up to knock, but stopped herself. She hated to bother him at this hour, but she would explode if she didn't talk to someone. She tapped lightly on the oaken panel. She waited and strained to hear sounds from inside the apartment. She was not disappointed. She heard footsteps approaching the door and the creak of hinges as the door swung open.

A tall man in his late thirties stood in the doorway. He had dark hair, a strong jaw, and an honest face. The eyes were Kilfrie's, though. Dark and mysterious like the druidess had been.

"Tolian," he said surprised. "Your Highness, I mean."

"Kiliordes, I'm so sorry to trouble you at this hour," she

apologized. "I just have to talk to you."

She tried not to sound desperate. "It's important. Well, to me."

A concerned look filled Kiliordes' eyes.

"Is everything all right?"

"Oh, yes. I'm sorry. Everything's okay. Really. It's just..."

The friendly smile added itself to the concerned face in a most receptive fashion. Tolian studied his face. There was no vestige of the evil there. No trace of cruelty or malice.

"Would you like to come in and talk about it?" He stepped back to allow her to enter.

"Thank you."

Kiliordes was dressed in a blue wool robe, which dragged the ground slightly as he walked. He led Tolian back into his den. He bid her sit on a comfortable chair next to the fireplace. Before she knew it, she was seated and had accepted a warm glass of wine from him. Kiliordes settled into the chair next to hers. He raised his glass.

"To your health, Your Highness."

"To yours."

They drank.

"And, please, you mustn't call me 'Your Highness' when it's just the two of us. We're friends, remember?"

"Well, yes, of course," he said. "Tolian, then. What can I do for you? I am at your service."

"I really do appreciate that, and I shall speak plainly," she said. "My father takes counsel from few men, but he listens to you, Kiliordes."

She waited a moment to see if she got any reaction from this. A modest flush, perhaps.

"I would never ask you to betray a confidence of the King's, but I must know. Has he decided on who is to be the Jarrels' Champion, yet?" she asked him. Her directness surprised her.

His brows knit a little.

"He has," he answered. "Though as a non-Lormian, I must admit to being baffled by the weight which you people afford such a relatively unimportant matter."

"Am I to be the Jarrels' Champion as I have been for the last five years?"

“That's not for me to say; yes, or no, Tolian. I'm sorry,” he answered evenly. “I’m not even sure exactly what the Yule Jarrels are. I don’t really like to ask anyone else. It reminds people I’m different.”

She could understand that. It was clear she wasn’t going to get her answer from him. The least she could do for his patience and hospitality was to answer his question.

“The Yule Jarrels are an ancient Lormian tradition,” the princess explained. “Every year, just before the winter solstice the King holds the Jarrels. It is his duty to appoint a Champion for the holiday. Warriors who wish a boon from the King must fight his champion. Those who win are granted their request. Those who lose go home bruised, bloodied, and empty-handed; though they are welcome guests to the continual feasting taking place before and after their Jarrels, or battles.”

Kiliordes nodded, smiling. “I thought it was something like that, but I wasn’t altogether sure. It sounds quite the extraordinary event.”

“Yes,” Tolian agreed. “It really is.”

“He’s going to announce the Jarrels’ Champion tomorrow,” Kiliordes said suddenly. “I did recommend you, you know. It is a politically difficult decision, though. I’m not sure what he’s going to do. But, I do know he’s proud of you and he loves you.” He looked at her squarely, kindly.

“What’s he proud of me for?” Tolian asked coldly. “You’re the one who saved the world. I would have sold it out.” She got up, turned away, and walked out without looking back.

“Tolian,” Kiliordes called sadly behind her. “You’re going to have to forgive yourself for that one of these days.”

Chapter 3

Kiliordes closed the door. Tolian still did not trust him and he knew it. He had no trouble understanding why, really. He still remembered watching helplessly as the Demon took possession of his body and used Brythia as a hostage against Tolian. The expression of hatred on Tolian’s face, directed at him, was burned into his memory. Such fury. Such outrage and horror. All directed at him. And Kiliordes knew Tolian remembered as well. Sometimes he could see it in her expression, hidden in the corner of her eye, maybe, but it was there. He knew Tolian felt bad about it, but she couldn't help it. It had placed quite a distance between them.

They had been close before. Before. Before there even was a Kiliordes. When he was two different people. As Rwiordes, he was one of the three bungling sorcerers who had allowed the Demon access into the world, and possession of their bodies to launch his hellish conquest. He had managed to warn King Tolris of the imminent invasion by the Demon's forces before he fell under the Demon's power, though. As Kilfrie, she was the druidess who had the gift of Hamfahring, the ability to take possession of any living creature. She had been one of Tolian’s original druidic captors sent to bring the prince (at the time) to Hyge Bryth for his transformation. It had been her assignment to use her unique gift to take possession of the then male Tolian and father his heir upon Myrthis, a fellow druidess. No doubt, the princess still bore Kiliordes some measure of suspicion over that. Nonetheless, she chose Kilfrie as one of her companions on her quest for the Moonsword, and the two of them became friends.

Kiliordes knew it had to be difficult for Tolian to deal with him. Tolian and Brythia were the only two people to ever encounter Rwiordes when he was possessed by the Demon. And Kilfrie, of course. Except that he was Kilfrie. Or she was him. It was only confusing when he thought about it. Normally the two personalities were unified and blended harmoniously into one being forged in the darkest depths of chaos, a vortex of entropy that was the Demon. Kilfrie had attempted to wrest control of the possessed Rwiordes' body to save Brythia from the fiend's wrath. For her trouble, she and Rwiordes were exiled into the pit of swirling evil from which the Demon was born. They unified what was not torn away of their personalities into one ordered being. One that could not exist in the realm of chaos and was, therefore, expelled. He was that new being of order who again took control of Rwiordes' body and saved Tolian and the world itself from the Demon. He could picture the severed head of his possessed friend Perelisk lying at his feet and in his hands, Tolian's Moonsword glowing with power.

He used the name Kiliordes now. It seemed like a name that made sense, given his situation. He had memories of both of them now woven into a fabric, which formed a new whole. He was different from either of the people he had been in some ways as well. It was not surprising, he reasoned, that the synthesis of the two parts would have some properties neither alone had had. For example, he now liked some foods, which neither Rwiordes or Kilfrie had liked. He had never before (nor had she) a taste for ale, but now it was a weakness for him. This, of course, he realized, may have had something to do with the superior quality of Lormian ale.

Another difference was that he had no interest now in many of the things that had been most important to his constituents. He had no wish to continue Kilfrie's druidic practices in general, and specifically none whatsoever to use her Hamfahring abilities. Kilfrie had been devout in her druidism and considered it her duty to practice her gift daily. He didn't even know if he could still do it. He didn't want to know. Rwiordes had a daughter in his distant homeland. She was a bastard child and lived in her mother's house, but he had visited her often. They had a good relationship. Even so, Kiliordes was surprised that he had almost no wish to see her since his...well, since his coming into being. He didn't know how else to describe it.

He was happy in Lorm. He was regarded as a hero because of his victory over the Demon in Keythion and because his timely warnings had helped prepare the palace defenses for the Demon's horrific onslaught. He was, as Tolian had pointed out, the King's most trusted advisor. A position not without advantages. He was popular at court. He had comfortable apartments (in fact, by far the most comfortable he had ever had). It was a good life. The Lormians may have been famous for being the bravest warriors in the West, but they were damn fine cooks as well. He enjoyed his popularity and the material comforts available to him. He simply had no longing for his faraway home.

In Lorm he had a new life. He found that suddenly being a national hero and the King's advisor had quickly immersed him, willing or no, deeply into Lormian politics. Court relationships were far more complex than he would ever have imagined, with such intrigue and hypocrisy in the noble classes that he shuddered as he thought of it. Everything in Lormian culture was based on ancient military alliances, histories, and warrior skills of the different Houses.

Tolian's return to Lorm in her new form had been an incredible destabilizing force in court politics, Kiliordes quickly discovered. King Tolris was having increased difficulty getting support for his policies from the other Houses simply because Tolian was his heir. There was open grumbling from the Houses of the Yeld and Jirtel. They claimed to be afraid of a druidic take over of Lormian sovereignty, with Tolian having undergone their magick, with her close association with druids. But that was a just an excuse. They were upset because they simply did not want a "woman king", even if she was the greatest warrior among them. There were even some in the highest houses, those of Hemris and Curdew, who were beginning to voice doubts over Tolian's nomination. Kiliordes was spending a great deal of time trying to keep everybody happy. And it wasn't working.

Chapter 4

Tolian awoke early to the sounds of the fire boy at work in their outer chamber. She pulled the warm covers tightly around her and listened to him. The fireplace was on the opposite side of the same wall as the bed, so the sound came clearly through, even though there were stone and heavy tapestries behind the bed. The shoveling of soot and ashes. The scraping and dragging of the metal across the stones. For a couple of moments there was silence, then the boy's grunting and the sound of logs (large logs, apparently) tumbling into to the empty fireplace. She inhaled deeply and sprang lightly out of bed.

The frantic nervousness of last night was gone. She was calm. Her obsession with the Yule Jarrels was diminished by her embarrassment at her actions of last night. She would have to apologize to Kiliordes, of course. Still, she was curious, she admitted to herself.

She pulled back the heavy window curtain and took a breath of the cold, clean air. The sun rose golden-red, shrouded in icy mist as it topped the distant hills to the east. A blanket of frost covered the fields, rolling hills, and rooftops of the many small villages surrounding the palace of Lorm. Twelve stories below her, a few merchants braved the cold to set up their wares in the main courtyard. A few small cooking fires sent their smoke curling into the air. A hunter with a deer carcass swung over his shoulder made for the butcher's tent. Tolian was generally a late sleeper and rarely witnessed such early morning views.

Before long, her handmaiden entered.

"Good morning, Milady." She smiled and curtsied.

"Good morning, Dovyse." Tolian smiled warmly in return. "What are you doing up so early?"

"Bilfk heard you up and about early again when he was preparing your morning fire, Milady. He woke me straight away, in case you needed anything."

"Well," the princess explained, "I've had a lot on my mind, and it seems to have ended my slumber early. I should be back to sleeping late again after today."

The girl looked at Tolian attentively as she spoke. She always did. The princess appreciated the attention. Dovyse was one of the few people in the palace who seemed to genuinely accept and like Tolian. It seemed to Tolian the girl almost revered her, not in a religious way but as a teenage girl might look up to a woman she admired. Tolian was fond of Dovyse as well. She was such a pleasant surprise. Having a handmaiden was a significant adjustment for Tolian. In Lormian society, princes required much less maintenance than princesses did. She was grateful for Dovyse for making that transition an easy one to adjust to. Both Tolian and Brythia depended on the girl to help them learn all they needed to know as Lormian princesses.

"Would you please make up a warm bath for me, dear?" Tolian asked her.

"Of course, Milady."

A short while later, Tolian was clean and dressed in a tight, brown, and green winter gown that accented her figure nicely. She was taking her breakfast in her outer chamber with Dovyse, which was technically inappropriate, but she was so lonely without her beloved Brythia, she needed the company. A door servant knocked and entered. She was a new girl and Tolian did not yet know her name. She looked a little surprised to see Dovyse seated next to the princess, but redirected her attention to her errand.

"Milady," she announced. "Lord Delorick is here to see you."

"Lord Delorick?" Wasn't he supposed to be at Hyge Bryth with Brythia, Relinder, and Myrthis?

"Yes, Milady. He regrets the early hour, but says the matter is urgent."

"Show him in please," said Tolian.

The girl bowed and left. Tolian looked at Dovyse, "Sorry, looks like you've been displaced. Take your breakfast and finish it in your room, dear."

She smiled, nodded, and went about her business.

Tolian rose and waited for Delorick. He entered immediately. He looked worried and it showed in his brown eyes. There were lines of unease on his face.

"Your Highness," Delorick said, greeting his friend as formally as always before lapsing into the casual tone.

"Delorick, welcome. I must admit I'm surprised to see you. Is everyone all right?"

Delorick shook his head and smiled. "No, no. Relax. They're fine. Don't worry. Brythia and Myrthis can take care of themselves, that's for sure. They are safely at Hyge Bryth, no doubt deeply involved in the druidic celebrations."

Tolian sighed in relief. "Well, what brings you back early and in such a hurry?"

Delorick looked squarely into Tolian's eyes.

"I have to talk to you. Before your father announces the Jarrels' Champion."

Tolian waited, her curiosity now piqued. Delorick bit his lip.

The Captain of the Royal Guard began, nervously at first, but gaining in control as he continued: "I know you have always been Jarrels' Champion. You've always done a great job. There's no one better than you with a sword. There's no one stronger than you. But... I would like you to do me a favor. I want you to refuse to be the Jarrels' Champion this year."

Tolian's head spun. While thoughts and questions bounced around in her mind, a servant knocked and then brought in breakfast for Delorick. The princess gestured for her friend to sit and join her at the table. "Why?" she asked at last.

"I am going to ask the King if I can be the Jarrels' Champion."

"You? But—"

"Let me explain," offered Delorick. "I have a boon to ask of the King."

A boon. What boon would Delorick seek in Lorm that he could not simply take by right as the Captain of the Guard? It must be something important.

"What boon do you seek of my father?"

"I promise you we'll get to that. But let me ask you something," he said. "If you were the Jarrels' Champion could I ever really hope to best you at combat and win my boon?"

"No, you couldn't," Tolian answered. "But if the boon is a

worthy one, I sometimes let people win."

Delorick looked at her and chuckled, "That was before, when people didn't know for sure you were doing it. Before you got your strength. Your power. Everyone would know I did not win my boon fairly. It is too important to me. However, the Jarrels' Champion always gets his boon, just for being the Champion. No one could say I didn't receive my boon fairly and with honor." He looked at her with an expression Tolian took to mean he was imploring her to say something.

"And you'll tell me what this boon is?" Tolian asked.

"Of course, for I must ask your permission before I can even talk to your father. Tolian, I want to marry Myrthis and she wants to marry me. However, since her legal status is essentially that of royal concubine, the matter becomes horribly complicated. Obviously, such a thing has never been done before. I'm not even sure it would be allowed, even with your father's and your blessings. But, of course, Jarrels' Boons transcend even the ancient protocols."

So that was it. She should have guessed. She did not hesitate. "Yes, you have my permission to marry Myrthis, even though she is the mother of my heir. And yes, I will decline to be Jarrels' Champion if we can convince my father to give you that honor in my stead. If he was going to give it to me to begin with. That is not as certain as you may believe."

"The King was going to announce you as Jarrels' Champion this morning," said Delorick. "At least that's what Kiliordes told me."

Chapter 5

It all felt strange to Brythia. To be back at her old room in the druidic temple stronghold of Hyge Bryth for the first time since Tolian's transformation. To have returned, even if briefly, into the daily lifestyle of the temple. The rigorous meditations, the politics of the hierarchy, the strict, bland diet. She looked down at herself. The plain white winter robe of the order had replaced the stylish dresses and gowns she had become accustomed to at the palace. She had to admit she had gotten used to being a Lormian princess, and, as a result, some of the more fundamentalist trappings of her religion had slid by the wayside. Despite that, however, she was still as an adept a tracker, fighter, or nature sorceress as any in the order. And she was still a Priestess of the Sun.

She had been there for almost two weeks now. Her life with Tolian seemed almost like a dream, fading slightly as she moved through the environs and trappings of her earlier existence. Engulfed, almost, by the power and simplicity of everything in Hyge Bryth. It had always been home to her, or the forests of the Haunted Mountains surrounding it. The temple, like Brythia herself, was named after her greatest ancestor, one of the founding members of the druidic order, Brythic. It had been her family's home since any one could remember. The place grounded her with its old familiarity, and gave her a sense of objectivity with which to view her life now. Still, it did not dull the sense of loneliness she felt without Tolian. She missed her desperately. Sometimes she marveled at how powerful the love magick that bound them together was. It was no wonder such magicks were forbidden by druidic law. She bore the High Druidess Magara no resentment for her magick; she and Tolian were perfectly happy. And Tolian probably would never have agreed to undergo the transformation and take up the mantle as druidic champion against the Demon, if it weren't for Magara's spell.

She was hoping that once again immersing herself in her druidry would allow her the opportunity to make some sense of the events since last year. She had told Tolian she wanted to return to Hyge Bryth for the Solstice celebrations, and that was true to a degree. The religious reason was valid. But she really wanted a chance to examine the original manuscript of Brythic's Druidic Prophecy, that potent work which had correctly predicted every major historical event since it was penned a thousand years prior, except one. It was the thing that had burned in the back of her mind since January. The question haunting her more than the memories of the horrors she had seen and experienced. Had the prophecy been wrong? It seemed impossible to believe it could be wrong in this one instance only, its last prediction. It simply didn't feel wrong to her, and she was as involved in the events as anyone.

And so Brythia had gone to Hyge Bryth to beg Magara to allow her to examine the original copies of the prophecy. For although all druidic teachings were passed on only orally, Brythic wrote down his prophecies. Even in the budding order this was considered highly unusual, and after Brythic's departure from the order, the scrolls, which contained the work, were studied, memorized, and locked away for safety, and thereafter solely passed along by mouth. On rare occasions druidic scholars were given leave to examine and study the work. Brythia had used the cover of the Solstice celebrations to come to Hyge Bryth under secrecy. But secrecy from whom, she did not know. And when Tolian wouldn't come, she dragged Myrthis and her stepson, Relinder, with her. Myrthis was glad enough to return to Hyge Bryth. She was a true lover of druidry and leapt at the opportunity to return to the sacred sanctuary.

Of course, it was next to impossible, as it turned out, to take the infant Relinder with them, but frankly, both Brythia and Myrthis raised such a uproar over it the King relented. The old man was adamant, and demanded they take Delorick as an escort. She thought it was amusing, but she accepted. She knew she and Myrthis could take care of any problems they might have. Delorick was an agreeable enough traveling companion, and Mythis was clearly happy about the King's choice of escort. Sometimes, Brythia disappeared ahead into the forest to allow those two a chance to be alone. They made a cute couple.

When they arrived at the temple, Magara was delighted to see them. It was all smiles, hugs, and greetings. Why not? Brythia thought. *She was like a mother to so many of us.* Yet even then Brythia wasted no time and asked Magara straight away if she could see the original prophecies. A curious and surprised Magara agreed, but said she had to wait until the new moon before she could do so.

All of these memories and feelings swirled through the druidess's mind as she was led into the deepest sanctuary of the Temple, a place few were permitted to go. Magara held a torch, providing the only light. It seemed as though they walked an impossibly long time, going deeper and deeper into the heart of the mountain from which the temple was hewn. Brythia could feel the heaviness of the rock around her. This passage was narrow and roughly cut, unlike the smooth polished stone characterizing most of the temple's spacious corridors. Neither of the two druidesses spoke for some time. At last, they came to the end of the passage. A simple but heavy wooden door with a silver opening ring stood before them. Both women considered the door in silence for a few moments. Finally Magara spoke.

"The scrolls are delicate due to their great age. We don't allow many people to see them. You are the fourth person to be allowed to see them this century."

"Have you seen them?" Brythia asked.

"I had no need," the older woman said. She began to recite the last prediction, her voice full of arcane power:

"On the night of the Equinox, in the Year of the Bear, when three comets fill the sky. Mark this day well, my children, mark it well. It is the beginning of the end of the world.

"A Demon shall enter human flesh in the Entrine Desert. No power can stop this. He shall lead vast armies into war, and bring great nations to ruin. He shall surround himself in death and suffering.

"By the time of the Solstice—He shall be Lord of the North.

"By the Spring Equinox—the skies shall turn black and the blood of the dead shall issue from the Earth. These shall be the last of days.

"Against this there is one hope: A Champion as no other.

The Demon shall be mighty, but not indestructible. He shall be killed by no man, and by none born female. No metal of the Earth shall harm him. He shall be slain, only, by one born of the dead, on a day not in the year."

Byrthia shivered slightly. There was such power in Magara's voice. And still such ominousness echoed in the words. A dread slithered past the back of her mind. It was that feeling which had brought her there. She sighed at the entrance. A question flashed. "Magara, you said I was to be the fourth person to examine the scrolls this century."

"That's correct."

"Well, have I heard of any of the others?"

The High Priestess nodded. "You should have heard of all the others. You may not recall Fenstyr, father to Pathik?"

"No, I'm afraid I do not," confessed Brythia. "Should I?"

"Probably. He was a great scholar of the prophecies. His notes will no doubt prove useful to you."

"His notes?" Brythia was surprised. "You kept his notes?"

"Of course, for the same reason Brythic wrote down the prophecy in the first place: for use by subsequent druids. All who examine the works are required to take careful notes of their findings. You, yourself are so charged. However, you may not take your notes out of the Library Room."

"I had no idea this was considered such a serious matter," replied the younger druidess.

"Serious, child? You have no idea. Every time someone examines the scrolls, a major controversy is started. Without exception. You certainly remember what was said of Demverstia's vision and the renegade Davlin? They were the other two who have examined the scrolls this century."

Magara looked at Brythia hard, but with a maternal kindness. She smiled, but Brythia knew the powerful priestess was worried. A new nervousness crept up on Brythia.

"Knowing now what I have told you," said Magara. "I must ask you if you wish to reconsider your request to examine the scrolls?"

She didn't hesitate. "No, I still wish to see them."

"Very well," Magara pulled on the door ring and opened the door. "You must enter alone. Only those who would read the scrolls may enter the library room."

The library room was a vast, largely empty cavern. It was illuminated by natural phosphorescence permeating the rock of the Haunted Mountains. Skilled manipulation with chisel and polish in certain key areas had allowed the early druids to bring light to the depths of mountain. This was all the druids had done to the cavern. They had left the few stalactites and stalagmites that had formed there.

The whole room was roughly two hundred feet in diameter, for Brythia determined its circular nature quickly. Across the chamber, a small stream of water rolled down the rocky wall and gathered in a blue pool glowing and casting its own strange light, and rippling in waves against the walls. A stone table stood off to the side of the cavern, which was best lit by the harnessed mineral radiance. Next to that sat a chair hewn into the center of a sizable stalactite. A great chest built of cedar sat close by.

Brythia turned back towards the door as she heard it pulled closed. She noticed immediately that, from inside, there was no means of opening the door. She smiled. "I wonder how long I'm in here for," she asked aloud. "Oh well."

It didn't matter really. She had intended to stay until she had found what she was looking for—the answer to the question that was haunting her.

As she turned away, a bag on the floor next to the door caught her attention. She bent down and tentatively examined its contents: a lamp and a small supply of oil, quills, ink, parchment, and a blanket. She lifted the bag and walked towards the table. As she neared the library portion of the cavern, she knew she would have little use for the lamp. She had seen several examples of druid cave lighting techniques, but this was the most astonishing to her. Just before she reached the table the history of the place hit her hard. She could feel the sheer power of the seat and table. The greatest and most curious of her predecessors had sat there and studied. She gently lifted the lid to the scroll box. She gasped as she saw the enormity of her task for the first time: there were hundreds and hundreds of scrolls neatly wound and stored in the chest. Brythia sighed. "I had better get started."

~~~

Was it hours later, or days? Time was of no consequence to her. She was aware that she had fallen into a trance. The scrolls had exerted the most awesome power over her. She was consumed by her task. Open scrolls lay all over the floor around her. She had no interest in the notes of others, if the scroll was not in Brythic's hand, she read no further. Even of those the legendary druid did write, if they concerned events of past times she had no patience for them. Part of her was amazed at the sheer ruthlessness in her handling of the ancient heirlooms. Yet she did not allow herself to be slowed in her quest by being overly careful. It was only the last prophecy that concerned her and she was determined to find it.

She did not even allow her body's natural appetites to interfere—not hunger, not thirst. She quickly opened and scanned each scroll, then threw it thoughtlessly out of her reach.

Finally, she found the scroll that began "On the night of the Equinox, in the Year of the Bear..."

She cleared the stone table of other scrolls, slowly sat in the great chair, and spread the scroll out over the table. She took a great breath and closed her eyes for a moment. She attempted to subdue the fervor that had hitherto marked her wild search. Now was the time for careful study; even in the depths of that strange trance, she understood that. She opened her eyes and brought her attention slowly and carefully to the scroll. Ancient it was, yet remarkably well preserved. Brythic's runic script was neat and methodical, yet Brythia suspected from the characters that he had been in a similar trance when he wrote down those dreadful words. She did not know how she understood this, simply that she did.

As she studied, she saw no surprises. The words were there, just as she had been taught them. Except two small marks. Two careless ink marks. Then the marks were all she could see. There was nothing on the page except the two marks. They were runes, tiny runes. The first rune was the symbol of "After Passage" and the second "One Year." Then their context became clear to her again. They were between the lines "By the time of the Solstice He shall be Lord of the North." and "By the Spring Equinox the skies shall turn black and the blood of the dead shall issue from
~~~

the Earth. These shall be the last of days."

Suddenly it became clear to her. Brythic probably didn't even realize he had put the runes there. But she knew what they meant. She was paralyzed by the implied horror for a moment. It wasn't over. And Brythia knew that Tolian was in great danger. The druidess ran to the door. "Magara, let me out."

As the words left her lips, she knew her pleas didn't matter. The door would open at the appointed time, whenever that was, and not a moment before. She prayed it wouldn't be too late.

Chapter 6

The celebration of Yule in Lorm always officially began with the boar hunt in the morning of the fourth day before Midwinter's Day. And if she couldn't be Jarrels' Champion, Tolian was doing the boar hunt, that was certain. It was customary for the noble warriors of the Great Houses to don their finest furs about their most ornate and decorative armor and hunt the fields and forests that surrounded the palace for boars which were then given to the townsfolk and peasantry. Tolian had always loved the spectacle—the mighty warriors questing forth, tall and resplendent, upon their mighty steeds decked in Yule armor, trailing beads and the banners of their houses. Dogs led the charge and screaming children ran behind. Of course, there were no boar left in the vicinity, so the King always had some brought in and released just for the event. At the first sighting of the sun above tree line to the east, the gates to the palace were flung open and out would fly the warrior huntsmen to the chase.

Tolian was quite a spectacle in her own right, and she knew it. She wore the immodest faerie battle armor given to her by Queen Ymrisiva. It was a tiny garment of an impossibly light chain mail, cut to leave little of her curvaceous form to the imagination. About herself she had draped the werewolf skin she had worn in her battle with the Demon a year ago, more for the shock value than for modesty or warmth. The magickal properties of the faerie armor afforded ample protection from the December morning chill. A pair of sturdy boots, a belt, and a sheath holding the legendary Moonsword completed her costume. Following her were the two finest hunting dogs in the kingdom, or so she reckoned; after all, she had raised them from pups.

A deep defiance of tradition moved through her that morning as she walked quietly out to join the noblemen gathered on horseback by the main gate. Let them gape. Let them mutter. With a graceful motion, she brushed back her roughly cut werewolf cloak to reveal more of her feminine charms. Perhaps she stood a little straighter and thrust her breasts out a little further. She knew her presence irritated most of her peers. Good, let them be irritated. So what if there had never been a woman in the Yule hunt before. There was one in the hunt now.

She caught sight of Misk, her stable boy, waving his arms in the dim torchlight of the main courtyard. As she neared him, she saw her silvery steed Whisper, a faerie horse (another gift from the Queen of the Faerie Realm) decked in the festive colors, dangles, and the royal blue banner of the House of Hemris, as well as another set of pendants, which Tolian did not recognize. They were purple with white crescent moons on them.

"Good morn, Misk," she greeted him. "What manner of emblem is that?" She indicated the new pendants.

Misk shifted a little uncomfortably, "Princess Brythia made them. She instructed me to use those colors as well as your own, Your Highness."

"Indeed."

"Aye, Milady, she said that they are your colors as well, them of the Lunar Realm."

Brythia. Her name brought a fleeting ache to her heart and a smile to her lips. There would almost certainly be a fuss made at court about the lunar banners.

Misk studied her face with much concern.

"Don't worry," the princess said, catching him. "They're fine. You've done a fantastic job with Whisper's Yule armor. You really outdid yourself this time."

The stable boy beamed with pride. "I thought I should do something extra special this year."

And so he had. Off the saddle and bridle hung the traditional beads, fresh fruit from far-off lands, and little bits of gold and gemstones. Most of the "dangles," as they were called, would fall off during the hunt. That was the point. Hordes of young children would travel behind the huntsmen searching the ground for fallen treasures.

The princess slipped lightly into the saddle. The boy handed up the reins to her.

"Thank you, Misk. You're exceptional," she said.

His cheeks reddened and his smile grew ever wider. He

straightened a dangle and gently rubbed Whisper's neck.

"It's easy to be, with a horse like this, Your Highness."

"Well, you make an excellent team; or the three of us do. Wish me luck."

With that, she trotted off to join the other huntsmen already assembled. She noticed the colors of the House of Hemris, and worked her way in that direction. Her cousin Kelvris was there. It was not easy to move through the throng of mounted warriors, their stable boys, and the assorted well-wishers who crowded the huge courtyard.

"Well met, cousin," said Tolian politely. Kelvris was tolerable enough. He was always friendly in person, though she knew that he had spoken sharply against her succession in his own circles. Everyone was entitled to his or her own opinion, no matter how ignorant it might be. At least she knew where she stood with him. And the false facade of niceness was still better than the rudeness she encountered from almost everyone else.

Kelvris smiled narrowly and nodded. "You look ravishing as always, Tolian."

She pulled her otherworldly horse next to Kelvris's steed. "Thank you," she said.

Kelvris leaned over, "Did you get a look at the boars your father got this year? They're monsters."

"I just caught a glimpse out my window yesterday, as they were releasing them. I do think they're the biggest he's gotten by far, in a long time. It should be quite the hunt."

"Let us hope so," Kelvris agreed. "Oh, here's the King now."

With a tilt of his head, he indicated a balcony, hanging off the royal residence over the main courtyard. Tolian looked to see her father emerge from a fourth story chamber onto the balcony used for public addresses. The balcony was well lit by torches and the Lormian King's golden robe, worn only during the Yule celebrations, reflected the flames in such a way that the robe glowed. Holly was woven into his crown, which Tolian knew her father hated, but even the warrior sovereigns did not often neglect tradition. Tolian strained to study her father's distant face, and could not clearly tell his mood at first, but his smile broadened unmistakably as he looked down upon his knights in their holiday finery. As always, the King's steward Miderick, and Kiliordes flanked him. A respectful hush fell over the courtyard. All eyes turned toward the balcony and the King. Tolris waited a few moments, his vision fixed upon the eastern horizon. The anticipation was a powerful force as the warriors tensed their muscles in readiness and everyone held their breath.

At last King Tolris bellowed the words all were waiting to hear. "The Sun breaks. Open the gates. Let the Yule Hunt begin. Ride."

Then the gates were thrown open and cheers echoed like thunder both inside the palace and out. The dogs rushed out barking like a large pack of wolves. Behind them, in a rush of excitement and power, sprang the huntsmen on their horses, galloping out of the palace into the town. Crowds gathered along the main thoroughfare, waving and screaming praises to the riders.

The hunt surged through Tolian's veins. She was lost in it. With wild abandon, she raced at the front of the huntsmen through the narrow streets of the outer palace, and through the siege wall gate. Breaking like an escaped predator, Tolian hit the field with such velocity she quickly distanced herself even from the dogs. She did not need the dogs. She brought Whisper on hard over the frozen ground. There was nothing but the wind, rushing cold at her face, and her prey.

The crowds in and around the palace were twenty times as great as they ever had been before; but to Tolian they were a blur. They were mere obstacles to maneuver around and vague images that distracted the eye from its quest for prey. Perhaps she saw the smiling face of an excited child, but the sight did not register in her brain as it usually did.

She had cleared the dogs by a considerable distance now, riding impossibly fast on her impossible horse. She turned her steed on some unthinking whim, wholly now a creature of instinct, driving hard towards the western tree line. The sun's earliest golden rays lit a sizable object between a grove of oaks and maples and the small but venerable hamlet of Lormthof. Tolian felt an irresistible fire burning within her, calling her on to even greater speed.

Deep inside, part of her knew what was happening. It was

the lunar power moving through her. She was the Goddess of the Hunt, pure and ferocious. Nothing could slow her from her quarry. When she became dissatisfied with the speed of her faerie horse, she leapt off his back and moved twice as fast over the wintry ground on her own legs.

The red-brown boar stood out plainly on the field, white from the heavy frost. The fresh dawn's light made the beast glow with an amber radiance most extraordinary. The distant sun's fury burned there, making the boar seem like a spirit of that solar fire roaming on the winter's garden. It moved towards the trees, where the grass was mostly shielded from the frost's ravages, hoping, no doubt, to find softer ground for rooting. It was unaware of Tolian's rapid approach. Just before the huntress cleared the last two hundred yards between them, the beast noticed her. Its primitive face evinced a mix of great surprise, alarm, and anger. Two jets of frosty steam issued from its snout and its eyes narrowed. Clearly, the boar sensed danger and turned fully to meet it. It lowered its head and ran toward Tolian.

A smile spread across Tolian's face as she charged the boar, her werewolf skin cloak flapping behind her like the wings of a bird of prey. And she felt like a bird of prey, too, as she practically flew over the frozen earth, fixed in her attack. Fifty yards from the boar, as she and the boar rushed at each other, she swiftly drew the Moonsword from its scabbard. The mighty weapon gleamed silver with a subtle purple sheen. Without slowing her step, the princess pulled the sword back and threw it with all of her superhuman strength at the charging animal. There was a flash of silver lightning as the blade passed through the boar. The fire went cold in the beast's eyes as the sword plunged through its body, burying itself in the frozen earth. The animal crumbled to the ground, instantly dead.

Tolian stopped in her tracks. She regarded the lifeless carcass of the prey for a moment, her face blank. The huntress extended her arm with hand opened towards the lunar blade. A wave of energy rushed through her arm and the sword shot back through the air and into her hand.

Then she was Tolian again, her normal perception of herself returned. She marveled at the shimmering blade in her hand. She shook her head mildly in disbelief. Its power (as well as her own) never ceased to amaze her. The sword, like so many of the things about her, seemed impossible. It was forged, if that was the right word, out of the substance of moonlight, distilled centuries ago by that legendary druid, Brythic. In a secret laboratory, he had devised a method of distilling the rays of the moon into a metal stone over the long ages of time. It was to be used as a weapon against the Demon, by the prophesied Druidic Champion, the only person who would be able to kill the fiend. The druids were sure that she was the Champion. It didn't matter now, of course.

What a quest that was, she thought, remembering the adventures of the previous year. Whatever had happened with the Demon didn't really matter; it was her weapon, hard earned.

She turned her attention to the boar. What a mighty beast it had been. She would not have been surprised if it was more than four hundred pounds. Already the folk of Lormthof (those who hadn't gone to the palace gate) were gathered around the animal. The first boar killed on the Solstice hunt was the luckiest, bringing with it good fortune to the hunter and those who partook of it. There was a round of applause for her, and a couple of children, a girl and a boy, came running up to her.

The girl could have been no more than seven and the boy four; both had the brown hair with copper highlights so distinctly Lormian. They wore their best winter clothing, well-kept, festive hand-me-downs which had almost certainly been in the family for several generations. They bowed as they neared her. The girl held a wreath of holly before her. "Thank you, Princess Tolian," the little girl said.

Tolian brushed the hair out of her face and smiled. "It was my pleasure, dear." The princess bowed low and the child slipped the wreath on to her head.

"You've brought us the Solstice luck, you know," the girl said beaming. "And for yourself, too."

From behind Tolian a familiar, but nonetheless vaguely unsettling, voice spoke, "If there was ever a person who had less a need for luck, I don't know who it would be."

Tolian straightened up, but did not turn around at once; she was enjoying the way the children's eyes suddenly looked all round and bulged in amazement.

"A faerie," shouted the boy, caught between terror and delight.

"Findelbres," exclaimed Tolian, now spinning around to get a sight of her friend.

There he was, a figure ghostly in appearance, almost translucent in the morning light. He seemed tall and thin, but sometimes seemed not so. His hair—was it gold or silver? In either case, it possessed highlights in colors that weren't known to exist in the mortal world. His smile was friendly, but with a mercurial curl at the ends that one could never be certain about. Those eyes—were they purple? Tolian was not sure about that, either. His clothes were woven of unknown fabrics and furs from animals that did not live in the world. His main garb, a heavy tunic with trousers in a strange earthen brown, possessed a vibrancy of unusual nature. His boots where of finely crafted dark leather and his cloak was the most amazing shade of sky blue. He wore no cap or hat, but had a slender circlet of white around his head. He held the reins to Whisper up to Tolian.

"Princess," Findelbres said, greeting her with a slight bow and a subtle inclination of his head.

Tolian stepped forward and embraced the faerie nobleman. He had been one of her companions in her quest for the Moonsword, a staunch, but peculiar friend.

"You know, I will never get over how fantastic you look," said the elf.

"Thank you," replied the princess, genuinely appreciative.

"Oh, that's right, compliments don't bother you anymore, do they?"

"No, they don't, and welcome, once again to Lorm."

"I thank you for your welcome, Oh, Glorious Goddess of the Moon, Empress of the Astral...."

"That still bothers me," Tolian said.

"Thank goodness, I was afraid there for a second I had lost my power to annoy you."

Tolian laughed, "I don't think that could ever happen."

Tolian turned, handed the still present little girl a small bag of gold, waved to the small crowd around the boar, and took the reins from Findelbres.

"Come on," she said, "I've got my boar. Let's go back to

the palace and relax. You must be tired."

"We of the Folk of the Sidhe do not get tired," he corrected her. "We get weary instead."

They walked slowly back across the field to the gates and towers of the Lormian capital.

"So friend Findelbres," Tolian inquired. "To what do we owe this visit?"

"Are you serious? How could I miss all of this festive slaughter, and see all of my favorite mortals in the process," answered the faerie. "And I have yet to be introduced to the baby."

Tolian raised her eyebrow and smirked just a little, "Well, you're out of luck, I'm afraid. Our druidesses have taken Relinder to Hyge Bryth for the Solstice. But, Delorick's here, and you know my father. And Kiliordes, of course."

"I'll get to see you as Jarrels' Champion, at least. That should be the sight."

Tolian chuckled. "Actually, Delorick is the Jarrels' Champion this year."

They took their time walking, Tolian leading Whisper along by the reins. It took them about an hour to transverse the distance that Tolian had just cleared in a matter of seconds. When they got back, Tolian was surprised. The palace of Lorm was crammed full of people. The mighty capital was never busier than at Yule. And this Yule was the busiest ever. Merchants and artisans plying their wares filled the streets and courtyards that stood within the fortress' walls. Jugglers, musicians, and all types of street performers crowded every corner. Delightful smells drifted from every restaurant and bakeshop. The fall of Keythion's Imperial Capitals to the north had left Lorm as the greatest city in that part of the world; a status it was ill prepared for. Tolian had never seen that many people in the palace before, not even during the siege last year. Suddenly Lorm was a cosmopolitan city bustling with hitherto unheard of economic activities. The princess led Findelbres through the throng of people.

"Well, you Lormians certainly know how to throw quite a party," observed the elf.

Tolian agreed, “Yeah, it sure looks as though we do. Just wait until the Jarrels, then you’re really going to see something.”

Chapter 7

Kiliordes watched the Yule hunt from the main courtyard balcony with the King. To him it was a quaint enough custom, perhaps a bit rustic, if not just a little barbaric, but with enough pageantry and tradition to make it an enjoyable spectacle. He mused it was exactly that combination that made the Lormians, themselves, such agreeable companions. They were the perfect mix of warriors and country-folk, with just enough civilization and sophistication to make it all work. They were a breath of fresh air for Kiliordes. It was perfect for him; as Rwiordes, he had known the more northern cultures, where the city-states were invested with the arrogance of modern, metropolitan attitudes, and as Kilfrie, the highly regimented life in the temples and woods. Both types of people would have looked down on the Lormians for this "blood-thirsty" celebration, but they would have been too "evolved" (or afraid) to say so to their faces. Yet, Kiliordes loved it all.

He swished his hot cider in its mug, and then gulped it down greedily. He watched the hunt with keen interest. He was not surprised at Tolian's amazing performance. She had killed the first boar before most of the huntsmen had cleared the second gate, and then immediately abandoned the hunt. The crowd at the palace, with a view of Tolian's kill, cheered joyfully.

He leaned over to King Tolris. "Your Majesty, is Tolian finished already?"

Tolris, clearly delighted at his daughter's hunting skills, could not help beaming.

"Yes, Kiliordes. One boar per huntsmen. Cuts down on the bad blood and hard feelings. I order one beast per huntsmen. Everybody gets a kill that way."

"Oh, excellent," commented the royal advisor. "That's going to save us some strife with the other Houses. Especially this year."

Kiliordes was sure there would be quite the ruckus raised about Tolian's participation in the event as it was. That girl was making all of their lives so much tougher than they needed to be. Did she have to wear that outfit? Tolian was irrepressible, and Kiliordes knew this. He couldn't be angry with her. He understood her motivations all too well. The other nobles' objections and ravings about the princess were based on chauvinism and jealously. Clearly, no one had ever dispatched the first boar so quickly. In the end, that would be the real reason for the rain of complaints they would doubtlessly receive from the Houses.

Kiliordes became distracted as he saw the green banners of Curdew House stream from the next huntsmen close in on the second boar. Thank heavens, Kiliordes thought. It was Lord Tathuwd. Bagging the second boar should help ease his envy and frustration at Tolian's superiority.

This hunt was different from the princess's. The boar had both the time and common sense to run from the galloping horsemen. Tathuwd rode down hard on the beast, bringing his stead right up next to the fleeing animal.

The warlord then used his spear, a weapon unique to the Lormian knights, capable as it was of being used either as a lance or a javelin. Tathuwd used his as both. First, he poked at the beast repeatedly, biting through its thick hide. The boar made a sudden wild turn from the huntsman and put enough distance between them to spare him from the lance prods. Now, of course, Tathuwd expertly released the spear with fury and buried the weapon in the boar's thigh, setting the animal to tumble to the winter-whitened ground.

Tathuwd pulled his mighty stallion next to the wounded boar and dismounted as he readied his sword. A plunge and the field's whiteness was marked with a quickly growing pool of red.

Kiliordes looked over at Tolris and Miderick. They were laughing and swilling a toast in Tathuwd's honor.

"Jolly fine kill, eh Kiliordes?" the King asked.

"A fine kill, Your Majesty," Kiliordes agreed.

The hunt took several hours. Most of the hunters had made their kill within the first hour, but Yewstrog of the House of Yeld bore the shame of the last kill, bringing the stigma of a year's bad luck on himself, his house, and the unfortunate villagers of Estbentk. At least the villagers, whose village was a long distance from the palace and had the most inaccessible tract of deer forest in the locale, were used to it.

After the hunt, all the revelers, spectators, and huntsmen retired for the afternoon, while the preparations for the Jarrels' feast were made. Kiliordes wandered the shockingly nearly deserted streets of the lower palace town for a while. It was eerie. He had never seen so few people there before. Apparently, even the foreigners and tourists knew well enough to get their rest. At last, realizing that he too would be up late for the evening's festivities, he decided that perhaps a nap might be a good idea after all.

A knock on his chamber door brought him out of his slumber. His head was groggy, seemingly filled with cobwebs. Wearily, he lifted himself upright and rubbed his eyes. The knock came again. Three quick raps, a pause then two more raps. It was his servant, Pilior. He yawned loudly, then mumbled, annoyed, "Yes, Pilior. What is it?"

The door opened and the boy entered, hesitating. "I'm sorry, your lordship. I truly am..."

"What is it, lad?" Kiliordes asked impatiently.

"It's just that there're people to see you, sir. They demanded to see you right away. I'm sorry. That and they're from..."

"It's all right, Pilior. Now, calm down and tell me who they are and where they are from."

Even as sleepy as he was, Kiliordes knew the boy was excited by his visitors' identities more than he was worried about his master's reaction to being awakened during his Yule rest.

"There are three of them, sir. Two men and a lady, sir. They're from the Solar Pilgrimage Festival."

The Solar Pilgrimage Festival. Pleasant memories of pilgrimage festivals past and the memory of the merry wanders following the course of the sun's journey, reveling and spreading joy and good fortune in their wake warmed Kiliordes' heart. He had traveled with them for a time. When he had first escaped from the Demon, he had taken refuge with them. The Chief Pilgrim, Krin Gul, had hidden him in their midst and had found a way to get him to Lorm in time to warn King Tolris of the Demon's approaching army. He had many a happy memory of his life with those merry travelers; it stood out as an oasis of cheer in the most harrowing period in Rwiordes' life. The Solar Pilgrims were universally welcomed to whatever region they visited. It was said that they brought good fortune in their wake, and to host the festival was considered an honor. The pilgrims loved the purity, energy, and joy of the sun, and any that wanted to join their ranks were welcome to join their bright caravan of feasting, drinking, and singing the sun's praises. They were free spirits, charged with spreading love and light to the hearts of all. He suddenly longed to see Krin Gul's ancient, jovial face once more. Could it be him?

"By all means, Pilior, show them to my parlor. I'll be there presently."

Kiliordes threw his robe over his disheveled bedclothes and was in his parlor before his guests were shown in.

Pilior ushered in three people, all outfitted in furs and wool garments dyed a hodgepodge of bright colors (though mainly shades of yellows, reds, oranges and pinks). The two younger pilgrims he recognized immediately; indeed, they were the first members of the Solar Pilgrimage Festival he had met on that bitter November morning when he wandered, hunted and exhausted, into their encampment. Their names? They were coming to him. Yes, Clonder was the young fellow, a bright-faced blonde man in his twenties, and his twin sister was Sornite, a Gestoan beauty. He jumped to his feet, delighted to see them. Now the other fellow, the third—there was something familiar about him, but Kiliordes could not place him. He was dark complected with a clean-shaven face. His jaw was square, and although his mouth was spread in the most friendly, joyous smile, it seemed somehow foreign to his face. The fun, mischievous twinkle in his eye seemed at odds with the deep furrows and lines around his eyes. And in the royal advisor's eye, his massive frame looked out of place in the brilliant colors he wore. A chill passed over Kiliordes' heart for a moment as he regarded the fellow, until the dark pilgrim stepped forward and bowed before him, leading his companions to do the same. An unpleasant rush of embarrassment chased away any other feelings Kiliordes had. He blurted out, “Get up. Don’t do that.”

Then, composing himself, “I mean, please... it’s absolutely not necessary.”

“But Lord Kiliordes...” began the large, dark pilgrim.

“No. No,” Kiliordes insisted, helping the fellow to his feet. “Any nobility I may possess is purely honorary, and doesn’t require such gestures of submission, especially for those who partake of the Sun’s own grand nobility. And please, Sornite and Clonder, my old friends, you must not spoil me so. It is I who have a deep debt to you, for the kindness you had for a weary fugitive.”

“Greetings, good Rwiordes,” exclaimed Clonder.

“Hail, Clonder, and to you, Sornite. Please, I go by Kiliordes now. What brings the Pilgrimage to Lorm for the Solstice? You should be in southern Surtiz or even Borean by now. And who is your friend?”

“The Pilgrimage is in northern Surtiz,” Sornite said.

“It is just we three who are here in Lorm,” added Clonder.

The dark pilgrim extended his hand towards Kiliordes. “Good Kiliordes,” he said, “my name is Pagyrus, and it is my great honor to meet the man who saved the world. Krin Gul spoke so kindly of you.”

The shadow chill again. “Spoke?” Kiliordes asked, understanding the message of the word, and in fear that he did so.

A look of concern replaced Pagyrus’ warm smile. Clonder and Sornite lowered their heads in uncharacteristic sorrow. Kiliordes had never seen such expressions on their faces before.

“It was most sudden...” began Pagyrus.

“He did not suffer,” offered Clonder.

It seemed as though his heart pooled with frozen lead, so heavy was it from this terrible and unexpected news. The vitality and joy of life that so marked the ancient pilgrim made the news of his death so much harder to bear. The color drained from Kiliordes’ face. He asked the first question that popped into his head: “What is the Solar Pilgrimage Festival going to do now?”

“What Krin Gul wished us to do,” answered Sornite.

“He spoke his last words to Pagyrus,” said Clonder.

“And these were?” Kiliordes asked.

"It was Krin Gul's will that the three of us should come to Lorm and entreat you to join the Solar Pilgrimage Festival as Head Pilgrim," Pagyrus said matter-of-factly.

"M-m-me?" Kiliordes stammered.

"Who better than the man who saved the world from darkness to lead us in merry pursuit of the sun?" Pagyrus asked. "Besides, you have traveled with the Pilgrimage before—you know our ways."

"You were Krin Gul's only choice," pointed out Clonder.

"You're perfect to lead us, Kiliordes," Sornite said.

Kiliordes' head spun. Panic and indecision stabbed at him, and overwhelmed him.

"Look, I'm sorry. You people have caught me off guard here," he explained. "I'm going to have to think about all of this."

The three Solar Pilgrim's eager smiles deflated.

Crestfallen, Sornite pleaded, "But we need you."

"I'm needed here too," said Kiliordes. "Why don't you relax, and be my guests for the Yule Jarrels while I think about it. I'll give you my answer after the Yule."

The Pilgrims accepted his offer graciously and took their leave.

Could things get any more complicated?

Chapter 8

The King held court in the Jarrels' Hall at sundown each day, during the Lormian Yule celebration. It was a sizable structure, vaguely dome-shaped with two mammoth fireplaces at both ends, and three terraced levels provided staggered viewing of the floor. The place seated five hundred at the tables and another three hundred standing. Red and green banners draped the walls and well-placed torches provided adequate lighting throughout the structure. His Majesty provided the most hospitable feast; the tables were always fully laden with meats, breads, and cheeses. Baskets of exotic fruits and nuts were arranged conveniently on every table, and no traditional horn tankard ever went empty (a custom which kept the servants ever busy).

The hall was already loud with the sounds of Lormian revelry when Tolian entered with Findelbres on her arm. It was almost deafening, and no one paid much attention to the herald's announcement of their arrival. The princess gently lead the faerie through the tables of the Houses Yeld and Curdew, across the Jarrels' circle, to the royal tables. The din quieted considerably as all eyes fell on Tolian. Her tight velvet gown shouted in scarlet that the Princess of Lorm had arrived. She wore the wreath of holly in her hair. The scabbard with the Moonsword hung off her belt. She almost always carried the sword with her out of both habit from her old warrior lifestyle and because of the strong connection she had with the lunar weapon. She did not like to be without it

As she made her way proudly to her seat, she saw stares of disapproval, of jealously, of wantonness and lust; looks of fear and respect. Tolian wondered if they were more or less pleased with Findelbres at her side, in place of Brythia. While most in the palace heartily appreciated the contributions of both the faeries and the druids to their victory in the war, they did not care for the amount of influence they perceived either possessed over the politics of Lorm. Findelbres whispered to her sarcastically, “Boy, you’re really popular here, aren’t you.”

“Oh, you noticed that, huh?”

She had sacrificed her manhood for these people, and received scorn for her trouble. Would it always be like this for her?

Tolian smiled in as friendly manner as she could muster at Kiliordes, seated at the King’s Guests Table with Miderick, Pont the Swordsmith, Urno, the Chief Bannerman, and three individuals who could only be members of the Solar Pilgrimage Festival. Their presence drew out the princess’s curiosity. She had not heard the Pilgrimage was in Lorm. Usually their travels did not bring them to Lorm until late spring. She was distracted from her examination of the pilgrims by Lord Talthuwd, who was already drunk and leaning over Kiliordes. Talthuwd, who did not notice Tolian as she passed, bellowed his complaints to a patient but disinterested royal advisor. “I tell you, that Tolian’s kill shouldn’t be considered as the first kill. He didn’t use a spear, as our custom dictates. It’s not fair. He or she, or whatever he is now, makes a mockery of our oldest traditions. I should, rightfully, be First Huntsmen.”

Kiliordes raised a hand to halt the warlord’s diatribe. “You make good points, my lord. Miderick and I will present your case to the King, for his consideration.”

Tolian had to admit that Kiliordes probably had the toughest job in the kingdom. He was constantly scrambling to put out the diplomatic fires that Tolian’s situation had caused. No doubt, there were many displeased that “the druidesses” had taken her son Relinder away from the palace during the Yule, adding to his workload.

Tolian commented to Findelbres, “I wouldn’t want his job for anything.” She indicated Kiliordes with a tilt of her head.

“You two don’t spend much time together do you?” inquired the elf.

That sort of question, exactly, was why this preternatural being sometimes frustrated her, and she knew it. “Not really,” admitted the princess. “No. I know Kilfrie is in there, sort of; I just can’t get past what he looks like. I try.”

“People say that about you, too, you know,” rebuked the faerie.

"Yes, I know—but that body has killed people, lots of people. Ah, here we are," she announced, glad to change the subject. She gestured, indicating their seats at the royal table. Already seated were her Uncle Keliof and his wife, Aunt Asbere, and their children (her cousins) Kelvris and Helbeflas. The latter averted her eyes as the princess passed her.

Keliof was beaming, "Tolian, my boy, you look ravishing tonight."

"Indeed she does, father," agreed Prince Kelvris.

"Thank you, and a Happy Yule to all," she said. She wanted to correct her uncle, but she was weary of it. It was Yule; she let it pass. He always referred to her with male pronouns and terms. It made it so much harder for her to be comfortable with herself, enduring the constant assault of confusion over her gender. That was one of the reasons she always wore obviously feminine and provocative clothing, to make a clear statement of her identity.

"Ah, hello, everyone." Findelbres bowed, and he and Tolian took their seats.

As if their seating was the signal, the trumpeters blared forth their call to silence. A hush fell over the hall. The herald's voice boomed, distinctly audible this time.

"His royal Majesty Tolris of the House of Hemris, King of Lorm, and Master of the Yule."

The assemblage sprung to their feet and let out a bout of cheerful applause. Out of the crowd strode Tolris, who walked in with his golden robe trailing and made his way next to Tolian, at the center of the royal table. He raised his horn tankard, and toasted:

"Warriors, nobles, ladies, and guests. I bid you all a Happy Yule. Let joy come to all within this celebration. Let no horn be empty. Let no heart be sad. In the depths of winter, let us gather here to keep one another warm with good company and good food. Let the Yule Jarrels begin."

Now the applause was deafening, echoing as it did throughout the immense hall. The King waited for a few moments for the din to lessen and waved his hands.

"Good Lormians and friends. I present to you, Lord Delorick, Captain of the Royal Guard, and my Jarrels' Champion."

Tolian was a little jealous of her friend as he stepped proudly to the Jarrels' Circle, his armor gleaming in the torchlight.

"He must have spent all week polishing that armor," commented Findelbres quietly to the princess. "I hope he found a little time to train."

Tolian laughed discretely.

Delorick bowed on one knee before the King.

"Rise, Jarrels' Champion, come join us in our feast, that you may find the strength to defend our court. Let the entertainers perform as the Jarrels' Champion takes his sustenance."

And at the King's call a host of jugglers, magicians, acrobats, and jesters seemed to come out of nowhere and move throughout the hall.

Tolris sat down and sighed. He looked at his daughter, "Thank heavens that's over with. I hate these bloody ceremonial orations. It seems like that's all I ever get to say sometimes."

Tolris leaned over close to Tolian. "That was a fantastic kill today, I'm proud of you."

And there was pride in her father's eye, though tempered as always with some discomfort in her appearance.

"I'm also proud of your letting our dear Delorick here take the honor of Jarrels' Champion this year."

What he didn't say was that Delorick's being Jarrels' Champion held down the hostility and bickering that otherwise would have ensued had Tolian been appointed. In any case, she was happy enough; it was Yule and she could relax for a change. "Thank you, Father, your pride is a true reward for me," she said. She then leaned past her father and queried Delorick who sat on the other side of the King: "So, my friend, are you ready for some action this evening?"

The captain of the Guard nodded with an uncharacteristic solemnity and purposefulness, "More ready than most have ever been." He added, "And more than you, certainly."

"Well, we'll see about that," she replied. "But I wish you luck."

They feasted for half an hour, before the roast boar was brought in. It was Tolian's right (and duty) to take the first serving, as she had made the first kill of the Yule hunt. As she rose to do so, she was startled by a voice raised above the raucous sounds of merrymaking.

"Wait."

It was Talthuwd.

The warrior stood at his place. All eyes were glued upon him.

"I call the right of the Jarrels," he bellowed.

The King now rose as well. "Good Talthuwd, surely we may feast on the boar before we begin the Challenges?"

"My liege," said the warrior, bowing to Tolris, then straightening proudly. "You have announced the beginning of the Jarrels. I am within my rights. I wish to fight to have the Princess's kill disqualified, and my own counted as first kill. I wish to take the first serving from the boar as is my right."

"Very well," said the King. "Prepare yourself. Let the Jarrels' Champion take the challenge. Tolian, sit down until the matter is settled."

She was surprised, but she took her seat obediently. The entire hall was startled, though delighted the Jarrels were off to an early start.

Only as Talthuwd removed his cloak did Tolian notice he wore his full battle armor and that his sword hung at his side. Clearly it had been his intention to make a challenge all along. It was risky as far as his personal honor went; and why he allowed himself to get drunk first, Tolian could not comprehend. Sober, Talthuwd would be a good match against Delorick. Perhaps he had merely considered the challenge earlier, and too much ale had inflamed his bravado and his pride. His challenge of Tolian's first kill was symptomatic of the effect of her transformed presence at court. It was a disease, this chauvinistic pride. She had felt it herself—the blind ignorant outrage as she learned of the druid's plan for her metamorphosis, and even initially after she had become female. Of course, she understood how wrong that attitude was, and now she despaired it would ever change. To her, Delorick was fighting this attitude as well as for her honor. She wished she could fight Talthuwd herself. She knew she could best him in a second, probably less.

"I hope Delorick humiliates that bastard," she said to

Findelbres.

"Ah, the Goddess grows angry," came the faerie's bemused reply.

The rules of the Jarrels were simple: the contestants battled with long swords within the Jarrels' circle until one disarmed the other or forced him out of the circle or to the ground. An errant foot placed outside the circle or one knee brought momentarily to the ground was sufficient to end the combat. The circle was eight yards in diameter. Armor was permitted; if someone too poor to own their own wished to challenge, a few pieces were available to borrow. Challengers must, however, have their own long sword, or one belonging to a blood relative. Lormian warriors, as a general rule, did not wear helmets (favoring the advantages of mobility and vision, and relying on their skill as protection), so none were permitted in Jarrels' combat. Anyone could make a Jarrels' Challenge. If the challenger was victorious, his boon was granted, provided the King sanctioned the boon before the match.

The clang of their long swords reverberated throughout the hall. Talthuwd made the initial attack, strong, but reckless. Delorick calmly parried the thrust and made a slight fete, feigned a low jab and then struck at his opponent's shoulder. The excess alcohol was obviously slowing Talthuwd's reaction time; his block failed and Delorick's blade crashed down on his shoulder armor. The drunken warrior shouted, more out of rage than pain. He brought a series of furious swipes down on his younger adversary, though, once again too high and with too much power. To Tolian's seasoned eye, it appeared that Delorick had not expected the force, which was brought against him at first, but had quickly turned it to his advantage. His sword blocked Talthuwd's first few blows, then he was able to deflect his last, leaving him open on his left side. Delorick got two rapid low hits on Talthuwd's hip. That caused him to explode in wild anger. Tolian was confident that Talthuwd's drunken rage would cost him the match.

Lord Talthuwd was an experienced swordsman, however, and his fighting instincts were dulled only so much by the considerable amount of alcohol that coursed through his veins.

After the first few blows Delorick delivered, Talthuwd, recovered his sword wiles, and fought with more precision and cunning. Rarely was there a fight of this caliber in the Jarrels. They fought fiercely, their grunts punctuating the loud music of their blades clashing. Delorick attempted to power Talthuwd toward the circle's boundary, but the older fighter would have none of it. Just as Delorick had done, early in the battle, the veteran deflected the strong blows, forcing the Guard Captain a trifle off balance, creating an opening through which Talthuwd's blade found his leg. The struggle went back and forth, first one man pressing the advantage, then the other.

For a half hour, they moved about the Jarrels' circle, engaged in their violent waltz of long swords and skill. Sweat poured off both of their faces. Delorick still had that look of indomitable determination, unchanged since the beginning of the match. Talthuwd's countenance alternated between a blankness as he fought from automatic instinct and a drunken rage, which occasionally returned, usually to the older warrior's detriment. Tolian's eyes were glued to the battle.

"What a treat," commented Kelvris. "Tolian, how about a wager."

"That depends," she replied. "Who do you want?"

"Oh, I know that you would want to take Delorick, obviously."

"A Jarrels' wager?"

"Of course, cousin," agreed Kelvris.

"Done."

"Done."

"A Jarrels' wager?" Findelbres inquired.

"A wager for a gift. More symbolic than anything. Usually we pay up all our festive wagers on the last day of the Jarrels," Tolian explained.

"Hmmm," said the faerie, his curiosity assuaged.

"Get me something nice this year, Kelvris," instructed the princess.

"If Delorick wins, I'll find you something out of this world, cousin," replied Kelvris. "I promise you."

"Look," exclaimed King Tolris, "Delorick's got him now."

"So he does. I think you've made a bad bet, my son," added

Duke Keliof, directing his latter comment to Kelvris.

Kelvris smiled darkly. "Oh, I don't think so, father."

Despite the prince's apparent optimism, the match was leaning towards the younger warrior. Delorick had launched a vigorous assault against Talthuwd, and the challenger was backed up to the edge of the circle. The Jarrels' Champion did not relent as Talthuwd struggled against his potent offensive. The ale had not helped the defender's stamina as he struggled to keep his balance. In just a moment more, Talthuwd fell backwards out of the Jarrels' circle, landing roughly on his posterior. His face turned bright crimson.

King Tolris stood up instantly.

"The match goes to the Jarrels' Champion," he announced.

The hall erupted in cheers. Delorick bowed, a big smile decorating his previously stern face. He reached a hand down to assist Talthuwd, who was not happy but was too big a man to refuse. He slapped Delorick on the shoulder and bowed to the King.

"Thank you, Your Majesty, for the opportunity."

"That was quite a fight, Lord Talthuwd, but your challenge is unsettled," said the King. "Tolian, take the first serving of boar as is your right."

Tolian was enjoying the festivities, but she missed Brythia bitterly. Her wife's absence seemed to weigh even more heavily upon her when she was surrounded by her family and the holiday merrymaking. With each passing day, it seemed that the pain grew more intense, the hole in her heart, larger. She was immersed in mirth and good cheer, and she laughed and made merry with those around her, but in the end, it only served to remind her of how much she missed her beloved Brythia. Even amidst the Yule fires, things seemed wrapped in dimness, an ever-growing emptiness emanating from her heart. After they had feasted on boar, she watched Delorick fight against a poor huntsman who wished to hunt the King's personal game tract for a white hart he had seen in the vicinity. Tolian could only think of Brythia. What mysterious druidic ritual was she engaged in at that moment? Was she having the same trouble that Tolian was, fighting the darkness of their separation, unable to focus on life unfolding around her? She hoped that the golden-haired druidess was having a great deal more fun than she was.

Chapter 9

There was nothing for Brythia to do but fret. She did not know how long she had been in the library. There was no means of gauging. It felt like forever. The steady, quiet pain of her distance from Tolian was augmented first by the darkest of foreboding and then outright panic as the druidess endured her confinement in the library chamber. She had long since quit her frantic screams and curses. Doubtlessly, no one was permitted even outside the door, lest they take pity on the captive scholar, and thereby interrupt the appointed period of sacred seclusion. If they could have heard her, would they have believed her wild cries of danger, or would they have dismissed them as the ravings of a delirious mind?

Hunger assailed her, worsening the torment of her confinement.

She alternated between the stone chair at the table, hugging her knees with a static worry, and pacing like a caged beast in frenetic mania. She prayed to the gods to let the prescribed time be over soon, and to let nothing happen to Tolian before she could get warnings to Lorm. The danger had not been averted last year, merely delayed. She had felt it all along. Some part of her had known, even in the toppled towers of Keythion. Questions forced away by the sheer force of joy and relief. They had all been too satisfied in their victory to allow even reasonable doubts to linger long.

She forced herself to think about those terrible days alone with the Demon, and that last moment of confrontation. Of nightmare. Of astonishment. Much of it she could still not access, so horrible were those events that they fled from her probing mind as rabbits at the approach of the fox. A few images were burned with supreme clarity in her mind:

The golden tassel. She remembered the remorseless winter air raging cruelly at her wind-burnt face. Her lips chapped, and nearly frost bitten, ached. She could picture the Imperial Palace of the Northern Empire of Keythion in ruins stretched out below her as the Demon brought her there on the back of a dragon on that cold December afternoon. Six other dragons, vast winged reptiles, circled the broken walls. Three of the Demon's Abominations roamed the burnt remains of the once most majestic city in the world. They were creatures formed by the Demon's dark power, towering several stories and comprised of the twisted bodies of the fiend's human prisoners, fused into a thing of madness and used as living siege engines.

The famed white spires of the North's greatest capital were scorched black from dragonfire. A few tattered pendants, now rags, waved in the icy wind. The largest army she had ever seen surrounded the once mighty walls, now crumbling and breached. The howling cries of the women and children assailed her even from high above the great city. She remembered having the impression that it could not have been more than a day since the Palace City had fallen to the Demon's forces. Soldiers moved in and out of the mangled gates. As the Demon brought his giant, scaled steed down towards the gate, she could see a corpse, garbed in gold, hanging from the entrance arch.

The warriors in the entranceway cleared the area as the giant reptile landed. The Demon threw Brythia roughly to the hard stone and hopped lightly down next to her. He scooped her up and, holding her by the feet, carried her roughly behind his back into the doomed city. She stared up at the corpse as they passed under it. Something caught her attention. Clearly, it was the Emperor of Keythion. The gentle swaying and flapping of the soiled robes of woven gold, worn for three centuries by the rulers of the vast and powerful land, mesmerized her. Golden tassels swinging gently. The scarred and eyeless face. The expression of terror was still evident by the grimace he wore. The golden tassels. The blackness gobbled up that memory.

Another flash of dawning recollection. Again on the dragon's back. The Demon, using Rwiordes' body, was holding her tightly from behind. They were once again circling the vanquished city. Was it a different time? Yes. There was something different this time. Something different. She looked into Rwiordes' face. His eyes were black. That and the cruel curl of a smile were all that indicated the Demon's presence there. The Demon had systematically possessed the three foolish, would-be sorcerers who had brought him into the world by their failed attempt at magick. Of course, the druidess knew that such works of evocation never failed completely—something always came, though usually a harmless elemental or sprite.

She had seen their sorcery through the Spirit Vision. The first of the three to succumb to the Demon's possession was Perelisk, who then raised an army and a host of dragons and conquered the great metropolis of Coertal City. The next to fall to the Demon's influence was Hertrid, who then contained half of the Demon's power and laid siege to the palace of Lorm. Tolian beheaded him on the battlefield before the fortress' gates. Why was this tangent related to the dragon's back?

That's what it was. She could see Perelisk's possessed form on the back of another dragon, flying directly across from them in the same orbit around the despoiled Palace City. There was someone behind him. She did not see him clearly, but she remembered her surprise by his presence. A swarthy rogue, bearded. Black armor. Who he was she had no idea. Could there have been a fourth? She did not think so because the Demon only had that sort of power against the three who were inside the broken magick circle. Besides, even from the distance his discomfort was evident, though he appeared to be no prisoner. Was this the difference from the last memory? No. There was something else. Something too horrible to remember. But she plunged backwards shattering the shields she had built around this image in her memory.

Below them the other dragons circled the Throne City of Keythion. And far below them she could see the vast army that surrounded the fortified walls. The soldiers looked like ants from the terrific distance.

Through the rushing air she could hear the Demon shouting something. The twisted howling of his words rang out: "CHALTRHADG HOOS IN UDEWSK THROUZ."

They were words of power, full of darkness. Vileness. They bombarded her with ancient hatred and wickedness. She did not know their meaning, but could feel their evil vibratory energy.

He let go of her with one arm and raised something over their heads. It was an earth talisman. She recognized it from the

Spirit Vision. The clumsy one the three fools had fashioned in their attempt to gain control of the cold, hard spirits of the tellurian darkness. They wanted treasure; it had been all about avarice for them. In the Demon's hands, the talisman became a potent tool for destruction. His vibratory shriek now became the call of the Earth elementals: "KILROP TY IROUD CURNIT VAZ EWRTY."

Then again: "CHALTRHAG HOOS IN UDEWSK THROUZ."

Rwiordes' lips kept moving and the barbarous words of evocation poured manically out, somehow growing louder and louder. Brythia's ears hurt from the powerful force of his cries, the volume now drowning out even the bitter wind.

He stopped his cries suddenly and the druidess lost her breath in the sudden, relative quiet. But, not for long. He began his shouts again. This time, however, the druidess could understand the bellowed words.

"Spirits of the Earth, I, who hold the Talisman, command you. Bring forth the fire that burns forever hot in the Earth's molten core. Let it pour up as from a well. Let the breath of these dragons ignite it. Let my legions stretch across and blacken the world. The Marriage of Fire and Earth. So mote it be."

And then it happened. She began to twitch violently in the subterranean chamber as the memory burned hot and dreadful, the pain of it searing her brain.

The dragons unleashed their fiery breath upon humbled Keythion. The dragonfire poured down from all directions engulfing the city in one instantaneous bonfire. The flames licked higher than the tallest tower. Clearly there was more than the dragon's breath at work. She had seen the dragon attacks at Lorm. Although there was a much smaller contingent of dragons there, the destruction she saw in Keythion could not merely be explained by more dragons. She thought of all the people still inside the city, burned to cinders in the blink of an eye. She did not wish to look upon the scene, but she could not divert her gaze. The leaping flames transfixed her. Their great heat reached even up to where the Demon in Rwiordes' body held her on the back of the dragon, circling the city.

In just a moment more of the surrounding army ignited in a

brilliant ring of fire, which took off at a burning run as a gigantic, ever-increasing circle of fire, scorching the land around the palace and racing as a vast wall of fire in all directions. The cries of the people burning below reached her ears. They had not perished as quickly as she had originally thought. They were now burning wraiths of flame charging all things in their ravenous rage and unyielding desire to consume them, undead spirits with the hunger of fire set ablaze to devour the world.

All at once the putrid odor of burned flesh found her and memory broke off—lost again in the dim shadow shields, which her mind had erected to protect her sanity as it fought to cope with the unspeakable horrors inflicted upon her.

Fragments. Shards of recollections. The scorched black room. The cold steel chains. The waiting, glad of the loneliness, so much better than when he came to gloat. A wave of repressed terror convulsed through her, as she recalled the ghostly silence broken only by the insane cackling of the fiend's two voices. She winced as she remembered being dragged out into the blackened courtyard, into the blazing sunshine and the cold north wind.

Then Tolian came and it all ended suddenly, like a brilliant flash of lightning. It happened so quickly. Tolian strode forward, wielding the Moonsword and issuing her challenge. But, the Demon was not afraid. He knew what he was doing. He used Brythia as a tool. He offered to spare her if Tolian would hand over the lunar blade, the only weapon capable of killing him. By that time the druidic love magick that had been used on them was already incredibly strong. As a result, Tolian was willing to sacrifice everything for her. The world. She gave the Demon the Moonsword and rushed to Brythia's side. With Perelisk's body the Demon wounded Tolian, and they waited together for Rwiordes' blow with the Moonsword to take off her head.

But that was not what happened. Somehow, and Brythia had to admit that she never understood this, Rwiordes' and Kilfrie's minds and spirits were united, and the new being created by their union threw off the Demon's control and brought the Moonsword down on Perelisk's neck. That was the end.

Even then there were questions. The prophecy could have conceivably referred to two Champions, one Tolian and one Kiliordes, but that explanation never did sit well with her. And where were the dragons? None were seen again after that day. What of the Earth Talisman? Though they searched, it had never been found. Everyone had dismissed these uncomfortable loose ends; they were too eager for the nightmare to be over. But it wasn't over; she knew it now.

The menace still lingered. If Kiliordes had not been a Champion, and therefore incapable of killing the Demon, then perhaps somehow the fiend had survived. Maybe there was something everyone was missing.

All at once, the door opened and a lanterns' light poured into the library chamber. Magara's voice startled Brythia out of her trance. There was a note of urgency in her voice.

"Quickly, child, we must hurry. Something has happened."

Chapter 10

"I have come to ask yet another favor from you, my friend," said Delorick.

Tolian was still in her robe. She had just awakened from her afternoon nap, surprised to find her friend calling on her. She rubbed the sleep out of her eyes, and mumbled, "Anything you desire, but you know that."

His brow was knitted and furrowed, "This may not be an easy thing for you, but it carries importance to me."

"What?" She asked with sleepy impatience.

He was uncomfortable, but he began, "I know it is your custom to carry the Moonsword with you wherever you go. I understand that it is a great source of power for you, there is no weapon its equal in all the world."

"This is true enough, yes."

"Well," he hesitated. "I ask you not to bring it to the Jarrels' Hall for the rest of the Yule."

Tolian was stunned by this request. Finally, she found her voice to ask, "But why on earth not, my friend?"

Delorick looked her straight in the eye, "It's hard enough being the Jarrels' Champion with you in the hall, but with the Moonsword on your belt, it reminds everyone that you should rightfully be the one holding that honor. The presence of the magick sword serves to bring that fact strongly into focus. I have overheard several people talking of it. I know it seems like a petty request, but it is a meaningful one to me."

Tolian sighed. He had a point, she had to admit. It would not be the first time she did not carry the weapon. She did not bring it to wedding banquets as a rule because it seemed out of place on such occasions. Still, she did not like to be without it, and it was not an easy decision for her. Nonetheless, she agreed, "Very well, my friend, I can see your concern. I will place the Moonsword over my hearth for the duration of the Jarrels, for your sake. I won't be needing it anyway, with you handling the fighting."

~~~

It was the third night of the Yule Jarrels. The aromas of honey-roasted pork, pheasant, and gingerbread mingled deliciously at the entrance to the hall with cinnamon and sweet potatoes as well. Tolian was late. Findelbres had arrived sometime ago, as had the rest of the celebrants. The princess stepped into the hall with all of her self-confidence and nonchalance. She faced the customary murmur, the staring eyes. That night Tolian cut a gorgeous figure in a white, lacy gown, matching slippers, and a holly wreath in her carefully coiffed hair. She felt naked without the Moonsword, though. She was already weary of the festivities, and were it not for her royal obligation to attend, she would not have done so. Nothing seemed to help the crushing loneliness that Brythia's absence caused. She told herself that she should have gone with her wife. Ah, but there she was, and regrets serve no purpose.

The herald, brimming with impatience, was livid at her tardiness, and told her so as acidly as a servant could address a princess. Did the princess not realize the time? Was she unaware the King could not enter to begin the evening's festivities until she was seated? Polite voice, angry eyes. Tolian directed her doe-eyes, big and brown, in as innocent a gaze as she could muster, and then said with bland coldness, "Well, I'm here now."

Again, she made her way across the hall and the Jarrels' circle. As she approached the King's table, she noticed a large open cistern, filled with what appeared to be wine, placed before the table. Two servants stood diligently next to the wine, if that's what it was. Tolian had never seen Yule wine placed so, and her curiosity was piqued.

"Tell me," she asked the servants, "where did this wine come from?"

"My Lady," answered the elder servant. "It was delivered this morning. 'Tis said that it is faerie-wine. A gift from a Lord of the Sidhe."

Tolian looked instinctively at Findelbres, seated across the table. The faerie shrugged. "It wasn't me. I'm not that thoughtful a guest."

"I've noticed that," Tolian agreed.

"Um, Princess?" squeeked the servant nervously. "I think
~~~

the herald would like you to be seated."

Sure enough, the fellow by the entrance was frantically signaling her to sit down. She shrugged her shoulders, but made her way around the table. Even her Uncle Keliof seemed annoyed at her for her disregard for the time. Kelvris was the exception of her kin; he was surprisingly cordial, and almost beside himself with uncharacteristic affection for her.

"Tolian. It's wonderful to see you. They feared that you had taken ill," said the prince. "But, you don't take ill anymore, do you?"

No, she didn't. Not since she had become a goddess, if that was really what she was now. She did not like those sorts of things being pointed out, however. Though she enjoyed her physical prowess, she longed to be like everyone else. She slapped Kelvris good-naturedly on the back, with just a little too much force. The prince lurched forward, barely able to keep himself from smashing into the table. Tolian smiled cheerfully, and noticed the extra chair next to the King's place.

"Kelvris," she inquired as she slid past him to take her seat, "who's sitting there?"

Her cousin regained his breath. "Ah, that's the mystery, isn't it? A special guest, though who it is, no one will say."

"Hmmm."

"Yes, exactly."

Tolian smiled brightly at Findelbres. Somehow seeing the elf always raised her spirits.

"Good evening, dear Master Findelbres," she greeted him. "I hope you are well."

"Oh Lady of the Silver Light, Empress of Clouds, who holdeth all the Realm of Faerie as a piece of her Kingdom, how could I not be well in thine radiant presence?"

"Please, Findelbres, spare me the epithets," said Tolian in a hushed whisper. For the King had entered the hall. "Well, what do you think of our little celebration?" she asked.

"The food and ale are fantastic, and I mean that. But, the entertainment, how many times can you watch Delorick rough people up before it gets old," came Findelbres' reply, shouted over the cheers that erupted with the King taking his place at the table and saluting the assemblage. Tolris waved down the applause and the polite silence prevailed once again.

"I bid you greetings, guests and folk of Lorm," boomed the King. "Tonight we have something different. For the first time in recorded history, we will have faerie wine served at the Yule Jarrels. And as all can see, we have an ample supply for the evening. I tasted this vintage myself not long ago, and it truly is something special. Now, our benefactor would like to enjoy our Lormian hospitality. I am pleased to introduce to you, a warrior who fought bravely for the cause of Lorm last year, the leader of the faeire forces, Lord Dowbreth."

Everyone there had seen faeries before, but this Lord Dowbreth was altogether different from those the people of Lorm had seen before. It was said that he had led the charge of the Elven warriors against the dragons at the siege, but if he had done so, he did not remain in Lorm for long. A deep uncertain quiet now took the hall as he made his entrance. Tolian could not see him at first as her cousin Kelvris had moved to the front of the table, next to the wine, blocking her initial view. He had leapt mysteriously from his chair at the King's announcement. Whatever he was doing there, Tolian did not care, but she wished he would stand somewhere else.

"Kelvris, get out of the way," she yelled to him.

He turned with a smug smile and promptly made his way back to his seat. Now Tolian could see the faerie warlord.

"By the Gods of Lorm," she muttered in astonishment.

"Dowbreth," hissed Findelbres in displeased surprise.

Dowbreth made a giant figure, standing between seven and eight feet tall; as with all of his preternatural race, it was impossible to judge his height with any degree of certainty. He wore full body armor, which glowed with an eerie green radiance and was accentuated by spikes projecting from its surface. His face was even paler than Findelbres' and marked by deep red scars across his cheeks and forehead. His nose, twisted and smashed, had clearly been broken numerous times. His eyes gleamed with red fire and his hair was deep black, darker than the night sky. He wore a smile, perhaps friendly on anyone else's mouth, but on the faerie warlord it revealed his teeth, which were filed to sharp points. As he crossed the Jarrels' hall with his confident, great strides, Tolian could see that what, at first, appeared to be several pouches or sacks suspended from his belt, were, in fact, severed heads, cured only by time, such that some were little more than skulls. Behind him trailed a green cloak that was either tattered or designed to stream behind him like the tendrils of some rare plant or sea creature. His boots clanged against the floor with resounding force as he walked.

Tolian felt a chill run up her spine as Dowbreth brought his gaze upon her. Their eyes met for an instant, and she could feel the wantonness and otherworldly menace that burned in his fiery stare. Did he smile more broadly as he perceived the haughty disdainful defiance in her eyes?

He stopped and bowed low before the King's table.

"Rise, Lord Dowbreth," entreated the King. "Receive our welcome and gratitude for your Yuletide gift as well as your past service to our realm."

Dowbreth rose again to his great height. And then he spoke. How different was his voice from Findelbres' bright and fluid cadences. The words still possessed a vaguely inhuman quality, but were a blended mixture of harsh cacophony and a jagged eloquence, beyond reconciliation from mortal lips. Gracious in tone, yet malevolent in timbre.

"Thank you, Your Majesty. I am honored to be received so warmly at your Midwinter's court," he said. He noticed Findelbres and nodded with familiarity in his direction. "I see that I am not the only visitor from the Faerie Realm present tonight, and I, as well, bring the good tidings of our Lord and Lady, and this gift from their own wine cellar. I wish nothing more than to enjoy your hospitality and share your proud and noble customs."

"Come," said Tolris, "please take a seat here at my table."

Tolian noticed that Findelbres' eyes narrowed with clear hostility. He leaned over to Tolian.

"You cannot trust him," he whispered in Tolian's ear. "He has no love of mortals, believe me."

"What, do you think he poisoned the wine?" she asked.

The King, overhearing their conversation whispered, "Please give us some credit, Findelbres. The wine was checked for poison as soon as we received it. He has not been near it since."

Dowbreth took his seat on the other side of the King, appearing almost ridiculous behind the table because of his massive stature, but menacing enough not to be. “Your Majesty, I should like to propose a toast,” he suggested with eagerness and humility.

“Of course, of course,” nodded Tolris agreeably. “Let the wine of the Good Folk be served,” he commanded.

With the celebrated Lormian efficiency, the servants set about the task of distributing the elfin spirits to everyone in the hall.

Tolian spent a few moments in discrete examination of Dowbreth as Findelbres addressed him.

“Lord Dowbreth, Our Lady had not mentioned your intention to visit Lorm as well,” he stated with clear curiosity.

“Naturally not, Lord Findelbres, for my errand is under authority of Our Lord, a matter of military policy. I do not believe Queen Ymrisiva was informed until after your departure.”

“A matter of military policy? How so? The Host of the Sidhe has never brought such dealings to the mortal realm before.”

In a patient tone, the warlord explained, “You’ll forgive me for my plainness, friend Findelbres, but perhaps the secret war councils of the Sidhe are somewhat beyond the providence of the Queen’s Guard. But, in any case, you’ll no doubt agree that a military alliance with mortals was formed last year, and that these mortals, these Lormians, have proven themselves to be mighty warriors, and worthy allies.”

There was a general muttered agreement with Dowbreth’s words among the surrounding tables.

“Do I detect a friendly rivalry between our faerie guests?” asked the King good-naturedly.

“Is it not possible, good Findelbres,” added Kelvris, “that his words ring true?”

“Actually, no,” responded Findelbres.

Tolian found herself torn. She trusted her friend’s opinion, but there was a brutal straightforwardness to Dowbreth’s manner that lent credence to him. Clearly, this man, or faerie, was a warrior; the folk of Lorm respected such people.

"His story makes sense, Findelbres," Tolian found herself saying quietly.

"You people don't know this creature..." began Findelbres.

"Ah," interrupted the King, "the wine is served. Lord Dowbreth, your toast."

"Excellent," said Dowbreth, "I'm quite parched from my journey." The warlord rose from his chair, towering above the table. When he addressed the assemblage, his utterances, though still rough, conveyed a sense of friendship and a savage, but mysterious grandeur. "People of Lorm," he raised his cup. Everyone in the hall did the same. "Here is to a new age of unity between our peoples, a new alliance hitherto undreamt of in either of our worlds. We have much to teach you, and you have much to offer us as well." As he said this he let his eyes fall briefly on Tolian.

Something in his eyes made her uncomfortable. She straightened herself in her chair and pretended not to notice him.

"May a great happiness come to our realms. To Lorm." He raised his horn to his lips.

"To Lorm and our faerie friends," offered the King.

"To Lorm and our faerie friends," echoed back the merry Jarrels' guests. And they all drank the wine.

When the wine hit Tolian's tongue, the flavors were unlike anything she had ever tasted. Yes, it was wine. It was fruity and sweet, and powerful. Waves of pleasure radiated from her mouth and throat as the vintage slid down. It sparkled with a hypnotic aroma, and a taste that seemed a combination of the melody of a songbird, the golden vista of a sunrise and the fragrance of honeysuckle, with a splash of mystery. Warmth stole over her body as the liquid reached her stomach. Clearly, the faerie beverage was stronger than the mortal version. The soothing warmth slowly blended with, and gave way to, a light-headed euphoria.

"This is a remarkable cordial you have shared with us Lord Dowbreth. We are indeed grateful," commented King Tolris. Tolian noticed that her father's speech was already slurred slightly from his first drink.

"You're very welcome, Your Highness. It is the custom of my people that friends exchange gifts on the Solstice," said

Dowbreth with a nod at Prince Kelvris.

Prince Kelvris stood up at once and spoke, "We have a similar tradition, Lord Dowbreth, and in the spirit of gift-giving... I should like to take this opportunity to give my esteemed cousin, Crown Princess Tolian, a gift which is due her."

He reached into his pocket and produced a bracelet that he held up for all to see. "Tolian, dear Tolian. I promised you something special, something memorable, for your Jarrels' gift. I shall not, I trust, disappoint."

He stepped next to her and bowed, holding the bracelet open for her.

Tolian held out her arm, allowing Kelvris to slip the bracelet closed around her wrist. It was beautiful, and clearly different from any other jewelry she had ever seen before. It was basic in design, a largish circlet of some dark metal or alloy, which was hinged closed, but now revealed no seam or sign of hinging. Its uniqueness was in its simplicity and its black shimmer that nearly radiated darkness.

"It's lovely, Kelvris. Thank you very much," she said with sincere gratitude. She held her wrist up for those in the immediate vicinity to view.

"Oh, you're welcome to it, I'm sure," said Kelvris. "It's the least you deserve."

Everyone at the table politely agreed. Dowbreth wore a satisfied smile. He was still standing.

"Your Majesty," the faerie warlord said. "In the spirit of sharing traditions, I should like to make a Jarrels' challenge."

Everyone in the hall gasped in one breath.

Tolris quickly recovered himself from his initial shock, "Oh indeed, Lord Dowbreth," he said. "What boon have you in mind?"

Dowbreth spoke slowly and calmly, "I wish the right to fight Lorm's greatest warrior, indeed this world's greatest warrior, in Jarrels' combat. I wish to fight the Moon Goddess."

Tolian leaped eagerly to her feet. "I will fight you Dowbreth," she declared.

"Not yet, you won't," the King said. "He must first best the Jarrels' Champion. You understand that this is our way, Lord

Dowbreth?"

"I do, Your Majesty."

"Very well," said the King. "We shall receive your Challenge; if you best our Champion you may combat Tolian using Jarrels' rules. Are you familiar with our rules of Solstice Combat?"

"I have recently been informed of them. This shall be most entertaining."

Tolian felt sorry for Delorick as he and the faerie warlord faced off in the Jarrels' circle. She knew that her friend was among the world's greatest swordsmen, but she did not think he could stand long before the legendary chieftain of the Sidhe. She shouted his name with the rest of the assemblage, though she both knew, and hoped, the match would be a quick one. She was eager to battle the giant.

Delorick once again gave the appearance of the determined veteran, showing no doubt in his own ability to handle himself and no deference to the stature or status of his opponent. He held his sword before him, waiting for Dowbreth to unsheathe his own long sword.

Dowbreth began to laugh in a most unwholesome manner, showing his filed teeth as he did so. His laughter was raspy, discordant, and entirely unpleasant. To Delorick's credit, he did not flinch, nor change his expression of confident concentration; he waited calmly with sword up and ready for Dowbreth to make his move.

Findelbres leaned over to Tolian's ear, "Remember, I warned you about this villain."

"I'm worried for Delorick," replied the princess, "but I am not afraid to face him. I've battled worse monsters than this rogue."

Findelbres agreed, "I know, but he must have something up his sleeve, my friend. You can count on that. Some treachery is lurking in the back of his mind. But for the present let us hope our Delorick doesn't get hurt too badly."

Kelvris, overhearing their conversation, interjected, "Oh, so you think our Jarrels' Champion can't stand up to one of your kind, Master Findelbres?"

"Few can," answered Findelbres plainly.

Kelvris smiled, almost slyly. "Well," said the prince, "perhaps, you would like to make a Jarrels' wager on the battle?"

Findelbres turned towards Tolian, "Your cousin, apparently has an abundance of Jarrels' gifts to be rid of this year." He brought his attention back to Kelvris. "You have a wager my friend. Another bad one, I fear."

"Done," said the prince with an uncharacteristic air of magnanimity.

Within the Jarrels' Circle the opponents slowly moved around, vying for positional advantage inside the boundary, locked eye to eye. The giant's unnerving cackle almost drowned out the shouts of support from Delorick's well-wishers. The Jarrels' Champion made the first move. With great speed, Delorick brought his sword down towards the faerie warrior's hip. Dowbreth's blade blocked his attack and with a mighty force pushed the Lormian's blade up and away. It was all Delorick could do to retain his grip on his weapon and keep on his feet.

Tolian frowned as she watched, for clearly her friend's sword was now too high to put up a defense should his opponent move to attack (which he would surely do). But Tolian was surprised (as was Delorick), for the giant made no offensive move. Instead, he merely returned his sword to a defensive position before him, and kept up his disturbing guffaw. *What is he waiting for?* Tolian wondered. It was now clear to everyone in the hall that Dowbreth could win the match whenever he desired.

Delorick produced a skillful fete to the right and then a quick lunge straight ahead to the faerie's midsection. However, Dowbreth now showed that he was not only the stronger of the two, but he was the more nimble as well. In a stroke that was beyond the agility of mortal sinew, the otherworldly knight parried the thrust and sent the Lormian staggering backwards. He then did something unexpected; he quickly caught Delorick before he toppled to the floor and set him aright on his feet. There was no motive Tolian could think of for this behavior, but, clearly, for some reason known only to him, the faerie was prolonging the contest.

"What the hell is he doing?" Tolian asked.

"I do not know, but he has a purpose, I assure you," replied Findelbres.

And so the match continued for another fifteen minutes, with Dowbreth making no offensive moves, but defending himself with impossible dexterity against Delorick's assaults. It seemed as though Dowbreth was playing with Delorick as a cat plays with its prey. Tolian had the impression that he was, somehow, playing with all of them. Then all at once the maniacal laughter ceased, and the giant in one swift attack sent Delorick flying across the Jarrels' hall, and smashing in to the table of the House of Curdew.

The giant's arms reached up in a victorious gesture. Attendants hurried over to aid Delorick.

King Tolris rose to his feet, "Lord Dowbreth is the victor. His Jarrels' boon shall be granted."

There was a polite, halfhearted round of applause for the faerie, though most of the people there would have much preferred to see Delorick best the otherworldly knight.

The King then addressed Tolian. "Prepare yourself, my child, to defend the honor of Lorm." He added quietly, "and show this elfish ruffian something of the power of Lorm."

The princess sprang to her feet. "I shall, father," she said. "Crud," she added, "I didn't bring the Moonsword; I didn't figure on fighting in the Jarrels."

"You can borrow my sword, cousin," volunteered Kelvris. "It is not as celebrated as your own blade, but it has seen me through many a fight to victory."

"Thank you, Kelvris," said Tolian, taking the weapon from her cousin.

"You're not exactly dressed for combat," observed Findelbres.

"That shouldn't be a problem," replied Tolian. "I don't think this fight will take very long."

She kicked off her slippers and with her borrowed sword, walked calmly towards the Jarrels' circle.

If there had ever been a more unlikely Jarrels' match in Lormian history, no one there could recall it. Princess Tolian slipped inside the circle without thought of changing out of her white lace ball gown. In her midtwenties and dressed in her party attire, she knew her foe thought she would be easily conquered. Smiling broadly, she stared up at the hulking faerie warlord. "So you want to fight the Moon Goddess?" she asked him. "I shall make this a much quicker fight than your last one."

He looked down at her and smirked most rudely, "Do not underestimate me, my lady. I may surprise you."

They raised their swords.

"We shall see, Lord Dowbreth, we shall see."

"Indeed."

The murmuring in the background grew strangely quiet as the match began.

Tolian struck first, her movements far too fast to be seen. She made three powerful swipes at Dowbreth's forearms, alternately, from both directions. Her goal was to disarm the warlord of the Sidhe immediately. No mortal warrior could defend or withstand her blows; Dowbreth, however, not only retained his grip on his sword though bleeding considerably from the wrists, but also had managed to deflect one of her assaults. Impressive, she thought.

With a series of light and easy flicks of her wrist she brought Kelvris's sword down on Dowbreth's defense with fury. In a few seconds his armor was ripped and blood trickled from numerous wounds. Dowbreth was backed up to the brink of the boundary, panting heavily for breath.

"Are you ready to finish this, Lord Dowbreth?" the princess inquired.

His speech was broken and punctuated with gasps for air, but his words carried no tone of defeat. "Oh, my princess, I never intended to finish this. I'm not so foolish as that. I'm simply biding my time, waiting from my preparations to come to fruition."

There was a powerful sense of menace tangible in his words. "Preparations? What are you talking about?"

"Well, to begin with, you'll notice we have lost our audience."

Tolian looked out around the hall. No one stirred; heads were slumped down or laid on tables, the low rhythmic sound of snoring could be heard.

"Fear not, they are only sleeping, nothing more than that. I have no quarrel with your people. They shall wake in a few hours."

"You arrogant fool," shouted Tolian. "I shall kill you for this." She wielded her sword with great agility and skill, but this time Dowbreth's blade was there to defend. She realized that for some reason her assault lacked the power and speed she normally possessed. In fact, the giant had already caught his breath and gone on the offensive himself. Now it was all Tolian could do to fend off his blade, as her own sword seemed to have grown heavier. This time it was Tolian who was out of breath after Dowbreth's frantic attack.

Fear grew in the princess's heart as the towering giant renewed his maniacal laughter and brought his sword once more toward her. Kelvris's sword was now almost too heavy for her to lift. With one more quick move, the faerie disarmed her.

What had happened? Where were her powers?

A great wave of exhaustion descended upon her. She fell to the floor. Dowbreth's scarred and laughing face was the last thing she saw before her eyes grew too heavy to keep open. Suddenly sleep could wait no longer. The princess succumbed to its irresistible beckoning. Dowbreth's sinister laughter echoed in her ears as deep slumber took hold of her.

PART II

THE DRUIDESS

Chapter 11

"Tolian has disappeared. Presumably, she has been abducted." Magara spoke the words calmly.

"How is that even possible?" Brythia asked. Her voice wavered in confusion and weariness. None of this seemed real. It was all like some fever dream had followed her out of the library chamber. A lingering of trance, the hauntings of a hunger and sleep-deprived mind. She could barely open her eyes in the blinding lamplight of her old room.

"We have no idea," was Magara's answer. "There seems to be some faerie involvement, but what happened is unclear."

"When? How long has she been missing?"

"Between two and four hours ago. Our scouts got word from the Lormians about an hour ago, and we just received their message right before I told you. We have no details as of yet."

The druids maintained a system of communication using the creatures of the wild to relay information over great distances quickly. The calls of the night birds, of frogs, of insects were their media. Using this method, the nature priests and priestesses were able to send messages to one another with incredible speed.

"I have to get to Lorm immediately," said Brythia in a distant, dreamy manner.

"That's not possible, dear. You need some time to rest, to build back your strength. Besides, you know as well as I do that it takes at least three weeks to travel to the palace," replied the High Druidess.

Brythia shook her head, "No, there is another way, and you know it. I shall use the flying smoke. I can be there in no time."

Magara sighed, "Or, it can kill you. I can't allow it. I'm sorry."

"Magara, I wasn't asking your permission. I am going to use the flying smoke, and that's final. You don't understand what's at stake."

"Well, of course, I do," said Magara. "Remember, it was I who bound you two by the forbidden love magick. You must feel torn in half. I do understand."

Brythia brought her most intense (and lucid) stare upon Magara. "It's not just about that."

"What else, then? Tell me."

"'By the Spring Equinox the blood of the dead shall issue from the Earth, these shall be the last of days.' It's not over yet. Somehow, the Demon is not dead. I'm sure of it, and only Tolian can stop him from destroying everything."

The color drained from the matriarch's face. Brythia quickly explained what she had learned from the scrolls in the library chamber. When she finished, the High Druidess took a deep breath.

"Brythia, do you think whatever has happened to Tolian is somehow connected with the Demon and the prophecy?"

"Yes, probably."

"Very well," said Magara. She paused for a moment. "Rest for a few moments, but do not eat or drink anything. I will prepare the flying smoke for you. It will only take a few minutes. Oh, what about Myrthis and Relinder? Should we send them back to Lorm under escort?"

It was then that Brythia became aware that their relationship had changed. Magara was uncharacteristically seeking direction from her.

"You must keep them safe here, at least until we find out what has happened in Lorm."

"Yes, I agree. All right, let me be about my task then. Luckily for us, you have already fasted, so that will not be a problem. I shall be right back."

When Magara left her, Brythia sat quietly in her old chamber, and waited. How she ached for Tolian. It had been bad enough before, when only distance separated them; now the uncertainties made it unbearable. How was it possible? There was no one in the world as powerful as Tolian. How could she be abducted? There were too many questions. She knew she would have to wait until she got to the palace before there would be any answers. Until she got home, she thought.

She remembered that she only had a few minutes to prepare herself. Quickly she garbed herself in her druidic winter robe, leggings, and battle armor. She slid herself into the comfortable boots worn in the cooler weather by the nature priest and priestesses. She draped a standard issue order travel pack over her shoulders and attached her sword (in scabbard) securely to it. She tied her small spell pouch to her belt. In five minutes, she was ready.

Magara did not leave Brythia waiting for long. She stepped back into the room without a sound, so Brythia thought.

"Are you ready?" she asked.

Brythia nodded solemnly. She was glad that Magara did not ask her if she was certain that she wished to proceed. The High Druidess evidently understood her well enough now.

They walked together in silence through the corridors of the Druidic Temple stronghold. Most of the other nature priests and priestesses were asleep, though a few stood here and there in silent vigil or traveled on their own nocturnal business. Some of the passing gazes revealed a degree of awe as they regarded Brythia. It was, of course, well known that she was the Moon Goddess' wife, and now her examination of the prophecy scrolls added to her mystique. How peculiar, the emotions she felt as they made their way through the polished stone passageways. A distant dread echoed in every footfall, growing louder with each step. It was funny, but for some reason, it had never seemed more like home at Hyge Bryth, yet some part of her was certain that she would never return. A twinge of existential sadness, a glimpse of the twilight of the transitory, and the subtle, bittersweet aroma of home grabbed her.

They exited the main building through the Forest Door and immediately the darkened woods surrounded them. The trees grew right up to that side of the temple, abruptly interrupted by the walls.

Magara broke the silence. "The clearing down here was designed for using the flying smoke. It was used much more often in the old days; I suppose people were more reckless then."

"Perhaps," said Brythia, "they were more clear on what needed to be done."

"Perhaps," agreed Magara. "Ah, here we are."

The forest path emptied into a small circular clearing in the midst a grove of birch trees.

"Sit down in the grass, dear," the High Druidess instructed.

They sat on the cold, brittle grass, cross-legged and facing each other. Magara removed a small marble pipe and leather sachet from the folds of her robe. She dipped the bowl into the pouch as she spoke.

"I know that you are not afraid to use the flying smoke; but your courage aside, you must be cautious," said the High Druidess.

She removed the pipe, now filled with a grey-brown power peppered with flakes of green, from the pouch and handed it to Brythia.

She took it.

"I will have to leave you before you begin, but first I must impart what little I know of the flying smoke and the instructions I have been entrusted with."

"I'm listening," said Brythia impatiently.

"I have never used the smoke myself, very few have in recent years, but Demvirstia, who was High Druidess before me, did so, successfully. The flying smoke powder is a mixture of the mushrooms we use for the Spirit Vision, our ritual pipeweed, and several herbs: wolf's bane, wild parsley, and elf-root. It is the responsibility of the leaders of our order to make certain there is a fresh supply of the flying smoke available at all times for emergencies. I am told the taste is wholly unpleasant, but you should hold each puff in as long as possible.

"From the first draw of the pipe on, you must keep your desired destination fixed firmly in your mind. This is the key. Before long you will feel the effects; they shall quickly intensify. The spirit of the flying smoke may or may not make itself known to you; if it does reveal itself, do not let your attention slip from your destination. Either the spirit likes you and allows you transport, or it does not."

A chill ran up Brythia's spine. She knew that some who used the powder were found dead while others wandered in madness. There were tales of those who ended up thousands of miles away, and still others who were never seen again.

Magara smiled reassuringly and stood up. "Do you have any questions?" Magara asked.

Brythia shook her head.

"Well, I shall leave you to it then. Good luck, dear. Get to Lorm and find her. This is your destiny, I know it." She turned to go, then stopped. She looked hard at Brythia. "There is one other thing you should know," Magara said with some hesitation.

Now what? Byrthia thought. "And that is?" Impatience bubbled in her voice.

"Tolian's transformation ritual did not go exactly as planned."

Why is she telling me this?

"There was an unexpected complication."

"Complication? What?"

"She was supposed to emerge from the ritual as the Moon Goddess manifested in the world of physical reality."

"And so she is."

"Well, yes, she is, and she is not. She was not expected to return to her old 'Tolian' personality, you know; we had originally expected her to have the mind of the Goddess as well."

"Well," said Brythia, "I for one am glad, for that is who I love."

"Exactly," whispered Magara mysteriously.

"Exactly?"

"We now believe that because of the love magicks we used to bind our Champion to our cause, Tolian's mind refused to be extinguished so great was her love for you. I don't pretend to know what will happen in the end, but I feel certain that this accident will determine the outcome of many things."

Silence.

"Well, I thought you should know," said the High Druidess.

She turned and retraced her steps down the forest path.

Brythia sighed. *No time for that now*, she thought. *Put it aside*. She closed her eyes for a moment and took a deep breath. She exhaled and opened her eyes. She brought her attention back to the packed pipe. She examined it. Intricate engravings decorated it, but were so worn as to be unintelligible. Clearly the pipe was old and had been touched by many hands in its time. Resinous deposits lined the bowl portion of it. She stared at the pipe for a second longer and reached into her own pouch and withdrew her firestones. With one hand, she expertly rubbed the two stones together over the pipe and instantly a fire ignited over the powder in the bowl.

She exhaled deeply and brought the lit pipe to her lips. She inhaled vigorously, drawing the flying smoke into her lungs. She continued inhaling until her lungs burned. She held her breath, holding the smoke tightly inside her. She removed the pipe from her face and blew out a sizable cloud of smoke, coughing as she did so.

Immediately she repeated this procedure, holding the hot and bitter smoke in even longer each time she did so. The entire time she held a vision of the palace of Lorm in her mind. She visualized the outer fortress walls, the great towers, the gates. She held the image firmly in her imagination as she began to feel light-headed. Shapes seemed to move vaguely in the surrounding darkness of the wooded circle. The air seemed comprised of tiny particles, which fluttered and flickered about, and then everything began to move in waves. The blackness of the night sky blended into the tops of the trees. A dizziness and nausea took hold of her. Still she did not allow herself to be distracted by the effects of the flying smoke; she kept the picture of the palace there vividly as possible before her mind's eye.

A strange humming noise came slowly in the background of her attention, growing louder and louder with each passing moment. Now everything was swirling around her, jumbled waves of energy, which were once the trees and the sky, seemed to lap like water at her feet. Was she standing now? Or no, had she fallen down? Was that the cold earth she felt all about her now? She was having difficulty breathing. The air that poured into her lungs stung and tasted foul. Was she still smoking? She could not be sure. She hung on to the image of the palace; it was her only anchor to sanity. Her regular vision was lost in blurs and a crashing hum of deafening ferocity raged so all other sound was drowned out. Now there came a sensation of movement and something raced just below her, rapidly, but nebulous.

Then there seemed to be a figure moving towards her in the blurred landscape that surrounded her. It struck her as an entity of some sort, but one who possessed no measurable characteristics she could hold in her affected mind. It possessed color and movement, but nothing even approaching shape. It flashed brilliantly through her mind.

"Who are you?" popped up in her thoughts. Did she ask it or did the entity ask her? She could not be sure. She attempted, at first, to ignore the presence and return her concentration to the palace, but again the question moved across her mind. "Who are you?" And then another question followed instantly. "Why do you wish to go to this place, this palace?"

She tried to move her lips to answer, but she found she could not. If she was making coherent sounds, they could not be heard over the din of the incessant humming.

The palace. Ignore the voice in your head and think only of the palace.

"Why? Why? Why?"

The strange voice in her head almost devoured her in its questioning. The humming became the question repeated at an incredible roar. Brythia formed an answer in her mind, and shouted it with everything she had: "For Tolian."

Her answer now echoed in the humming. She remembered to bring her attention back to the palace. "The palace, the palace, the palace, the palace, the palace," she screamed over and over again.

And then that was all there was. The words ringing throughout eternity. There was nothing else.

The palace. The palace. The palace. The palace. The palace. Her mantra rang over and over again.

A barrage of quick images danced across her consciousness. A rolling sea of clouds stretched out in the darkness below her. A carpet of trees. A flash of light.

Suddenly she felt tears on her check. She felt her foot on solid ground. The screamed mental mantra faded with the sound of a twig snapping under her. The crackle of leaves beneath her feet. The blur of her vision shifted into uncertain shapes before condensing into trees all around her. It was still night. She became aware of the cold wind rushing down on her. She stepped, from the midst of the tall barren oak trees surrounding her, onto a paved road. She turned right on to the path and continued walking. Her head still spun and a violent wave of nausea took hold of her. She had to stop and vomit.

She retched for several minutes, regaining her normal

consciousness in the process. She had, of course, eaten nothing, so she suffered from the dry heaves. The odor of her own bile assaulted her. She continued down the road for a few minutes only, before the forest around her gave way to fields. And there, two miles away, stood the towers of the palace.

The light-headed feeling retreated. She shook her head, breathed the cold, clean air and began running.

Chapter 12

The early morning quiet held the palace, though groups of soldiers moved hurriedly through the capital. Brythia moved quickly through the streets of the outer gate village; it felt as though she were gliding. She still felt residual effects from the flying smoke, making it seem as though she belonged to some separate reality. She traveled as softly and as lightly as a ghost in the night. The simple houses and shops were dim and closed up and the villagers inside their warm and comfortable homes asleep.

The druidess looked up at the stars above, glaring brilliantly in the chill, clear sky. Here and there the smoke from the many chimneys wafted together as a cloud and obscured the night sky in its communal ascension to the starry heavens. Judging from the position of the stars and planets, she gauged the hour to be close to three o'clock in the morning. Only a few moments had passed since she left Hyge Bryth.

She moved with gliding haste towards the main palace building, passing closely to guards who appeared not to even notice her. As she entered the building, the bows of the door guards reassured her of her own visibility.

"Where is the King?" Her inquiry sounded harsh and unceremonious.

"In the Jarrels' Hall, Milady," responded one of the men.

With quick thanks, she turned towards the direction he indicated and resumed her determined pace.

The Jarrels' Hall was in chaos. As she entered the hall, she could hardly comprehend what she was seeing. The tables were still arranged for feasting, and strangely, fully one third of the places were occupied by sleeping Lormians. Around them moved soldiers and servants tending the newly awakened. The King's table had been converted into a command center. The King, Miderick, Kiliordes, Delorick, and Lord Talthuwd were huddled around the table. From the Jarrels' circle, their words were inaudible. Four unusual people standing a little apart from the others distracted her. Three were dressed in the costumes of the Solar Pilgrimage Festival, and the other, whose back was towards Brythia, wore his clothes and held himself in such a way as to indicate he was not human. After a few moments, it dawned on her who this entity was—it was Findelbres.

She pulled back her hood as she reached the table. She did not wait to be acknowledged before asking the question that burned like a fire within her. Nothing else mattered. "What has happened to Tolian?"

Everyone gathered at the table (and those in its periphery) turned their attention towards her, all with signs of great surprise on their countenances, mixed with different emotions on each. The King's deeply furrowed brow loosened briefly into a look of happy recognition, Miderick and Talthuwd offered an annoyed frustration, while Delorick and Kiliordes looked noticeably relieved. Findelbres' look of worry was replaced by one of optimism.

"At last," said the faerie, "someone who will heed my counsel."

"Brythia?" How is it possible?" asked the King, appearing astounded by her presence.

"As always, Your Majesty, I have some magicks of my own," she answered mysteriously.

"It is well, my daughter. We have need of such magicks," commented Tolris.

Miderick and Talthuwd rolled their eyes.

"Such magicks as I have are at your service, but you know this. What has happened? Where's Tolian?"

"Well, that's the problem, isn't it?" said Talthuwd. "Perhaps your powers can divine Tolian's location?"

"Perhaps they can, and I certainly could follow whatever trail there is, but I still need to know what has happened. So, would someone please tell me, or do I have to put a spell on someone," Brythia directed this last remark at Talthuwd.

Findelbres cast a glance at the others, then spoke, "Tolian has been abducted by a renegade faerie warlord, Dowbreth. He somehow drugged everyone in the Jarrels' Hall, though how is not completely clear, probably Tolian too. We don't know where they went or exactly how long they have been gone."

"I still do not understand how Dowbreth could have stood against Tolian and the Moonsword, drugs or no," Brythia said.

"Tolian did not have the Moonsword; she left it in your room." Delorick lowered his head in guilt. "I asked her too. I had no idea."

Brythia turned back to Findelbres.

"Why would this Dowbreth do this, Findelbres?" the druidess asked.

The elf shrugged his shoulders. "I have some suspicions, but..."

"Tolian would produce powerful offspring..." offered Miderick.

"Mated with that giant, her children would be invincible," said Talthuwd.

"You're suggesting that this was done for...for procreation?" Brythia's voice grew noticeably louder as she spoke.

"We know nothing," interjected Findelbres. "We will not be able to determine Dowbreth's motives, it is useless to try."

It had become apparent to Brythia that they had no more idea of what was going on, or of what to do, than she did. She was wasting precious time. The trail was getting cold. Action was needed, not debates. Especially as some of those involved in the discussion would just as soon Tolian never came back to Lorm. Her patience was already worn thin. Her tone made that clear.

"Look, I don't have time for this. I assume you have troops searching for them?"

"Um, ah, yes, of course. Keliof and Kelvris are leading troops in the search."

"Good," said the druidess. "Then you wouldn't mind if I took Findelbres here and did a little looking myself."

Tolris smiled. "I'm sure that I'd have to clamp you in irons to stop you, my dear, and most likely that wouldn't work. In the end, none of us are better equipped to find her than you. Go, take whomever you want, but find her. Bring her home."

"Thank you, Father." She bowed.

Delorick coughed. "I would go with you, Princess Brythia," he volunteered. "If my Lord allows it."

"An excellent idea," agreed the King. "You, who are Tolian's three best friends, shall venture forth to her rescue."

"Make that Tolian's four best friends," Kiliordes said, stepping forward. "I would go with my companions of old, if you will have me?" He looked at Brythia.

"Absolutely. You are welcome to join us, both of you. We shall be glad of your companionship. But you must be ready quickly."

"Fifteen minutes?"

"That will be fine."

One of the nearby Solar Pilgrims walked behind Kiliordes. He was a large man. *More of the stature of a warrior than a merry wanderer,* thought Brythia.

"My name is Pagyrus," he said, bowing to Brythia. "And if Kiliordes comes with you, I shall come too. I am charged to bring him to the Solar Pilgrimage Festival."

"Very well," said Brythia impatiently. "But that is all. And I warn you that we shall travel quickly, and rest little. All of you be sure you can travel at my pace. I will not be slowed for anyone."

"We shall keep your pace, Lady," Pagyrus assured her.

"Oh, one quick question," said the King. "My grandson and Myrthis? Where are they?"

"Safe at Hyge Bryth, Your Highness, until you send for them. I think I would wait a little longer just to make certain that Dowbreth had no Lormian aid, if you take my meaning."

"A wise precaution, my daughter's wife," nodded the King in agreement. "We shall investigate that possibility."

"That is well," said the druidess. "Now gentlemen, gather your things, I'll see you in the courtyard in fifteen minutes. If I may take your leave, my lord, I must get one more thing from our chambers before I depart."

"What would that be?" asked King Tolris.

"The Moonsword."

Chapter 13

Brythia could not help but cry when she entered the rooms that had been her and Tolian's home for the last year. The room still smelled like Tolian—her favorite perfume still lingered there, pulling out ever deepening levels of longing in the druidess. If she closed her eyes, she could imagine Tolian there, coming up behind her, whispering softly in her ear. She had to take a moment, and sat on the bed they shared. The tears rolled down her cheek and her sobs sounded unabated. They had been so happy here. Of course, palace life was not without its difficulties, and Tolian's situation hadn't made living there any easier. But this was their home, the place that symbolized their life together. They had lived as though their happiness would be eternal. Instead, it was all too brief an oasis in a desert of nightmare.

She was weak and tired. Even the strength that her considerable will afforded her was waning now. Not now, she thought. Not now. She felt all used up, like she had squeezed every ounce of energy from her body and her soul, and now there was nothing left. Now, when she needed all the energy she had ever had. There was no time for weakness, no time for tiredness, no time for tears. Tolian needed her. She would find what strength she needed somewhere. She forced herself to get off the bed. As she did so, a familiar voice chimed brightly behind her.

"Milady, can I get you anything?" It was Dovyse. Her kindly voice was like a balm.

Brythia turned to face her. She couldn't help but notice the girl's startled reaction when she saw her face. "What's wrong, Dovyse? Do I look that bad?"

"Oh Princess Brythia, you look hard. Like all the warmth and kindness has gone out of you. Like you could murder someone. I have never seen you look so. You frightened me, Milady. There, that's better. Though, you still look starved to death. Let me get you something to eat, at least."

"You are so precious, dear. Thank you, but I don't have the time."

The girl knitted her brows. "You're off after Princess Tolian, then?"

"I am." Brythia nodded, touched by the young girl's bright eyes and caring expression.

"You must eat something, before you go. I will not let you leave unless you do. Wait here, I'll be right back."

"I don't have time, dear, really."

"I'll just be a minute, wait here."

Without waiting for an answer, the girl hurried out of the room.

Brythia shrugged and turned to the business she had come for. She moved a stool next to the fireplace, and climbed up on it. With one hand balanced on the mantle place, she reached up and took down the sword that hung there.

Her fingers tingled as they touched the hilt. A strange energy radiated from the weapon. She thought she would have felt it even if she had not been trained in handling such mystical forces. It exuded an alien power, a magick not rooted in the natural world, yet soothing and oddly reminiscent (in some ways) of Tolian. She removed the lunar blade from the hooks holding it above the mantle place. Such a placement was the custom of the warriors of Lorm. Brythia had always thought that a more ceremonious and convenient place would be more in keeping with the Moonsword's status, but Tolian had insisted. She had maintained that if the hearth was considered the sacred heart of the home, then the warrior's sword should mark the defense of the same by its customary position. Brythia suspected that Lormians simply loved their swords so much that they had to keep them within their view if they weren't on their belts. Well, in any case, it was Tolian's sword after all, and her explanation of the traditional placement did make some sense. Of course, Tolian was tall enough not to require a stool to fetch it down when she needed it.

Brythia climbed off the stool and regarded the weapon. When on the wall it was inert, remarkable only for its mysterious beauty and imaginative styling of the hilt (forged as it was by the power of Tolian's will), but in her hands it seemed to glow dimly with a purple radiance and pulsed with something akin to a life force. She stood transfixed, mesmerized by the sword's strange aspect. She could feel the ebb and flow of a wondrous energy. Several minutes passed before she pulled her own sword out of its scabbard with one hand and slid the Moonsword in its place. Now looking at her own trustworthy blade, she smiled. She climbed back up on the stool and hung her sword on the hooks above the mantle. Just as she was doing so, Dovyse returned bearing a tray.

"I'll leave this in the outer room for you, Milady."

"Thank you, dear."

Brythia followed the servant girl to their small table. She stood as Dovyse laid out the food: two eggs (hard-boiled), bread, butter, cheese, and slices of rare oranges imported from some far-off land.

"How did you have time to prepare this?" Brythia's surprise sounded in her query.

Dovyse giggled and said, "This was nothing, Princess. 'Tis what I'm here for."

Brythia had no time to sit and take a meal, but she was ravenous. She picked up a few handfuls of food as she stood and she proceeded to eat it, far too fast than was healthful. A bite, at first, seemed only to make her hunger worse. She had to admit that even this simple fare (by palace standards) tasted better than the best of the Temple cooking in the order. She had devoured her meal in only a couple of minutes, plus drained two tankards of water. She turned away from the table when she had finished.

"I've packed you some more food. Is there anything else you require, Milady?" Dovyse popped back into the room as she did so.

"No, that was perfect, Dovyse. Thank you. Never overeat after a fast," Brythia said. "Now, I've got to get moving."

She looked at the girl. "Now, Dovyse, promise me you'll take good care of yourself."

"I always do, Princess. But, please don't talk like you're not coming back." A single tear ran down the girl's cheek. "You'll find her, I know you will. When you do, I'll be here to take care of you both."

"I hope you're right."

She could see that only Findelbres was waiting in the courtyard as she stepped out of the main palace building. Her ears picked up the footfalls of boot on stone behind her.

"Ah, there you are. You mortals take a long time doing everything, don't you?"

Delorick's voice sounded behind her, "Master Findelbres, that's because we are more thorough in our preparations. At least a mortal thought to secure some provisions for our journey."

Brythia let the others carry on their conversation. She immediately set herself to find some trace of Dowbreth and Tolian's passing from the cold cobblestone of the courtyard. She crawled about on all fours for several minutes, searching for some clear sign, in vain. She was climbing to her feet as Kiliordes and the pilgrim Pagyrus emerged.

"There are no signs of them here," Brythia announced. "We'll have to try our luck outside the palace."

With her eyes focused on the stones, she led the way through the inner gates, paying no more attention to her companions. She would have felt better if there were some trace on the stones. There should have been. Even on the hard stone, a giant's step should have left a small mark—a clip or scuff. But there was nothing discernable. She was just about convinced that she must have missed something. She grew afraid that her concentration was dulled by the lack of sleep she had experienced. As she stopped before the outer gatehouse, an obvious question entered her mind.

"Delorick," she said lifting her gaze off the ground for a moment. "The guardhouse is empty. We don't protect our gates anymore?"

"There are no guards posted during the Jarrels, Princess, except during wartime. All the men are encouraged to participate in some Jarrels' festivities. That has been our tradition for centuries," responded the Captain of Guard, with more than a measure of guilt in his voice.

Brythia hurried through the gate.

"How fortunate for Dowbreth, or how well-informed he seems to have been," noted Brythia. "Oh, and Delorick, let's skip the titles, for now, okay? We're all friends here, right?"

The others moved forward to follow, when she stopped and

bent down towards the ground. "Oh, here we are, though your men seem to have done their best to trample over the tracks."

There was one set of footprints distinct from the general traffic. They were huge, the biggest prints from a humanoid she had ever seen, and they were sunk deep into the earth.

She shook her head. "Well, I don't know how, but your men seemed to have missed these tracks; they went in the wrong direction."

"They weren't my men," Delorick corrected her. "Prince Kelris led this party. My men went with Prince Keliof out the Warrior's Gate."

"Well, Kelvris's troops then, went straight out to the west. Dowbreth and Tolian seem to have traveled back along the outer walls and to the southeast, to start with. Gentlemen, let's run for as long as we can see the trail clearly."

"Watch carefully, Brythia," warned Findelbres, "it is an old faerie trick to make a strong trail in one direction, then turn off and give no indication of direction or trail after that."

Dowbreth's tracks cut across the surrounding field for about three hundred yards before joining a road leading south. The prints became immediately more difficult to follow as they continued down the road called, if Brythia remembered correctly, Doveshyre-Palace Road. Suddenly, the footprints disappeared altogether. Brythia held a hand to stop the others, and knelt down to examine the last visible prints.

"It seems you were right about the old faerie misleadingly-clear-trail trick, Findelbres," she remarked.

"I usually am, dear druidess," he replied.

"Modest, isn't he?" commented Pagyrus, coming up with Kiliordes.

"Oh, you've noticed that," said Kiliordes.

"Modesty, sir, is a character flaw we faeries do not possess. It is a completely human foible."

Their conversation brought the tiniest of smiles to Brythia's face. She studied the ground along the sides of the road. "Damn, he's good," commented the druidess. There was no trace of the massive faerie's tracks. "How can he obscure his trail like this?"

"You must remember, first off," explained Findelbres, "that we of the Good Folk do not exist in the normal sense in your world. We may enter it yes, and when here most of the same laws that govern your actions apply to us as well. But, there is a buffer of sorts keeping us partially insulated, most of the time. With enough concentration and practice, it can be utilized for various purposes for brief times."

"How long? How far could he possibly go, carrying a mortal, before he would have to leave a trail?" Brythia felt her patience wearing thin as the question poured across her lips.

"If he was carrying a mortal, he could probably go, I don't know, maybe a hundred yards or so. But, I caution you to remember that which you choose to forget, Druid-Princess. Tolian is not mortal, so I hesitate to say for certain. And, trust me, Dowbreth's trail will be almost imperceptible without his concentration."

"All right, fine," she said. "You gentlemen, wait here, I'll go and check a hundred yard radius and see where that takes us."

It was discouraging. Never, in all her considerable experience had she even encountered such a difficult trail to follow. She crawled low to the grass, bringing her eyes and nose close, for what seemed to be a painfully slow pace, to search for a spore or scent. With each minute she searched thus, she felt the distance from Tolian grow greater. Her intestines began to ache in tune to the anxieties growing in her heart. How could they hope to pursue Dowbreth and Tolian with any sort of rapidity under such conditions? Hopelessness bit at her as the first signs of lightening in the eastern sky came in softly. She went out another fifty yards and began another circle of what was escalating into a frantic hunt.

Just as desperation was moving toward despair, an idea flickered like a candle in the night. She slowly got up off the ground. She straightened out her frame and stretched her muscles a little. She reached back and drew the Moonsword out of her scabbard, and raised it straight up over her head.

It took all of her training to still her mind. Slowly a mental clarity and quiet replaced her churning apprehension. In her mind, she questioned the Moonsword: *Where is Tolian?*

She repeated it several times, as she attempted to tune into the blade's lunar nature. At first, she could sense a subtle vibration gently throbbing in response to her query.

She stood there and stood there. She must have stood there like that for several more minutes before she noticed the intensity of the vibration begin to fluctuate. Brythia got a sense of confusion from the sword. She rephrased her question.

Where is the Moon Goddess? she asked mentally.

There was no hesitation. No doubt. Immediately upon the initial formulation of her question, the sword pulled itself so that it pointed, in her grasp, to the east.

Yes. She smiled and called to the others, "Gentlemen, let's go to the stables, first. I think we can make up some time."

Chapter 14

It was noon before Brythia quietly signaled them to stop with the raising of her arm. Kiliordes was glad enough for the break, though he could almost feel Brythia's dread and her reluctance to do so. She had led them at a breakneck gallop through the villages, woods, and farmlands that comprised most of the southern portions of Lorm. They would not have been able to keep up with Brythia's faerie horse if it were not for the spell that Findelbres placed on the other horses, though he called it merely words of encouragement. Always the druidess held the Moonsword extended before her as a divining rod to guide them. The further they traveled from the palace, the sparser grew the signs of settlement. Their route tended to avoid the more populous areas; clearly, Dowbreth had used the wooded byways and lonely forest roads for that precise purpose.

Brythia slid off her steed (actually it was Tolian's horse Whisper); she nearly stumbled as her feet hit the ground. Composing herself, she led the horse to a small grassy field off the road and immediately let out a tired sigh. "Gentlemen, rest your horses," she said.

Kiliordes dismounted immediately; after all, Kilfrie had always obeyed Brythia's commands. He noticed that Brythia could barely stand up. He saw the dark circles around her bloodshot eyes. He had never seen her look so exhausted before.

"Yes, the horses need to rest, but so do you," he said.

Brythia turned her weary gaze at him. So pale, so fraught with worry. Yet, through the fatigue, her eyes shown with a fierceness and determination.

"We'll give the horses an hour," she said flatly. "Oh, and Kiliordes, I do appreciate your concern, but we simply don't have time for anything more."

"Princess, um, I mean Brythia," broke in Delorick, "I think I agree with Lord Kiliordes. You need to take some sleep, or you won't do us any good."

Brythia sighed and addressed Findelbres, "When do you think Dowbreth will stop for rest?"

The faerie spoke solemnly. "He may not stop today, or tomorrow. If he is mounted on his own faerie warhorse as I believe, we will be hard-pressed to catch him, even if we do not rest at all."

"But surely, he would have to stop sometime for Tolian..." Kiliordes stopped himself. Brythia flinched noticeably as he pronounced Tolian's name.

Once again the faerie spoke in an uncharacteristically subdued manner, "I can vouch that Tolian can survive for at least three weeks without food or water. She did so when she was buried under the palace last year."

Pagyrus, the pilgrim, who had been a silent observer of the conversation, now spoke. "You know, if she was merely drugged like the rest of us, I wouldn't be surprised to see the Princess walking back this way, carrying that rogue of a faerie on her shoulder."

Did Kiliordes see hope flash now in the druidess's eyes?

"Yes, that would almost seem likely," agreed Findelbres, "But I know Dowbreth too well. He is always well prepared. I'm sorry to say that if Tolian could have freed herself, she would have already done so."

"Yes, she would have," murmured Brythia.

"But, I think the point is how long can we afford to rest, is it not?" asked the faerie. "And in what condition we'll be in when we catch up to them. The point, which Pagyrus brings up about Tolian, may afford us some hope. If Dowbreth has found a way to somehow restrain or diminish the Goddess' powers, then he may well be required to stop more regularly to provide her with sustenance, etc. That should give us some hope.

"Also, Delorick, Kiliordes and Pagyrus, I know, have only slept the few hours our foe's drug induced. They need rest, at least a couple more hours to be of any use to you." He directed this at Brythia.

"And what of you, friend faerie? You have slept the same short nap as we have," pointed out Delorick.

"Neither Dowbreth nor I need take sleep in your realm, at least, not regularly," he answered. "But, what of our leader, when did you get any real sleep, Brythia?"

"I honestly don't know the last time I have slept, though I

did eat something earlier," she admitted.

"What do you mean?" asked Pagyrus. "Surely you slept sometime yesterday or so?"

"No, it's probably been—I don't know, a week maybe since I've actually slept. But we don't have time..." She had to stifle a yawn as she finished speaking.

"Oh no?" Findelbres asked. "And what are we going to do when we catch Dowbreth, yawn him into submission? You need some rest. Sleep for a couple of hours, at least. I'll have some supper ready for you, and we'll ride through the night, if we need to."

"This is sound counsel, Princess," agreed Delorick.

She gave in.

Once she agreed to rest, she moved quickly to unpack her sleeping gear. Scarce had a moment passed and she was huddled under the blanket.

Part of Kiliordes was amazed, yet he had the recollection of moving with the same skill and efficiency at one time.

Her voice came muffled through her bedding cocoon, "Findelbres, get that fire going as soon as you can, thanks. And just a couple of hours—no more."

Kiliordes looked at the others and shrugged. He began to prepare his own bedding. Pagyrus offered to help Findelbres gather firewood. Delorick seemed torn between the two activities. He idly gathered a few sticks of kindling, and then gave up to take his own rest. Kiliordes dozed off with surprising ease in the cold winter sunshine.

Kiliordes awoke to the crackling of a nearby fire. For a moment, he could not remember where he was. Grogginess. He felt the hard, chill ground beneath his blankets acutely. He uncovered his head and the smell of meat cooking struck him. The feeble, afternoon winter sun shone wearily over the trees.

"Ah good, he's awake at last," said Delorick brightly. "Good morning, Lord Kiliordes."

"That leaves only the princess asleep," commented Pagyrus. "Should we wake her, then?"

"Yes, yes, by all means, she'll be quite cross if we don't," answered Findelbres. "And believe me, you don't want to see her cross."

"I heard that," came Brythia's voice from beneath her blankets.

With some effort, Kiliordes slowly pulled himself out of his bedding as the druidess quickly did the same.

"What are you cooking?" asked Kiliordes as he caught another whiff of whatever it was they were cooking. "It smells delicious."

"Roast boar. Leftovers from the Jarrels' feast," replied Findelbres. "We're just warming it up a bit."

"I'd say it's there," said Delorick, poking the meat that he turned on a makeshift spit, with a stick.

"That's good," said Pagyrus. "For I am hungry. And, I must say that you people do eat pretty well for non-pilgrims." He hovered over the fire inhaling the meat's aroma.

Brythia walked over to the fire. "If it is ready, we should eat. We have no time to waste."

"So much for healthful digestion," commented Pagyrus, good-naturedly, or so it seemed to Kiliordes.

Brythia, however, shot the Solar Pilgrim a nasty look of complete impatience. "You are welcome to relax here as long as you like, but if you intend to come with me, I suggest you eat quickly and be ready to leave immediately."

Afterward, they ate in a hurried silence following the druidess's lead, gulping down the meat and taking a few swigs of water. To Kiliordes, the meat tasted even better than it had at the Jarrels' Hall—there was always something tasty about food eaten (and prepared) outside. No doubt, he mused, one's body is extra happy about the nutritional support to help battle the effects of exposure to the elements. Several of Kilfrie's druidic memories came back to him: countless days and nights spent in the forest and many, many meals cooked in the wilds (though clearly druidic culinary skills paled with this Lormian fare).

He had hardly swallowed his last bite when Brythia leapt up and straightaway set to putting out the fire. Kiliordes found himself jumping up and helping her...both of them using their feet in the method their druidic training had imbued in them. Kiliordes was surprised—he moved his in concert with hers.

"You remember, huh," said Brythia, with a trace of a smile

on her lips and pleasantness in her voice, the first such expression to mark her since her arrival in Lorm last night, or this morning, whichever it was.

He smiled back. "Yes, much of the old training is coming back to me out here."

"You'll have to join Myrthis and me on our druid outings," the golden-haired nature priestess suggested. Then her countenance changed as dark thoughts seemed to gather on her brow.

Poor girl, thought Kiliordes, *Poor dear Brythia.* He tried to sound as encouraging as possible. "Don't worry Brythia, we'll catch up to them soon, get Tolian back, and before you know it, you, Myrthis and I will be out in the woods practicing our nature magick and aggravating the Lormian nobility."

"Thank you," she said, "I need to believe that."

How must she feel? There were no magicks more potent than love magick. The magick that bound Brythia to Tolian. In the Druidic Order, such spells were strictly forbidden. The severity of the effects made so much more the grievous moral objections of interfering to such a degree with the individual's free will. The folk charms of the uneducated, of course, rarely possessed the necessary power to be effective or lasting, but to a skilled practitioner of the magick arts, it was too easy to bind two people together in eternal love. Eternal Love. Pure love that lasted for all eternity. And that was precisely the problem with such undertakings. If such a spell is cast and one of the lovers should perish, the other will quickly follow them into death. It is said that even beyond the shores of death, and through all of their lives are they so bound. For some, mere separation can cause physical pain and extreme psychological torment. Kiliordes had heard from Myrthis, who had received her information from Brythia, that the High Druidess, Magara, had been sanctioned to use exactly those formulae to bind Tolian to Brythia, and thereby secure his (at the time) cooperation. Kilirodes could see the signs of her suffering in her face as they spoke.

Kiliordes couldn't help but notice that she was giving him that look. The one she always gave him. The look. Straight in the eyes, determined to be accepting and warm, despite the fact that he wore the face of her deepest nightmare. She always tried so hard to not be affected by him. Bless her.

"Let's go," Kiliordes suggested. And it was he who hurried the others to gather their gear swiftly and get moving. Then it was back on the horses and off in pursuit.

They rode harder and faster than Kiliordes had ever ridden before. In her haste, Brythia pushed her faerie horse far faster than the mortal horses, which the rest of them rode, could keep pace. Yet, the beasts did their best to hold that dizzy gallop steady. They passed a sizable tavern with an inviting inn just as the sun dipped below the tree-lined horizon, lighting the clouds with deep orange and pink highlights. Kiliordes imagined the warmth of the hearth inside the inn and the taste of fine Lormian ale they no doubt offered. Imagination would have to suffice, for there was no denying the urgency of their quest afforded them no time for such distractions.

Now they turned off the road and forced their horses down what amounted to little more than a deer path. Despite Brythia's attempt to force them to continue her frenetic pace, their mortal horses, Elven spell notwithstanding, could not do so. He was surprised that Pagyrus was able to keep up with her at all. What a horseman he was. Clearly, he had done a great deal of riding in his past before he joined the Solar Pilgrimage Festival.

The chill set in deeper as nighttime took hold of the thick woods they recklessly navigated. No one else seemed to mind the tight path or the almost constant barrage of branches leaping out of the darkness and smashing into their faces. He had almost lost sight of Delorick, who was riding right in front of him. He thought of his warm bed, of the Jarrels' feast, of all the comforts he was already missing. Darkness and the cold were his only comforts. He felt guilty for feeling sorry for himself. Think of poor Tolian, he thought. *In the clutches of that villain.* And he was feeling sorry for himself. No, his discomfort was voluntary. He would gladly endure as much of this wearying journey as was necessary for the sake of his friend.

A strange quietness came over him. The darkness of the deep woods tightly around him, the pounding of hooves, the crashing of branches. Crazy speed. It was almost hypnotic. He became numb to the danger and the scratches and welts, which adorned his exposed skin. He lost himself to the thrill of the ride, to the obsession of their determination. Just going on. Racing through the night.

Voices in the distance. He strained to hear. Pagyrus was shouting something. Kiliordes caught his words.

"Brythia, we must stop."

No answer. Of course not, thought Kiliordes.

"We must stop."

Defiantly she screamed back, "No, we can't. We can't. We're catching up to them. I can feel it."

Then, Kiliordes heard a snap, even before he felt the branch strike him in the shoulder. A moment of acute pain, followed by the sensation of flying through the air. He panicked and yelled in surprise and fear. The biting blackness of the underbrush. A barren bough torn through his trousers and skin. Another crash and a thud as he felt the impact of the frozen path. His head hit hard.

He attempted to raise himself and a surge of dizziness brought him back down.

Now, there was more yelling and shouting up ahead, but he could not focus on it—he was slipping into unconsciousness.

Chapter 15

A strong odor. Rather like a sweaty horse. Stronger, yet more delicate. Subtle. And fouler. A horse. An impression of speed. Coldness. Sleep slowly faded from Tolian's mind as her senses returned. She gradually became aware of being in an uncomfortable position, and of being jolted and bumped with considerable regularity. This even before true wakefulness took hold of her—a state that bridged the gap between the depths of her drug-induced slumber and her normal thought processes.

She was slumped over the back of a gigantic horse. Her wrists were bound, as were her ankles. A rope strung below the horse's belly tied to each of her bindings, secured her to the beast. From her position, each hoof fall slammed her stomach into the beast's back and knocked the air out of her.

When she opened her eyes, she was struck by how little she could see. It was dark. At first, she could only make out the deep black hide of the horse against her face, and maybe a few quick snatches of blurred and shadowy ground passing below her. Mostly vague and confused glimpses. A turn of her head and she could see a little more of the gravel road. A lonely forest road at night.

As more and more of her consciousness returned, she became aware of her physical discomfort. A jolt of pain in her gut, the tangled ache of the stretched muscles in her arms and legs, it seemed as though they were almost being pulled out of the sockets. She had not known such intense pain since before her transformation, her alleged deification. Another stride, another jab of pain. The air was pushed out of her lungs. She gasped for another breath and her ribs screamed their displeasure. Probably just badly bruised, she diagnosed. Still, it hurt her. She could not stifle her cry and let out a loud groan.

Suddenly her hair was pulled roughly, jerking her head up towards the front of the horse. She let out another gasp. She could see little more than the giant silhouette, the flash of fiery crimson eyes.

"Ah, the Goddess awakes." That voice. Dowbreth. Of course, Dowbreth. *The second most disturbing voice I've ever heard*, she thought.

"I trust you slept well."

She could see his sneer by the dull gleam of his filed teeth.

She turned her head to speak, but the painful tug of her hair pulled her neck at such an angle that she couldn't get words out at first. Her mouth made only a pitiful, hurt-filled peep of anguish. This produced a great wave of anger that radiated through her being. Now she was mad. How dare he. She pulled at the cords around her wrists. She expected them to rip apart as though they weren't even there. They should have. Instead, they dug roughly into her skin. Another noise, this time an unmistakable whimper.

"Oh, what's wrong, Divine One," he asked mockingly. "Are your wrists tied too tightly together?"

He let go of her hair. That, at least, was a relief. But, what had happened to her? Where was her strength? She should be able to easily free herself and give her captor one serious thrashing, faster then most people could even see her doing it. She should be able to. Then why couldn't she? Now, fear and confusion blended with the intense pain and cold racking her mind and body.

Dowbreth began to laugh most vilely, sending shivers down Tolian's spine. He must have sensed her helplessness and apprehension, for his laughter grew louder.

Her voice came back to her muffled, of course, as she was speaking directly into the horse's hide. "Laugh now, fool, while you can, for you will die for this." Brave words, but how weak and ineffectual they sounded even to her.

His laughter stopped. "Will you kill me, Oh Goddess of the Silver Light?" asked the faerie. "Then, why not kill me now, why endure this hardship any longer? Smite me with your slender arms. Free yourself and use your shapely, tiny hands to strangle me, if you wish."

He waited for her to respond. She fumed quietly, refusing to give him the satisfaction of a reply.

"No? Perhaps you enjoy my company, then?" he suggested. Tolian felt pressure on her thigh. In horror, she realized the rogue was stroking her roughly. A wanton caress, full of savageness. He let his hand rest on her bottom. Now new fears and a deep sense of vulnerability took hold of her. His gnarled fingers touching her. Unclean and vile. Tolian had never known this feeling before. Until last year, she had been a man, of course, and largely immune to this fear of violation. After her transformation, she had a strength that exceeded everyone else's. She had not known personal trepidation. Suddenly, everything was different. Somehow she had lost her power and now she was frightened in a way she had never been before.

"No," she pleaded. Pleaded. She hated the sound of her voice. She hated the begging and the terror that rang clearly in her tone.

"No? So you do not enjoy my touch, Princess?" the faerie inquired. His hand lingered. A threat. "Very well." He lifted his hand away.

Tolian sighed.

"You were right," Dowbreth murmured. "It will work."

His words made no sense to Tolian, nor did they seem as though they were directed towards her. There was something sinister about his words, spoken to no one. Perhaps insanity was the explanation. Still, in her current situation, that idea was hardly comforting. Her mind raced with questions and doubts. What had happened to her? Why was he doing this? What did he hope to gain? She was afraid of the answers. What if he meant to rape her? Rape. It was inconceivable. She fought the panic welling up inside her. She was simply too vulnerable. For the first time since her initial displeasure at her new form, she cursed her femininity, her weakness. This sense of vulnerability, of powerlessness, seemed like it would swallow her. She fought it.

She struggled with her emotions and with the pain in silence for considerable time. She refused to cry or let any sound to express her discomfort escape her lips. She would not give into that villain. And at last she became numb to the situation.

The softness of morning light replaced the darkness, but from her position, it did little to increase her view of her surroundings. The cold was becoming unbearable, even as her anxiety and aches receded. She was dressed still in her white Jarrels' gown, which offered scant protection from the elements.

Her exposed skin burned with the frosty chill. The frigid air was making her need to urinate even stronger. She had to say something, stubbornly defiant or not.

"If you do not mean to kill me, Dowbreth, then you're going to have to let me down. I'm freezing to death. I'm thirsty, and I probably won't survive much longer like this." All true enough. "You won't get much ransom if I'm dead."

The faerie warlord chuckled. "Ransom, eh? What makes you think I'm going to ransom you? What paltry treasure has Lorm that would interest me? No, your Highness," he hissed, "I have other uses for you."

Fight back the fear, she told herself. She tried to keep the bravery in her timbre. "What uses?" she demanded

"Fear not Princess Moonchild," he said. "If you cooperate, you will not be harmed. In fact, I shall insure your comfort."

With these words, he brought the giant horse to a stop. The sudden halting caused Tolian enormous pain as her bindings pulled harshly at her wrists and ankles.

Dowbreth dismounted and cut the rope that held her to the horse's back, and with one hand, lifted her off the beast and set her down gently on the ground in a sitting position. He then cut the bindings around her ankles, took another length of rope, tied one end of it to her wrists, which were still bound, and the other end to a branch of a nearby wild cherry tree, ten feet in the air. The giant faerie easily reached the branch with no effort, by extending his arms their full length. He left plenty of slack for her to move around. Dowbreth went about this work in complete silence.

While he did this, Tolian took advantage of the opportunity to stand up and stretch her legs, as well as examine her surroundings. They were just off a small forest road lined with bare black oaks, sassafras, cedar, and wild cherry trees. Clearly, they were still in Lorm. Even with his faerie horse, Dowbreth couldn't hope to clear the kingdom that quickly. Probably, they were in-between the capital and farming towns of the East, for to the west of the palace, the Pine Lands held sway over the terrain.

Dowbreth's faerie horse. Now that she could see, it was much bigger than she had expected. A lot bigger. It stood tall enough that she could not see over its back; it was fully twice the size of the biggest warhorse she had ever seen. It was outfitted in armored head and neck gear and a saddle matching the faerie's dark green gear. It was deep black in color and possessed that strange ethereal quality of the faerie that her own Whisper had, but in this beast its glamour took a disturbing aspect that inspired a deep aversion in the princess. Various saddle packs hung in disarray around the sides of the beast.

As she stood there shivering, quietly observing the horse and Dowbreth's activities, the faerie knight pulled a huge woolen cloak from one bag and a small package wrapped in cloth from another. He set the cloak around Tolian's shoulders. Warmth immediately stole over her body, quickly easing the frigid chill which had a hold over her. It felt good, but Tolian allowed herself no feelings of gratitude. The cloth package he unfolded, revealing a small loaf of bread and some cheese. This he set down carefully on the ground (on the cloth) before Tolian. She said nothing as Dowbreth set his water skin down next to the food, and inclined his head slightly in a semi-bow. He then walked back to the horse and unhooked yet another bag from the saddle. This sack appeared to contain a fair-sized object, evidently vaguely spherical—rather like a melon. This bag he carried with utmost care and gentleness. He stopped a moment and regarded her.

"I recommend you eat and drink quickly, Your Highness. I shall leave you alone for a few moments. When I return, we resume our journey," said Dowbreth. "I wouldn't waste any of your time attempting to escape. You will not be able to, and I shall be back soon."

With that, he turned and headed into the surrounding woods, carrying the sack in an almost gingerly manner. She watched him disappear into the trees. She sighed heavily in relief as soon as she lost sight of him.

She examined the cords wound tightly around her wrists and the rope Dowbreth had secured to the tree. Even if a superhuman giant hadn't tied the rope, she wouldn't have been able to free herself. She tried anyway. She wiggled her wrists the little bit they could move and tore at the cords with her teeth. It was no use. The rope was tied high enough into the tree that she could not hope to reach it. Enraged by her weakness and helplessness, she began to bang her tied wrists against the cherry tree's trunk. Futility.

At last, she gave up, crouched low to the ground, and with her bound hands, brought the waterskin to her lips with some difficulty. She was parched and the water was cold and refreshing. She gulped the water, and then turned her attention to the bread and cheese. They were clearly Lormian in origin; no doubt, the villain took them from the Jarrels' feast.

She had not finished her meager meal when Dowbreth returned. She hadn't even heard him come up behind her, but there he was.

"Have you finished, Goddess?" he asked.

She did not turn to look at him. "No, not yet."

"No? Then perhaps next time you will learn to eat quicker."

She felt her arms jerked roughly up by the rope, causing her to drop the cheese she was bringing to her mouth. He kept pulling the rope until she was standing, almost teetering on her tiptoes. He pulled her right before his pale, scarred face.

"Now, I would advise you to tend to any personal business you need to, for we will not stop again until tonight." His bloodred eyes. Inhuman. The unearthly voice filled with violence and bubbling impatience.

Tolian stared back at him in defiance. "Where are we going, Dowbreth?"

The faerie smiled, revealing his pointed teeth, "You'll find out soon enough. Now don't waste your time as you did earlier. It is not my wish that you should hate me. But we are in haste."

He released the rope and set her down on the flats of her feet. Dowbreth left her and reattached the sack he was carrying to his horse's saddle with the utmost care. Tolian went around to the other side of the tree she was tethered to and urinated, all the while trying to pretend that her faerie kidnapper wasn't there. But he was, and she had never been more self-conscious in her life.

"Quickly, Great One," he commanded, "We must hurry. Your friends are in hot pursuit. I am quite surprised."

He came around the horse, took the rope off the cherry tree, and tied it around his own waist above the dried heads that hung from his belt.

"You did not expect pursuit, after kidnapping the heir to the throne of Lorm?" Tolian inquired. She was puzzled by his words and tone. They indicated that this was news he had evidently just learned. How was that possible?

"No," he answered frankly, "I did not expect them to be able to track us. I used great care to conceal our passing, but it seems your druid girlfriend is tracking us, nonetheless."

"Brythia," Tolian shouted. Her heart leapt for joy. Her Brythia was following them. "And she's my wife, not my girlfriend, as you put it, knave."

"I do not recognize your sham marriage, beautiful one. Two females cannot be wed," he stated. "But we must move on. Here, get up." He hoisted her into the saddle and jumped up in front of her.

"Dowbreth," Tolian asked, "how is it that you know that Brythia is leading the party? That doesn't even seem possible; she was three weeks journey from Lorm."

Dowbreth turned to face her. "I do not yet know how the nature witch arrived so quickly at the palace, nor for that matter how it is that she follows our trail. But I will know soon, and I do not care to say how. At least, not yet." He laughed ominously.

Dowbreth rode like madness itself. They flew down the road and the trees were a blur to Tolian. She was so afraid that she held on to the rope that bound her to the faerie with all she was worth. They rode so hard and fast that it was nearly impossible to fix her eyes on any landmark. Occasionally, she thought she could see a building here or there, but they passed them so quickly that it was difficult to be certain. Speed. The echo of the hooves that moved so fast that they sounded like a dragon's roar, but yet stirred no dust on the dry road behind them.

After several hours, Tolian finally had become used to Dowbreth's frightening pace. She slowly loosened her grip so her fingers did not hurt so much. Despite the biting chill of the air, the cloak the faerie had given her protected her adequately from the cold. At length she was even able to think about something other than falling to her death off the great faerie horse.

Her first thoughts were of Brythia. How she missed her. Such pain in the depths of her soul could not be assuaged. She remembered their last kiss, their last embrace before Brythia had left for Hyge Bryth, a month ago now. If she closed her eyes, she could invoke the memory clearly. The sweet press of her soft lips. The gentle squeeze of her hug. The longing that enveloped her even as they released each other. She had wanted to have sex with her badly then, but Brythia was in a hurry. Tolian remembered her assurances that there would be plenty of time for lovemaking upon her return.

I miss you so badly, my love, she thought.

And now, somehow, at least according to Dowbreth, Brythia was close on their trail. How could the druidess possibly manage to return from Hyge Bryth and launch a search party for her so quickly? Tolian could not fathom how this was possible, though she had to admit Brythia was full of surprises of her own. She did not think that any search party would be able to catch up to them. Wherever they were headed. Then she found herself thinking in circles again. Where were they headed? Why was Dowbreth doing this in the first place? She needed more information before she could figure out exactly was going on. Dowbreth had promised to stop later; she would try to glean the information from him then.

Tolian was distracted from her thoughts by the sudden turn that Dowbreth maneuvered his horse into. In an instant they had gone from the gravel paved road to a narrow game trail that did not seem capable of allowing the giant horse (let alone the oversized faerie himself) access. Yet the horse tore down the path as well as he did the road, moving with a powerful grace through the dense foliage. Tolian ducked down low behind Dowbreth, who rode seemingly oblivious to the hardships of the trail.

Hours passed as Dowbreth urged his dark ethereal steed through the tangled, overgrown game trail. Just as the sun sank below the tree line and the edges of the twilight crept up around them, Dowbreth slowed the beast to a halt in a mossy glade of white birch.

The cold, dark winter's quiet suffused the forest. Clouds had rolled in to extinguish the starlight. Dowbreth once again tied the rope, which held Tolian to a high tree branch, leaving her enough room to move in a ten-foot radius. He proceeded to build a fire without comment. Tolian huddled by the warming flames. She was tired and the warmth, which stole over her entire body, began to draw her towards sleep. She dozed then in unthinking torpor, staring into the small fire. She barely paid attention as Dowbreth cooked something on the flames. Her eyes were heavy as the faerie handed her the leg of some sort of poultry. She nibbled on it absently. Tiredness weighed upon her. She was having difficulty keeping her eyes open. A couple of times she dozed off with the food still in her mouth.

Sleepily, she noticed that Dowbreth sat quietly across the fire from her. He, as well, gnawed on a leg of the unknown poultry. She struggled to wake up so she could attempt to question the brute. She yawned. As she fought to awaken, she heard something quite strange. A voice.

She could not swear she was awake for the voice sounded like a voice from a nightmare, a subtle impression, frightening her. A muffled cry.

"Quickly, you fool, they are near. Leave. Hurry. Now." A hiss, muffled, yet malevolent. Strangely familiar. Yet, Dowbreth had not spoken the words, and he seemed as surprised as she was.

The faerie looked down at the bag sitting next to him on the ground—the same mysterious bag he had taken into the forest with him. Yes, it did seem the voice had come from the bag. Impossible.

Tolian had little time to ponder this for Dowbreth leapt up with great urgency.

"Hurry," he cried, "get up."

Tolian starred at him dumbly for a moment.

"Now," he shouted.

The faerie knight picked up the strange bag and quickly, but with care, secured it to his horse. Tolian slowly climbed to her feet, clutching the wool cloak tightly around her. Dowbreth rushed over to the tree where her rope was tied and worked feverishly to release it.

What is going on? Tolian thought.

In the distance, she heard shouting. Dowbreth grabbed her

roughly and tossed her up on to the horse. Tolian strained to hear the distant voices in the dark of the forest. Did she hear the name "Brythia"? She could not be sure for in a second Dowbreth jumped behind her on the saddle and the faerie horse charged away into the thick woods.

Chapter 16

Brythia examined Kiliordes' leg under the light of the torch Delorick held behind her. A nasty cut, some abrasions, and probably a slight sprain, she diagnosed. She washed the area out with a little water Pagryus offered her. Not too bad—it certainly could have been a lot worse. Pretty much just the leg and a knot on his head. No concussion. Still, she felt guilty over the incident. Clearly, she had been reckless driving them on at an unsafe speed in the dark of night. They were lucky that Kiliordes wasn't more seriously injured in the fall. She removed a sprig of elfroot from her pouch and rubbed it over the wound. "That should help with the pain," Brythia explained to him.

"Elfroot?" Kiliordes asked.

"Ah, yes, so you remember that as well," commented the druidess. "Though, as I recall, healing never was your specialty. How's that? Any better yet?"

"Yes," he answered. "It feels cool and soothing."

"Good," she said, pulling his pant leg back down. "Can you ride a little further? At the very least, we need to find someplace to set up camp."

"Absolutely," he answered, "I'm fine, really, no problem. Here, um, Pagyrus, give me a hand."

"Of course," responded the pilgrim. "Up you go." Pagyrus extended Kiliordes his hand.

"Easy does it," cautioned Brythia as Kilordes was lifted to his feet. He staggered a little as he put his weight on his leg. Clearly, the sprain was worse then she had thought.

Brythia was torn. She wrestled with the guilt, yet was ready to get back on her horse and course through the thick, stygian woods to find her beloved. Her mind churned with strife and uncertainty before settling on an answer to her internal conflict. "Look," she said, "this is too dangerous for you."

She met the gaze of each of them with a tilt of her head. Delorick, in particular, shot her an indignant look. Ah yes, the male pride, she thought. "I can't let you travel any further," she continued. "Especially under these conditions. Follow me at your own pace at daybreak. It's just too dangerous in these thick woods. This game trail isn't safe to ride. But I know we are close to them, and I can't let them slip away." She got to her feet and handed the elf-root to Findelbres, who numbly took the weed from her. She walked over to Whisper.

"Brythia, don't do this," begged Findelbres.

"Please listen to reason," Delorick said.

She slipped into the saddle. "Gentlemen, thank you, but it is reason I'm listening to. I'll see you soon, I'm sure." She urged her faerie mount to tread the black trail once again. The way seemed even darker than earlier, but she did not need to see. Whisper maneuvered the narrow stretch with ease, holding a speedy gait. Faerie horses had the valuable ability to provide their riders with a smooth, steady ride despite rough terrain or other obstacles. Neither the nighttime nor the thorny brush along the trail interfered with this skill. Nor did Brythia require light to sense which way the Moonsword pulled her arm with urgency.

She was hardly settled fully in her saddle when she saw the flicker of a fire. A small campfire, she discerned, off the trail to her right, partially concealed by a small grove of white birch. The Moonsword almost jerked her off her horse as she slowed the beast, directing her further down the narrow path, but she had to investigate the camp. She halted Whisper and dismounted. Holding the sword before her, she cautiously approached the fire. She could see no sign of anyone around the flames. She cast her gaze warily behind and around her. No one. She listened to the winter's quiet and the crackle of the fire. No other sound disturbed the chill silence. Then a pop as one of the burning logs sent a small shower of sparks into the air. Startled, she held still, then furtively crept closer. Shadows danced on the trees cast there by the fire's whimsy.

She scanned the campsite in the ample lighting the fire provided. Though there were no signs of anyone there now, clearly someone had left in a hurry, only moments before. Her skilled eyes caught the marks of a woman's slipper and prints much, much larger than any human could possibly make. Signs of a hasty departure. A half-eaten turkey leg lay discarded near the fire.

"Damn, they're gone," she said out loud.

A whiff of perfume caught her nose. Tolian's perfume.

She ran back to Whisper. She bounded up into the saddle.

"Tolian," she shouted and kicked the great mare. With the Moonsword outstretched before her and pulsing with an anxious vibration, she urged the faerie equine forward at a terrific speed.

Her heart was pounding and nervous energy coursed through her veins. Her thoughts raced. She was so close now she knew it. She tried to focus on the Moonsword, but scarcely needed to. There was nowhere else for them to go, no offshoots, no more off-trail glades or meadows. Just the trail which was getting even narrower, yet impossibly her horse galloped unconcerned. The occasional branch or thorn vine tore at her face, but she considered such assaults as mere annoyances. She did have to be certain to grasp the magick sword with the firmest grip or it would have pulled itself out of her hand and flown towards Tolian of its own power.

Occasionally, she yelled Tolian's name at the top of her lungs. Her shouts seemed to fall behind her, so fast was her pace. Nonetheless, she strained to hear a reply. Her heart begged to hear Tolian's husky voice echoing from the darkness ahead of her. She heard nothing.

As she rode, she could feel the moisture in the air increase and the temperature rise slightly as clouds moved in, creating a gray ceiling high above her. It would snow sometime that day. She was still a good enough weather witch to know that. The thought of snow did not particularly trouble her. With the Moonsword doing the tracking, and Whisper handling the travel with little instruction from her, the impending snowfall should be little worse than a nuisance. Certainly, it was nothing to be concerned with, and she did not allow such thoughts to occupy her mind for long. Nothing did. Except, of course, for her poor Tolian.

"Tolian," she intoned softly. "Hold on, my love, I'm coming. Just hold on."

Images of Tolian, powerless and in the clutches of that villain, prompted her to urge Whisper to undertake even greater speed down the now twisting game path. She was still baffled as to how Dowbreth had managed the whole thing. Tolian was the epitome of power, of strength. She was a goddess. How was it possible, even for a faerie, to rob her of her vast strength? From the evidence she had seen at the hastily abandoned campsite, it was clear that Tolian was no longer unconscious. Yet, perhaps the drug the faerie warlord had used had somehow blunted or neutralized her divinity. Perhaps, but the Moonsword seemed still focused on her trail. It was a mystery to her. Brythia was tormented by this question and by her imagination, which pictured her love at the mercy of the enigmatic Elven knight.

"Faster, Whisper, faster," she said to her steed.

Fatigue began to tug at her after a couple more hours of the pursuit had passed, but not enough to check her manic resolve. She could not let her concentration flag now else the lunar sword, which guided her, would slip from her weary grip. It seemed that even the incredible speed of her horse could scarce keep up with the blade's urgency.

Then it happened. Suddenly the eager vitality seemed to diminish from the Moonsword's vibrant pull. Brythia sensed a deep confusion from the otherworldly weapon. Something was wrong. Uncertainty. A sense of shock, of loss, of pain. It became clear to Brythia the sword was suddenly at a loss. She reined Whisper to a much slower pace. Perhaps, she surmised, the sword just needed a moment to recollect its bearings, but she felt there was a more significant cause for the blade's behavior.

The reduction of speed did nothing to aid the Moonsword. It was now inert in her hand. She attempted to communicate mentally with it again. She quieted, then opened her mind to the sword and "listened" for any impressions she might receive. There was almost no effort necessary. The Moonsword was sending a strong signal. An overwhelming feeling of confusion and worry poured from the blade to her mind. She tuned herself in, even more, to the stream of the weapon's energy. She projected a thought, a question. *What's the matter?*

The Moonsword answered her mental probe immediately. *She has closed herself to me. She doesn't want me to find her.*

"No," replied the druidess, out loud this time, "She does want us to find her. Please try again. Please."

The sword sent its answer to her. "She told me to stop, and she cut herself off from me. It hurts me. She is afraid. It hurts.

Please, Brythia," the Moonsword begged, "please help her. I cannot."

She sighed, brought the sword to her lips, and kissed it gently. "I will find her," she assured it. She slid the blade back into her sheath. *But how?*

It was clear, at least, that the faerie would be unable to leave the narrow way of the game trail, so tight and thick was the forest in that region. With some optimism, she simply followed the trail, until it ended a scant two miles later emptying (as well as Brythia's hopes) onto a more typical and well-maintained country road. There was, of course, no clear indication of their path.

She had already discovered she would be unable to track them in the traditional sense, and to renew such an attempt would only waste more valuable time. No, she needed to employ more arcane techniques to pursue them. She could employ several methods if she had more time. She could use the Spirit Vision, if she could find the right mushrooms quickly enough; but the impending snow would likely render such a course of action impossible. She forced her fatigued mind to concentrate, to think of the way. Then, it came to her. *Ah, yes*, she thought. There was only one choice. She had to attempt the Whole Forest Assumption. A difficult meditative practice under ideal conditions. Yet, she could think of nothing else.

She slid off Whisper, and cast a last, less than hopeful look in either direction down the road. She could feel the tiredness around the edges of her consciousness, eating away her ability to concentrate. "Wait here," she instructed the horse. "This could take a few minutes."

The Elven steed whinnied in response. The druidess gently stroked the beast's neck, before turning her attention to the task.

Brythia walked a few yards away and sat cross-legged on one side of the gravel road. She drew a couple of deep breaths in an attempt to calm her frantic mind. She looked around her as she did so, almost as though she was breathing the surrounding landscape into her lungs. The air was cold and hung heavy with the sweet icy scent of the coming snow. The sky had brightened now as the heavy snow clouds seemed to glow with anticipation, for it was still too early for the sun to be responsible. It afforded her enough light to see the gray, bare branches of the trees, almost twiggy fingers, interwoven and reaching solemnly up to the sky.

Steadier, deeper breaths. She closed her eyes. She had to quiet her worries and thoughts. She focused solely on her breathing. *Deep breath in; count to four. Hold for four. Exhale for four. Let the stress and anxiety fade, get past the sleepiness,* she ordered herself. *Let there only be the breathing.* Slow, steady, deep. With each breath, a gradual simplicity took hold of her tumultuous mind. It occurred to her she had not practiced even basic meditation in some time; most novices could calm their minds more easily. Then she reminded herself that such thoughts were a distraction to the calming of the mind. She let the thought go. With more breaths, she let everything go. It was coming back to her, now. Inhale, Hold, Exhale. The quieting of thoughts.

Once there was only the breathing, and nothing more, Brythia allowed herself to become conscious of the shadowy forest around her. First the cold hard ground. She opened her imagination and meditated on what it must be like to be the frigid, leaf-covered ground. A great blanket of icy coldness seemed to descend upon her as she did so. Cold, hard, and dead. No, not dead. There was a quiet network of life nestled inside her, roots twisting and delving, asleep in her chill embrace. Down deep in her being it was warmer, and larger creatures were nestled in their burrows, dens and nests. She was all of these creatures as well, she reminded herself. By realizing this and incorporating them into her awareness, she felt a powerful wave of sleepiness take hold of her. She could not fight this feeling as it was equally part of the meditation—she had to realize fully every aspect of the forest and every creature in it, even those in hibernation. She followed the roots back up—climbing the tangled maze back to the trees and out of the ground, though she tried to hold all that she had felt beneath the Earth in the back of her mind.

Now she was the trees, still the delving root ways, but now also the proud trunks and noble branches. The sap ran so slow through her wooden veins. The trees were sleeping as well. Another powerful urge to sleep. This time she had to fight it to some degree or she would fall asleep herself. In doing so, her doubts began to creep in to her consciousness, the nagging feeling that it was all just her imagination. This was a perilous doubt; it could disrupt the entire work.

She felt herself as the thousands and thousands of branches reaching in silent entreaty for the return of the sun, or at least for the snow. It had been a dry autumn, and Brythia could feel in her countless wooden limbs the subtle yearning for water, a primordial thirst, less in her great oaks than in the maples and smaller trees and undergrowth. She began to feel the strain in her mind. Attempting to experience the perceptions of an entire forest was no easy task, and, as a rule, the trees were where the mind began to get bogged down. Clearly, the winter should be easier than the summer, but there was still the winter-slumbering lassitude to contend with. In any case, somehow, Brythia was doing it, and the assumption was unfolding splendidly.

Her mind raced down the gentle banks of a brook. She was the frozen stream, flowing beneath its icy surface. She was the fish and frogs asleep in the deeper regions. She was the wood mouse searching the dried leaves of the forest floor for food. She was the great owl. She felt the rush of air beneath her wings as she swooped down on her unsuspecting mousey self. She cast her consciousness out further and further into the surrounding forest, attempting to catch some glimpse of her beloved and her captor.

The hibernation instinct was so diffused over the nighttime woods that Brythia had to find as many nocturnal creatures as possible simply to maintain some state of wakefulness. Many such creatures moved through the darkened woods even at night. Was she imagining the family of possum that slipped over the log as she looked through their eyes? She battled her own skepticism, her amplified tiredness, and the enormity of her undertaking, almost constantly now. The druidess did not stop, however. She kept expanding her consciousness so that she was the entire forest for at least a three-mile radius.

Then the snow began to fall and she was the snow. She drifted, first idly, as a thousand timid flakes moving down through her outreaching branches. Her pace quickened and she danced through her forest self in crystal patterns of infinite variety. She became almost dizzy. Her animal selves moved in haste to find food before all was lost in the frozen white blanket.

Suddenly, it happened—she was no longer the forest; she was Brythia once again. But she was not as she would have expected, sitting cross-legged along the roadside. She was, instead, moving through the tightly knotted trees, searching. She was surprised by this, and wondered how long it was that she had been doing so.

The snow fell all around her, moving with its gentle hush through the trees. Brythia tried to remember the feeling of being the snow, of being the trees, but the Whole Forest Assumption had faded, and she was left with only a few vague, vestigial impressions. There was something magical, perhaps divine about snow. An infinite variety of unique icy crystals covered the world in a white blanket of purity. It seemingly wrapped everything in an innocence that briefly hid even human hypocrisy and hatred. One of her favorite weather magicks was the Call to the Snow. She roused herself from this reverie, and tried to concentrate on her situation. Where exactly, was she? How far had she wandered from the road? Fog clouded her brain, making the task of thinking difficult.

A nearby sound caught her attention. She turned towards the sound. She could just see it. A white shape, now holding still, in the dim light and falling snow. It was a great white hart staring intently at her. Brythia stood motionless and casually regarded the remarkable creature. The druidess uttered a greeting in the subtle clicking language of the deer-clan and waited for the customary response. She was surprised by the white hart's reply.

"Hail to thee, Brythia, Priestess of the Sun, and well met," the animal said plainly in human speech.

Chapter 17

They could not have ridden for more than half an hour before Dowbreth stopped his dark steed. As the giant faerie reined in the horse, Tolian could hear the strange, malevolent voice almost shouting from the bag. She was certain she was not imagining it. A string of foul curses and epithets colored the mysterious cries. "Fool. The druid-bitch still follows. It's the damned sword. She's using the sword."

Dowbreth looked at the bag for a moment and considered the words coming from it. Did a look of doubt briefly flash across his face? She could not be sure. He brought his gaze to Tolian and narrowed his eyes. In a quick motion, he shoved her off the horse and sent her tumbling to the frozen ground.

Tolian was caught by surprise. She hit the ground hard and was instantly winded by the fall. Stunned and confused. Then Dowbreth was on top of her, straddling her prostrate form. He hit her hard in the face with the back of his hand. The princess cried out weakly. "Quiet, wench," the faerie said.

She lay there staring up at him. She was as afraid as she had ever been. She could read the threat in his eyes, and knew her own eyes shone with fear and a soft, but urgent plea. There was only the two of them and the moment. The awful string of curses and unintelligible ravings had ceased coming from the bag. It was quiet.

With great violence, the Elven warlord jerked Tolian's gown up above her waist. She was frozen in terror. He spread apart her legs and crawled over her, bringing his face right next to hers. He whispered coarsely, "Do you want me to do this, Princess?"

She shook her head. She was shaking and trembling.

"Then you must do something for me," said Dowbreth. "That sounds fair now, doesn't it, O Beautiful One?" The villain paused. "You must stop your girlfriend from following you," he commanded. "At once."

Tolian had no idea what the faerie was talking about. How

could she stop Brythia from following them? Confusion now joined fear manifesting in her body language.

"You see," explained Dowbreth, "your girlfriend is using the Moonsword to track us. But, the sword will obey your command. And you must tell it to stop. Do you understand?"

"I've lost my powers, remember?" she said.

"Not quite," Dowbreth corrected her. "Your power is being blocked; its outward expression is being absorbed, but you still control you inner powers, child. You can still control your sword. And you must, do so now, or...." He let his lust-filled stare complete his sentence.

It had never been clear to her exactly how she was able to do any of the preternatural things she could. Usually she tapped into her "powers" without thinking; she never had to concentrate on them. The sword. Her connection to it had always been unconscious, instinctual. She had no idea how to begin to tell the sword not to follow them. "I don't know how," she said, fear dripping from every word.

Dowbreth looked down at her with scorn. "That's too bad, princess..." He leaned back a little and began to unfasten his belt.

"Please no," she pleaded. "I'm sorry. Please just give me a minute. I'll try to do it." She hated herself for begging, but her fear was complete. She was afraid for herself, but also for Brythia. What if her beloved did track them and confront Dowbreth? Tolian knew the druidess would be no match for the Warlord of the Sidhe. He would kill her and continue on his way. No, there was no hope of rescue anyway.

Dowbreth completed unfastening his belt buckle, but still he hung a little away from her. "Do it now."

She closed her eyes and attempted to steady her frantic breathing and compose herself. She pictured the weapon in her mind's eye. The long blade, the purple sheen, and the hilt, which fit her hands so perfectly. The image came easily to her mind. Her sword. Yes, there it is, she thought. That it was a living thing of its own right, she did not doubt. There were times when she could sense its emotions clearly.

She formed a mental command and visualized herself imparting it to the Moonsword, "Do not follow me; don't help Brythia track me." She felt love radiating from the sword and was warmed by its happy glow. Then she heard Dowbreth shout at her, "Now."

She was shaken. Fear swirled inside her, yet the sword seemed to be holding their connection fast. As her fear grew, it seemed the sword's presence in her mind strengthened. In terror she shouted, "Stop, you must not follow me. Do not follow me."

She felt the lunar blade's confusion and its own reflective fear. The clear impression that the mystical weapon was not happy about her command came to her. She heard herself screaming her final order, "Do as I say."

The vision of the Moonsword faded, and her own harsh words echoed in her ears. She opened her eyes. Dowbreth still hovered over her, too close. His red eyes burned scornfully down upon her.

"Is it done?" he asked.

Tolian lowered her eyes. "Yes," she replied. She hated the meekness in her voice.

The faerie nodded as a crooked smile played on his pale and scarred face. He reached over and pulled her gown back down below her waist.

"Good girl," he said. "If you keep obeying my orders, our relationship will go well."

There was such power and authority in his tone, such superiority.

"Come," he said lifting her up off the ground, "We must continue on our way."

They rode on as night ceded its place to morning. They traveled now over paved roads again, traversing forests and fields. Tolian was surprised to see a farmer driving a cart full of winter cabbages on the roadway, though she was certain that she was not as surprised as he was. Her eyes caught his—saw his shock as the faerie steed raced past him. Could he see the despair in her eyes?

The snow began falling shortly after that. The first few flakes slipped from the sky as a gentle flurry, but the pace quickened to a steady snowfall. The landscape became a white blur to Tolian in her position in front of the faerie on the dark warhorse. For the first time in her life she was helpless, carried beyond her will towards some unspeakable doom. A great numbness took hold of her. She had her fear, but that was all; it was clear there was no hope for her. No one could help her, let alone find her. *Is this what it really means to be a woman? Are we weak and powerless? Are we to be preyed upon and victimized without recourse, a plaything for the strong?* She shivered, as much from fear as from the cold. *No, I can't accept this. We are so much more*, she thought, but her fear threatened to overtake her. She fought hard against it.

After a while, some part of her brain reminded her that she was a warrior, that as such she had known fear many times in the past. She had fought her first battle as a young boy, no older than thirteen. He was terrified out of his mind. His father taught him the warrior's mantra before the fighting and he held it firmly in his mind, "Fear is for my enemy. Fear is defeat, and the forerunner of defeat. I will hold no fear." The warrior's mantra.

She tried it now, gradually bringing it around her mind: *Fear is for my enemy. Fear is defeat, and the forerunner of defeat. I will hold no fear. Fear is for my enemy. Fear is defeat, and the forerunner of defeat. I will hold no fear. Fear is for my enemy. Fear is defeat, and the forerunner of defeat. I will hold no fear.*

She moved her lips in a secret whisper with the mantra. It was helping. Slowly, her panic diminished. The slightest trace of hope grew in her heart. She would not be this weak and helpless thing. She would wait and watch. She would study her enemy and his mysterious speaking bag. She would be patient, resolute, and calm. She would find a way. *Use your perceived weakness against him*, she thought. *He thinks he has me beaten. Perhaps, I can determine how he has robbed me of the use of my powers, and restore them.* Above all, she told herself, *I will not give up. I will kill this villain and return to my Brythia's side. Somehow.*

The snow fell, a force of heaven. Even the dark faerie stallion was having trouble making progress through the fierce snowstorm. With a curse, Dowbreth reined in his horse and slowly guided it to the protection of a copse of tall but bent evergreens just off the road. He dismounted and lifted Tolian off the saddle and set her standing next to him. He methodically tied the rope from her bound wrists to a branch about ten feet in the air, leaving her, once again, with enough slack to move a few feet away from the tree, but little more.

"Wait here," he barked, as he turned his attention to unfastening the strange, but now quiet, sack from his saddle. "I will just be a moment."

Then taking the bag, he disappeared into the heavy snow.

Tolian looked around her. The snow was really coming down, placing a coating of white over the entire landscape. The tree branches were laden with almost five inches of snow, bowing them under the frosty weight. Despite this, however, the canopy made by the snow-covered pines protected both her and Dowbreth's horse well from the precipitation. Still, it was cold; even with the heavy cloak wrapped around her, her ears hurt, as did her feet, which were afforded almost no protection by her delicate slippers.

She looked up at the rope, her leash, as it were. Instantly, an idea entered her head. Yes, it would be bad if it didn't work, probably very bad. She drew back a little as the fear played about the edges of her mind. Thoughts of Dowbreth touching her.

She had little time to decide. It was now or never. She looked quickly around her and set a suspicious glance at the faerie horse. Yes, she had to try. It could well be her only chance. Perhaps, she thought, *Brythia has conjured up this storm to give me just such an opportunity*. Her fear came back with a rush. A quick look up at the branch again, and she grabbed the rope and began to pull herself up.

She whispered the warrior's mantra as she did so. "Fear is for my enemy. Fear is defeat, and the forerunner of defeat. I will hold no fear. Fear is my enemy. Fear is defeat, and the forerunner of defeat. I will hold no fear."

It was tough going, arduously pulling herself up the tree trunk, and using her legs to help her. She struggled, again cursing her weakness, but using her frustration to fuel her efforts all the more.

Hurry, girl, she told herself. *Hurry*.

At last she had reached the branch, and, with great difficulty, she managed to pull herself up to it. Once there, she fought her way over to a branch on the other side of the tree, about four feet higher, the whole process made challenging by her securely tied wrists. She wrenched herself into a crouched position, perched perilously on the narrow branch. She slowed her heavy breathing and attempted to calm herself.

Fear is for my enemy. Fear is defeat, or the forerunner of defeat. I will hold no fear.

She waited, peeking around the tree. She peered as best she could through the snow. Visibility was poor. She would have to keep her vigilance up. Timing was going to be everything.

She kept the mantra going through her head, but she no longer allowed herself to vocalize it, lest she give her position away. She was not as well protected from the snow as she had been, and she could feel the flakes quickly accumulating on her head and shoulders. Her hands were bitterly cold. She looked again warily at the horse. It seemed unconcerned. Tolian had not freed herself from her bindings so it made no alarm. She hoped it would have no time to give Dowbreth a clue to her whereabouts until it was too late.

Come on. Come on, she urged in her thoughts.

Doubts came again and she fought them back. "*I will hold no fear...*"

Suddenly the faerie's massive figure emerged from the blinding snow. At first, he showed no surprise that he did not see her at once as his great steed hid most of the site from vision. Then Tolian saw his eyes grow wide, and then narrow. Now he was close enough. Now, it was time.

She made a loop in the rope and jumped down at the giant.

"*Fear is defeat, and the forerunner of defeat....*"

She just managed to get the loop of rope around his neck as she slapped down into his back. She pulled with everything she was worth.

Clearly, the faerie was not expecting any such attack, and he was ill prepared for one. At first, she thought it might just work, as she watched him gag and drop his bag on the snow-covered ground. Tolian put all of her concentration into pulling the rope as hard as she possibly could. "Die, you bastard, die," she shouted.

Once, however, Dowbreth realized exactly what was happening, the situation quickly changed. With an easy shrug,

Tolian went flying off the faerie's back, and hit the ground hard, despite landing in a small snowbank. The air rushed out of her lungs, and the rope jerked her wrists so painfully she was sure one had broken instantly.

Dowbreth leaned over her. "Will you never learn, girl?" He growled. He pulled her up by the rope and punched her in the eye. The pain was excruciating. He dropped her back into the snow, and stroked his own neck. "I see that I cannot secure your cooperation without using my leverage. Very well."

Chapter 18

To his surprise, it was Kiliordes urging the others on to greater speed. His own impatience astonished him. No doubt, Brythia's sense of urgency had been contagious. He had to assure Findelbres that he was well enough to resume their trek and Delorick that the horses had had enough rest. As for Pagyrus, well, he seemed content to follow Kiliordes' lead and made no protest one way or the other.

He was worried about Tolian, certainly, but now Brythia had become the focus of his anxiety. Clearly, Dowbreth needed Tolian alive for some purpose. But the druidess...what if she managed to catch up to them? The giant faerie would surely have no difficulty dispatching her and continuing on his way undisturbed. As they made their way down the narrow game trail (at a much slower pace than under Brythia's lead), his eyes scanned the dark, fearfully searching for Brythia's lifeless and bloody corpse. How could she have even entertained the notion of confronting Dowbreth by herself? *Stupid. Stubborn,* he thought. Even with the Moonsword, it was an errand of folly.

These thoughts forced Kiliordes to pick up the pace of their pursuit, just as the snow began to fall. The flakes became more visible in the gradual lightening of the sky, bringing memories of both his childhoods to his thoughts. He normally didn't indulge himself with reflections on his old life as two people. It often brought on the feeling of disunity he loathed. It was stressful. In many ways, it was more convenient to think of himself as having come into existence on that bitter day in January. But something about the magick of the snow called the memories out and allowed him to wander there without the discomfort. He remembered himself as young Rwiordes, maybe seven, dashing through the woods behind his father's house, throwing snowballs at Perelisk and Hertrid. How strange they seemed to him from the shadows of his memory, Perelisk so damn cocky, yet so innocent, and Hertrid, ever the stout follower, but how young. He had not liked to think about them since, well, last year, but here in this memory there was only innocence, except the well-thrown ice ball from Perelisk, which hit him square in the chin. He could easily recall how it hurt. Then the passing shadow, the guilt. He had cut off Perelisk's head. It wasn't Perelisk at the time, of course, he always told himself that, but it rarely helped. He was obliged to remind himself that if he hadn't done it, the Demon would have destroyed the world. Even that didn't help.

He was happy enough to escape that line of thought by a reminiscence from Kilfrie's girlhood. So different she was from Rwiordes. She was alone in the deep forests of the Haunted Mountains. It was so clear. How old was she then? Five. So young. Practicing, always practicing. Walking alone through her favorite part of the forest, a thick deer woods, moss-covered green in the warmer weather, but in this memory, snowbound in fresh powdery cover. Ah yes, he thought, this was that day. She had felt so strange that day. She knew then that that would be the day. All the practicing would pay off. She felt it in the deepest core of her young being.

The snow was falling, just an idle snow shower, amongst the birches and the grapevines of her little valley. The rabbit should have been tucked away in its warren, cozy and warm, but it wasn't. It had felt like they were drawn to each other. They came upon each other as if the gods had set an appointment for them. He remembered dropping down to her knees, bare knees in the snow. She didn't care. She stared into the rabbit's eyes.

He stopped himself. He didn't like to remember the Hamfahring, the Gift. That power that Kilfrie had possessed. It made him nervous. He didn't like thinking about it. He refocused his attention to the game trail and signs of his friends. But his mind, it seemed, was uncooperative, enjoined by the snow's power to pull memories unbidden into the light of the conscious mind. And so another reverie unfolded before his mind's eye. He remembered the last time he had seen Serendi, his daughter. They made a snowman together. The snow was too dry and did not pack well, resulting in quite a pathetic figure. But what a jewel Serendi was, so beautiful, maybe six years old. Luckily, she took after her mother. What fun they had that day. He felt a pang of loss and then he heard Delorick exclaim behind him, "Ho. A campsite. You passed it, Kiliordes."

The campsite had been abandoned, and was largely snow-covered, offering few clues to who may have camped there. The smoldering remnants of a small campfire were all that could be seen. There was nothing to be learned there. They studied it and paced about for a few moments, but quickly resumed their path. It offered some hope that they were still on the right trail, and for that Kiliordes was grateful.

Nonetheless, it stood as a reminder to Kiliordes of what a different person he had become. To Kilfrie, it would have been second nature to see the campsite, even in the snow-packed morning twilight. Despite his reluctance to access her druidic training, he needed to use any resource at his disposal in the current situation. His friends' lives depended on it.

The snow grew in intensity as the morning wore on, weighing down leafless branches and evergreen boughs, and making it even more difficult to detect the various obstacles of the poorly kept trail. Kiliordes was ecstatic when he could see the path empty onto a snow-covered road. At last to be free from the oppressive tightness of the game trail (a thought, he realized, which would have been alien to Kilfrie).

Despite the now heavy snow, he could see there was something in the road. Was that a horse milling about in the close vicinity to the object? As they brought their horses on to the road, he could see it was Whisper, and the object in the road was none other than Brythia, covered in several inches of white powdery flakes. She wasn't moving.

"Oh Gods, no," he thought. "Please no." He yelled back to the others, "Hurry, quick. It's Brythia." He immediately dismounted and rushed to her side.

She was sitting in the druidic meditation position—cross-legged. Her eyes were closed tightly and her face had a reddish-blue tinge, which immediately set Kiliordes to worrying. As he reached her side, however, it became obvious that she was breathing rhythmically; in fact, she was snoring slightly. His heart lightened with relief.

"Bring blankets. Get a fire going," he called back to the others, and he returned his attention to the near frozen druidess. "Brythia," he said in a quiet voice next to her ear.

No response.

"Brythia," he said again, but louder. He gently brushed the accumulated snow off her head and shoulders and delicately squeezed her arm.

Her eyes popped open. Bewilderment and sleepiness played there.

"What?" she mumbled in confusion. "Oh no, Kiliordes. The white hart was going to tell me something important."

Now, it was his turn to be confused. "I'm sorry, Brythia. What did you say?"

She blinked a couple of times and shook her head.

Findelbres stepped up and wrapped a blanket around her. She paid him no attention, but continued speaking to Kiliordes.

"You interrupted me; I was doing the Whole Forest Assumption and I would have had something... if you hadn't broken the trance—"

"You weren't in a trance, you were asleep. People don't snore in meditative trances."

"No, you wouldn't think so," agreed Delorick, now standing behind him. "Princess, are you all right?"

Delorick's question caused the druidess to shudder involuntarily and pull the blanket snuggly around her.

"I guess so, I'm not sure," she replied. "I fell asleep. Damn."

"Brythia, get up off the cold ground, while we get a fire going. You'll catch your death of chill," said Findelbres, taking some kindling from Pagyrus and placing it in a small circle he must have just cleared in the snow.

"What, oh yes." Kiliordes helped her to her feet. She still seemed disoriented and angry with herself.

"You attempted the Whole Forest Assumption?" he asked her. With Kilfrie's power, she had never bothered to learn the more traditional meditations of that sort, but Kiliordes remembered hearing of others attempting it. It was supposedly a difficult procedure under the best of conditions.

Now despondency colored her voice, "I failed, and now we have no way to track Tolian."

She started to sob, softly at first.

"But," inquired Delorick, "what of the Moonsword? You

were using it to track them, were you not?"

"It doesn't work anymore," she said. "Tolian commanded it to stop..." Now tears flowed freely down her frozen cheeks. "Now we can't find her, that's why I tried..."

"Calm down, dear," offered Kiliordes. He felt so sorry for her. "You're not making any sense, you know."

He put his arm around her. She shuddered slightly as "the look" flashed across her face. Kiliordes sighed. "Take some deep breaths, try to relax, and calm yourself," he suggested.

Then something in her changed, her eyes lit up, and she stared into his eyes. "You," said the druidess. "You can do it. You're Kilfrie. You have her power."

Kiliordes let go of her, his face went blank, and he stepped back. He instantly found himself getting nervous. Agitated. "I can do what?" he asked with a surprisingly accusatory tone.

Her eyes grew wide, and a smile touched her lips. "You. You can find them," she exclaimed triumphantly.

"She's delirious from the cold," said Delorick. "Here. They've got the fire going already."

"No. I'm not delirious," she exclaimed, almost gleefully. "You can do it, Kiliordes. You're the only one who can. You can use the Hamfahring. Use Kilfire's gift. Your gift."

He stared at her as though she had committed the most heinous of crimes. He could say nothing. He wanted to protest, but the words would not come.

"Yes, of course," said Findelbres. "She's right. That is provided you can still do it. Can you?"

There it is, isn't it? He had been afraid of the power. For some time, he thought it just been a rebelliousness in him, something that did not, once having been freed from the harsh regimen of always practicing "the gift", wish to be so obliged once again. Something in him wanted to be this new being, a creature of unity, not some synthetic thing, two separate souls stitched together, but someone new and complete. But, it was fear. He was afraid of the gift. He could not explain why he was afraid either. He just knew that he was afraid for some reason. "I can't do it," he said. "I don't think I can do it. I don't really remember how."

How hollow his words sounded, even to him. Empty words

formed of fear. Cowardice, he thought. No, now was not the time to pander to his selfish worries. Tolian was in real trouble. His friends were right—it was the only way. "I'll try," he said finally.

Brythia smiled and hugged him. She held him in her embrace and whispered a soft "Thank you" in his ear.

"Come, Princess Brythia," said Pagryus. "You must warm yourself here by the fire."

Kiliordes disengaged himself from her embrace gently. "Yes," he agreed, "you should warm yourself. I'll try, but first let's just warm up for a minute."

Brythia had summoned a crow with a few loud caws and a piece of leftover pork. It regarded him through the snow on its position on the druidess's forearm. Of course, Kilfrie would have been able to summon the crow herself, and probably he could still do it, but it seemed more important to concentrate on that which he alone could do. It was a good-sized bird, and it was likely no easy task for Brythia to hold her arm as steady as she was. First, the druidess asked the crow with a series of croaks and caws whether the bird had seen two people traveling through the area. Kiliordes was surprised that he largely understood their conversation. If the crow had encountered them, it could save him from having to undertake the use of Kilfrie's "gift".

"What is she doing?" Pagyrus asked.

"She's asking it if it's seen them," Kiliordes replied.

"Then, why not just ask all the animals in the forest until we find one who has?", inquired Delorick.

The question made sense, on the surface, but Kiliordes knew it was impractical, at best.

Brythia answered him softly, so not to disturb the bird on her arm. "It would take a long time to summon forest creatures and in turn interrogate them. Yes, maybe we would get lucky early on, but more likely probably not. That was why I attempted the Whole Forest Assumption, to try to do it all at once. No, this is the only way. Kiliordes, are you ready?"

He sighed to relieve some of the stress building up in him. Was he sure he could even remember how it was done?

"Yes, I'm ready. We're both of us going to need to sit

down, I'm afraid."

"Fine," answered the golden-haired druidess, and she dropped gently into the staple cross-legged position to one side of the fire.

Kiliordes eased himself into a similar position (but, with much more difficulty). He made a sharp click with his tongue to get the crow's attention, and, sure enough, the black bird brought its wandering eyes to face him. The eyes. That was the secret. As he caught the bird's gaze and held it, everything came rushing back to him.

The eyes were the gateway. He steadied his breathing. Slow and calm. Slower. Match up with the crow's breathing and slow it down. He stared deeply into the eyes. The eyes. The old trick. The eyes were the gateway. Blackish purple. He imagined himself walking into the crow's eyes. As soon as he did so, the "gift" went to work. It was automatic.

Kiliordes was the crow staring back at his own human body sitting motionless, save for the slow and rhythmic breathing. The crow's body fit him as if it has always been his own. The old joy of achievement came back to him. The thrill of being something else, something alien. Different.

With a joyous caw, he hopped off Brythia's forearm. She smiled at him.

"Go. Find them," she said.

He walked a few steps and unfolded his wings. He noticed that he was much warmer now, his feathers fluffed to maximize his insulation from the frigid air. He tried a couple of experimental flaps of his black greasy wings, to accustom himself to the crow's body. Then, he leapt up into the air, flapped his wings, and rose into the sky with a caw, leaving them on the ground.

Higher and higher he flew. The exhilaration was complete. He was flying. He allowed himself to fly no higher than he could easily see the others clearly through the falling snow. He circled them twice and then went in search of Tolian and Dowbreth. It was pure freedom, pure magick. He felt the crow's blood pulse through his veins. He felt alive. He rang out a few more caws just for the sheer thrill of it.

How beautiful the world looked from this perspective. The

world painted crystalline white, bathed in a blanket of divine innocence, pure and wholesome again. Flakes of infinite variety danced in the air around him. Life at its most peaceful, yet full of its coldness and harshness. The air moved beneath his mighty wings and he felt like singing. How could he have ever forgotten the glory, the power, and the freedom of the Hamfahring? The sharing of life. This was true communion with nature. He could not remember being happier. He cawed again.

Chapter 19

Dowbreth pulled Tolian by the hair, dragging her next to the warhorse. She cried out in pain. He deposited her and picked up the mysterious sack. His normally pale face was bright red with rage. "We are finished with these games, my Lady of the Silvery Light," he hissed. "You will obey me without question, from now on."

She was terrified and hyperventilating. She knew she did not want him to have that victory over her. No matter what he would do, she had to find a way to be strong, to fight back her fear. She ran the warrior's mantra through her mind. *Fear is for my enemy. Fear is defeat, and the forerunner of defeat. I will hold no fear.*

Bravery was the only recourse for a warrior. She had to summon whatever courage and defiance she could muster. *No matter what he does to me*, she told herself, *I will not be defeated. Fear is for my enemy. Fear is defeat, and the forerunner of defeat. I will hold no fear.*

The faerie towered over her. His rage was quelled already, and replaced by an expression of sadistic glee. He held the bag over Tolian's head. She had no clue what he was doing.

"You think you can be strong. That there is nothing I can do to you that can break your spirit, is that not so?" His words were full of a triumphant savagery.

He grabbed her by the back of her neck and hoisted her up to a sitting position. Every time he touched her, every time he laid his filthy hands on her, she was seized with an indescribable revulsion and experienced extreme apprehension. She felt like she thought a dog must feel, always waiting for the next beating.

"There is another," he said, "better method of obtaining your cooperation—your true weakness ... your lover—Brythia." He spit the words, his voice full of violence and threat.

"Do not defile her name with your tongue," Tolian commanded. "By what power can you affect her? Now that she can no longer use the Moonsword to follow us, she is safely out of your reach."

"Is that so?" Dowbreth asked. He seemed pleased with himself. "Perhaps, what you say would be true if it were I alone involved in this conspiracy. But I have many accomplices, one of whom is quite well trusted by you and she alike."

Another wave of panic engulfed Tolian. She managed to hold it in check this time. Anger replaced it. After all, the faerie was most likely bluffing.

"You lie," she shouted at him.

"Right now," replied Dowbreth, "you have the luxury of believing that if you wish. In a few moments I shall demonstrate the truth of my words."

"And how can you prove such lies?" Tolian demanded.

"Ah, such fire in you. I thought you had already succumbed to meekness and fear. I am grateful that your spirit is not yet broken. It gives me something to look forward to. But for now, your fair question deserves a fair answer." He held the mysterious bag for Tolian to look at—a plain, drab gray-green fabric, mostly filled, seemingly, by a single oblong object. Wholly unremarkable. "As you are no doubt aware by this time, this bag has some magick to it." He paused, looking to see if his statement caused a change in the princess's new skeptically defiant pose.

"I had rather gotten that impression, yes," she said casually.

"One of my fellow conspirators has a similar bag, and we are able to communicate with each other utilizing these bags. Oh, and if I had neglected to mention it, my friend is among your precious Brythia's trusted companions."

Tolian was determined to keep her face brave.

"You still haven't offered the slightest proof of your claims, and frankly, I don't see how you can. What, will your magick bag second your claims with expletives? I shall not trust it, either."

The faerie smiled, revealing his filed teeth. He was evidently enjoying himself a great deal.

"What if I show you the danger your druidess is in, the power I hold over her? Would you then call me a liar?"

She stared at him blankly. *Give him nothing*, she told herself.

"Humor me, then, princess. Close your eyes."

Dowbreth held the bag a few inches over her head. "Close your eyes," he repeated. "The bag's magick will allow you to look through the eyes of my friend, to see what he sees. You will learn firsthand, my power."

She closed her eyes. At once, she was looking through someone else's eyes. Using their sense of sight. It was snowing there, as well. There were several people huddled around a small fire. From what she was given to look at (she could sense the conspirator was being deliberate about it), she could not discern anyone's identity. It was clear, however, that they were all men. Except one person. The one person in the entire world Tolian longed to see.

She was garbed in her battle armor, though her white, winter cloak was pulled tightly around her. Her face seemed cast in granite, in a grimness etched in the pink marble of her chill resolve. Even that cold hardness did nothing to diminish the beauty in Tolian's view. Just seeing her, even with this borrowed sight, made her blood burn twice as hot with her desire. Her hair spilled golden like honey from her hood and about her shoulders. A few snowflakes glittered there, caught in her blonde tresses. And those eyes. Blue. The clearest, brightest blue. Pools of sapphire brilliance.

It seemed to Tolian that she could reach out and touch her beloved. But no, the person whose eyes she looked through moved casually behind the druidess. He looked down and allowed Tolian to see the point of a sword just inches from Brythia's back.

Tolian wanted to scream a warning to her, to rush to her side, to protect her. She could do none of those things. There was nothing she could do to help her wife. It was agonizing.

Apparently, Dowbreth and his ally felt that they had shown Tolian enough and the vision vanished. Her eyes were closed and saw only blackness. She felt a jolt of malice like a bitter aftertaste. The hairs on the back of her neck lifted.

She opened her eyes. The faerie was beaming, which made the most unpleasant aspect on his face.

"So you see," he said calmly, "I can have your little playmate killed at my whim. You believe me now; I can see it in your expression. Now you are truly afraid."

She said nothing. There was no need. She knew her face was transmitting her fear and this new vulnerability all too well. He was right. Yes, of course, there was the possibility that she had been shown an illusion. She could not take that chance.

"Do you wish me to exercise my power? Do you wish her killed?"

"No," she said sharply. "Do not kill her."

"And you will do as I ask?"

"I will." She said it flatly, without emotion.

"No more tricks, no more escape attempts, my little goddess?"

Tolian exhaled heavily. "I will do as you say. I won't try to escape. No tricks. I give you my word, but no harm must come to Brythia. You must give me your word, if it has any value."

He tried to fain hurt at her accusation. That expression also did not work well on his countenance.

"The word of Dowbreth, Warlord of the Sidhe, is better than gold. If you cooperate fully, neither myself, nor my associate will harm your druidess. I swear it." He said it like he meant it, for what that was worth. A sense of relief, though tempered with some uneasiness and uncertainty, flooded her consciousness. "We have a bargain then, Lord Dowbreth," she declared.

The giant smiled again. He set his bag down lightly on the snow and removed a jagged blade from his belt. With one motion, he cut the bindings from around Tolian's wrists.

"You will find that cooperation offers many advantages, Your Highness," he said, his tone much less harsh and savage. There was less implicit violence.

Tolian watched the cords fall into the snow with disbelief. They were speedily buried beneath the heavily accumulating flakes. She moved her sore wrists to loosen them up. One was at least badly sprained. She was surprised that she still wore the bracelet Kelvris had given her. It had been obscured by her bindings. Even in the dim light, it shimmered slightly. It was simple and elegant. She never would have suspected Kelvris of having such good taste in jewelry. The pain of her red and swore wrists distracted her from the gift. They were badly rope-burned. She stuck them into the snow. The cold felt almost good for a moment.

She was still worried, of course, and unsure of what this "cooperation" entailed, but she was happy that her Brythia would be safe. Nothing else mattered in comparison; Dowbreth had reminded her of that. He had helped her find her courage again. She would willingly submit to anything for her wife's sake. Anything. She shuddered. Gods, how she missed her.

Dowbreth reached into the snow, took her hand, and helped her to her feet.

"Come, Princess," he said. "This snow is becoming a nuisance. There is an inn nearby, we shall rest and warm ourselves before embarking on the next leg of our journey."

"Where are we going, anyway?" Tolian asked.

"I wish to surprise you," answered Dowbreth. "You will see soon enough."

The Tanslynt Inn was a modest coach and wagon stop on the trade road between the vast farmlands of eastern Lorm and the palace in the interior of the kingdom. Throughout the growing season, the road was jammed with farmers, merchants, and tradesmen bound for the markets of the capital with their produce and wares, but, in late December, it was desolate. There were no crops to be sold (save for cabbages), and if the merchants had not already made the trek to the palace, it would be too late to set up shop for the Solstice by that time.

The inn itself was comprised of a large building, built three quarters with stonework dating back some three hundred years, and a wooden portion (most of the second floor and all of the third) rebuilt within the last ten years. There were also a stone stable building and two wooden outbuildings of recent vintage. All four of the structures were topped with snow. There were no other signs of civilization in the vicinity. The main building, or inn proper, sat right up on the road (which in the near blizzard conditions, was all but obscured). What was visible of the well sat halfway between the inn and the stable, and next to it stood a trio of snowmen, the tallest nearly seven feet tall and the shortest just less than five. They were crudely fashioned of three snowballs each—work obviously having been suspended because of the worsening snowstorm.

Snow stuck to the sign hanging just above the door, making it all but impossible to read.

Tolian was surprised that Dowbreth would consider stopping at an inn. He must have felt the word of her abduction could not have reached so far so soon, and that their pursuers would have no means of tracking them there. Nonetheless, as the raging snowstorm stung her cheeks, nose and ears, she was comforted by the prospect of shelter and warmth.

Dowbreth brought his dark steed close to the door. He gently lifted Tolian from her position in front of him, to the ground.

"Go in and order us some food and a room. I'll stable the horse," he directed.

She turned and obeyed him. She opened the door, and the warmth from inside hit her in a most welcoming fashion. She stepped forward into the inn, feeling detached from reality.

Chapter 20

The cold air rushed beneath Kiliordes' wings, making him feel more alive than he had in some time. Flying. He had forgotten how much fun flying was. This was true freedom, gliding on the wind, the snow swirling like heavenly dervishes around him, rushing against his feathers. The sky was empty but for the snow and him; other avian creatures were clearly too wise for this sort of frolicking. He was alone in a sea of dazzling whiteness, his streamlined black wings cutting through the blizzard. Like the first crow that danced at the advent of the Universe. The crow was one of the archetypal tricksters in druidic lore, he remembered. He felt the same joy the first crow must have felt. To be so alive.

In the midst of his joy, he remembered his urgent mission. He returned his attention to the landscape far below him. How small things looked from his vantage point. White-capped trees dominated the miniature scene. The solid band that cut through the forest was obviously the road; the other band that twisted and turned all over the countryside was clearly a frozen stream.

Once he pinpointed the road through the raging snow, he followed it from high above. His eyes focused, constantly scanning the white strip for signs of travelers. Movement out of the corner of his eye distracted him temporarily. He caught a glimpse of something rare— a thing the human eye could almost never see. A pair of snow spites played joyously in the air, dancing from flake to flake. They were barely discernable, more like air currents of crystal aspect, vaguely human in shape, but adorned with wisps of wings. In a moment, they had vanished into the storm. Kiliordes brought his attention back to the road below.

He lost track of how far he had flown when at last he saw the first signs of habitation. A large building, with three other structures close, sat right up next to the road. He descended to take a closer look. With a little concentration, he alighted upon a sign hung by the door of the largest of the edifices, which was clearly an inn.

His ears caught the hoof falls of a horse approaching. He took to the air once more. Against the blizzard, it was hard to gain altitude once again. He peered through the snow. He could see two figures approached the building on horseback. His heart leapt. He flew lower to be certain. Yes, it was them. Dowbreth and Tolian on the great faerie warhorse. Without a sound he skimmed the air above them, turned, and headed back to the others as fast as his wings would take him.

Chapter 21

Brythia huddled between Delorick and Pagryus around the fire. Slowly, she turned to warm both her front and back, pausing for a few moments for the benefit of each, and trying desperately to summon whatever patience would attend her. She spoke to no one; indeed, an anxious quiet pervaded the scene. Findelbres paced around the fire, sidestepping lightly to avoid Kiliordes in his trance, but exhibiting a nervousness Brythia had never seen in him before. She alternated her gaze between the fire, the faerie, and the sky where she strained through the snow for some glimpse of the returning crow whose body Kiliordes had borrowed. A task made more difficult by the Solstice's early twilight. She struggled to keep her eyelids open as she searched the sky. Her earlier, unwitting nap had served to only make her feel worse and more in need of real, prolonged sleep. Slumber. Her body craved it.

She faced the fire and stared into the orange-red embers in its depths. Suddenly, she heard the loud caw from above. She wheeled about just in time to see the crow alight on the road, and then sink several inches into the snow. It looked displeased with the frozen precipitation on its feathers. It hopped to a position in front of the immobile Kiliordes.

In an instant Kiliordes leapt up, throwing much of the snow that had accumulated on him back into the air.

"I've found them," he announced gleefully. "They're at an inn, about, oh, maybe six miles up the road. They just got there."

Brythia wrapped her arms around him.

Delorick who had been squatting by the fire, jumped to his feet and rushed to the horses.

"Hold there, Delorick," Brythia commanded. "Wait a moment."

Everyone looked at her as though she had gone insane, but she knew exactly what she was doing. Still, it was a gamble.

"Why are we waiting, Princess?" asked Pagyrus in confusion.

"A good question," agreed Findelbres.

Delorick simply stood by his horse with a look of perplexity on his face.

"What is your plan, Brythia?" asked Kiliordes. She stepped away from the fire and sat down, cross-legged once again, in the road. She took her crystal from her pouch. She looked up at the others with grim determination.

"I am going to notch this snowstorm up a few intensity levels," she said. "Try to keep them there until we can get there."

"B-b-but won't that slow us down and make it tougher for us to travel there?" asked Delorick.

"Nothing is going to slow me down," she said, and she meant it.

Findelbres stepped forward. "Wait," said the faerie. "I have something to tell you. I think I have figured out where they are going."

This caused her to pause. She looked squarely at him. Her curiosity suddenly erupted violently.

"Where?"

Findelbres held her gaze. "I think he means to take her to Faerie. To our realm, though I can't imagine why."

Faerie. A new dread took hold of her. Faerie. Where few mortals have ever gone, and from where none have ever returned.

"If that inn is the Tanslynt Inn, then they're almost there," the normally cheerful Findelbres added dourly.

"Why didn't you mention this before?" Brythia demanded, though she was able to keep her voice calm. Inside she was boiling. Her gaze was glued to him. She knew she was glowering, but she could not help herself.

"Well, I um...I mean... I wasn't certain exactly where we were, not until just now. Almost ten miles past the inn, to the left of the road is a field of ancient barrow tombs." He paused. He looked uncomfortable, as if he were having an inner debate. At length, he continued. "There is a secret entrance to Faerie there, though it is our most serious crime to reveal this to mortals. The penalty is banishment forever," he added quietly.

She barely heard his last sentences.

"Then we must get to them before they can get to Faerie,"

Brythia said. She resumed her spell.

Though she was an apt enough weather-witch to bring on a snow on an otherwise clear day, the task of increasing the intensity of a snowstorm was a relatively easy one. Essentially, it wanted to be snowing anyway. She ignored the others who were presumably breaking camp and concentrated on the white crystal in her hand. She quietly began to hum the hymn of the snow sprites. She focused her attention solely on the crystal and the hymn. Inside the crystal, she envisioned a terrible blizzard. She hummed her near inaudible melody, expressing a love of cold, of ice, of the snow sprites themselves. At last, she sprang up with outstretched arms and cried out, “Krious.”

She slipped the white crystal back into her pouch and walked over to Whisper. The others were standing in readiness next to their respective horses, holding the reins. She jumped into her saddle.

“Gentlemen, I do not expect that you will be capable of keeping up with me,” she said. “Especially after it really starts to snow. Catch up as best you can.”

She did not wait for their protests. She gave Whisper a gentle kick and a hearty, “Yah,” and galloped away.

The wind, which had already begun to pick up, was to her back; the snow was blowing horizontally now, but it could not keep up with the faerie horse. It was as if she were racing the snow itself, and handily besting it. She focused on her riding, though in truth the horse needed scant guidance. The snow, which was kicked up behind them, rose as a cloud of icy dust.

She had to catch them. If Dowbreth was allowed to escape to Faerie, it was likely that she would never see Tolian again. The thought caused her insides to knot with worry. She could not bear that. She had to stop them. She had to. It was that simple.

Despite the near whiteout conditions now raging with her own fierce fury around her, Brythia noticed something amiss as she rode furiously towards the Tanslynt Inn. Redness. The color seemed alien in the landscape of white. Redness in the snow just ahead, not so far from the door to the inn. She slowed Whisper and dismounted right beside the scarlet anomaly. It was blood, a lot of it. So much blood, that despite the frantically falling and drifting snow, it soaked the whiteness with crimson as fast as the flakes could fall.

She took in the smell of blood as she stooped to examine the area. Something was buried in the snow. She brushed the snow gently away, her heart frozen with fear. An image of Tolian's face, bloody and lifeless, flashed across her mind. She dug a little faster.

There were three bodies. She breathed in relief when she discovered that Tolian was not among them. They were huntsmen, garbed in gray leather, bows hung at their sides. One had a small clutch of winter coneys tied at his belt. They had not been there long, for blood still trickled from the wounds. The eyes and jaws had been removed and the mouths and chins had been hacked off. There was a large incision from their chests to their navels, the internal organs had been removed, and the arms severed at the shoulders.

A quick scanning of the snow showed bloody footprints going back into the inn and another set of tracks, those of a horse of magnificent size, judging from their appearance. Dowbreth's horse. She cast a look back at the door to the inn and up the road where the horse prints led—in the direction Findelbres had indicated the secret entrance to the Faerie Realm was hidden. The mystery of the inn murders would wait. She could not allow them to get to Faerie.

She fought the elemental force to find her way back into the saddle. She was off, the wind at her back. She rode like a missile towards the barrows. She could not be too late. She begged to all the gods. She begged the Universe itself. *Please don't let him take my Tolian away forever. Please let me get there before they can get away. Please. I need her.*

There. There was something ahead of her. A large dark shape, a patch of green. She urged her own faerie horse to even greater speed. Faster, faster. She was closing in on whoever or whatever it was, but only gradually, suggesting the object was moving fast as well.

She lost sight of them for a moment. It seemed like eternity. It was so hard to see. Panic racked the druidess's being. No, there they were. They turned off the road. Into the barrow field.

In a moment, she had reached the spot where they turned off. She followed them. The green of the faerie's cloak flashed in the snow and wind. Peering into the blinding whiteness, she saw her. Her. Tolian. She was seated before Dowbreth, for clearly that was who it was, on a great faerie warhorse. They sat there as if waiting for her.

"Tolian," she called. She could barely hear her own words; they were blown away by the wind. She pushed her horse to cover the distance between them. Dowbreth held his horse patiently, waiting for her. Now that she was moving against the wind, the snow stung her face.

"Greetings, druidess," called Dowbreth as soon as she was in earshot. The violence in the rough tone sent a shiver down her spine.

Brythia saw Tolian's eyes light up and widen. "Brythia." She struggled futilely in the giant's grasp. Her face was bruised and she had a black eye. Her lip was swollen.

Brythia unsheathed her sword. "Let her go, or taste the bite of the Moonsword." She moved closer to them, slowly now.

Tolian squirmed in the faerie's grasp. She shouted to Brythia, "No, he's too strong. You can't..." She turned to Dowbreth. "You promised not to hurt her. You promised."

"Now, now, Princess," Dowbreth chided her with a vile hiss, "Fear not, it is not necessary for me to hurt her. We shall let them do it."

The druidess looked about her. She could see nothing through the blizzard.

"This reunion has been quite touching," noted Dowbreth, "but I fear that we have another engagement... in Faerie."

Tolian looked up at Dowbreth in shock and horror.

"Say your goodbyes, for you shall not see each other again," scoffed the faerie.

"Unhand her," demanded Brythia.

Dowbreth spat at her and rode between the adjacent barrow mounds.

Brythia watched as Tolian, her face streaked with tears, disappeared in the snow. Brythia called out to her, "Fear not, my love. I will find you." But as Brythia moved to follow, arms grabbed her and pulled her from her horse. Into the snow. Disoriented. Winded. She heard Tolian call back, "Brythia, someone close to you may be a traitor. Be wary. I love you."

Brythia looked up. Looming over her stood three figures. At first glance, they appeared to be nothing more than snowmen, but another look assured her that was not the case. Bloody arms hung at their sides. Their heads were accentuated with eyes and jaws dripping gore. She cast a look in the direction Tolian had disappeared and then back at her assailants. They slid over the snow—to her horror, she saw they had full use of their macabre limbs. She gripped the Moonsword, swallowed hard, and waited as they neared.

PART III

The Tower

Chapter 22

The largest of the nightmarish snowmen lunged down on Brythia with arms flailing and jaws gnashing, while the other two moved to flank her. Monsters of blood and ice. The druidess rolled over and flipped herself to her feet. Shimmering lunar blade ready in her hand, she backed up. It was difficult to see them in the snow; she looked around her warily.

She turned to run after Tolian. She had only taken steps in the drifting snow before she was bowled over by one of the animated snow ghouls. The thing glided over the deep snow with remarkable ease. Another of her frosty assailants grabbed her as she fell and set its eager teeth upon her neck.

She cried out in pain and jabbed the horror's head with her sword. The blade passed through the snowball, causing some snow to fall away from the left side of its head. The thing scooped up some snow from the ground and restored that portion of its head in one easy motion. It barely slowed the creature. She swung the blade again and sliced at its arm, severing it just above the elbow. Her attack only served to eliminate that one limb—the thing maintained its vigorous offensive with the remaining arm and its snapping jaws. The largest snow fiend came down upon her once again, moving in so fast: it prevented her from regaining her feet. She had no choice but to lay half buried in the snow and swing the Moonsword with everything she had. She was able to keep them at bay, but, clearly, the things had the advantage. She had to figure out a way to defeat them, and fast. Fatigue tore at her fighting skills and her brain as she considered her situation.

She stared into the eyes of one of the snowmen. Human eyes plucked from their owner, their icy sockets lined in blood. What sorcery could create such sinister creatures against the laws of nature? Her sword thrusts to their snowball torsos did little to slow them. How could such things move with the life force? What engine did the dark magick use to animate them? One of the icy ghouls grabbed her leg and pulled her towards it, temporarily catching her off guard and leaving her open to attack by the smallest of the creatures. Its teeth clamped down on her wrist, on the hand that held the sword. She fought the pain to maintain her grip on the lunar blade's hilt. The snow poured from the heavens relentlessly. It was difficult to see them in the whiteness.

She called out, "Whisper. Get help, quick."

She balled up her fist and landed a strong punch in the middle of the little snowman's head. The snow gave some, crumbling half the head away. One eye fell to the ground and the teeth released her other arm. It retrieved its eye and repaired the damage to its head, pausing only briefly to do so. Throughout this struggle, however, the other monsters had not been idle and fought her kicks to gain a position of advantage. One of the creatures brought its arms down and its blood-covered hands found her throat. A firm grip for a snowman with a cadaver's arms. Brythia began to lose consciousness.

There was a loud whinny and Whisper reared up out of the snow behind her. She watched in surprise as a well-placed hoof sent the thing's head flying ten yards away. Its attack did not lessen. It did not release its strong hold on her. She was quickly losing the ability to defend herself. As her kicks and sword slashes became more infrequent and ineffectual, the punches, bites and slams by the snowman increased.

Something clicked in her brain. An image appeared. The three bodies in the snow. The organs had been removed. *Why*? *Because the snowmen needed them. Needed the organs. Part of the black magick that animated them.*

Whisper reared up again and leveled a square kick at a snowman (it was impossible for Brythia to tell which one at this point), but did little more than knock the thing back a few feet. It did afford her a moment, however, long enough to make her move.

She lurched forward and stuck the point of the Moonsword deep into the center of the middle snowball of the creature. Right where the heart would be if it were a person. The fiendish snowman reeled backwards clutching at its chest. It stopped moving, held frozen once again. Brythia looked at the sword. It was soaked in blood. Now she knew what she had to do. She drew a deep breath.

Another kick from the faerie horse bought her enough time and room to gain her feet once again. She held the Moonsword with both hands before her and waited for the remaining two animated snow monsters to make their moves. Luckily, she realized she was facing the headless one, who seemed to be moving around more or less aimlessly, and the one-armed one.

Brythia felt the energy of the mystic weapon pulsing up her arm. She saw the eyes through the snow. A jab. She spun around and struck again. Both remaining snowmen instantly stopped in their tracks.

She paid them no further attention. With a soft and perfunctory, "Wait here," to her horse, she made her way through the deep snow following Dowbreth. His horse's tracks were easy enough to see, but the blizzard made for slow going. Although they were difficult to see, two dozen or so ancient tomb mounds surrounded her in the field. The tallest stood maybe twelve feet high at the top of the dome-shaped barrow. For the most part, all were snow covered but one; the one toward which the tracks led, appeared to have an opening in its side—a glimpse of cavernous darkness in the otherwise pure white vista.

She forced her legs to move even faster through the drifting and blinding whiteness. In her eagerness, she did not see the great black warhorse moving behind her from her right side. She stood, momentarily, just before the opening. It was narrow, but just big enough for a person to squeeze through. As she puzzled over how the giant could have gotten through, she heard a sound behind her. She turned at the same instant Dowbreth's horse struck her in the head with a hoof.

She collapsed into the snow. Numbness took hold of her as she watched the black beast leap through the narrow entrance in the snow-covered tomb. It should not have been able to do so. But it did. Brythia struggled to rise, but she could not. Dizziness and nausea. She had failed. Tolian was lost to her forever. It was just as well that she would die here in the snow. Extreme pain burned in her head. Then darkness.

As consciousness returned to the druidess, she became acutely aware of a considerable discomfort on the side of her head. A throbbing that sent occasional jolts of pain deeper into her brain. She did not open her eyes right away. She was tucked in a comfortable bed with blankets piled upon her. A crackling sound and warmth told her that a fireplace was across the room. She could hear muffled voices and she had the sensation of someone's eyes upon her.

"Good morn, Princess," said Findelbres softly. "How's your head?"

"It hurts," she replied. "Could you put some elf-root on it for me? It's in my pouch."

"We did."

"Use more, then."

"Of course, dear druidess."

She opened her eyes. The wooden beams of the ceiling came into focus, and then the faerie leaning over her, applying the herb to her wounded cranium. A soothing sensation slowly replaced the ache and discomfort. She tentatively sat up. Some dizziness. Not too bad.

"That's doing it," she said. "Now where are we, the Inn?"

They were in a small room with a bed, a table, a chair, and the fireplace. Heavy blue curtains covered the windows.

"You're good," observed the elf. "Yes indeed, we are enjoying the hospitality of the Tanslynt Inn."

"We have to get after them, Findelbres. I have to get into Faerie," implored the druidess. She felt galvanized, but exhausted, and the dizziness was coming back.

"Well, first off, you need some rest. A fair amount of rest."

She shook her head. "There isn't time."

"My dear, time is all we have. Time moves differently between the worlds. There is no telling how much time has passed in Faerie since yesterday. It could be two minutes, or it could be a month, likely even more."

"A month. More," she cried. "We have to get back to the barrows now."

"We can't," replied Findelbres.

"What do you mean, we can't? We have to. I know what you're thinking. And, of course, I know the others can't go. I would never ask them to—but you and I—we have to get into Faerie."

"Calm yourself, druidess," the faerie warrior said. "The way into Faerie is closed. I could not take you there if I wanted to, at least, not through the entrance in the barrow."

"What do you mean, 'the way into Faerie is closed'?" Brythia asked. She was incredulous.

Findelbres nodded. "When we found you, I attempted to follow them into Faerie. I thought I could notify the King and Queen, and have our troops find them, one, two, three. Nice and simple. Except, I couldn't get in. The way is closed. Not only can't we get into Faerie to find Tolian, I can't get back home."

"How is it possible, Findelbres?"

"I don't know. To my knowledge, only the Queen of Faerie controls the Gates of the Realm. Even the King cannot control them. They are only sealed at times of crisis."

The room was beginning to spin. The dizziness was getting much worse. She struggled to remain sitting up. I must think clearly, she told herself.

"Could the Queen be in league with Dowbreth?" she asked herself. Out loud. She hadn't meant to.

She had met the Queen of Faerie, Ymrisiva. Both the King and Queen were guests at her and Tolian's wedding. She did not seem at that time to be plotting some treachery. Still one could never tell with the Good Folk, they had their own motivations. That thought made her cast a suspicious look at Findelbres. Dowbreth and he were both faeries, after all. If Ymrisiva was somehow involved in this conspiracy, there was the possibility that Findelbres could also be involved. He had proven himself a loyal friend. Still, she would watch him carefully.

Findelbres had paused to consider her question. Finally, he answered. "Queen Ymrisiva is in no way in league with Dowbreth, I would stake my life upon it. But, admittedly, something has happened in Faerie."

Trust him, but keep an eye on him, she thought.

Begrudgingly, she had to lie back down. She sank into the mattress, her head resting on the pillow.

"Okay, so how else can we get into Faerie?" Brythia inquired.

"You ask this question too lightly, Princess. What makes you think there is another way?"

"There must be another way," Brythia insisted.

"Of course, there are other secret entrances," offered the faerie reluctantly. "But it is likely that those ways are closed as well."

"Yes, Findelbres, I had that figured out," she said. "But your kind aren't the only beings who move between the Astral and the Physical World. There are others. What about the Pine Devils? They are said to live in both realms."

The faerie pondered her words, "The Pine Devils, or the Winged Satyrs as we of the Sidhe call them. Yes. The Blue Holes. That could work."

"The Blue Holes?" the druidess said. "What do the Blue Holes have to do with the Pine Devils?"

Findelbres was beginning to get excited by the possibility. "The Winged Satyrs use the Blue Holes to travel between the worlds. It is their gateway."

"There's a Blue Hole in Southwestern Lorm," exclaimed Brythia.

"We'll go as soon as you are feeling a little better, and you get some rest."

Brythia did not argue this time. As urgent as their mission was, Findelbres was right. She had neglected her health for too long. She was exhausted, in pain, dizzy (when not lying down), and she realized, she was starving.

"Findelbres, is there anything to eat around here?"

"Ah, well, I see that you're starting to feel better already," he said. "And you're in luck—the innkeeper's wife is a wonderful cook. I'll go see what she can whip up for you. Meanwhile, rest."

"I will. Oh, but first just a pinch more elfroot, if you please."

"Certainly, my lady," replied the faerie. He immediately set about applying more of the healing herb to her head and a little to her neck where she had been bitten by the sinister snowmen. When he finished, he made his exit, promising to send the food in as soon as it could be prepared.

She closed her eyes, half listening to the fire's soothing crackle. She could only pray the gods would protect her beloved from harm until she could get to her.

It was not long before Mrs. Gelstrit, the innkeeper's wife, came into the room, carrying a tray of food. As soon as she entered, Brythia caught the delightful aroma wafting towards her. The scent of cooked beef, carrots and potatoes—probably stew. Her mouth began to water almost instantly.

Mrs. Gelstrit was a fit-looking woman in her late fifties. Her face was surprisingly robust and free of wrinkles, and there was only a trace of gray in her dark hair. She wore a kindly smile that appeared genuine.

"Well, hello there, dear," she said as she brought the tray to the bed. "You gave us quite a scare. It was lucky your friends found you when they did. You were bleeding aplenty when they brought you in, I'll tell you. Can you try to scoot up a little there? Here, I'll help fix your pillow."

She set the tray on the table and helped Brythia lean up a little in bed. With great care, she arranged the pillows to provide some support for her, yet in such a way to keep her dizziness to a minimum. When satisfied with her work she retrieved the tray from the table and set it in Brythia's lap. There was a big, steaming bowl of beef stew, some fresh-baked bread, newly churned butter, and a large tankard of clear, cool water.

"Thank you so much," said Brythia.

"Oh, you are so welcome, dear. I've been doing my share of nursing here lately. I must say though you look even worse than the other girl we had here yesterday."

"The other girl?" inquired Brythia with her mouth full of food. She realized at once the woman had to be referring to Tolian. Her heart raced with the prospect of news of her beloved.

"Yes, we had a strange couple here yesterday. Of course, we're used to having the Good Folk here, but that fellow that brought this poor creature with him—he was something else. Big. I swear I ain't ever seen anyone near the size of him. Rough he was too, but gentlemanly enough in his own way I suppose. We get all kinds in here. Oh yes, but the girl, she was awfully beaten up, but you could still tell how fair her features were. It was such a shame. The faerie who brought her said he had rescued her from some barbarians. I suppose he was taking her home. Well, I took one look at the poor girl and put her in this very bed."

Brythia pictured Tolian lying there. She tried to feel her presence as she gorged herself with the delicious food, and listened to Mrs. Gelstrit's rambling narrative.

"She seemed so sad," continued the older woman, for whom talking obviously came naturally. "It's funny, you would have thought she would have been much happier, what with being rescued and all. Well, I tended her, and fed her. And the big gentleman, he sat in a chair, right over there and guarded her. I guess so she wouldn't have to worry 'bout them barbarians."

"Did she say anything to you?" The druidess asked.

"Well, she had real manners, like a lady, and she was quick to say thank you and such, but, no, she wasn't much of a talker really. You could just tell by looking at her that she was beside herself with worry and sorrow. Poor girl, I hope he gets her home right quick."

Brythia smiled at her with a cheerfulness and optimism that she did not feel, "Don't worry, ma'am. She'll get home soon. I'm sure of it."

"What a strange thing to say," remarked Mrs. Gelstrit, "though I hope you're right. I'm sure her husband will be glad enough to have her back—as pretty as she was."

"Her husband?"

"She had a wedding ring, actually quite like yours, dear," the innkeeper's wife said. "I pay attention to details. I imagine your husband must be worried about you—traveling with that odd assortment of friends of yours."

Brythia considered her response. She thought briefly about not saying anything. Instead, she said: "Actually, the girl you're talking about is my wife and that faerie ruffian kidnapped her.

The other woman's eyes went wide. "Oh, my, you're Princess Tolian then."

"No, I'm Princess Brythia, her wife. And I'm going to find them, kill him, and take her home."

Chapter 23

The hospitality at the Tanslynt Inn was as fine as Kiliordes had encountered (in Lorm, anyway). When he was not helping Findelbres tend to the unconscious Brythia, he was sitting in the common room enjoying the toasty fire, the delicious food, hearty ale, rowdy talk, quick wit, and the good company of his companions. At that moment, he was sprawled over a comfortable chair, his feet propped up, and his belly full of stew and beer. Pagyrus was finishing a dirty joke. The dark pilgrim was surprisingly affable and jolly, characteristics that seemed like they would have been foreign to his long, broad, and taciturn face. Laughing, Delorick left to use a chamber pot.

Pagyrus was still smiling when he addressed Kiliordes, "Have you had an opportunity to consider our offer?"

"Your offer?" asked Kiliordes. "Oh," he remembered after a moment, "about joining the Solar Pilgrimage Festival?"

Pagryus's smile spread even wider. "No. About leading the Solar Pilgrimage Festival."

Whenever he heard the words Solar Pilgrimage Festival, his heart warmed. The days he spent with them were the happiest he could remember. He was growing weary of all the bickering and infighting back at the palace. All the commotion about Tolian being the heir. He had done his best there after all. Now, it seemed likely the problem of Tolian was settled. Dowbreth had taken her to Faerie. There was nothing else they could do. No mortals ever returned from Faerie. Relinder would be named the heir, with Kelvris named as second. They had tried damn hard to save Tolian, but she was beyond their power to help her. Poor child. Perhaps it would be best to put all of this Lormian business behind him. Yes, he could envision himself immersed in the continual celebration of the Sun's journey.

He looked at the pilgrim's face, and nodded gently. He felt warm and good. The beer was surging through him, making him feel lighter, more cheerful, perhaps than he should have been.

"Pagyrus," Kiliordes announced, "as soon as we get

Princess Brythia safely back to Lorm, I will come with you to join the Pilgrimage."

"You mean, lead the Pilgrimage," corrected Pagyrus.

"I mean join the Pilgrimage. We can discuss the rest later."

"I fear you make your plans too soon," chimed Findelbres, coming up behind them. "The princess is not giving up. She will not be returning to Lorm."

"What do you mean, she's not giving up?" inquired Kiliordes. "What choice does she have? Even if she was brave enough to enter the Faerie Realm to pursue them, she could not. You yourself said the way to Faerie is closed."

"Indeed," agreed Pagyrus, "I do understand the princess's drive. I have never seen such determination, but what more can she hope to do? Except try to find a way to carry on without Princess Tolian. That's the business she should be engaged in. Perhaps she would like to come with us and forget her troubles by following the righteous course of the Sun. Kiliordes has told me that Brythia was a priestess of the Sun in the druid's order. She should be well inclined to our company."

"Well," Findelbres answered, "perhaps she would be so inclined if she had given up hope as easily as you two have. But, she and Tolian are my friends and I mean to help her as long as I am able. We have determined to make our way into Faerie by other means. A way that should be unsuspected, and unguarded by the Folk of the Sidhe. Perhaps we can gain entrance that way."

Kiliordes gulped. "Enter Faerie?"

"Not you three, no," replied the Elven warrior. "Once we reach our entrance point, Brythia and I will go on alone."

"Where is this entrance point?" Delorick, who had just rejoined them, asked.

"The way we are going to try is hidden in the Pine Barrens of Southwestern Lorm," Findelbres said.

"I will see you safely there," Delorick stated.

"Yes, of course," agreed Kiliordes. "I shall do so as well. And if you will accompany us, Pagyrus, I shall go with you once we have seen them safely off."

"Excellent," exclaimed the Solar Pilgrim.

Kiliordes took another pull on his ale. "How is she feeling," he asked the faerie.

Findelbres cracked a smile finally. “She is the toughest damn mortal I’ve ever met.”

Chapter 24

Brythia dreamt. She was in the snow-drenched forest—deer woods with birch, ash, and elm trees so thickly situated as to make moving through them difficult. Although it was nighttime, the air was aglow with an astral luminance, indicating the presence of mystical energies. The snow covered branches cast twisted and bizarre shadows in its eerie shimmer.

She was looking for something. She reasoned that she was probably searching for Tolian. She wandered the woods for a while before she remembered that Tolian was in Faerie. Even so, it did not stop her from searching, though it struck her as strange that she did so. She treaded through the knee-deep snow, twisting herself between the close tree trunks.

Wait, she thought. There was something there, not too far away, moving towards her. It was white and large. Recognition dawned. That was what she was searching for, though she did not know why. It was the White Hart.

"Well met again, Princess Brythia," it called out to her.

She was startled only slightly this time. "Well met indeed," replied the druidess. "What can I do for you?"

"For me?" The White Hart asked. "Why nothing, but how thoughtful. I have come to you on a mission from my lady. I believe that we both serve her."

"Well," said Brythia, "since I don't know who your lady is, I can't well say. Is she Magara, the High Druidess?"

The beast chuckled—unusual for a deer. Ah, but so was talking in human language, she remembered.

"No, no," said the White Hart. "My lady is no mortal. She is the Queen of the Night Sky, the Empress of Clouds, the Mistress of the Hunt, the White Goddess. She has dispatched me to bring you to her as quickly as possible. Unfortunately, with the abduction of her earthly manifestation, and the suppression of her powers, my lady is now a prisoner in her own tower. This is why you have been summoned. She needs your help. And she wants to help you."

"I'm confused," stated the druidess. "I thought Tolian was the Moon-Goddess. Who's this other lady?"

The animal nodded. "Yes, she told me that you would be confused. These matters are complicated for mortals. If you come with me, I will attempt to explain as we go. It will take us some time to reach the Moon through the Dream-gate, probably several night's dreams."

"That's fine," agreed Brythia. "I can't think of a better way to spend my dreaming hours."

"Excellent," said the White Hart. "My Lady will be well pleased. Come, we should start at once, we have a long dream-journey ahead of us and you have many questions I am sure. I will do my best, but for some you must wait until we arrive, for the Goddess to answer."

Without further ceremony, the white animal stepped right up to the golden-haired nature priestess and lowered its head. "Climb on my back, Princess, I can carry you."

"You don't mind?"

"Quite the contrary, I am honored to carry you who are my lady's earthly consort."

"But, you said..." Brythia began.

"Please, we must hurry."

Brythia did as she was bid and climbed upon the hart's back. It was a sufficiently large enough animal to accommodate her completely. As soon as she had done so the talking beast began to dart through the narrow trees with easy strides, yet in such a way that Brythia had no difficulty in keeping herself on the creature's back.

"Now," she said, leaning forward toward the hart's head. "You must explain exactly what's going on..."

"I shall endeavor to, Princess, but unfortunately we have already used all of our time; you are beginning to stir already. You will be awake in a few moments. We will have to pick this up in your next dream."

"Already?" she asked out loud, as she found herself awake in her bed in the inn.

Chapter 25

Vivid colors swirled around Tolian—all the hues of the rainbow and some with no correlation in the mortal world. Dowbreth held her securely in front of him on the horse, but she had stopped struggling. Her tears still gushed down her cheeks in a veritable torrent as they progressed through the portal between the world and the Realm of the Fay. Flashes of prismatic light danced before her eyes. A powerful sound permeated the air, like the rush of a strong, steady wind, yet the air around them was still. Physical sensations now moved throughout her being—a tingling feeling that started at her toes and shot up her body until her head was spinning. The sound, the colors, and the tingling all merged into a single wave of energy, and then passed quickly. She was left with a sinking feeling in her stomach. And blurry vision.

She rubbed her eyes, but it did nothing to relieve the indistinct images swimming there. Lights and shapes, but without order or cohesion.

"It may take a little time for your eyes to become used to seeing here," explained Dowbreth.

She said nothing. What was there to say? She was in Faerie. Beyond hope of escape or rescue. Forever apart from Brythia. To have been so close to her, and then to lose her in an instant. She closed her eyes. She could envision Brythia charging after her. Her face full of fury, but still Brythia's face, graceful and delicate. Then she was lost in the raging snow. Lost to her for all time. The agony of that knowledge tore at her bitterly. She coughed in broken sobs.

"Oh, don't worry yourself about your girlfriend," said the faerie. "I'll make sure she doesn't get hurt. She is my insurance. Perhaps that will comfort you."

Comfort. She knew she would never know comfort again. Not without her beloved's sweet embrace.

She attempted to look about, but things were still far too blurred. It was disconcerting. She could see nothing whatsoever.

She could hear the sounds of the horse's hooves on a stone-paved road. She could hear the songs of birds, but these melodies were far more intricate and lyrical than those of terrestrial avians. Distant shouts of greeting sung out from several voices.

"We draw nigh to my house," announced Dowbreth. "We will rest there, at least until your vision returns."

They rode on for only a few more minutes before Tolian became aware that a small crowd of people surrounded them. She could not see them and rather than strain to comprehend the jumbled images her sight gave her, she kept her eyes closed.

"Lord Dowbreth is home." Fay voices shouted in surprisingly (to Tolian) mirth-filled tones.

"Well met," said Dowbreth with much less malice than usual in his voice. "This is our special guest. She is an important lady. You must treat her with the utmost care at your disposal. See that she has no wants."

A murmur of agreement and obedience ensued; calls of welcome greeted her.

Tolian felt Dowbreth's grip tighten about her as he lifted her off the horse and put her down on the ground.

"Be careful and gentle," the faerie warlord commanded. "She is still blind with the mortal world. Capreesh and Delotti, you shall be her handmaidens. Have her bathed and dressed as befitting her status. Make note—there are none in Faerie who are her equal. None."

"Yes, my lord," the two faerie women chimed in unison.

Each of the women took one of Tolian's hands.

"Come, Lady," said one.

"We shall guide you well, fear not," said the other.

She allowed herself to be led wherever her two elfin guides desired. They were filled with a bubbly enthusiasm, which was, initially, annoying, but which eventually lightened even Tolian's heavy heart.

"We're turning right, my Lady."

"Now, left."

"Duck, my Lady, the doorway here is low."

"We're about to head up a flight of stairs."

"Another right, my Lady."

They punctuated each advisory instruction with a round of

giggling. But they proved to be careful guides, and they led her without incident.

"Here we are, my Lady."

"Where is here, precisely?" she asked with a weary indifference.

"The finest guestroom in Lord Dowbreth's estate," answered one of the faerie girls (though Tolian still could not tell who was Capreesh and who was Delotti).

"Would you like a bath first or some rest, Lady?"

Tolian had to admit that a bath sounded like a wonderful idea, but she was exhausted, both emotionally and physically.

"I think I need to sleep first," answered Tolian.

"Very well, Lady, we'll help you get undressed. Delotti, would you fetch a nightgown for her Ladyship? Oh, and I think I should treat your injuries first. But, don't worry, Faerie medicine is speedy."

Before Tolian could tell what was happening, they had removed her soiled and tattered gown and replaced it with the softest, silkiest nightgown she had ever worn as a woman. Cool compresses were applied to her bruises and wounds. Tolian could not tell if they were cool or hot after a few seconds, but they were soothing, that much was definite. The girls treated every injury, every cut, every bruise, even her broken wrist and cracked ribs. The wounds felt better immediately. One of the girls tugged on her bracelet.

"How does this come off, my Lady? I can't seem to figure it out. It doesn't seem like mortal technology, and it's not faerie. It is lovely though."

Not mortal technology? The girl is obviously mistaken. "My cousin gave it to me," Tolian explained. "I'm sure it is mortal craft, but I haven't tried to take it off."

"Hmmm," said Delotti (Tolian was beginning to be able to distinguish their voices—Capreesh's voice was higher, had more of a lisp and a slightly more melodious tone). "I can't get it. It must have some sort of mortal magick to it. It's glowing a little."

Capreesh came and tugged at the bracelet for a few moments. "I'll get it," she said, but she had no success either.

"Look, let's not worry about it right now," said the princess. "We'll figure it out after I get some sleep."

They led her over to a comfortable bed and helped her into it. The sheets had a sensual quality to them, and the mattress provided the most astonishing support.

"Sleep well, Lady," said Capreesh.

"We'll be right here if you require anything," added Delotti.

The princess's head hit the pillow and she fell asleep immediately. She slipped right into a dream.

In the dream, Tolian was walking through the palace of Lorm, but something was not right. She was, once again, male. He starred down at himself in surprise. No, this wasn't right. Or was it? He was a woman, wasn't he? Hadn't the druids transformed him? What was going on? Where was Brythia? Perhaps all of that had been some sort of bizarre dream. Maybe none of it had really happened. No, Brythia was real. There was nothing more real than her memory. Then why was he a man? It felt so strange now, but still familiar enough. People smiled at him or bowed low with great respect as he passed them.

Wait, he wasn't even in the palace was he? What about Dowbreth? He walked on. He saw a mirror hanging on a nearby wall. He looked at his reflection. His rugged, bearded face stared dumbly back at him.

His father's voice came from behind him, "Ah, you're yourself again, at last."

Tolian turned to look at him. "Is this who I am?" Tolian wasn't so certain. Why was he feeling this way? He was born male after all. He had always been happy enough as a man. Already, he was feeling the strength in his male muscles and the respect that shone it the eyes of those around him and enjoying it. The feeling of vulnerability was gone. He felt strength and confidence grow in its place. This was all well and good, but he had been transformed into a woman, hadn't he? What had happened to him? Confusion boiled and churned.

Now he was wearing a blue silk dress. It looked out of place on his muscular body. He started to run frantically throughout the palace, his dress fluttering behind him and shouting, "Brythia, Brythia, Brythia."

She awoke with her shouts echoing on her lips. She opened her eyes. The blurriness was gone. *Good. I can see again.*

In fact, everything was more distinct than she had ever seen it. Images were sharper and colors more vibrant, with the occasional hue that had no parallel in the mortal world. She starred up at the canopy over the bed. It was a deep azure and, unless her eyes were deceiving her, white fluffy clouds seemed to blow across the canopy's surface with a slow, gradual pace. Sunbeams streamed in, golden bright, through the nearby window. The room's walls were a glistening, polished stone, mostly covered with rich tapestries depicting fantastic scenes. They appeared to move in some impossible animation, similar to the clouds in the canopy. On one tapestry, a field of sunflowers sprouted from the ground, grew tall and blossomed. On another, the one nearest to her in fact, was a structure that resembled the palace of Lorm. The sky around the palace was filled with dragons. Out of nowhere, an army of winged faerie warriors appeared and began to battle the reptiles.

Her observations lighted quickly across her consciousness. Her hand went instinctively to her crouch. She was somewhat disappointed as her hand found her soft, feminine genitalia. It had been a dream, after all. She sighed.

Capreesh and Delotti appeared on either side of the bed. Capreesh, on her right side, had a thin, delicate face, pale and framed by her short, silver-metallic hair with pointed ears protruding. Delotti had a rounder face with more color than most of the faeries Tolian had seen. Her cheeks were positively rosy, her bright purple eyes were beaming with concern, and she had long, black hair. Both appeared to be young, but Tolian knew enough about the Good Folk to know that they could be a great deal older than they looked. Their faces were both cheerful and worried when they looked down at her.

"Is everything all right, my Lady," asked Delotti.

Tolian quickly, yet discretely, removed her hand from her womanhood (though hidden under the covers) before she replied. "Yes, everything is fine, I suppose. Or as fine as it's ever going to get."

"Are you sure?" asked Capreesh. "You look so sad. Like all the sorrow of the mortal world has found a home on your brow."

Tolian directed a half smile at her. "Well, let's see. I've been drugged, kidnapped from my home, separated forever from the woman I love, robbed of my magically enhanced strength, beaten up, coerced, threatened. And that's since the day before yesterday."

The elfin girls' jaws dropped in shock and disbelief.

"Don't worry, Lady," Delotti said. "You're safe here. Lord Dowbreth won't let anything happen to you."

Tolian sat up in bed and looked into her eyes. She saw only sincerity and honesty. She reminded herself, once again, to not necessary trust what her eyes showed her when it came to dealing with faeries. Take what you see as a starting point, she told herself, but be wary and keep an open mind.

"Dear," Tolian shook her head slightly. "Lord Dowbreth is the person responsible for all my problems. It was he that kidnapped me."

Delotti took no time to defend her master. "Our master is a noble faerie. Perhaps his ways are not always clear to us, but we can be assured that his purposes are directed towards the best interests of the realm. Now, my Lady, if you would like, the bath is ready for you."

There was no use arguing with them, she could sense that immediately. They obviously had a great deal of respect, if not love, for Dowbreth. And, a bath sounded like a wonderful idea. With a turn, she brought her feet to the floor.

"A bath sounds excellent," she said.

"I'll go get the bath, then, Lady," declared Capreesh. With a remarkably light step, the girl left the room.

"She won't be a minute, Lady," stated Delotti. "Would you like to take off your nightgown?"

"Oh, yes, of course," Tolian replied.

She stood up and raised her arms, and the faerie pulled the gown up and off her. Recalling her dream, the princess looked down in fleeting regret at her ample, shapely breasts.

"Ah, here they are already," said the servant girl, glancing to the doorway.

They? thought Tolian. She turned just in time to see Capreesh enter the room followed by a large, bronze bathtub walking under its own power. It would have been a marvelous piece of craftsmanship for the intricate etchings adorning it alone, but the four sturdy legs by which it propelled itself flabbergasted Tolian. It was full of sudsy, steaming water, fragrant with the scent of honeysuckle and lavender. Tolian felt herself relax the moment she first detected the fragrance.

"I think by the window," Capreesh advised the tub. "But mind you, not too close."

The tub located itself precisely where the faerie indicated, with complete obedience, and then lowered itself to an easily accessible position. Capreesh gestured. "My Lady, your bath awaits."

Tolian crossed the room, and with just a little timidity, climbed in to the tub. She sunk herself into the warm water, immediately feeling the tension melt away from her limbs. She submerged herself so only her head remained above the soapy foam. It felt fantastic. She had to admit the faeries had perfected bathing. It was almost as though the water itself were massaging her muscles, unknotting the stress from her neck and shoulders.

"Oh, my," she cooed.

Capreesh's smile spread across her face. "I took a chance," she explained. "I wasn't sure you liked undines in your bathwater."

"Undines?" Tolian asked.

"Undines are the elemental spirits of water."

Normally, the thought of mysterious creatures in her bathwater would have filled her with dread, but she had to admit the undines knew what they were doing.

"Yes," said the princess reassuringly. "The undines are fine."

"Shall we shave your legs and wash your hair, Lady?" Delottie asked.

"Oh, absolutely," replied Tolian.

With precision, Capreesh ran a fine razor over Tolian's legs while Delotti washed her long, curly chestnut brown tresses with the most delightfully scented shampoo Tolian had ever smelled. As she worked the lather through the princess's hair, Delotti asked her, "May we know your name, Lady, so we may be more polite when addressing you?"

"Of course," agreed Tolian, who was so relaxed she would have agreed to just about anything. "I am Princess Tolian of Lorm."

Delotti stopped lathering the princess's hair. Tolian opened her eyes to see what had happened. She was surprised to see both girls on the floor in the lowest bow she had ever seen.

"Great Goddess, forgive us," they cried.

"We did not know it was you," explained Delotti.

"Oh, please, not you too," Tolian said.

Much to Tolian's chagrin, the girls groveled lower to the floor, and Capreesh shook with fear.

"This isn't going to work," sighed Tolian. "I don't want you to do that. Please get up."

They scrambled to their feet, awe and terror mixed in their eyes.

"Well, that's a little better, but I still have shampoo in my hair and it's starting to run into my eyes," noted the Princess of Lorm.

"Oh," Delotti shrieked in horror.

"You're burning the Goddess' eyes," Capreesh screamed, handing the other girl a pitcher.

"Great Goddess of the Moon, I beg your forgiveness," apologized Delotti, rinsing the lather out of Tolian's hair.

"Relax, please," suggested Tolian with her softest, most reassuring tone.

"Of course, O Holy One," whimpered the terror-stricken girl.

And Tolian had thought the druids were bad enough with their adoration and worship. This was even worse. She had to stop this behavior immediately.

"Look, I don't know how long I'm going to be here. Or what's going to happen," she said. "But you two seem nice, and I'd like us to be friends. Do you think that's possible?"

The faeries looked at each other, as if unsure of how to respond. Capreesh spoke first. "If that is your wish, O Magnificent Goddess of the Astral Light."

"Great," began Tolian with as much patience as she could muster. "You're going to have to drop all the epithets, at least when it's just us. Please call me Tolian, or Lady Tolian, if you must. Even Princess Tolian would be fine, that's my title in the mortal world, though some people still use the male version of the title being as I was born the son of a king."

Again the girls exchanged doubtful looks, before Delotti finally said, "If that is your wish...Lady Tolian."

Tolian looked for agreement from Capreesh, who avoided eye contact, but nonetheless whispered, "We live to obey you ... Princess." She squirmed as her mouth formed the syllables.

"See, isn't that better?" asked Tolian. "Now, we're all friends."

Delotti smiled. "Thank you, Princess Tolian, for the honor you have shown us." She punctuated her comment with a curtsy.

Capreesh was still quiet, frightened, and uncomfortable.

"Pshah," dismissed the princess, "now, although I was considering spending the rest of my life in this tub, I should probably get out and put some clothes on."

"Yes, Tolian," agreed Delotti. The girl was starting to take a delight in the familiarity Tolian had allowed her.

Capreesh produced a towel and wrapped it around Tolian as she emerged from the bathwater. Delotti immediately wrapped another smaller towel around her wet hair and then immediately removed it.

Much to Tolian's amazement, her long brown tresses were completely dry. "Incredible," she exclaimed.

"There are no towels in the mortal world?" Delotti asked, confused by her reaction.

"Of course, we have towels in the mortal world," explained Tolian. "It's just that, well, they take longer to dry hair there, a lot longer."

"How inconvenient for someone like yourself to have to endure, Your Majesty," sympathized the faerie.

Capreesh finished drying her off and then wrapped and tucked the larger towel around her so it kept her covered. "I'll go and get the dress Lord Dowbreth wishes you to wear today, Princess Tolian," she said. She curtsied and disappeared into what was presumably a large closet. She emerged with a brilliant purple gown that seemed to throw off sparks of iridescent energy.

Tolian removed her towel and handed it to Delotti as Capreesh pulled the garment over Tolian. It was the most sensual, mesmerizing material she had ever felt, and it fit her like glove. They led her over to a full-length mirror, where she stared at herself in wonder. She knew she was beautiful, but the faerie gown made her radiant. The neckline plunged down below her navel, and revealed much of her cleavage. Every curve of her body was accented perfectly. And, it was no trick of her eyes; sparks of purple and silver arced and leaped from her. Delotti stepped up to her and ran a comb through her hair. With one pass, her hair was teased, styled, and held in place. Capreesh speedily applied eyeliner and painted her lids and lips with complimentary shades of purple. Lastly, she added a light blush. Tolian had to admit that she looked like the Goddess of the Moon.

"To be true," confessed Capreesh, "O Glorious One, um, but, well... As I was saying, I thought it was the height of fashion cheek for someone to wear this dress, when our master ordered us to make it. It seemed sacrilegious for a lady, faerie or mortal to assume the colors of Our Most Holy Goddess, but now it makes sense. You look magnificent, Empress of Faerie. I'm sorry, but I cannot look at your brilliance and call you anything less."

"She's right," agreed Delotti. "You cannot deny your Goddesshood now."

Capreesh slipped crescent-shaped earrings through her pierced ears, then a necklace, also moon shaped around her neck. She held up a matching bracelet.

"Oh, Princess, did you want to show us how to take your magick bracelet off? Or would you prefer to wear it instead of this one?" she inquired.

She had forgotten about the bracelet again. How odd. She examined it carefully. There appeared no seams or fasteners to hold it secure, yet some mechanism must exist, or how else could she have put it on. Then she remembered that Kelvris had put it on her. How would he have even come across a magick bracelet to begin with? She tugged at and twisted it, but she could not figure out how to remove it either.

"Huh?" she said.

"You don't know how to take it off, either?"

"No, like I said, my cousin gave it to me right before I was kidnapped by your master. I haven't tried to take it off since," said Tolian. A slow dawning of understanding was entering her brain. That bastard. Kelvris was in league with Dowbreth, of course. He had drugged the wine as Dowbreth entered. He gave her the bracelet. Now she was pulling at the suspected jewelry with all her might. He had gotten rid of her to progress his status, and get that much closer to the throne of Lorm. She became worried for Relinder, suddenly, and then sad as she realized that she would probably never see her son again. Or anyone else that had ever mattered to her.

No one had ever returned from Faerie, or if they did, it was three hundred years after they left. Findelbres had once confirmed to her that time did indeed run differently between the two worlds, sometimes more, sometimes less, sometimes one way, and sometimes the other. It was impossible to predict, but the immortal faeries were untroubled by the discrepancy. To them, time was without consequence or real meaning. That said, he had pointed out the Good Folk could in fact control the temporal fluctuation to a large degree, allowing them to enter and exit as they saw fit. The disorientation and the despair at her parting from Brythia and her trek between worlds were suddenly diminished. Hope flickered. The Folk of the Sidhe could, in fact, travel between the worlds at will, and Findelbres, and Dowbreth had been able to control the timing of their visits with great accuracy. But no mortals could. Of course, he had added that. He had said that even if the Fay wanted to transport mortals back from Faerie (he didn't deny many were taken) they could not be returned with accuracy. But she wasn't mortal anymore, as the faerie maids had reminded her. Or at least she hadn't been mortal. Before Kelvris gave her the bracelet.

Her wrists were badly bruised already from her vigorous assault. Delotti and Capreesh stared numbly in horror as the princess tore madly at the stubborn jewelry.

"Holy One," shouted Capreesh, "You're going to hurt yourself."

She stopped her frantic efforts. She tried to seem calm and reasonable, though her emotions and thoughts were churning. "You're right," she agreed. "Do we have something sharp around here? I think I could pry it open right here." She held the bracelet up quickly as if to show them, but took it away before they could get a look at it, for there was no crease to pry.

Tolian smiled brightly and batted her eyelashes innocently at Delotti, who seemed to have taken charge. "You know, like a knife, or maybe a sword," Tolian sang out her request in her most melodic tone. She had formulated another plan already. It was desperate, and it depended on Capreesh and Delotti believing her to be far too rational to do what she was indeed intending. "Something pointed, sharp, that will give me some leverage. Yes, I think I could do it with a sharp sword. Can you get me one, please?"

The girl looked at Tolian and then over at Capreesh, who shrugged. Tolian knew they wanted to obey her. As long as they didn't suspect she would try to do what she was going to.

"Of course, Holy Goddess," Delotti replied.

As she left to fetch a sword, Tolian tried to put Capreesh at ease.

"That bracelet matches this gown perfectly," the princess said, indicating the one Capreesh held.

"Yes, Goddess of the Silver Light Most Blessed," agreed the girl cheerfully.

"I can't wait to try it on," Tolian added in mock anticipation.

Delotti offered her a short sword. It wasn't as sharp as she was hoping for, but it would have to do.

"Hold out your arm, and I'll get it for you," the servant offered.

"Oh no, that's okay," said Tolian brightly. "I know just what to do, and where I have to do it. I'll get it."

She held her hand out for the sword. Delotti handed it to her with a bow.

"Great," she said examining it in closer detail. She walked over to a nearby table. "Fine, I'll just use this to hold it still, so I can get at it."

She lay her wrist down on the table. She inhaled. She knew what she had to do, but she had to admit that she was frightened. It was not an easy thing to do. She could only hesitate for so long before the girls would become suspicious.

"I will hold no fear," she began silently in her mind. "Fear is for my enemy. Fear is defeat, and the forerunner of defeat. I will hold no fear."

She looked one last time at her wrist and at the bracelet. She pulled the short sword back, held it high in the air for only a moment, then brought it back with as much strength as she could muster towards her wrist.

Chapter 26

Tolian closed her eyes just as the blade was about to strike her wrist. She steeled herself for the inevitable pain, but it did not come. Instead, she felt something grab her arm and pull it back the other way with such force that the blade fell from her grip. She opened her eyes.

There was Dowbreth. He was not happy. He held her arm at an uncomfortable angle.

"Our Wondrous Deity of the Mystic Energies," he said with ill-concealed anger, "must use more caution when handling sharp objects. You could have hurt yourself. Do not fear, we shall allow no such harm to come to you."

She stared at him fuming, her lip curled in rage. "Now I know how you have sapped my strength, it is only a matter of time before I find the opportunity to free myself and take my vengeance upon you. And, I will not be merciful, I assure you, Dowbreth."

His look of displeasure was replaced my smugness.

"Perhaps you have forgotten, though a world away, your lover is still under my power. You have given me your word of honor against her safety. Have you forgotten, Radiant One?"

"You ensnared me by treachery and now you talk of my word of honor," spat Tolian.

"The treachery that 'ensnared you,' as you say, was not mine. You were betrayed by your own blood kin, not by me," replied the warlord.

"How am I to know that you have not broken your word and already killed Brythia?" the princess asked. The thought of that possibility sent a wave of fear and anguish through her.

"I had come to assure you that that was not the case as I require additional cooperation from you, Your Magnificence," answered Dowbreth. "So first, I should ease your concerns for your beloved's well-being."

He held aloft his magick sack in his other arm.

"Would you like to see for yourself that she is well?"

"Yes," came her immediate response.

"And you'll behave yourself as a lady should and not attempt to cut your hand off again?" Dowbreth asked.

"Not at least until I see that Brythia is safe and unharmed."

He released his tight grip on her arm.

"Fear not," he said, "I will see to it that nothing nasty happens to her as long as you continue to cooperate. But, I feel that we must remind you that it is within my power to have her killed quickly should you cross me."

Tolian rubbed her arm where the giant faerie had held it.

"You two, out," Lord Dowbreth commanded to Capreesh and Delotti.

They curtsied and hastened out of the room.

He redirected his attention to the princess. He raised the bag so it was just above Tolian's head. "Now close your eyes."

A sudden, sickening feeling passed through her, like a thousand worms crawling around inside her. It passed just as quickly and she was seeing through someone's eyes. Dowbreth's fellow conspirator's eyes. They were focused on Brythia deeply asleep in a bed. Her angelic face in perfect peace. A strong wave of desire stirred in her. She wished she were in bed with her. Though it clearly wasn't their bed, it looked familiar.

"Where is she?" Tolian asked Dowbreth, keeping her eyes closed and "looking" down at the sleeping druidess.

"She is in the very bed you slept in yesterday in the Tanslynt Inn. Perfectly safe. Unless..." The conspirator held a sword next to Brythia's head just for a moment, and then quickly removed it. A threat, nothing more.

Tolian wanted to keep watching the golden-haired druidess sleep. She felt so close to her. It was impossible to imagine that they were worlds apart. She swore to herself that somehow, someway they would be reunited. She had to believe that. She would be patient. Dowbreth's vigilance would drop at some point. All at once, the image of Brythia faded to blackness. The disturbing sensation and now nausea came and went once again. An alien, lingering, and powerful malice receded more slowly from her consciousness. She opened her eyes. Dowbreth was looking down at her expectantly. "Our deal stands," she announced. "What do you want me to do?"

He smiled wide, baring his ghastly pointed teeth. “Excellent,” he said with triumph. “We are going to call on the King and Queen of Faerie this afternoon. All that you have to do is follow my lead and agree with whatever I say. That is all.”

She nodded.

“Capreesh. Delotti,” bellowed the Faerie lord.

They reentered the room almost instantly.

“Finish getting her ready,” he ordered. “We leave immediately.”

“Yes, Lord,” again in unison.

Tolian watched them. They feared him, too, that was clear. But, they respected him. There was something in him that had earned respect, even admiration from the girls. She could not imagine what it was.

He turned and left them, taking the sword with him. Tolian breathed a long sigh of relief. She was so intimidated by him. She hated herself for it.

The girls were stressed and concerned by her previous behavior, yet more afraid of her, Tolian knew, than they were of Dowbreth. They said nothing to her, but set about making the final additions to Tolian’s outfit. Delotti set a silver circlet crowned with a crescent moon upon her brow, while Capreesh slipped the most peculiar slippers Tolian had ever seen on her feet. They were purple and silver and matched her gown perfectly. And as she moved across the floor her slippers shot off sparks just like the gown. But that wasn’t the most unusual thing about them. The heel was high and pointy, raising it fully three inches above the toe. They angled her leg in the most fantastic manner. She quickly noticed that they were difficult to walk in. She admired herself in the mirror for a moment. She loved looking gorgeous. It was an extraordinary feeling; there was no real equivalent in male existence. She puckered her lips up into a pout and posed in front of the mirror. It helped to take her mind off her present circumstances. And it seemed to put the two faerie maids in a more relaxed state, as they also admired her beauty.

Dowbreth’s voice caught her off guard as she examined herself. “Come, Powerful Queen of Tides, your chariot awaits.” His voice was booming and deep, but a mocking theatrical tone joined the violence underneath. He gestured to the door.

Tolian had to concentrate carefully to walk in the high-heeled shoes. They required precisely placed steps, not the confident, long strides she was used to. *Tentative, and dainty little steps*, she thought. But, even she was aware how sexy that walk was. It made her aware of her own sexuality. And of how difficult it was to walk in those shoes. Now, she teetered too far forward, or her ankle wanted to roll over this way too far. She followed Dowbreth back through the great house, doing everything she could to keep up with his giant steps, and not break her neck doing so. The warlord was muttering to himself. Tolian could only make out a few of his words.

"You are certain that this is the best plan?" he said to no one in particular.

She could hear doubt in his voice for the first time. She strained to hear more of his words, but he was too far ahead of her, and she could not make them out. She was so preoccupied by these tasks, that she paid little attention to the household, or its furnishings. All that changed, however, when they stepped outside into the bright sunshine.

It was dazzlingly brilliant outside. Golden rays of sunshine spilled down like rain. Energy poured out of the sun and visibly moved through the air like droplets, touching each blade of grass, tree, and faerie with a hint of its own luminance. Everything glowed with life and energy, bathed in the shimmering grandeur of the sun's light. Yet Tolian's eyes did not squint nor burn. They took it all in as though it was natural. Objects still possessed their own distinct colors, but more vividly than in the mortal world. The trees lining the cobblestone walkway to Dowbreth's door appeared to be some faerie version of magnolia trees, their pink and red petals in full bloom. Their fragrance tantalized Tolian with a sweet, potent delight. The sky was clearer and bluer than any sky she had ever seen before. The birdsongs rang out with symphonic complexity.

Dowbreth strode next to a mammoth chariot, carved from wood with an interlocking pattern of crescent moons outlined in painted silver. Four spears arranged in the proximate inside corners were decked with purple banners emblazoned with silver crescent moons. Thirteen faerie horses were harnessed to the mighty chariot. The faerie warlord gestured towards the chariot and held his hand out for her. With great disdain, Tolian took the giant's hand and stepped up into the chariot. Her shoes caused her some difficulty; she almost toppled right back out as soon as she had climbed in. She squeezed Dowbreth's hand firmly and caught her balance. She quickly pulled her hand away. With a light easy step, Dowbreth was next to her. He looked down at her and smiled. Tolian turned away from his stare. It was filled with lust, and a degree of nearly clinical satisfaction as he examined her. She did not like it. He lifted the reins and with a flick of his wrists, brought the horses to a slow walk. The chariot moved forward.

Tolian looked back to stare at the big manor house behind. It was clearly an ancient structure. A thick layer of green ivy, which had encompassed the entire structure, save the windows and the doors, covered the stones of its construction. It stood four stories tall, and spanned all of a hundred yards. But far more interesting, at that moment, was the sight of the long line of people emerging from the house, each carrying a purple moon banner on a pole, and all of them marching two abreast behind the chariot.

"What's going on?" she asked.

"As I said, we are visiting the King and Queen of Faerie," answered the warlord. "The Goddess of the Moon making such a visit is an event of great magnitude, my Lady. Of singular importance."

"Is that everybody from your household?" Tolian queried.

"As a matter of a fact it is. They have nothing more important to do than attend you, I assure you."

She gasped in wonder as a dozen winged faeries leapt into the air in formation. She had, of course, seen the faeries launch an aerial assault on dragons before, but that she had witnessed from far below. This was taking place just a few feet behind her. Their wings, presumably designed to fit the motif of the day, were purple and silver, and were constructed of the finest Elven gossamer and a framework of wooden sticks to hold their shape. They were strapped onto the faeries, who despite the seemingly dysfunctional manufacture of their wings, flew like kites in the wind. They appeared like massive butterfly wings, with tendrils of gossamer, streaming resplendent in the golden light.

Now many behind them handed their pennants to their neighbor and retrieved musical instruments from their packs as they walked. Some pulled forth flutes and some stringed instruments of a design Tolian had never seen. Others righted drums hanging from their belts. A large, bald faerie shouted off a count of four and a tune was struck up. Upon hearing the thick texture of the musical melody, all assembled sang out a joyous anthem.

Tolian was enraptured by the lush and powerful melody of their music. Though she did not understand the words, Tolian sensed that their song was about her, or more accurately about the Moon Goddess.

"You like the song?" Dowbreth asked, seemingly, for once without malice, violence, or lurking motive.

"It's the most wonderfully beautiful piece of music I have ever heard," she answered honestly, her own voice without the bitterness with which she usually addressed the faerie. She was too caught up in the phenomenal assault on her senses. The smells so deliriously acute. The sights and sounds beyond all equal in the mortal world.

As they passed through the gate in the wall surrounding Dowbreth's estate, Tolian was able to get her first real look at the countryside of Faerie. Rolling green hills abounded, some with castles situated upon their crests, some with manor houses, and some with cottages set upon them Copses of trees and brush were interspersed here and there. A great range of majestic snowcapped mountains dominated the western vista, but it was what lay to the east that captured Tolian's attention. Perhaps three miles away stood the largest, most amazing structure Tolian had ever seen. A palace of unearthly grandeur. Its innumerable spires reached dizzying heights, yet were dwarfed by the main tower which was the highest by far she had ever seen. It glistened in the sun as though it were encrusted with diamonds.

Her mouth hung open in disbelief. Dowbreth took notice of her incredulity.

"Yes, the palace of Jurthys and Ymrisiva, King and Queen

of Faerie is without equal," he commented.

"Yes, it is," agreed the princess.

Now that they were on the open road, more and more of the Fay soon joined them. Some wearing wings of countless colors and designs, followed in the air, while most fell in behind the members of Dowbreth's household, and took up the song of the Moon Goddess. In a short time, a legion of all shapes and sizes of faeries fell in with them (behind the chariot). Most were the sort of faerie Tolian had come to know, while others ranged from tiny pixies to giants bigger than Dowbreth. There were creatures that looked like pumpkins with faces, arms, and legs. There were centaurs, and faeries dressed as flowers and human-sized flowers that walked alongside them. Tolian was getting dizzy trying to process all her senses were presenting.

Something whizzed by her head. She twisted to look at it, but it was no longer there. As she turned back to look ahead, she saw it. It was a cat. Perhaps it was a little smaller than the average terrestrial feline, but that was not what was unusual about it. It had wings. Not the artificial variety like the humanoid faeries wore, but actual feathered wings, tan in color and matching its tan and gray tabby markings.

The flying cat hovered just a few feet in front of Tolian's face, keeping perfect pace with the moving chariot. "Meow," it said.

Tolian's gaping smile of amazement, brightened to express even greater delight. "Hello there," she said with cheerful enthusiasm despite herself.

The flying cat lowered its head in humble subjugation, then did an aerial flip and brushed its face gently against Tolian's cheek. She reached out and petted the creature.

"He is so cute," she remarked.

"They fly wild here in Faerie," explained Dowbreth. "Keep him as a pet, if he will stay with you."

"Really?" she gushed. She sounded like a little girl, and she knew it. She became aware of the casual manner in which she conversed with her captor. Why was he being so nice to her? Almost gentlemanly. It seemed to beyond what was required, even if he was trying to get her to do something for him. She sensed some conflict in him. Perhaps there had been goodness in him at one time, and he was closest to it at his own home.

Why they were going to see Ymrisiva and her husband was beyond her comprehension as well. Surely, they would simply command Dowbreth to release her. She knew Ymrisiva. She had met her in her dreams first, and she had proven herself a staunch ally against the Demon's menace. What could Dowbreth hope to gain? Perhaps the faerie warlord only needed her to make some point or to gain some boon or favor from his King and Queen. Maybe, she would be able to leave once he had obtained whatever it was he wanted. That did not seem likely, but it did afford her a small measure of hope. In any case, she was sure to discover whatever it was that he was planning in a short while. In the meantime, she would content herself with watching the unfolding spectacle around her, listening to the delightful music in her honor, and petting her new cat, who seemed as pleased with her company as she was with his.

"Do you name cats in Faerie?" she asked Dowbreth.

"Some do. This one has been hanging around my property lately. I believe the servants call him Pilt or Wild One, in your tongue."

Tolian found it difficult to believe that this daunting warlord of the Sidhe would ever bother to know something like that.

"Pilt," she repeated. "I like that. Pilt."

Pilt meowed his agreement and nuzzled Tolian's neck.

A vast throng moved behind the chariot as it passed through the gates of the palace. The guards moved aside and bowed deeply to Tolian as they did so. It seemed as though they had been expected, for a pavilion had been erected in the field between the gate and the palace proper, which towered impossibly, so it seemed, high above. The King and Queen sat in thrones within the pavilion. They stood up and bowed low as Dowbreth brought the chariot to a stop just before them. The faerie warlord leapt down off the chariot and assisted Tolian off.

Dowbreth whispered to her, "Give them leave to rise."

"Rise, Noble Monarchs of the Faerie Realm," said Tolian.

They got back to their feet. How regal they looked. How beautiful. Ymrisiva had long silver hair down to the base of her back. She was not so pale as she had appeared in the mortal world. In fact, Tolian realized, none of the faeries had that same unearthly pallor in Faerie. Even Dowbreth had some color to his cheeks in the crisp, golden sunlight. The Queen's features were fine and delicate. Jurthys resembled her so nearly, a masculine version of her, that they could have been brother and sister. The King wore a long, gleaming white robe and the Queen's gown constantly shifted colors as Tolian looked at it.

Ymrisiva's eyes fastened onto Tolian's. The depth and wisdom there was unfathomable. And power. But kindness and curiosity shining also. Tolian smiled uneasily at her.

Ymrisiva addressed her. "Hail unto thee, Holy Goddess of the Moon, who reigns sovereign over Faerie, Mighty Empress of Clouds, we your loyal subjects welcome you. We were surprised when your messengers advised us of your arrival. Is it wise for you to come so to Faerie? Your influence will quickly begin to make its effect obvious in the Astral Plane of which this realm is a part. It must be a vital and urgent mission."

Tolian glanced furtively at Dowbreth. His sneer returned as he stepped forward.

"My Queen," the warlord spoke, "The Goddess wishes that I speak for her as this situation is somewhat awkward for her."

Tolian had to agree with him on that point.

"Is this so, Holy One?"

She nodded, "Yes, Dowbreth speaks for me."

She wished she knew what he was up to.

"Very well," the Queen said.

Dowbreth cleared his throat roughly and began. "Our Empress is, of course, aware that her power and divine essence will begin to dominate her surroundings in this mutable kingdom, but, as you say, her mission is an urgent one. She will, naturally, attempt to have as little effect on the fabric of our world as possible."

The Queen's eyes narrowed as Dowbreth spoke. It was obvious to Tolian that she did not trust him. The King's brow carried great concern, but he remained silent. Tolian found herself fidgeting uncontrollably, causing a great commotion of sparkling energy to fly from her dress and shoes.

"The Goddess," continued Dowbreth, "has decided to remain here in Faerie. She will take all precautions to prevent contamination of others. As Empress of Faerie, she will no longer require Your Majesties services. She will be occupying your palace, as it is the only suitable residence for her. You are welcomed to use my estate, if you like, until you can find other accommodations."

To her credit, Ymrisiva did not flinch. "Where will you be staying, Lord Dowbreth?" she asked.

"I will be staying in the palace with her Holiness. After the prescribed engagement period of seven years, we shall be wed."

Tolian's head started to spin. Dowbreth subtly placed his hand on the magick bag, hanging off his belt, surrounded by the severed heads of his enemies. Tolian understood his silent message.

"This is true, Tolian?" asked the Queen without formality.

Tolian swallowed hard. "Yes, I suppose it is."

Chapter 27

After four days at the Tanslynt Inn, Brythia could no longer be persuaded to remain for any reason. No plea carried any weight with her. Findelbres's arguments that she needed more time for healing and rest were politely brushed aside. Just as soon as she was able to stand without dizziness, she was determined to set off. She could not get the image of Tolian's tormented and beaten face from her mind. Additional rest was a luxury she could not afford when her love needed her. They stocked up on provisions, paid their bill, said their farewells, and went on their way. She noticed that Kiliordes and Pagyrus looked back with obvious regret as they turned and began their new trek.

Brythia set her eyes on the road. She was filled with cold determination, yet tempered with optimism. Somehow, she was going to find Tolian and rescue her. As she stared at the snow-covered pathway ahead of her, she tried to nurture that feeling of hope that time would be on her side and that she would find Tolian before it was too late. Take each step, one at a time and everything else will fall into place, she told herself.

The landscape was still blanketed in white; the bright sunshine played upon its lustrous surface and made the snow crystals glow with gleaming brilliance. She squinted. The wind had cleared the tree branches of their white burdens, though a few icicles dangled off the larger boughs here and there. A blue jay landed on the limb of a black oak, just off the road and squawked a harsh territorial protest. Brythia chirped a greeting and an apology. The jay returned her greeting and, satisfied that they were friends, took off once again.

Findelbres pulled his horse up next to the druidess. "Are you positive you're ready for traveling?" he inquired with genuine concern.

"I'm going to be fine," she replied. "Remember, I do know a thing or two about healing, too. We just can't afford to wait. Tolian needs me."

"I know, I know," agreed the faerie. "And her presence in Faerie could cause the greatest havoc," he added in an ominous whisper.

She cocked one eye quizzically, "How would Tolian's presence be a problem in Faerie?"

Findelbres glanced nervously back to make certain that Kiliordes, Delorick, and Pagyrus were far enough behind to be out of earshot, before speaking. "You know the Realm of Faerie is different from your mortal world in certain fundamental aspects," he began.

Brythia nodded. "Sure, in the Order they teach us that Faerie lies in the Astral Plane, on the border with our own world, and the Land of Dreams. Presumably many of the laws of the Astral govern your world as well."

"Yes, exactly," Findelbres concurred. "The problem with Tolian visiting Faerie is a simple one. The Astral Plane is the prototypical version of your world. It receives the influence from all the higher worlds, as well as from your world. That is precisely its function. But a creature of great mystical power, like a goddess, for example, can exert undue influence upon Faerie itself if she stays too long. Short visits aren't a problem, but a longer stay could warp the fabric of Faerie's reality. People nearest her would be influenced first, with those with minimal contact least affected."

Findelbres sighed. "I hope, Brythia, the powers of the Moon Goddess cannot be easily thwarted in the Astral Plane which is part of her domain. I do not know, but I fear there is danger here for all of Faerie as well as for Tolian. I wish I knew what Dowbreth was up to. It makes no sense."

Brythia studied the elf carefully. He had always been a good friend; she needed to trust him. She had to confide in someone about what she had learned at Hyge Bryth, about her suspicions.

She leaned close to him as she rode. "Findelbres," she said almost inaudibly, "I'm not sure how to say this, but I looked at the original scrolls of the Druidic Prophecy when I was at Hyge Bryth

Surprise registered on his face. "And..."

"And, I don't think the Demon's dead. Somehow, he is involved in this business with Dowbreth and Tolian. I don't know how, but I know it. I'm certain that your Warlord of the Sidhe is in league with the Demon. And, I'm not sure who else is. Clearly, there is some Lormian involvement. I just don't know how extensive this conspiracy is."

She tilted her head vaguely back toward the others and winked at the elf. "So don't mention this to the others until we can be sure. I hope I can trust you."

He smiled. "My dear, if you can't trust me, then you are in deep trouble. I am your friend, and I am Tolian's friend. I would never betray either of you. But, I agree. I smell a conspiracy. Best to be careful."

Their pace was swift, but with nowhere near the urgency that marked their journey to the Tanslynt Inn. Just about noon, they dismounted for lunch. They let the horses wander in a field just off the road where last year's ryegrass, dry and brittle, stuck up from the snow like the spires of a palace. Kiliordes and Delorick wanted something hot to combat the chill of the day and Brythia saw no reason to deny them. In fact, she leaned well over their small fire and inhaled the emerging scent of the cooking stew (sent with them by Mrs. Gelstrit from the inn). Her mouth started to water.

They crouched along the roadside and ate their stew. It was still delicious, a sturdy, beefy broth and lots of potatoes, carrots and, of course, chunks of tender beef. Brythia felt warmed with the first spoonful. The winter's chill slowly receded within her as she ate.

"Someone's coming," announced Findelbres.

A moment later Brythia felt the vibration in the ground and the slightest sound, almost like distant thunder.

"Horsemen," she said. "A troop. Get the fire out and be ready," she added.

Delorick protested, "Princess, we are well within the borders of our kingdom. These will surely be friends."

"You're probably right," she agreed. "But do what I say, just in case."

Kiliordes and Pagyrus quickly removed their cooking gear and put out the fire. Brythia hastily swallowed the last bite of stew in her bowl. She wiped her mouth with her hand, and realized when she did so, that she would never have done anything of the sort back at the palace, back home. Home. Without Tolian, there it would never again be home for her. Wherever Tolian was, that was home. She felt tears begin to well up. She stifled them. She had to be in control.

They did not wait long before the riders could be seen heading toward them from the direction that they themselves were headed. From central Lorm, the palace. At first, she was tense. She had some unspecific feelings of caution, and the shadow of potential trouble. She breathed a sigh of relief as she saw the outriders' banners, those of Lorm and the House of Hemris.

Delorick resheathed his sword and waved a greeting. The others all noticeably relaxed as well. The troop of horsemen was a sizable contingent, perhaps fifty men. Brythia recognized Kelvris as their leader. She also raised an arm in greeting. The Lormian horsemen slowed their steeds as they neared, but then did something unexpected. They immediately surrounded Brythia and her companions. With the famed Lormian military precision, they all pulled their swords in one motion and extended them towards the smaller party.

Kelvris, smirking, said, "You are all under arrest for conspiracy and treason. We have reason to believe that you were involved in the kidnapping of Princess Tolian, Heir to the Warrior Throne of Lorm, not to mention the Royal Prince Relinder. You will come peacefully with us."

He dismounted and almost gleefully held his sword up to Brythia's throat. "Attempt no tricks, sorceress. Or, I will kill you where you stand."

Brythia felt the cold steel against her neck. She held still.

"Take their weapons," commanded Prince Kelvris.

"Wait," shouted Brythia.

The men stopped and looked at Kelvris for further instructions. They were clearly uncomfortable.

"This is ridiculous," Delorick said.

"What is the meaning of this?" demanded Kiliordes.

Pagyrus said nothing; he simply appeared confused and at a loss. Findelbres regarded Kelvris with narrowed eyes and nodded quietly.

Kelvris addressed Kiliordes, "Dear Lord Kiliordes and Lord Delorick, you must forgive this inconvenience, but until we know who was involved with this witch and her inhuman accomplice" (with a nod towards the faerie) "we must take you all into custody."

"Kelvris," said Brythia, "I wasn't even there when Tolian was abducted, and she's my wife. How can you even suggest such a thing?"

"Oh no," retorted the prince, "you were hundreds of miles away, weren't you? Yet you arrived at the palace only a few hours later, and then immediately you and your faerie conspirator departed."

"That's circumstantial at best, Kelvris," stated Kiliordes. "I hope for your sake you have more proof than that."

"You will hear my proof soon enough, before the King," the prince said. "Meanwhile, must I remind you how badly Brythia wanted Tolian to accompany her to the druids' stronghold? When the princess wouldn't cooperate, she had no choice but to have her abducted. It is a druid and faerie conspiracy. Now, take their weapons."

Brythia reached up and touched Kelvris on the forehead. She concentrated and visualized the prince suddenly turned to stone. It was an old druid technique of self-defense. Kelvris immediately could not move anything other than his lips. He was effectively paralyzed. Brythia stepped away from his sword, but kept her hand upon his forehead.

"Stop," the druidess commanded.

"What have you done to me, witch? I can't move," asked the prince in horror. More horsemen pointed swords at her.

"This spell is only temporary, but my next one won't be. Tell them to back off, Kelvris, or else," she said.

Kelvris was not giving up control that easily.

"Or else what, my cousin's treacherous wife?" he asked, his voice still full of swagger and fire.

"If you don't let us go right now," she said with a dawning smile, "I'll use the druid spell to transform you into a woman. Just like I did to Tolian. How would that be?"

"No, you wouldn't," he pleaded. The change in attitude was astounding. "Back off men," he added nervously. "Get back."

She was, of course, bluffing. She hadn't participated in the ritual of transformation for Tolian. Only the High Druidess knew the magickal formula employed, and to accomplish the ritual took thirteen days, a special chamber, potions, and almost the entire female population of the druidic order.

"You'd make a lovely girl, Kelvris," she added. "Shall I transform you, then?"

"Please, no, no," pleaded the paralyzed prince in terror.

"Of course," Brythia continued, "you won't have Tolian's powers, and you'll just be a woman. Oh, and I can work the spell from half a mile away."

She traced a pentagram on Kelvris's forehead. She turned to her companions, "Gentlemen, I suggest you get on your horses."

"But," asked Delorick, "wouldn't it be better to simply go with them and sort this out back at the palace? We know you and Findelbres had nothing to do with Tolian's abduction. We can resolve this and get back on the trail."

"Delorick," replied Brythia, "you are welcome to do that, but I don't have time right now. Anyone coming with me, get on your horse immediately."

Findelbres, Kiliordes, and Pagyrus went without hesitation to their horses. Delorick delayed but a moment, an expression of conflict on his face, then did the same. Brythia slowly made her way through the brandished swords towards Whisper.

"You know," she told the surrounding Lormian troops, "I can just as easily turn all of you boys into girls if you give me any trouble. It's a quick spell, too. Think your wives, mistresses, and girlfriends will be as understanding as Tolian's?"

Brythia held back her smile as more and more space opened around her. She got to Whisper's side and mounted.

"No takers then?" she asked. "You might like it, you never know. No? Then, gentlemen, we shall see you back at the palace, when we return with Tolian. Then we shall properly address this issue of treason and conspiracy." She leveled that last remark at the still paralyzed Kelvris.

She glanced over at her comrades. "My friends, I think we should be going."

And finally, to Kelvris, "If we even hear you behind us, I will cast that spell. Think long and hard about pursuing us. In the meantime, I recommend the hospitality of the Tanslynt Inn, a few miles down the road. Farewell, Kelvris, my wife's cousin. The paralysis should wear off in a few minutes."

They were off, galloping into the heart of Lorm. Brythia did venture a look behind to make certain the Lormian troops weren't moving. They hadn't budged. She exhaled vigorously. *Thank goodness for male pride*, she thought.

They rode too hard and too fast for conversation, and the rest were hard-pressed to keep pace with the druidess. Brythia was lost in her own thoughts of Tolian, of course, when she heard Delorick's voice calling behind her.

"Princess. Hold."

She reined Whisper to a slow pace and waited for him to catch up.

"Yes, Delorick, what is it?"

"Unless it is your plan to transform the entire Lormian army into women," he said with a wink, "we should get off this road as soon as possible."

"I would agree, but I do not know another way across Lorm" she stated plainly.

"I know another way, a hunter's road that cuts across this road just ahead and follows a track through the King's Forest and provides a direct route southwest to the Pine Barrens," he said with earnestness. Evidently, he had resolved his conflict and was prepared to be as helpful as possible. She was encouraged by his suggestion. That was exactly what they needed. She did not think her bluff would work indefinitely, and they were certain to meet more Lormian forces if they stayed on the main road.

"Lead the way," she said.

Chapter 28

Once again, the forest's sparse winter canopy crowned their passage. The path was wide enough for them to travel one by one, without the constant assault of limbs and bracken. For that much, Kiliordes was grateful. He rode second to last, behind Pagyrus, and just ahead of Findelbres, who stationed himself in the rear to listen for sounds of pursuit. The cold seemed to be bothering Kiliordes more and more. He supposed he'd gotten spoiled by the days of relaxing at the Inn. The memory of the excellent beer made his mouth water. But he knew where his duty lay, and he was going to do everything he could to help Brythia find Tolian. Well, everything, within reason. He did not intend to enter Faerie with Brythia and Findelbres. It was an established fact that no mortal had ever returned from Faerie.

His future had become much more complex now, since their encounter with Kelvris. Or perhaps, it had become simpler. Unless Brythia did find Tolian and somehow returned with her to Lorm, there was no way any of them could go back. And although he wore his most determined expression, he knew in his heart that Brythia didn't have a chance. To be clear, he did not doubt the druidess's resolve. She would no doubt find a way into Faerie. She would probably even be able to track down Tolian and Dowbreth once there, but he did not see any way for Brythia to best Dowbreth in combat, Moonsword or not. Tolian had all of her power when she faced Dowbreth, and she could not vanquish him. What chance did Brythia have? It was unlikely that he would ever return to his newfound home at the Lormian palace.

It seemed that events were leading him to the Solar Pilgrimage Festival after all. In his heart, he knew that it was what he desired. To live the carefree existence of the joyous pilgrim. To be free from the shadow of the past. To live somewhere where he could just be Kiliordes, and not have people look at him as though he were someone else. He wasn't Kilfrie, he wasn't Rwiordes, and he wasn't the Demon. Yet, in subtle, perhaps unconscious ways, the people closest to him did not really know who he was. They looked at him and saw ghosts. With the Solar Pilgrims, he could start anew. Sure, they had known him briefly as Rwiordes, but only briefly. And yes, they thought of him as the person who saved the world, and they expected him to become their new leader, but those expectations he could live with. To travel with the sun, spreading joy and mirth. To revel in the rays of the Daystar, bringing the glad tidings of those golden rays to all who would receive them. He was decided: once they made certain of Brythia's passage into Faerie, he would go with Pagyrus to Southern Surtiz and rendezvous with the Solar Pilgrimage Festival.

When they stopped to camp that night, Kiliordes was overjoyed. A bitter cold had set in, and he was already tired of riding. They lit a large fire that Brythia made certain was well controlled. They ate the last bit of stew and some bread, and stared into the flames. There was something so magickal about fire, Kiliordes mused as the warmth wrapped around him. Mesmerizing. He had seconds of the stew, washed it down with a little wine, and then wrapped himself up in his blanket for the night, close enough to the fire, yet not so close that he would catch aflame. The last thing he remembered hearing was Brythia's voice.

"Delorick, you are sure this path will soon turn west, right? We've been going pretty much south."

He didn't hear the Captain of the Guard's answer.

Kiliordes' dream. He was on a ship. A sturdy vessel with a broad hull and two masts reaching high; sails full with the wind. How real it was. One of those dreams that possess that vivid lifelike quality, a certain lucidity. Was he dreaming? He hadn't remembered dreaming in a long time. Had he even dreamt before? As Kiliordes? He didn't think so. The warm sea breeze kissed his cheeks. He inhaled the delightful salty air. The sun on his face. So pleasant. He looked out over the port rail. The blue ocean water spread out as far as the eye could see. Maybe this wasn't a dream after all. Perhaps, everything else had been a dream. Maybe there was no mad trek through the winter's forest, no formerly male, kidnapped princess, no faerie warlord, no obsessed and beautiful druidess. Maybe there never had been a Kilfrie or a Rwiordes. Maybe he had always been Kiliordes. Maybe there had never been a Demon. It hit him. It did not matter. Dream or reality, he wanted to hang on to this sweet respite, this oasis of tranquility.

It occurred to him that he should try to find someone else on this ship. He could find out exactly where they were sailing. That might, indeed, be important information. He looked about, but there was no one to be found. He headed towards the front of the boat. The bow, he remembered. Yes, that was what it was called. The bow.

It was difficult to take his gaze from the ocean. The rolling waves kissed the azure vault of heaven, while a thin string of puffy white clouds lined the horizon. As he walked, he quickly scanned the deck around him, and then stole looks over the sea. The pitching of the ship as it crested waves produced an uncomfortable feeling in the pit of his stomach. A slight queasiness, nothing more. He leaned over the rail and looked down into the ocean. A blue-green abyss full of mystery and power churned below. What monsters moved in those depths? A chill ran down his spine.

Finally, as he approached the wheel, he saw someone else. A lone figure, standing at the helm. He was tall and thin, and oddly familiar from the back.

"Hail, captain," Kiliordes shouted over to him as he walked.

The fellow turned his head back to face Kiliordes and smiled. It was Perelisk.

Brythia's dream. She was on the White Hart's back. As soon as she realized this, they broke out of the forest and on to a grassy plain. Patches of snow, glowed and shimmered in the moonlight, like ghosts dancing below them.

"Welcome back, Priestess of the Sun," the hart said in greeting. "It has been days since you have dreamt deeply enough to resume our trek, but nonetheless, some progress has been made."

She was surprised. "How is that possible? If I have not been dreaming how could we have progressed in our dream journey?"

she asked.

"You came close enough a few times," answered the hart, plainly. "Not enough for us to converse, but your spirit is driven by an insatiable fire; it is always bending towards my lady. We have moved as the dream shadows through the tangled forests of your unconscious fancy. Your heart ever strives to reach her."

"Okay, you said her, but who do you mean, exactly? Tolian or your mistress, the Celestial Aspect of the Moon Goddess? I am confused."

"They are the same," replied the beast cryptically.

"Look, they can't be the same," said the druidess. "Tolian doesn't know anything about being the Moon Goddess, she's just her earthly manifestation, right? They are different."

"They are the same."

"You're not very good at explaining things, are you?" Brythia asked in frustration.

"I do not see the confusion. I am sorry. It is clear to me," said the White Hart apologetically. "My Lady will explain when we get there."

"Where exactly are we going, again?"

"To the Moon," answered the deer.

"And how long is it going to take to get there?"

"Several long dreams, Princess. Several long dreams. The Moon is far even in the country of dreams. Very far."

Chapter 29

Tolian, surrounded by her new retinue, climbed the long spiraling stairs towards the top of the highest tower. She moved there in numb shock. They had been walking for hours it seemed. Capreesh and Delotti walked next to her. Two other faeries went before her spreading white rose petals and jasmine on the steps. Behind them followed a collection of faerie women and three male warriors, who did not seem at all happy about their assignment when they received it from Dowbreth. No one spoke. The silent procession wound its way higher and higher.

At length, they reached the topmost suite. One of the warriors went in first and a moment later returned. "It is secure," he announced. "The Goddess may enter."

The flower girls went in first, spreading a profusion of potpourri on the threshold. Tolian stepped forward into a room large enough to be a great hall, but was clearly a parlor. The servants and her "bodyguards" filed in behind her and instantly spread out, some disappearing into other doors from this main room.

"This was the Queen's private suite," explained the warrior who had entered first. He was tall, not a giant like Dowbreth, but a looming presence. A narrow face, with close-set eyes, and a serious cast. A distinct brooding quality hung over him, but he was clearly attempting to be genuinely welcoming. "You should be comfortable here. I am sorry for the long walk, but the Queen only came here when she wanted to be alone, so we are isolated from the rest of the palace. We are all assigned to you as your personal servants. If you require anything whatsoever, you have merely to ask for it, Divine One."

As Tolian looked about, one thing was immediately apparent; it was the most expansive, most luxurious room she had ever seen in her life. The walls were covered in tapestries, depicting one continuous scene, which gradually changed from forest to seascape to sky as she watched. She redirected her attention to the faerie, knowing that she would have plenty of time to explore her new apartments.

"My name is Kreel," he said. "I have been assigned the honor of being your chief bodyguard."

You didn't seem so honored when you were given the assignment, Tolian thought, but she said, "It's a pleasure to make your acquaintance, Kreel. I'm sure we'll get along famously."

The faerie smiled despite his obvious conflict over the situation. He gestured to indicate the other two guards. "This is Mesdor and this Gredalon," he said. The two faeries looked even unhappier than Kreel, but they bowed nonetheless.

"One of us must always be in the same room with you, Great One, without exception; on Lord Dowbreth, your betrothed's, orders."

"Even when I'm going to the bathroom?" asked Tolian.

"I am afraid so, Holiness," replied Kreel. "We have been entrusted with your safety; we shall be as discrete as is possible, but there will be no opportunity for you to do anything foolish. Beyond this you have few restrictions."

"Oh, I find that difficult to believe," the princess said.

"You have free access to this entire suite. Upon request, with suitable notice and approval, and on special occasions, you will be permitted access to other areas of the palace or Faerie. This is primarily to protect and insulate our world from the effects of your Divine Lunar Energies and the magick that transformed you."

"What exactly are you people afraid of?" she asked. She kept hearing people talk about 'her influence on the fabric of Faerie.' What did it mean?

He seemed surprised by her question. "Beings charged with magickal or divine energies forever retain them. In Faerie, such energies are infused into the surrounding environment. People and things here absorb these energies and it changes them. That is why you are quartered here in the highest tower. The isolation should minimize the effects."

"What about you and everybody else here with me?" she asked.

"The females should suffer few negative effects from exposure to you. We," here he indicated Mesdor and Gredalon, "will most likely be significantly effected by our continual proximity to you. But, we are Dowbreth's most loyal men and we are honored to serve. We are prepared to accept the consequences."

Consequences. Tolian still wondered what they might entail.

"Is that it for the rules then?" Tolian asked with a yawn.

"There are a few others," answered Kreel. "You must remain in pure, both to protect your status as a virginal goddess and as preparation for your upcoming wedding."

"Well, it may be too late already," said Tolian triumphantly. "I am certainly not a virgin."

"Have you ever had sex with a male?"

"No."

"By our laws you are still a virgin then." He said it flatly without emotion. "And lastly, you are never allowed outside, or near a window, if the moon is out. These are the only restrictions I was advised of. Beyond that, you are free to do as you wish. Anything that you require, or simply desire shall be brought to you. Now, allow me to introduce the remainder of your new servants."

She stood there politely, smiled, and nodded at each of the faerie women who came before her. She was beginning to get tired, however, and she remembered no one's name. When they all had been presented to her, she looked over at the small assemblage, cleared her throat, and addressed them as a group.

"Well," she said, "here we are. I want us to understand one another. The way I see it, we are all prisoners here. I'm sure none of you want to be stuck up here anymore than I do; that said, I hope we can all get along, until such a time as either I manage to escape, or you do. If you must treat me as a goddess, so be it, but understand that I do not regard myself as such. Now, I am tired and hungry; probably you are as well. Let's do something about that."

Capreesh stepped right up and took charge, "You heard the Goddess, let's get supper ready."

Once again, the servants scattered throughout the suite and busied themselves. Kreel leaned forward. "Would you like to see your bedroom? We can show you everything else later."

"Sure, that sounds fine, Kreel. Let's go."

She followed him across the parlor and through a door into another grand room. It contained the largest bed she had ever seen. The canopy and matching bedspread and sheets had a starry sky motif. As she gazed upon it, she noticed shooting stars moving here and there across the pattern. The walls of the room around the bed were white marble, dotted with columns, large panel mirrors and a few tapestries hanging there, mostly depicting garden scenes. Of furniture, there was much; the room held an array of dressers, bureaus, and wardrobe closets. There was a large ornate desk, several comfortable looking sedan chairs, a small breakfast table and chairs, and behind a silver curtain, a balcony of great size.

Tolian was dumbfounded. She stood there with her mouth hanging open and gaped. When she had conquered her sense of grandeur, she did manage to say, “This is amazing.”

“Yes,” agreed Kreel. “The Queen likes her luxury. Now, all this is yours. You should try to enjoy it. At least you have that.”

She appreciated his compassion. “Well, am I allowed to look out the balcony?” Tolian asked.

“Yes, it is still daylight out and the moon is not in the sky,” replied Kreel.

She strode across the room, her dress still shooting off sparks as she walked. After all the walking she had done that day, she had mastered walking in the high heels. The swinging glass doors were opened, so she stepped out onto the balcony without obstruction. She was greeted by the kiss of the cool evening air, refreshing and deeply sensual. She held tightly on to the railing as she looked out. She was shocked at how high up they were. Faerie was spread out like a child’s model. Towns, castles, lakes, forests, mountains, and rivers stretched out below her, tiny and most unreal. Wisps of clouds moved around her.

She felt her guard move closer to her.

“How is it possible we are this high up, Kreel?” she asked. “We climbed many steps, but not enough to account for this altitude.”

“You are correct. Like most things in Faerie, the stairs to this tower are magickal. Without the magick, it would take the better part of a day to get up here. As it is, it takes a little more than an hour.”

She stared below her, straining for details, held in a state of marvel. She did note, however, that clearly there was no means of escaping this way.

Delotti came out and joined them. "My Lady, your supper is ready. Would you like to take it out here?"

"Oh, that sounds wonderful. The air up here is so invigorating." Tolian turned to her bodyguard, "Given that you have to hang around me anyway, Kreel, would you care to join me?"

He looked surprised. "Of course, my lady, if that is your wish, I would be honored."

He was already more relaxed, less conflicted, Tolian thought. They walked over to the wrought iron table and chairs. Kreel politely held the chair for her. She smiled and was seated. He tilted his head in a semi-bow, returned her smile, and sat across the table from her. He had a nice smile. Despite his delicate faerie features, there was a definite masculinity about him. She caught herself looking at his strong jaw, broad shoulders and well-muscled arms. It was the first time she had ever looked at a man like that. What on earth was happening to her? She felt a sudden physical attraction to Kreel. She found herself wondering (just for a second) what it would be like to... No, she had to stop herself from thinking like that. She could not believe that she was having thoughts about having sex with a man, faerie or not. A man. Since she had become a woman, she had equated her sexuality in terms of her relationship with Brythia; it was something special that they did together. Thoughts of Brythia made her yearn for the druidess, her wife. She felt a pang of pain at their separation. But they were separated, that was the fact. Probably forever. The realization came to her that her entire female sexual experience had been with Brythia. They had always satisfied each other's needs. She had never even masturbated as a woman. And now, her hormones were starting to make her want things she would never have imagined that she would want. Despite herself, she wondered what it would be like to have Kreel inside her. She felt herself moisten at the prospect. She felt guilty immediately.

She was distracted from this line of thinking by the arrival of their food. It was the most unusual plate of food she had set her eyes upon.

"What is this?" she asked.

"It's chicken and mushrooms with pasta in a creamy tomato sauce," answered the girl serving her.

"Well, I know what chicken and mushrooms are," she said.

Kreel chuckled, "I don't believe pasta or tomatoes have been discovered in your world yet. You are in for a treat, Lady. But first, a toast, if I may?"

"Please," offered Tolian. She batted her long eyelashes, without even thinking.

Kreel raised his wineglass. "To the most beautiful woman in Faerie, Daughter of Heavens, Empress of Clouds, who reigns from on high."

"That's nice," she commented softly, "but I'm not going to drink a toast to myself. Where I come from, that's bad luck. And I don't mean the Moon. But since we are both essentially prisoners here, let's toast to freedom."

His eyes twinkled. "To freedom then."

"To freedom."

They gently tapped their glasses together. Tolian brought the wine to her lips. She paused for a moment as she took the first sip of the rich, dreamy faerie wine. She remembered the last time she had tasted that particular vintage. It reminded her of her kidnapping and her present situation, and served to cool her building passions somewhat.

The food was the best she had ever tasted. The new tastes filled her mouth with delight. They ate, drank their wine, talked, and laughed. They talked about battles they had fought, as two veteran warriors might. Tolian stared into his eyes as she listened to him tell of a nasty battle against the Goblin hordes. She found herself focusing on his maleness, almost unconsciously examining everything about him that made him male. She was getting aroused again, and she knew it. In fact, it gave her an idea. If she could seduce Kreel and have sex with him, she would no longer be a virgin, and therefore, she would be of no further use to Dowbreth. It might work. Yes, she would feel guilty if she betrayed her marriage vows to Brythia, but if her plans worked, she and her beloved would be reunited. In her mind, she begged Brythia's understanding. *Please forgive me for this my love*, she thought.

Still, she was too intoxicated by the wine to think clearly. There was a nagging thought she couldn't pin down. Some flaw in her plan. She took a deep breath to help her think straight. It didn't help. How much had she drunk? Two bottles between them. Nonetheless, she was determined to begin her plan. She allowed herself to submit to the power of her feminine desires. She flipped her hair and gently stroked one of her breasts absently.

"Do you like to dance, Kreel?" Tolian asked.

"Dancing is considered one of our greatest arts," he answered, "and one I am fond of. I was not aware the warrior-folk of Lorm danced, however."

"We're not barbarians, you know."

"That is obvious, Lady."

Was he feeling the attraction she was feeling? She could not tell. Everything was different now that she was a woman. She had no idea how to read a man's signals.

"Would you care to dance, my Lady?" Kreel asked.

"I'd love to, but what are we going to do for music?" she asked.

"That's easy," he said. "First, however, I'm afraid we must go inside and draw the curtains. The moon will be rising soon."

"Rules are rules," she said agreeably.

They both rose from the table. Kreel escorted Tolian back inside. He suavely placed a hand on her back to guide her. She felt a surge of electricity from the contact.

Once inside Kreel said, "Okay, now wait right here, and I'll get the music."

Get the music? How was he going to do that, she wondered. How many of the servants were musicians?

Kreel returned carrying a small copper chest. "What sort of music do you want to hear? Something fast? Something slow?" he asked.

"Something romantic," she said without missing a beat.

A sly, half-smile graced his face. He commanded Capreesh and the other girl standing in attendance to leave. He set the box on a nearby table and opened the lid. A wall of music rose from the box. It was as if two-dozen invisible musicians had entered the room and were now playing. Lush, vibrant tones filled the room.

Kreel bowed and extended his hand, "My Lady..."

Tolian stole towards him, but paused. "Ut-oh," she said. "It just occurred to me...I don't know how to dance like a girl."

Kreel laughed, "I'll help you. It is hard to believe, to look at you, that you were ever a man."

"I guess those druids did a good job," she remarked.

"A good job," he echoed. "Come on, come here then, if we're going to dance," Kreel offered.

"All right then, it's easy," he insisted. "Stand there. Good." He stepped up next to her. The proximity was enticing. "Now give me your hand." He took her hand in his. "Now put your other hand on my shoulder. Good. Now my hand goes here just above your hip. The rest you know, right?"

That depends on what you mean by the rest, she thought. They danced for some time. Tolian had no idea for how long. She was having a good time. It felt good pressing her breasts into his torso and having his arms around her.

The music flowed around them as darkness crept into the room; more candles lit themselves one by one. There was a powerful magnetism at work between them. That was obvious. She couldn't figure out why she had never felt this kind of attraction to a man before now (it was powerful, very powerful) and second, who was seducing whom.

They stared deeply into each other's eyes. Tolian could feel Kreel's erection through his jerkin and tunic, pressing against her. She understood that signal, at least. Her nipples were hard and erect as well. She pressed herself more snugly against him.

Then they kissed. He slipped his tongue inside her mouth. She burned for him, craved him, needed him, and had to have him at that moment. She broke their kiss and pulled Kreel towards the bed, wild with passion. She wanted him inside her. No, she needed him inside her. She smothered him in sweet kisses and he her. He tossed her, in his excitement, almost roughly onto the bed; the candles dimmed automatically.

Tolian kicked her shoes off, pulled her gown over her head, and flung it to the floor. The shower of sparks that resulted illuminated the room. She lay there naked, her heart pounding with anticipation. Her head spun and she had the passing realization she had drunk too much. It seemed to be taking him a long time. In the dim light, she strained to see him taking off his shirt. He stood still.

"Oh no," he said. His voice sounded strange and panicked. "Damn, too late."

"Kreel, what's wrong?" Tolian asked. "Aren't you coming to bed?"

"There's no point," Kreel said. His voice wavered in almost a falsetto. "Lights."

The candles relit themselves. Tolian's eyes went wide in horror (and to be true, disappointment).

Standing where Kreel had stood was a tall and comely faerie woman with her shirt off. She was staring down at her breasts, a look of surprise and dismay playing on her features.

"Damn," she said.

"What's going on?" Tolian asked. She sat up at once, her eyes searching for her lover.

"What's going on is that my plan to free us both has failed. I never expected to be so affected by your power," the faerie woman explained while still unable to take her eyes off her own breasts. She slipped her hand into her trousers, a look of sorrow taking hold of her face.

Understanding filtered in through the dense clouds of heated passion and alcohol in her brain. "Kreel?" Tolian asked. She hoped that she was mistaken.

"Yes," said the woman. "It's me, Kreel. I hope you can forgive me. I lit lust incense in here when I first came in, and I had the girls cook more of the lust drug into our food. The drug makes a person sexually attracted to the opposite sex and willing. We drew straws. I won. We thought that if I could seduce you, you'd be no more use to Dowbreth and we could end this mess, before...well, before this happened."

"If it makes you feel any better I was willing to seduce you for the same reason," confessed Tolian. "Wait, it could have been the incense."

"Probably," agreed Kreel.

"How long will this drug last?" Tolian asked.

"Too long, I don't want to have sex with Mesdor and

Gredalon, though right now, maybe I do. But you won't be able to anyway. They'll be simply transformed in your embrace as I was. I've only been female for two minutes; I'm not ready. I've got to get that antidote."

She put her shirt back on, and yelled for Capreesh, who entered immediately and stared at Kreel in surprise. Kreel looked so uncomfortable asking her to fetch the antidote. Tolian normally would have been amused by Kreel's discomfort with her new femininity. She had gone through that herself. But, she had wanted him so badly. She ached still to have him. To make love to him. And, now because of her, he was a she.

"Kreel," asked Tolian, "are you sure I couldn't try to have sex with either of the other two? Maybe if we skip the dancing and dinner, we could do it before he..."

"My Lady, I am so sorry to do this to do to you. Capreesh will have the antidote here in just a moment. Please try to wait for it. You can try after that if you still want to. How's that?"

Tolian reluctantly agreed. Capreesh returned with two small cups of liquid. The two formerly male women drained the cups. After a few minutes, Tolian's intense need eased. As Kreel warned her the draught, combined with the wine they had drunk, could result in drowsiness, Tolian fell asleep.

Chapter 30

Tolian awoke to the warmth of the sun on her face and the most unusual sensation on her cheek, as if she were being licked. She opened her eyes to see Pilt standing there. He stopped his licking as Tolian stirred and focused his big eyes lovingly upon her. There was no disorientation, she knew exactly where she was. She reached over and scratched the winged cat behind the ears. He emitted a soft purr. She looked over at the open curtain as fresh air and warm sunbeams poured in through the balcony door.

"Good morning," said Kreel from a chair, not far from the bed.

"Good morning," mumbled Tolian sleepily. "Did you stay up all-night, sitting there watching me sleep?"

"That's my job. Someone has to watch you constantly. Our orders, remember," Kreel responded.

"You were willing to break the rules last night," Tolian pointed out.

"Actually, I didn't. I didn't put the lust drug in the food. I was a victim of its effects, just like you. You could say that I had the lust drug put in the food. It's a technicality, but, under our laws, I would have been declared innocent. Deliberately and willingly breaking an order, now that's a different story."

Tolian sat up and pulled the covers away from her, revealing her naked body. Pilt scooted to the other side of the bed. "How are you handling, um, everything, this morning?" Tolian asked with kindness.

"It's quite an adjustment, but I've decided not to be bitter about it," her newly female bodyguard answered.

Kreel tried to stifle her sigh of discontent, but Tolian caught it. She ignored her. Pandering to her dissatisfaction wouldn't help her adjust any more quickly. Tolian had fought her own adjustment the entire way, and it had served no purpose.

Kreel said, "You might want to take your bath now, while I'm still on duty, my Lady, so you don't have to have Mesdor gawk at you."

"That's a good idea. Thank you. Oh, and Kreel, I think we're on our way to becoming friends; please call me Tolian."

"Well, since as far as I know, you're the only other person who has undergone this type of transformation, I'd say we have a fairly strong basis for a friendship. We were almost a little more than friends there, last night," Kreel joked. "Tolian, then. I am honored to call you friend. But understand that I will not break any orders for you, friend or not."

"I won't ask you to," Tolian promised. "When I escape, I'll make sure you're off duty."

"Fair enough." Kreel addressed the servant girl who had been silently waiting. "Assist the Goddess in her bathing."

"Yes, sir, I, er, ma'am," said the girl. "Right away."

The girl presented herself to Tolian, and led her to the pool.

After Tolian had bathed and was dressed in a white silken gown that clung to her curves, Mesdor came in and relieved Kreel. As he came in, he noticed Kreel and assumed a startled and nervous expression. Kreel shrugged, bowed to Tolian, and left without saying a word. Tolian's breakfast was served on the balcony. Mesdor said nothing to her and did his best to keep his distance. When she had finished eating her scrambled eggs and sausage she looked at Mesdor.

"Mesdor, let's explore my new prison," she said.

"As you wish, my Lady," he said. He was as nervous as it was possible to be, or at least he appeared so to Tolian. He clearly did not relish this assignment and was determined to resist his unavoidable transformation.

Nonetheless, he dutifully and politely led her around the suite. The whole place seemed impossibly big. In addition to the parlor, bedroom, bathroom with pool, there was a library filled with books by faerie and mortal authors (some of which hadn't been written yet in the mortal world), a dining room, kitchen, and numerous servants' quarters. However, Mesdor refused her access to one door that piqued her interest.

"That door," he explained, without malice, "leads to the Queen's private garden." She would have to obtain Dowbreth's permission before gaining access, he told her.

Tolian was curious about how the door in the highest tower could lead to a garden, the Queen's famed garden, but she was beginning to accept such oddities as normal. Besides the last time she visited that garden, she got there through a dream. Still her curiosity was burning.

"Well, can we ask if I can go to the garden today?" she inquired.

"Certainly, Goddess," said Mesdor. "I don't see why not. I'll get Gredalon to ask for you."

He was as good as his word, for in two hours Gredalon had returned with Dowbreth's authorization for Tolian to visit the garden for two hours. Mesdor and Gredalon were both to escort her, and she had to wait another half an hour for the royal gardeners to finish their work and exit the grounds.

Gredalon unlocked the wooden door yet, as the door opened, the garden was clearly visible through the egress. Tolian blinked and glanced around her to make certain her eyes weren't deceiving her. Mesdor went through the door first and, sure enough, walked right into the garden, turned, and gestured for Tolian to join him. Tolian walked through the doorway. Immediately she felt the warmth of the sun upon her face and was caught up in the heady fragrance of thousands of blooming flowers. She spun around at once and there was the doorway in a small section of ivy-covered wall. Behind the wall, more gardens stretched for a couple of hundred yards before the tower rose to impossible heights. Tolian watched as Gredalon slipped through the doorway.

"The Queen's private garden," Mesdor said, "or, I suppose, your private garden now."

The vast profusion of floral fragrances and blossoming colors was mindboggling. The sensory rush was almost beyond her capacity to withstand. The garden was sizable, like everything at the Faerie palace. Stone paths and walkways cut through the vast assortment of botanical arrangements and flowers. Right next to her was a circular collection of sunflowers, ringed in casing stone. To her left was a pond brimming with healthy water lilies. As far as she could see, assortments and exhibits of vastly differing plants, many of which she had never encountered before, and many had no correspondence in her world. And butterflies flew everywhere. Their colors were so bright and vivid they seemed to jump off their wings. Pilt immediately popped out of the tower door and began chasing the butterflies through the air. Tolian laughed as she watched the cat scamper on wing after the brilliant insects.

There was such serenity and beauty there. For the first time since her ordeal began, she relaxed. She strolled idly through the garden, marveling at the wonders around her, or chuckling at the antics of Pilt. Capreesh walked a little behind Tolian, with Mesdor and Gredalon some little distance behind her.

Finally, she had a moment to contemplate her situation. Evidently, she was to be a prisoner here forever, surrounded by incredible luxury, to be sure, but a prisoner nonetheless. The agony at her separation from Brythia seemed to wax and wane, but was always present. Unless she could find a way to escape or render herself useless to Dowbreth, she would never see her beloved again. Or anyone else that she cared about: Relinder, her father, her friends. She would have been happy to see Lord Talthud at that moment.

She stopped before another even larger pond and sat on a stone bench. She stared with a faraway gaze at the water. There was something barely perceptible moving beneath the surface. She focused her attention on it and strained to peer through the murky water. It was a large fish, with rainbow-tinged scales that changed hues as she watched. It was feeding. Once she determined what it was, her focus dwindled and she returned to her thoughts.

She gradually came up with a plan. A good plan, thought Tolian, one that could end her captivity almost as quickly as it began. She leaned back and called, "Gredalon."

"Yes, Moon Goddess?"

"I need a favor," she said. "I need you to ask Lord Dowbreth if he could join me for dinner this evening. I need to speak with him on a private matter of some importance. We may as well dine."

Gredalon seemed surprised by her request but said, "Of course, my Lady, I shall ask him when you are through out here."

"That's fine, thank you," replied the princess. "Oh, and let's not mention Kreel's transformation to him just yet, okay?"

"As you wish, Lady," he agreed compliantly.

Without her great strength, she would have to rely on her cunning and wiles. Just like any other woman in her position would. The irony of the circumstances made her smile wryly. Just like any other woman, she thought. How easy it had become to think of herself as female. Yet, little more than a year ago she had been a man's man. She had even attempted suicide to avoid the transformation. And once she had become a woman, she refused to accept her new femininity. She had fought against any feeling of acceptance within herself. It wasn't until she and Brythia made love for the first time that she found that she could find some pleasure in being a woman. The memory brought rosy warmth to her cheeks. After that—almost like magick—she began to accept the change. But why? In what way had their lovemaking changed her, or was it simply the catalyst? Had some other force been brought to work on her, merely triggered by her initial acceptance? She was distracted by a voice coming from the pond before her.

"Greetings, Holy Goddess of the Silver Light."

She looked up and was startled by the sight of a prismatic, large fish sticking halfway out of the water, talking to her. She was becoming inured to such things, so she quickly recovered her composure. "Hello," she replied, trying to sound cheerful, but with melancholy lingering in her tone.

"Don't look so sad, Great One," said the fish, with a doleful voice.

"Why not?" she asked.

"Because, I see hope in you," the fish said. What first sounded like a somber tome was simply the slow manner of speaking the multicolored fish possessed, she realized. "And vast powers untapped," it continued. "Fear not, I foresee a time when you will be reunited with your lover."

"How can you see this, fish?" she asked, surprised by his remarks.

"I see many things under water. I see what is to come. I am old, among the first of my kind. I have the gift of true-seeing. In you, I see a creature of unequaled glory and of immeasurable power. When you tap those energies, you will find all things are possible."

"If I have this hope in me," Tolian said, "it comes from your kind words, fish. Thank you."

"I am honored to be your servant, Holy Lady," said the fish, and with that, he disappeared beneath the waters.

Tolian felt a new optimism. She prayed the fish was correct, but even knowing he could be wrong, she was prepared to proceed with her plan.

Tolian was dressed as provocatively as possible, without being obvious about it. Her formfitting scarlet red gown was so low cut that she had to concentrate when she moved to keep her breasts from toppling out. And it was, without a doubt, the single shortest gown she had ever seen, being cut enough above her knee to reveal a fair portion of her thighs. She had instructed Capreesh and Delotti to apply her makeup with subtle allure. Her perfume was heady and intoxicating. Enough so, she hoped, that Dowbreth wouldn't smell the lust incense burning discretely in a nearby brazier. Tolian admired herself in her full-length mirror as Delotti made the final additions: diamond earrings, and a matching choker. Capreesh stood a few feet away admiring their handiwork, while Kreel (who was sitting on the bed) watched with some interest and newfound curiosity at the process.

"I'm never going to be able to do all that," Kreel said, discouraged.

"Of course, you will," said Tolian, hoping to provide reassurance. "It will be good for you to start trying soon. It will be so much easier if you just embrace it and stop feeling guilty about being a woman. You may start to like it."

"It's easy for you to say," Kreel said, "You seem to like being a woman."

"Now, Kreel," Tolian said, eager to change the subject, "you're certain Dowbreth doesn't know about you, right?"

"For the fourth time, yes. I'm sure. Gredalon didn't mention it. No one else has gone downstairs, since we came up. Besides, he's upset about the King and Queen's disappearance. Seems that they cannot be found."

"I would think that Dowbreth would be happy about that," said Tolian.

At that moment, the door maiden entered. “Queen of the Astral, High and Holy One, Lord Dowbreth has arrived, at your invitation for dinner.”

Tolian nodded. “Fine, I’ll be ready in one second.”

She turned to Kreel. “Wish me luck.”

“Looking like that, you don’t need luck. I don’t think you’ll even need the lust drug or the incense,” Kreel replied.

“Thank you, now, go hide somewhere. Oh, first go find Gredalon to take your place. Go, hurry.”

Kreel hastened out of the room and Gredalon returned in her place. He bowed.

“You ready, Gredalon?” Tolian asked.

“I serve,” he acknowledged.

“Excellent. Let’s go,” Tolian said.

Dowbreth was waiting for her in the parlor. His scowl was more pronounced than usual. He was wearing his usual costume, his green armor, tentacle-like cape, and belt of heads around his waist. Tolian shuddered when she saw him. She could feel the violence and impatience radiating from him like a palpable force. She steeled herself to keep from expressing her revulsion. Instead, she gave him a slight smile. “Lord Dowbreth,” she said with graciousness, “thank you so much for coming. As I said in my invitation, I have some questions for you, so I do appreciate your attending me.”

His bloodred eyes glared at her with hatred, yet his words were cordial. “‘Tis I that am indebted for the invitation, my Empress, my betrothed. I am your servant.”

“Come,” offered Tolian, “Let’s eat. I hope you don’t mind, but I’ve been taking my meals out on the balcony of my bedroom. It’s comfortable for me, so I thought it would be suitable for us.”

“As you wish. Lead the way.”

Tolian did just that, with Gredalon tagging dutifully behind.

“Oh, can we let Gredalon go and eat his dinner with the others? You can watch me, for a few minutes, right?” she asked.

Dowbreth shrugged.

It was clear to Tolian that Dowbreth had given the matter no more thought. *Perfect*, she thought. “There you go, Gredalon; you are dismissed,” she said.

He bowed and walked in a different direction as Tolian and Dowbreth entered her bedroom and headed toward the balcony.

The servant girls seated them. She had made certain there were plenty of girls available to serve the meal and see to its presentation, yet they were advised to keep their distance when not needed. The magic music box was also placed nearby to provide relaxing (and amorous) dinner music.

Bread, soup, and finally grilled steak and lobster tail were served. Tolian watched to make certain Dowbreth was eating. She had to fight to keep the smug grin of satisfaction off her face.

They said nothing to each other until they partook of their main course. It was Tolian who began. She wanted to keep him off balance, not paying attention to how he felt until it was too late.

"Lord Dowbreth," she said, "I've been thinking. It seems to me, that you don't need to keep me here. You kidnapped me so it's obvious that through me you could take control of Faerie, which you have done. Why can't I just make you my regent here, or whatever, and I'll go on my way, and you can have what you want. It means nothing whatever to me who rules Faerie. I'm sure you'll do a good job. Why not just let me go home?"

Even before she had finished that sentence, she could feel the lust drug beginning to work. She felt the raw masculine energy Dowbreth exuded. She was disgusted with herself as attraction to him replaced the revulsion she normally felt. *This has to work*, she prayed.

"Why not let you go home?" He laughed with obnoxious gusto. "Why should I let you go home? What can you give me that I do not already possess? Besides, I have made another bargain to gain this already."

Another bargain? Tolian thought.

He leaned close to her. The simmering rage in him was sexy. She wanted him badly now. She leaned close to him. His body odor was rank, but she did not care. *I want you, Dowbreth; I want you, so bad.* Be strong, she thought, fighting herself. *Don't be obvious*. Was it affecting him? He didn't seem to be responding to her in the same way Kreel had. Perhaps it needed more time. "What other bargain?" she forced herself to ask, more to keep the pretense of a conversation going than out of curiosity.

"You want to hear about my bargain? You want to hear Dowbreth's story?"

"Yes," she whispered with way too much husky sexuality in her voice.

"But, you don't really want to hear my story do you? You want to make love to me, don't you, Tolian?"

Her burning heart sank, but her desire for him did not. Now her plan was almost a small matter to her. She needed to make love to Dowbreth. What was he saying now?

"Your ill-conceived machinations have failed, Princess," he hissed. "You see, not only did I take an antidote for the lust drug, but, in something of an amusing practical joke, I made certain the entire supply of that antidote, in this tower, was destroyed. I don't think you're going to be feeling good for some time. You should be in great readiness for our wedding day, however."

"Why wait for our wedding day?" Tolian panted. This is how a dog must feel in heat, she thought. It was as if she would burst into flames if her need to copulate were not acted upon. She needed a man. Part of her knew the plan had failed, but that part was not in control. *Rationalize, Tolian, Think. No, I need him. Think.* An idea flashed across her mind. It would satisfy her wanton lust and her desire for freedom. She stood up, leapt over the table, and threw herself at Dowbreth.

The giant caught her by the shoulder with one hand, and threw her down on the hard stone of the balcony. With his other fist, he punched her hard in the face. That sent her sprawling even further. Blood spewed out of her nose.

She was dizzy, in pain, scared for her life, but she still wanted him. She crawled towards him, trying to suppress the bloody fountain shooting from her nostrils. She looked up at Dowbreth.

His hideous grin spread across his entire face. His filed teeth glowed as he smirked in triumph. "Do not try my patience again. Dowbreth will not be trifled with." He untied his magic bag from his head belt and held it up over Tolian's head.

She could barely think, but the bag's magic worked just as well, anyway. That sickening feeling, that trace of malice, and then there was Brythia. Her heart leapt. The druidess lay sleeping. By a fire. Out in the woods somewhere. A sword held next to her head as a reminding menace. A threat that penetrated Tolian's muddied head.

"Brythia," she croaked in misery. "Brythia." Tears now mixed with her blood. Then the image was snatched from her. There was just Dowbreth leering down at her, holding the bag. Her face hurt. He was maliciously toying with her, she was aware of that, but it didn't stop the all-consuming need to have sex with him—or with any man.

He kicked her in the shoulder. She felt a snap as it was dislocated. "Do not forget, wench, that I hold your girlfriend's life in my grasp."

"I hate you," she cried. And she did, but she still needed him.

"I am not so affected by your presence as others in Faerie. I am protected by my own magick."

She shivered in the corner, glaring at him with hate and lust. "What magick do you have? Your bag?" she hissed back at him.

Dowbreth held the bag aloft. He unfastened the string that tied it closed. He reached in with the other hand and began to remove that which was inside.

"Behold," said Dowbreth, "the source of my magick."

For a second, all the pain, the rage, the fear, the lust that she was feeling went instantly numb. There was nothing. No feeling. No emotion stirred. Just a heavy coldness descending on her like a curtain of unfeeling dread.

It was a head. Dowbreth held it by the hair. Tolian recognized it even before it had been removed from the bag. She had seen that person before. It was Hertrid's head, the second person to become possessed by the Demon. The one she had killed. Black orbs for eyes fixed upon her. To her horror, the head began to laugh, with that familiar evil hissing snarl of a laugh. "Greetings, Tolian of Lorm" said the Demon's head.

PART IV

The Moon

Chapter 31

Tolian lay there, racked by desire and pain. Her eyes were wide and transfixed upon the new nightmare that leered down at her. She held her nose in a vain attempt to staunch the bleeding.

"What's wrong, Moon Goddess?" mocked the Demon's head, foul and reeking. "Nothing to say to an old friend?"

"You're dead," she mumbled, almost incoherently. "I killed you."

"A minor setback, nothing more. Now not only do I have you at my mercy, safely removed from interfering in my plans, but I have a whole new world to twist and defile. And now there is no one to stop me in the material world either. You should have done a more thorough job, he-bitch."

"Put that thing away," Tolian shouted at Dowbreth. "Or is it your master, Dowbreth? How did you fall under its thrall?"

Dowbreth grimaced but a second, then his confident sneer returned to his own ghastly features. He set the head on the table on top of the bag, pulled one of the chairs around, and sat down (facing the chair back) right next to Tolian.

"Dowbreth has no master," he said quietly, his rage steeping behind his words. "Dowbreth is Lord of Faerie now. The Demon and I have a mutually beneficial relationship—as equals. But if you are curious about my tale, I shall tell it to you. You should know, really. It will help burn you up with despair as you wallow in your own failure. It is fitting that you should lose your divine powers; you are not worthy of power. You are now the worthless woman you deserve to be."

"Hah-he-he-ha-hah, worthless woman," interjected Hertrid's head from the table. "We are going to have such a fine time with you. Hah-ha."

Dowbreth shrugged off the interruption and continued. "I discovered my true destiny on the battlefield of Lorm. I led the forces of the Sidhe to aid your puny Lormian men against the Demon's invading army. Thanks to our troops, your palace was saved and your enemy defeated. After we cleared the skies of dragons, we brought the fight back to the ground. Soon, we were triumphant."

Not exactly how Tolian remembered it, but she did not bother to contradict him. It was difficult for her to have him sit so close to her. Fear and lust for him battled for control of her emotions.

"On the battlefield, I watched as the Demon almost killed you even then, but for your lucky strike which felled him. But then, when you could have made certain of his death, you fled to the palace to rescue your beloved. I, at that time, assumed the Demon had been killed, and I thought to add his head to my trophy belt, a memento of the conflict. As I took my prize, the eyes opened and the black orbs fixed upon me. I remember that moment well.

I asked the creature plainly, 'What are you looking at, villain? Your day is done, your army here destroyed, soon the rest of your forces elsewhere shall fall as well.'

'Is that what you believe, Lord Dowbreth?' it hissed at me. 'You are wrong. My defeat, my impotence—they are a shroud to hide my true schemes from my enemies. One day all will be mine; mark my words.'

I laughed at the head's face. 'Brave words for a defeated foe,' I said 'I do not wish to hear your false boasts.' And I stuffed the head in this bag and proceeded with cleaning up the last of the Demon's troops while you were letting his other incarnation escape with your girlfriend. I supervised the establishment of the Faerie camp on the perimeter of the palace and secured the arrival of my King and Queen into your world.

Once the fighting was over, I grew restless. I had no wish to associate with our human allies, so I spent most of my time in my tent awaiting orders to move north against the Demon's other incarnations and army. It occurred to me that I might be able to gather useful intelligence from my trophy. I pulled it out of the bag. Again, those black eyes gazed upon me.

'Dowbreth, has found the wisdom to seek my counsel,' the head said. 'Excellent. I will tell you what you want to know, and more.'

'You may as well,' I responded. 'You shall be defeated soon enough. Tell me where is your other army going to strike next? Reveal to me your plans.'

'Indeed, I shall, Dowbreth who could be Lord of Faerie. I shall reveal all of my plans to you. I plan to devour this world, twist it into a nightmare of beautiful chaos churning in the infinite night. And I plan to use you to help me, brave warrior chieftain.'

I grew impatient with the head, for even as I demanded he give me the information I required, he kept telling me that he would, but also that I was a part of his plans. In frustration, I once again stuck the head in the bag and tried to ignore it. But I found I could not leave it long. I was determined to be master of the Demon's head, a foolish notion I now know, but at the time, it did not seem so. I pulled the head back out of the bag. I interrogated it for another two hours without making any progress. I threw the head around the tent, but that simply made it laugh hysterically. I held it still, for I did not want anyone else to know of my prize.

Finally, the Demon began to make sense to me. It was not giving me the military information I wanted, but was instead laying out the framework for a scheme that would work to both of our advantages. He was right—I was meant to be Lord of Faerie—and with my new ally, his vast knowledge, cunning, and, yes, powers, it could be so. He made me understand. I had no love of my King and Queen in any event, and he helped me see there was no true honor serving them. I asked Kreel, who was my best lieutenant, to take charge of the army of the Fay, while I tended some personal business. I told no one where I was going, nor did I bother to ask leave of my Lord and Lady. Who were they to Dowbreth now? Dowbreth would conquer them in due time, the Demon promised, and he has proven to be true, has he not?"

"I am Dowbreth's truest ally," came a cackling outburst from the head.

Dowbreth looked at the head for a moment, and then continued. "I decided to trust him and join him. First, he needed me to obtain something for him. Something rare. I set out in quest of it. It took me several months of journeying across the wastelands of the North and beyond, to a land locked in perpetual winter, somewhere so cold and bitter that it could only be located in your inhospitable world. For three weeks, I saw nothing but the whiteness of snow. I rode across the frozen surface of a sea to find what the Demon wanted. And find it I did.

A witch lived, somehow, in an ice castle set upon an island in the midst of the frozen sea. The crone was half alive, and she had some power to her. The Demon protected me from her spells, however, and it was with great joy that I wrung her neck with my bare hands. It felt good to do so, since it was some time since the battle of Lorm, and I have always relished the giving of death. She struggled futilely in my grasp, but she could not resist the strength of Dowbreth. No one can. I searched the castle until I found that which the Demon had sought. A dark metal stone. Black and cold. It seemed such an insignificant thing for such a harsh quest.

'What is this that you have had me trek across the mortal world for?' I asked the Demon. 'In what way will it serve our ends?'

'This is the key to our victory. It is the Dark Moon Metal.'

I had not heard of it, so I repeated his words, 'Dark Moon Metal?'"

"I see by the look on your face that you have not heard of it either," the faerie said. "You make a poor Moon Goddess indeed. Listen and you will learn much."

Continuing, he said, "The Demon explained it to me: 'This witch hath distilled this stone over three hundred years from the darkling rays of the new moon. Her schemes for it are irrelevant now, but through her craft she has delivered to us the means to destroy my enemy and gain you control of Faerie. We shall use it as a weapon against the druid's champion.'

'A weapon?' I asked, 'Will we use it as a projectile?'

'No, my friend. The Dark Moon Metal will absorb and nullify the external manifestation of her lunar power. We shall fashion it as a piece of jewelry, a gift, and bind her forever.'

And he told me more of his plan, much of which I am sure you have gleaned yourself. I stayed in that ice castle for another month forging the Dark Moon Metal into the bracelet you now wear. The Demon carefully instructed me in the proper techniques of manufacture. It had to be perfectly designed and made. While there, the Demon revealed to me that we already had an ally with whom I could communicate using his head as the magickal means. Other dark secrets he taught me, and we planned more together. He told me of the defeat of the other demonic incarnations and the outcome of the war, but assured me that it was not unexpected. Now, more than ever we needed you out of the way."

Tolian listened from her position on the floor. "What about Kiliordes? Aren't you afraid of him?" she asked at last. "He is the other Champion, isn't he?"

The Demon's head began laughing with malicious humor. "There is no other Champion, my sweet," it hissed. "And we have no fear of the conglomerate being. Don't you get it? Everything was part of my plan. I allowed Kiliordes to kill Perelisk. It bought me the time I needed to remove you from the equation."

Instinctively, Tolian shrunk up against the balcony railing. Terror now flowed wildly within her. She started to shake.

Dowbreth stood up, tossed the chair out of his way, grabbed the head, rather roughly by the hair, and stepped towards her. "You need to be taught a lesson for what you attempted with Kreel yesterday, and what you tried to do to me today, wench." He knelt down next to her. She tried to squirm away from him, but he was too fast and far too strong. He struck her hard again in the face.

She was paralyzed by fear. She was helpless. There was nothing she could do. She closed her eyes and summoned the warrior's mantra to her mind. She struggled to find the courage within herself to endure. *Fear is for my enemy. Fear is defeat and the forerunner of defeat. I will hold no fear.*

"Mark my words."

She could barely croak out a shattered whisper. "I shall kill you both."

The head spat upon her.

"Understand," said the faerie giant, "with the Demon's head I am immune to your transforming energies. You are nothing compared to the Demon." He kicked her hard, several times, following her body across the balcony.

The Demon screamed, "Kick her. Kick her like a dog."

The last blow landed in her abdomen. The pain echoed throughout her body, until her senses were overloaded with it.

Dowbreth grabbed her by the hair and brought her face close to his. "In seven years, we will be married. You will not escape. There is nothing you can do to change this. Remember, the injuries you suffered today were the result of your own treachery."

"Come, Lord Dowbreth," said the head, "Our business here is completed."

Dowbreth stared down at her with utter contempt. "Do not attempt to escape. Do not attempt to render yourself useless to me. Or we will be back. Do you understand me?"

She tried to hold his stare, but she could not. She looked away submissively.

"Capreesh," bellowed Dowbreth. "Get out here."

As the Elven girl hurried out to the balcony and seeing Tolian rushed to her side, Dowbreth said, "Farewell, my betrothed." He turned and left.

The pain was intense. She could tell that some of her injuries were extensive.

More servants came running out. Kreel was among them. She lifted Tolian and carried her with great gentleness to the bed. "Quickly," she snapped, "get bandages, get pain suppressants, get the healing drugs. Hurry, she's already lost a lot of blood."

Tolian could barely maintain consciousness. She looked into Kreel's eyes and saw genuine concern there. "How bad do I look?" she asked weakly.

Kreel smiled reassuringly, "This is not your best look, but you're going to be fine. We'll have you better in no time, okay?"

Tolian nodded slightly, before unconsciousness engulfed her.

In the morning, she awoke to excited voices.

"She's moving," Delotti said.

"She's awake," said Capreesh.

As she opened her eyes, Kreel's smile was the first thing she saw.

"Good morn," the bodyguard said with feigned cheerfulness. "How do you feel?"

"I don't know," Tolian replied. She felt remarkably improved, physically. The wounds to her face felt better, but she felt considerable discomfort in her belly. "Yes, I do feel better. A lot better than I did last night."

"Last night?" Capreesh repeated.

"You've been a sleep for a week, dear," said Kreel. "Most of your wounds have healed perfectly. We still don't understand why, but you have developed some internal condition that isn't responding to our medicine."

She was trying to sound as clinical as possible. She was obviously deeply distraught.

"You're weeping blood from your ...um, female regions. It's not just internal injuries and it's not your period—we have drugs that would have worked if it were because of either of those. It's possible, since you are the Moon Goddess; your exile from the Moon's rays is causing the problem. At this point it doesn't seem directly related to Dowbreth's attack."

Tolian flinched immediately as the memory of her attack poured fully into her consciousness. An abyss of darkness, a scar across her soul. A psychic pain radiated throughout her being. Tears streamed down her cheeks. Kreel leaned over and embraced her. She could not stop crying. She sobbed and sobbed, clutching firmly onto the feminized faerie.

"It's going to be all right, Tolian," she said in reassuring tones. "I won't let this happen ever again. I promise you, he won't touch you again."

"You can't understand," the princess muttered. "It's just not just what he did to me, it's what's going to happen to everything. Dowbreth is in league with the Demon. He has the Demon's head. Oh Gods. What have I done?"

She knew she wasn't making any sense, but her three faerie friends seemed to understand her nonetheless. Crushing guilt. Now confusion. Fear. And still a lingering desire for a man burning in her womanhood.

"Can you eat, Lady?" Delotti asked, ever practical. "You do need nourishment badly,"

"I'm not hungry," she whispered.

Kreel released her, stood back a little from the bed, and regarded her. "Delotti is right, Tolian," she said. "You have to eat. We'll do a little something to get your appetite up, okay?"

Tolian wiped the tears from her eyes with a handkerchief which Capreesh handed her, "I don't know what."

"Leave that to me." Kreel turned to one of the attendants who stood in waiting by the door, "Fetch the pipe weed. The Queen's best."

The girl departed at once. A few moments later, she returned carrying a tray. Upon the tray: an ornate stone pipe, a pouch, and a lit candle. She handed the tray to Kreel, who sat down on the bed, just next to Tolian, and expertly packed the bowl with the pipeweed from the pouch.

It was not the first time Tolian had seen pipeweed. Indeed, she had even partaken of it at the Druid's Temple of the Stars, Hyge Nuyt. Under the influence of the druid's smoke, she had traveled either astrally or in a dream (she wasn't certain of the difference) to the Queen's Garden and first met Ymirisiva.

"Is this anything like the pipeweed the druid's use?" she asked.

Kreel smiled. "It's similar, but, of course, better. You know how to smoke then?"

"Yeah, I did it once before."

"Very well, let's get started."

Kreel used the candle to light the bowl, took a big pull of it, and handed it to Tolian. She took it from the faerie and inhaled the smoke deeply into her lungs, holding it there. It burned and stung. With a cough, she released it.

Immediately a feeling of euphoria stole over her. Everything seemed outlined in the faerie rainbow spectrum. She was enjoying these new sensations when Kreel handed her the pipe once again. She was beginning to relax, to feel more herself, but at the same time less so.

When they finished smoking, Tolian found she was hungry and soon was eating breakfast in bed. She felt insulated from her problems and after breakfast laughed at a joke of Kreel's that wasn't even funny or was it? When she tried to remember the punch line, she realized he had forgotten what it was.

She glanced over and saw Kreel looking distant yet vexed. "What's wrong?" Tolian asked. "Brooding over your sex change?"

"Always, but that wasn't it, right then," she replied. "If the Demon is truly in Faerie, our world is in serious trouble. The effects of your presence here in isolation seem to be minimal, well, except for me of course, but the Demon's evil will quickly spread and corrupt all of Faerie. With Dowbreth in charge, there is nothing we can do about it."

A calm certainty came to Tolian, growing stronger as she spoke. "I don't want you three to leave our suite without me. None of the servants are to leave; send Mesdor and Gredalon for supplies or whatever. But, Kreel, rest assured, someday, somehow I will free Faerie from the Demon's evil and slay Dowbreth in the process."

And she knew that she spoke the truth.

"Well, right now," said Delotti, "you're going to soak in the tub. It should help heal your wound, if that's the right word. Lots of soaking is what you need."

Tolian summoned a tiny smile. "More food first, please?"

Chapter 32

The Pine Barrens. That was what the folk of Lorm called them. A strange name, Brythia thought, as short, scrub oaks were more populous than the pitch pines for which the landscape was named. And it was anything but barren, though the white sandy soil resembled that of a desert; the druidess was always surprised when she traveled through those woods at the incredible variety of exotic wildlife and plant inhabitants they possessed. Even in the depths of winter, signs of life were never far. The air smelled of sand and pine.

Delorick's path had run true, and brought them without incident to the borders of that unique wilderness. The weather had turned milder, and it had obviously not snowed anywhere near as much as it had to the west, for only here or there could Brythia could detect a few patches of snow scattered on the brown leaves that lined the bases of the trees. The oaks climbed to just above eye level, their bare and twisted limbs looking almost alien against the winter's gray sky. There were a great variety of birds that wintered there: crows, grackles, jays, and quail. Mostly she saw them as they took flight, frightened by the approach of her companions (for she could move soundlessly).

How melancholy and grim this wild expanse seemed. Not like the friendly forests of eastern Lorm, or her favorite woods around the Haunted Mountains. Here, even she, a nature priestess, felt unwelcome. Few people made this tract their home, mostly berry farmers, and those who liked to keep their own company. Strange tales of the area abounded. Tales of mysterious homicidal blue mists that rose off the lakes and streams, of folk so twisted by isolation and inbreeding that they no longer looked human, of ghostly apparitions, and, of course, of the winged satyrs, or Pine Devils.

There was a time that the Pine Devils and the druids were friends, but that was a long time ago, and none of the Order had encountered them in several hundred years. They had become almost mythical. Certainly, in Lorm and its neighbor, Therasia, they were more regarded as legend than fact. *That was the problem with Lormians*, she mused, *they never believe anything until they see it.* Tolian had never believed in trolls until one almost killed him (him, at the time) and Delorick, she recalled. Ah, but Brythia was a druidess. She had seen her fair share of preternatural creatures through ritual summoning and spirit visions. She was certain the Pine Devils existed, and on top of that, Findelbres claimed to have known a few of them.

They journeyed two more days. They barely spoke to each other so solemn was the mood of the desert of brush, sand, and trees. The skies held fast to their gray shades, but at least the cloudy canopy held in the heat and kept it from getting too chill. Brythia reflected on her last trip through the area, though still many miles from were they were now. Her friend Kalabred had died there, and Kilfrie's body was destroyed, at the hands of the Demon's werewolves, in that region. Delorick almost died; in fact, if it were not for Tolian's intervention, she, Findelbres, and Myrthis would be dead too. She strained to remember, but she had only seen so much, fighting for her life. Somehow, Tolian, in the pit of despair, found a way to access her divine power. There was a sudden blast of silver radiance, and the werewolves were dead, Tolian standing in their midst. So much power. She simply could not fathom how Dowbreth had managed to take that away from her. Her thoughts always took her back to Tolian. Always.

"We are nearly there," announced Findelbres suddenly. "I think we should probably walk the horses the rest of the way, or leave them here, better yet. The way will be difficult, the trail narrow."

In silence, they slid off their horses.

Findelbres led the way. Brythia crouched and bent to follow him down the tiny path. Green briar and thorn joined the crowded underbrush as they neared a small stream. Black deer moss replaced the white sand underfoot. The druidess looked back to see Delorick and Pagryus struggling to proceed while Kiliordes obviously remembered enough of Kilfrie's training to avoid the snags. Barren and leafless raspberry vines grew in profusion around the stream flowing with rusty brown cedar water through the lonely expanse. The thorns were so heavy the travelers had to crawl on their hands and knees over the tiny brook spanning no more than three feet at the point of their crossing. A short distance past the stream, the path turned and headed towards its source and, luckily, the briar, raspberry, and thorns lessened and the way became clear enough that they could once again rise to their feet.

It was, of course, all the same to Brythia, who could move as nimbly on all fours as she could on two legs through any terrain, but the others were clearly relieved.

The pale circle of the sun, shrouded in gray, hung low in the sky. It would dip below the horizon soon. It occurred to her that she had fallen out of the habit of saluting the sun in its course, as was the druidic custom. Some Priestess of the Sun she had become. She stopped in midpath, stretched her arms out wide, and faced the quickly fading orb.

"Hail unto thee, mighty Sun in thy Setting. Travel with joy to the kingdoms of Night."

The others waited patiently for her to finish and all resumed their quiet trek.

A few minutes later, they had arrived at their destination.

The Blue Hole. A circular pool of water twenty-two yards in diameter. Even in the dimming light, the water practically glowed with an eerie bluish luminance. Brythia knelt down and dipped her fingers into the water. Bitter cold. It was said that the water of the Blue Hole was always cold, even in the heat of summer. Other tales claimed there was no bottom to the pool, that it simply could not be sounded, that it was infinitely deep.

"Well, here we are," said Pagryus matter-of-factly. "Now what?"

"The Blue Hole is useless to us without the Pine Devils to guide us," replied Findelbres. "So, we have no choice, but to wait."

"How can we be positive that one of these Pine Devils, if they exist, will come, and even then, will help us?" Delorick asked.

Brythia watched all of them stare at the unearthly pond. There was something so strange, unnerving about it, yet captivating to the eyes.

"Trust me, friend Delorick," said Findelbres, "they exist.

They are the guardians of the Blue Hole. They are already aware of us. In fact, I can hear one coming now, my skeptical Lormian friend."

A chill shot down Brythia's spine. She strained to listen, but at first could hear nothing. Then the sound became just audible. Like the leathery flapping of bat wings, only of a large bat and another sound, movement in the low pine and oak trees.

"What are these Pine Devils? Where do they come from?" Delorick asked, a quiver in his voice revealing his nervousness.

"The Winged Satyrs, or Pine Devils, are denizens of many worlds," explained Findelbres. "They are powerful beings, who keep largely to themselves. Even the faerie folk know only little of them. In any case, you are about to learn a great deal more than most people know about them."

Brythia could see a shadowy form moving just over the tops of the trees, heading towards them. Lights flashed around the creature. As it neared, the details of its nature became increasingly clear. It was taller than a man, almost eight feet tall, she estimated, but was similarly proportioned. Its torso was the most human part, save that it was lightly covered in hair. Its legs resembled those of a goat, ending in cloven hooves instead of feet, and its head looked like amalgam of a horse and a human's. The creature's eyes glowed bright red. Black wings, like those of a bat, spread over twelve feet. It appeared to travel by flying and lightly stepping on the tops of the trees. Strange flashing lights clustered around it, though she could not determine the source for this phenomenon.

The Pine Devil let out a loud, piercing scream that cut through the gathering dusk like a knife. Brythia's hand instinctively found the hilt of the Moonsword. Findelbres stepped forward in a friendly manner. "Hail friend," he addressed the Pine Devil, even as it alighted on the ground.

How fearsome he is, Brythia thought (for Brythia perceived the creature to be male).

His penetrating red eyes quickly scanned them and then leveled his gaze upon Findelbres. "This place is forbidden to all, mortals and faerie alike." His words were perfectly pronounced, and his voice rough, but human sounding.

"We have an errand of some importance," Findelbres

explained. “We are in pursuit of the Moon Goddess.”

“She is in Faerie,” the Pine Devil replied. “She has taken claim to the throne there, as is her right.”

Brythia stepped forward. “She is a prisoner. Anything she is doing is done under duress. We have to get to Faerie to rescue her. Please, you must help us. She’s my wife.” The desperation in her voice was obvious.

The Pine Devil turned to her. He then did something that took the druidess by surprise. He bowed low before her.

“I am your humble servant, Consort of the Goddess,” he said with sincerity. “But, I cannot do what you ask. I beg your forgiveness.”

Brythia was taken aback by his complete change of attitude, and though she had become used to such demonstrations of abeyance as a Lormian princess, it had not prepared her for a situation like this. Nevertheless, he said he could not help her. Nothing else mattered.

“You have only to take me to Faerie, that’s all I ask of you. Please, I’m begging you.” She fell to her knees. Tears gushed from her eyes. “Please, she needs me. I can feel it. Something terrible has happened to her. I can feel her pain across the worlds. You’ve got to get me to Faerie.”

The Pine Devil gently took her hand and, rising himself, brought her to her feet.

“It will not do to have the Goddess’ wife kneeling or pleading to me,” he said softly. “I am your willing servant, if it is within my power, I shall do anything you ask of me. Through the Blue Hole, I can take you to any world you wish to visit, but I cannot take you to Faerie.”

Shock. Not to Faerie.

“Why not?” the druidess demanded.

“The way to Faerie is closed,” the Pine Devil said with finality. “There is no way in or out.”

Chapter 33

Tolian leaned against the railing of her balcony and watched the wispy clouds pass by. It had hit her hard that morning when Kreel advised her that it was the one-year anniversary of her captivity in the tower. One whole year. Gone. Lost to her forever. A year of restlessness, of loneliness, of yearning and pinning, of drug-induced numbness that soothed her aching soul. A year spent dealing with a wound that would not heal—a wound that bled and ached everyday—that had transformed her womanly center of pleasure into a source of pain. That robbed her even of the desire to pleasure herself. Mercifully, the effects of the lust drug had worn off. The theory that the problem was caused by the lack of moonlight seemed to be true. Everyday she felt physically weaker. Everyday it seemed to ache a little more. She could feel the need for the Moon as a physical requirement, like hunger, or the need to sleep. It seemed logical, as she was, after all, the Moon Goddess. And the Moon ruled the womb.

She was comfortable for the most part. Her meals were always first-rate; she could swim, read, sleep, or watch plays and events in Faerie by means of the magickal tapestries in her rooms. She found that she spent most of her time watching the tapestries and smoking the faerie pipeweed. She never missed watching the aerial combats between two winged faerie warriors. They reminded her of the Jarrels back home, but with an extra dimension. Essentially, they had the same rules, however, with combat concluding when one warrior hit the ground. Over the course of the year, she had picked her favorites, and often bet with Kreel on the outcomes of the matches. Only friendly wagers, of course. Tolian could have anything she wanted, within the guidelines of her imprisonment, so her fellow gambler had nothing to offer her.

She loved watching the Will-o-the-Wisp hunts on the tapestries—of all the activities she watched, these were, by far, her favorite. She had a great fondness for the mysterious light-shrouded, hovering amphibians, ever since her encounter with them in the Great Marshes on her quest for the Moonsword. She always rooted for them to get away from the faerie horsemen in pursuit. She had to respect the determination of the faerie huntsmen and the astounding lengths they would put their steeds to. Tolian was amazed at how much more faerie horses could do in Faerie. They were faster, more agile, and able to bound such significant distances that they gave the impression of flight. The hunts always took place at the twilight of soft summer evenings on the fields and in the forests that surrounded the Queen's garden. The faerie huntsmen went out on horseback armed with their ornate capture jars. They set upon a wild chase of the small luminous beings, springing off their steeds with jars open in often vain attempts to snag the nimble creatures. The huntsman to capture the most in an hour was declared the victor. It was, as Findelbres had once told her, the most beloved sport of the Faerie Realm. The huntsmen were held in the highest honor in Faerie, and deservedly so, Tolian thought. For their acrobatics were extraordinary, and fascinating to watch. But, Tolian always cheered on the Will-o-the-Wisp.

She watched plays (both dramas and comedies), processions, and trained monster battles on the tapestries. She made a few visits to the garden, but was disappointed in that she never again encountered the multicolored fish. She spent many hours playing with Pilt, who was now a female cat.

She did everything she could to help Kreel adapt to her new womanhood. The faerie tried to appear comfortable with the change, but Tolian could tell she still suffered from the initial reluctance to accept the situation that Tolian had endured. Evidently, even faerie boys were taught that girls were lesser creatures, and such conditioning was difficult to overcome. There was guilt for even feeling slight acceptance of the transformation. There was so much more to it than that. The sense of loss, at first was crushing. She remembered that well and from time to time, it still echoed through her.

Tolian realized that Kreel's transformation provided an excellent opportunity to examine her own feelings. There were many things she hadn't thought of before. Was she still the same person she had always been, just in a different body? Was she fundamentally different as a woman than she was as a man? In many ways, she was forced to admit she was a different person now. As a man, she had been more reckless, less concerned with the effects of his decisions, and less caring in general. The male Tolian was selfish and determined to succeed at all costs; the female version had learned compassion and concern for others. And perhaps she felt some resentment that people treated her as a lesser being, less worthy of respect, but that was something within them, not her, she reminded herself.

The physical changes were not an easy adjustment to make either. With her goddess strength, she had not at first experienced the difference in physical prowess her sexual transformation had wrought. Now she had less muscle and the corresponding lack of strength. In place of those muscles, she felt the strangeness of soft curves accompanied by a new vulnerability. *If I were a man, I would not be in this situation.* But, there were positives to being a woman and it was her job to make Kreel see that, too. Feeling beautiful, though taking a little getting used to, was an enjoyable feeling.

Kreel was quieter than Tolian had been about her discomfort, her dysphoria, but it was taking her much longer to come around than the princess had. With Capreesh and Delotti's assistance, she instructed Kreel in dressing in fashion, applying makeup, adjusting her movements to those more graceful and appropriate for a lovely faerie lady. As work on Kreel progressed, Tolian found herself realizing that both sexes had advantages and disadvantages and that everyone had aspects of both genders as parts of their personalities. Once she gained this awareness, she found herself feeling more whole and balanced. She shared her realization with Kreel.

She explained. "You have to embrace the feminine parts of yourself now."

Over the course of that first year, she had begun making that adjustment that Tolian remembered so well. It gave Tolian a project to help keep her mind off her captivity and the hole in her heart that cried for her baby, for her family and friends, but mostly for Brythia.

Mesdor and Gredalon began to feminize slowly during that first year, as well. Subtle changes at first, but they progressed until they were noticeable. Their features softened. Obviously, they had grown breasts, but beyond that, Tolian could not say. They were clearly dismayed and unhappy at the changes they were experiencing, but they made no effort to befriend her and tried to avoid contact with her as much as possible. As per Tolian's order, they were the only two allowed to leave the tower for any business required. Their breaks from Tolian's presence worked to slow their inevitable transformation. Tolian also studied them to see if the Demon's energies showed any signs of affecting them in appearance or attitude. Towards the end of the year, harshness worked its way into their softening facial structures, a hawk-like, predatory aspect in their features.

It was by watching the tapestries, however, that she first saw the corrupting power of the Demon's presence, about two months before her anniversary in Faerie. She was watching the day's aerial combat. Her favorite winged warrior, an undersized but feisty competitor named Chatrul, was seized with a bloodlust and beheaded his opponent in midair. The tapestry zoomed up on his face as he did so. His expression had changed from friendly to almost bestial in its demeanor and structure. The savage grin he wore, not only revealed his fangs, but resembled only too well the expression of wanton malice the Demon had worn. She shuddered involuntarily as the realization hit her that eventually all of Faerie would be corrupted by his evil. Distressed, she commanded the tapestries to show a pleasant natural seashore scene, and left the room.

After that she watched the tapestries less and spent more and more time in the library, or on her balcony staring down on Faerie (from her vantage point there, it still looked peaceful and beautiful) or up at the clouds. The Empress of Clouds, she mused, lighting another bowl full of the faerie pipeweed and reflecting upon her year of impotence of languishing in the limbo of her captivity. A powerless creature, not so different from many other women, perhaps, she thought, trapped by circumstances and physical weakness, devalued as a person, recast as an object—a thing—a tool of power for others to use, as they will.

She released the smoke from her lungs. "Hail unto me, Tolian, Empress of Clouds." Looking out over the clouds, a sense of wry humor passed over her. With a regal tone, she addressed a small puffy white cloud passing by, “Pay abeyance, my wispy subject. Pay homage to your empress.”

To her shock, the cloud paused in its movement, held itself suspended still, and then the front part of the cloud (nearest to Tolian) dipped down. She blinked in astonishment. Unless she was mistaken, the cloud had just bowed to her. She leaned over the railing further and stared.

The cloud held its position.

“Um, rise,” Tolian said.

The cloud slowly raised itself higher in the air.

Kreel, who had been staring off in the other direction, asked, “Who are you talking to?”

Tolian looked at her, “This cloud.”

She again addressed the cloud, “Move to the left.”

The cloud did so.

“Interesting,” observed Kreel.

At that moment Mesdor came out to the balcony, shot Kreel an evil glare and announced to Tolain, “The Moon will be rising soon, you must come inside, Goddess.”

Tolian smiled and whispered, “Thank you,” to the cloud, which bowed once again and then continued in its quiet trek across the Faerie sky.

Chapter 34

Prince Kelvris lifted the small parchment scroll off the trail and smiled. His confederate had come through for him once again. The prince was well pleased with him. He had never much cared for the fellow when he was staunchly in Tolian's fold, but Kelvris had to admit he was proving to be damn useful. He was deserving of the position and rewards Kelvris promised him. Now that Tolian was out of the way, it only remained to capture the druidess for Dowbreth's plan to come to fruition. If, of course, the infant Relinder returned to Lorm, he would be dealt with. There was already enough doubt about the child in the minds of the noble houses, that he shouldn't be an issue. They feared the baby was far too tied to the druids to become King. Once the old man, Tolris, was removed, the combined armies of Lorm and Faerie would wipe the order of the nature priests and priestesses off the face of the planet and make certain that any vague threat Relinder posed to Kelvris's rule was eliminated.

Such thoughts churned almost constantly in the prince's head. He was amazed at how well Dowbreth's elaborate scheme was working. Of course, the failed capture of the nature-witch and her companions the day before was the first thing not to work as planned, but the note he was even then unfolding would reverse that setback.

The penmanship was hurried, obviously written hastily and furtively, but it contained all the information he required. So, he thought, they are headed to the legendary Blue Hole of the Lormian pinelands. Dowbreth had assured him that Brythia would be unable to follow the warlord and the captive princess into Faerie. They would be trapped there like fish in a bowl. His smile broadened. He slipped the note into his belt and remounted his horse.

"Follow me, men," he commanded. "Our prisoners await us."

The last lines of the note secured his confidence. They read: "The witch does not have the power to transform anyone. It takes an elaborate and time-consuming ritual. She was bluffing."

Soon, Kelvris would be King of Lorm.

Chapter 35

Brythia cried the entire way back to their horses. The briars tore at her in the darkness as she crawled over the cold ground. She paid them no attention. Occasionally, behind her, she heard curses from Delorick or Pagyrus, but they barely registered on her consciousness. Her hopes were crushed. There was no way to get to her beloved. Nothing else mattered. Nothing else would ever matter. Despondency and despair began to strangle out all other emotions in her soul. Her love lost forever. *Tolian*, she sobbed, *Tolian*.

Kiliordes was surprised how well he was progressing through the thorny underbrush with no light to guide him. It was clear that this time in the wilds was bringing the skills he had learned as Kilfrie to the forefront of his mind. Mostly, though, he worried about poor Brythia, and, of course, Tolian. What a crushing blow it must have been for the druidess to hear that her wife was beyond her reach. What could he possibly say to console her? She could never be consoled. There would always be a gigantic hole in her heart. The love magick would eventually cause her to waste away and to pine for Tolian throughout all eternity. He felt a pang of sorrow at the knowledge of the sad fate that would befall her. How long would it take before the druidess took her own life? Kiliordes was determined to prevent that from happening at all costs.

He was glad enough when the narrow, overgrown trail from the Blue Hole gave way to the wider, sandy pathway marking their entrance point. He heard the neigh of a horse and rose to his feet. A short distance more and they had arrived at their waiting steeds.

A torch was lit behind him and illuminated the scene. Kiliordes turned to see Delorick carrying the flame. He looked at Brythia. Gods, how miserable she looked. He rushed to her side and put an arm around her. She pressed herself against him and sobbed quietly. He squeezed her shoulders supportively.

"She's lost to me, forever, Kiliordes," she whispered. "She's lost. Oh, my Tolian, lost."

"There, there, dear," he said reassuringly. "Maybe you could join Pagyrus and me with the Solar Pilgrimage Festival. Help you get your mind off things."

He was almost surprised to hear himself suggest it, but it was a good idea. It would be good for her to be around the joyous pilgrims in their near constant merrymaking. She said nothing, but buried her head in his chest and gripped him tightly. She was a strong girl, he realized.

The others stood around forlornly, uncertain what to do next. No one knew what to say. They milled around in sympathy and discomfort.

Findelbres broke the silence.

"Horses approach. We've been followed," he cried out.

Then chaos erupted. Before Kiliordes could figure out what was going on, Delorick had drawn a sword and directed its point against Brythia's back.

"Drop your swords, all of you," commanded Delorick, Captain of the Royal Guard. "In the name of the King of Lorm, I place you under arrest."

Kiliordes turned himself and the druidess in his arms, so that Delorick's blade was directed into his flank, not her back.

"This is preposterous," he exclaimed.

Brythia's tear-streaked face wore a look of shock.

"Delorick," demanded Findelbres, "What manner of joke is this?"

Pagyrus said nothing, but slowly and quickly maneuvered himself closer.

"Hold there, Pilgrim," cautioned the Lormian. "I don't want to hurt you, but I'm not afraid to if I must. None of you are a match for my sword."

"Do not do this, Delorick," warned Findelbres. "This will not turn out well for you."

"Brave words, my friend," retorted Delorick, "but I do not fear you. Let her go, Kiliordes. I have no quarrel with you."

The sound of many hooves pounding over sandy trails, though muffled, was growing louder in Kiliordes' ears. He held Brythia even more tightly.

"Delorick, please," Kiliordes implored him. "Stop this madness and we can still be away."

Brythia suddenly broke free from Kiliordes' grip.

"How dare you," she yelled at Delorick, walking right up to the point of his sword. "You who were Tolian's best friend. She would have done anything for you. You traitorous swine. You can kill me if you like. Why not? You betrayed Tolian and now me. You've already destroyed my reason to live; you might as well end my suffering now. But first, tell me why you ruined our lives and betrayed your rightful liege. What exactly did Kelvris promise you? Tell me that much before you kill me."

"This is all your fault, witch. All of it," answered Delorick. "If you hadn't ensnared Tolian's heart and reduced him to that mockery of existence—as a mere female. How can Lorm have a Woman-King? How can the bravest warriors of the entire world be ruled by a woman's whim? A woman who is merely a puppet of you druids. Do you think we Lormians are that stupid? We are not."

"Oh, no, not stupid. Ignorant, backstabbing, chauvinistic traitors. But not stupid," she snapped.

Kiliordes could not but marvel at her bravery.

"So, that's it?" she asked with venom. "You betrayed your best friend, who has saved your life innumerable times, I might add, your princess, your King, your honor, for nothing but ridiculous rhetoric. You are a fool then. Kelvris's lapdog, no more."

She spat in his face. He scowled and wiped the spit off his cheek.

"Before you die, you will know what I was promised. I was promised a Lorm returned to its glory, and a bride, untarnished—Myrthis."

"But you already won the right as Jarrels' Champion," protested Kiliordes in astonishment.

"I will not be wed into disgrace. My wife will not be the concubine of a woman's child. What sort of marriage would that be? Kelvris has promised me that once Tolian is removed, he will deal with the infant. Myrthis will be all mine. And with the might of Dowbreth's Faerie army at our side, none shall stand against the power of Lorm."

Brythia shook her head in disgust.

Kiliordes could hear the voices of the approaching Lormians. There was little time. No doubt, they could see Delorick's torch and had hastened their approach. He had to do something. He was not going to sit back and watch Brythia be killed. But the raging hate that burned in the warrior's eyes showed there were only seconds left to act. Acting without thinking, Kiliordes leaped forward, shoved Brythia roughly to the ground, and made a desperate grab for Delorick's sword arm. The warrior easily blocked his attack and hit Kiliordes in the head with the bottom of the torch. He pulled his sword back to strike at him. Kiliordes watched helplessly as Delorick's blade came down toward his head.

Pagryus screamed, "No." The pilgrim rushed over and stabbed his long dagger into Delorick's back. The warrior turned and stabbed the pilgrim through the heart. Both collapsed to the ground.

Then the Lormians were upon them.

"No one move," shouted Kelvris as his troop of horsemen surrounded them.

Chapter 36

"Lord Dowbreth is here, My Lady," said Capreesh.

Tolian froze. Every muscle stiffened at once. Her heart skipped a beat, and suddenly she could not catch her breath. A slight spasm ran up her spine and produced a twitch in her face. Hardly noticeable, but nonetheless reflective of the jolt of terror that just passed through her. He had not come to her chambers since that time, two years ago now. A violent shudder took hold of her, like an earthquake after a tremor, or the full force of the blizzard after a flurry. She hated that she was afraid of him, hated it almost as much as anything else. She hated that he held such power over her simply because she was smaller and weaker than him. She hated him for what he had done to her. Another involuntary shudder raged through her. She hated him for another year spent in her prison in the sky.

Kreel looked at her with concern. Her brow knit in an instant fit of worry. Her eyes revealed her fear for Tolian.

The Empress of Faerie was determined to show no fear. She tried to steel her soft, quivering muscles. She would not feel this fear if she were still a man; this was a fear that she could never have fully understood as a man. She set her book down and stood up from her comfortable chair in the library; a twinge of pain issued from her wound, still weeping small amounts of blood and slough. As time passed, felt as is she was growing increasingly weaker. She exhaled to calm herself.

"I'll see him the parlor," Tolian replied to Capreesh finally.

"Very good, Milady," said the faerie girl, with a curtsy. She turned and left the room.

Tolian stood there a few minutes to regain her composure. She battled her fear, which wanted, more than anything, to send her cowering, hiding away somewhere safe. She fought that impulse back, but was surprised at how powerful it had been. She was no coward.

Fear is my enemy, she reminded herself, silently. "Come" she said to Kreel.

She walked slowly out of the library and towards the parlor, with Kreel following just behind her. *Thank the gods for Kreel*, she thought. *I don't think I would have kept my sanity this long if it hadn't been for Kreel.* Her kindred soul, her closest friend in Faerie. It had helped, to have her there, always by her side. Only she could truly relate to Tolian, truly understand what it is to go from being a man, a warrior at that, and become a woman. Helping Kreel adapt, to accept her new body, her new gender, had been a project Tolian had enjoyed. Occasionally Kreel provided insights Tolian had not yet gained.

"Are you going to be okay?" the faerie asked. "I can tell Dowbreth that you're ill, or something."

"I will see him," Tolian replied with a sternness that surprised even her. "I will not live in fear."

"Do you want me to get Mesdor and Gredalon?" Kreel offered.

"Oh, do you think they would help me? I think they've become far too corrupted by the Demon to protect me from Dowbreth," the Princess of Lorm answered. "Besides, they give me the creeps now."

Mesdor and Gredalon had changed significantly in the last year. Their proximity to Tolian had indeed feminized them, but their frequent visits to the lower palace had exposed them to the twisting, foul influence of the Demon's head. They now had fanged beaks on their gnarled faces, fully developed breasts and female characteristics, but ragged, greasy wings sprouted from their shoulders, their legs ended in talons and they smelled like dung on a warm day. Since Kreel kept constantly by Tolian, their presence in her vicinity was kept to a minimum. Still, when Kreel slept, one or the other of them kept a vigil on Tolian. She tried to have as little to do with them as possible, not because of their physical transformation, which Tolian understood they couldn't control, but because of the changes in their attitudes and personalities. They had become downright mean, though Gredalon retained her natural quietness, so she wasn't quite as bad. They constantly snapped and barked at the servant girls, and seemed to take great delight in belittling others. Tolian had to repeatedly command them to leave the servant girls alone. No, Mesdor and Gredalon would be no help to her if Dowbreth did mean to hurt her again. A twinge of trepidation. *Fear is for my enemy. Fear is defeat and the forerunner of defeat. I will hold no fear.*

She hated to think what Faerie must be like now. There were still some bastions of sanity left, she knew. It had only been a week since she was seated, as so often, on her balcony playing with the clouds or staring down at Faerie from her vast height, from where it still looked mostly normal. But she knew it only looked so because she could see no details. Well, there she had been sitting, when she noticed something strange about a passing cloud. It was a huge, big white and fluffy cloud. And upon it were a castle and a small village, situated around a lake, all set right in the middle of the cloud. She could descry a few trees and a sizable field filled with the abundance of the harvest there. The sight held her transfixed. The cloud passed just below her and when some of the inhabitants of the cloud island beheld her they waved. They appeared to be normal faeries in every respect, showing no signs of the Demon's vile corruption. Tolian waved enthusiastically in return, a smile brightened her face for the first time in months. A father, presumably, held up his young daughter so she could see Tolian. Tolian blew her a kiss. The little girl locked her gaze lovingly on Tolian. Pilt wanted badly to fly down to her, but Tolian held the flying cat tightly.

"No, Pilt," she said. "You know I don't want you to leave the tower. It's not safe."

She almost thought of the faerie cat as her child. This realization brought thoughts of her real son, Relinder, to her. She prayed he was safe, but she knew that Myrthis would allow no harm to befall their child. She missed him terribly. She missed Myrthis. She missed everyone. Then thoughts of Brythia came back once again and she cried for the thousandth time.

She had turned to Kreel then.

The faerie saw her tears. "What's wrong?"

"You're my friend, right?" Tolian asked, balancing her glances between Kreel and the cloud village maybe two hundred feet below her as she spoke.

"I would die for you, but you know this. You are my Empress, my Goddess, my best friend, yes."

"Then, why can't you help me escape from here?" Tolian

questioned with an almost begging tone in her voice.

"We've been over this before," replied the faerie. "You have commanded all of Faerie to obey Dowbreth. I will not disobey your command. Now if you order me to help you escape, I will do it immediately, but how far could you get? And could you live with the consequences? We both know what will happen to Brythia the moment you try it. It is up to you. I am your servant."

"I know," said Tolian, wearily.

Still, she could not help but think about jumping down to the passing cloud. She could summon it to come closer, but who knew the havoc it could wreak on the village. At this distance, she might make the lake, or it could prove fatal and end her misery. Kreel would stop her, no doubt, before she could do it. Perhaps, it would be best for both her and Brythia if they were both dead—if their suffering were finally ended. She could not bear the thought of Brythia dead, of those pure blue eyes closed forever. No, she had to endure; she had to find a way. Somehow, deep inside her she held on to the slender and tattered belief that she would once again feel Brythia's embrace.

Those memories faded as she strode into the parlor. She made certain to straighten her back and stand as tall as she could. There was Dowbreth, looking unchanged by the Demon's power, save perhaps for even more cruelty and malice burning in his red eyes. Tolian noticed the bag containing the Demon's head still hung from his belt with the heads of his slain enemies. She held herself still, calm, and composed and met Dowbreth's scornful gaze with defiance. Kreel stood just behind her.

"Lord Dowbreth," she said with formality. "Welcome. What can I do for you?"

He seemed almost surprised, at least a little disconcerted, by her straightforward manner. His gaze strayed to Kreel and a lustful sneer took his lips as recognition dawned on him. Tolian protectively stepped over to obstruct the villain's view of her friend.

"It has been some time, two years, since you accepted my proposal, and I thought I should pay you a visit to remind you why you are here."

"I do not require reminding as to why I am here," Tolian said flatly.

"Do you not even want to see your girlfriend, just to make certain that she is safe?" the warlord asked.

"Yes, I want to see Brythia more than anything, but I will not do so through your master's cursed eyes, not ever again. I cannot trust such visions in any case. I assume by your willingness to show her to me that she is still at your mercy and still alive."

Dowbreth was nearly crestfallen. He seemed to be at something of a loss.

Tolian continued. She felt her voice wanting to waver, but she held it firm and maintained her cold stare into the giant's glaring red eyes. "Well, if that's all, and if you will excuse me, I'm in the middle of a chapter in the book I'm reading and I would like to finish it. You can spare yourself the trip up here next year, if you like. I will not use the Demon's magick for any purpose ever. Trust me, I will feel it in my heart if anything happens to Brythia. And if she dies, I will gnaw off my hand and free myself from your Dark Moon Metal. Nothing will save you or your master's head. Now, may I return to my book or would you care to assault me first?"

Dowbreth said nothing, and he was too mad to pay any more attention to Kreel's obvious feminine charms. Finally he said sourly, "I will be back in five years, then, on our wedding day. Enjoy your book." Without another word, he spun round and exited the parlor, his translucent green cape trailing behind him.

Tolian could scarcely believe it. Relief poured into her muscles and her soul. "Whew," she said.

"I second that," agreed Kreel. "I've never felt anything like that in my entire life. I was so afraid of him, of what he could do to you, or," she paused, "to me."

"Yes, well, this time he didn't," said Tolian. "And, somehow or other, I am going to figure out a way out of here before another five years passes, I can tell you that. A way that doesn't risk Brythia's life."

"I am your servant," replied Kreel, "always. Come on," suggested the Lormian, "let's have some more pipeweed. After that I think we both could use it."

Once again, on the balcony. They sat and smoked bowlful after bowlful of the fine faerie pipeweed. It soothed Tolian's jagged nerves, and helped her forget about her pain for a little while. It helped numb her feelings, so the separation from Brythia did not hurt so terribly. She hoped Brythia wasn't feeling it as badly. She didn't think time was passing as quickly there as it was in Faerie. She kept picturing what the Demon's head had shown her, running the images over and over in her mind. Clearly, little time had transpired from Brythia's perspective. Her garments were the same all three times that she had seen them, it was obvious. She could not be sure if somehow the fiend had merely projected images from that one time into her brain. Still, there seemed to be an element of truth in the images, as if she were seeing something that was happening at the same time. Not unlike the Spirit Vision of the druids. Kreel had verified that such differences in time between the two worlds did occasionally occur. So, perhaps the agony of the separation was not as acute for her wife.

Another puff of smoke and the thought was gone, buried, or forgotten. Tolian began to stare dreamily at the clouds. With her mind, she bid them form the fanciful shapes of giant birds and dragons.

"We can't stay out here too long," Kreel said. "The Moon will be up soon. Mesdor will be coming to make sure that you're not outside when it does."

"Of course she will," responded the princess. "She always does. And you're a good little soldier, so you make sure I'm locked away before she gets here. How long do we have?"

"About a fifteen minutes."

"Let's try something—an experiment," Tolian said

"Sure, what do you want to do?" inquired the faerie.

"I'm going to find out exactly why I'm not supposed to be exposed to the moonlight," stated the princess.

"You know I can't let you do that."

"As of right now, I command you to no longer accept that Dowbreth is in charge, but I want you still to act as though you do in every situation save when I give you specific orders not to," said Tolian.

Kreel was surprised. It was as if a light of understanding slowly descended upon her. "As you command," she eventually responded with a wide smile.

"Good," Tolian said, struggling to gather her thoughts. The pipeweed often clouded her reason; that it did so, was part of the reason she smoked it—to escape. But now, since she had stood up to Dowbreth, a new courage had taken hold of her. She would be cautious, she would be meticulous, but she would figure out a way to escape her prison.

"First, we need to stop smoking this pipeweed for a little while and clear our brains," Tolian offered. She detected a frown darting quickly across Kreel's features.

"Kreel," she addressed her sternly. "We are getting out of here, and I am going to figure a way to do it that will get us out of Faerie, but that will keep Brythia safe from Dowbreth's secret confederate. To do that, I need to think clearly. To think clearly, I need to stop smoking. You may continue if you like."

"What about your pain?" questioned Kreel.

"I am a warrior," replied Tolian. "I shall deal with the pain." A confidence swept over her, such as she had not felt in a long time. There would be a way. First, to experiment and plan.

"Come let us go in before Mesdor comes," Tolian said, while standing up. "We want her to think that we're being good girls."

"Well, aside from plotting to escape, we are being good girls," laughed the faerie as she followed Tolian in. "Oh, and Tolian, I'm still not going to let you hurt yourself. I don't care what you command me to do. You're going to have to come up with a plan that doesn't involve self-sacrifice or self-mutilation."

"I'll see what I can do."

"So," asked Kreel, "do you want to go back to the library?"

"No, we need to stay in the bedroom; we'll send Ristin to get our books and bring them here."

They did just that. When Mesdor came in, they were lying on Tolian's bed, propped up on pillows and next to each other. Mesdor's odor crept into the room with her. Her face twisted in malice. She skulked into the room, walked over to the curtains, and pulled them tightly. Her bird-like gait was disturbing to watch.

"Hello, Mesdor," greeted Tolian. "How are you today?"

"Terrible as always, Goddess," she screeched hoarsely.

Tolian ignored her bad attitude and returned her attention to her book.

"Kreel," growled Mesdor, "the Moon is almost rising, fool girl. Always make certain that these curtains are closed."

"I would have, Harpy," Kreel said, "but there are still two minutes left."

Mesdor scowled and left. Tolian was always grateful when Mesdor left.

"It's time to go outside for a couple of minutes," Tolian announced, once she was satisfied the cruel harpy-faerie had left.

She slid out of bed. "You can stay there if you like."

"But, I..." then Kreel stopped herself. "I'm not following those rules anymore, am I?"

"No, ma'am."

"Then, I guess, I'll stay here. Now, don't be out there too long. You know the warden will be back before long," reminded the faerie.

As soon as she stepped outside, she felt it—a surge of power moving deep inside her. There to the east a half-moon was rising yet dimly in the daytime sky. It was difficult to see, but she focused in on it immediately. It shone to her mind's eye like a lamp of silver brilliance, even in the hazy assure of the summer afternoon sky. A current seemed to bubble up from within her soul. Flashes of ideas, of images. Fast flung impressions, vague like ghosts, but enervating.

She decided to test to see if this feeling of power translated to strength. She grabbed at the Dark Moon Metal bracelet that imprisoned her powers and tried to pull it off. She pulled as hard as she could at it, but to no avail. It wasn't coming off. She stepped over to the heavy, wrought iron table and tried to lift it. It was far beyond her ability to move. No, the Moon power she was feeling did nothing for her strength.

A cloud passed before the moon. "Damn," she mumbled under her breath. She wished the cloud had not interfered with her experiment. She silently projected a command to the cloud and it quickly passed the Moon

She turned her attention to the table again. She calmly

projected the idea that she wanted the table to raise itself a few inches from the floor of the balcony. Instantly, the table did as commanded. She smiled.

It was a start. She went back inside, satisfied with her day's work. I am going to do this, she thought. *Brythia, my love, I will do this.*

Chapter 37

"Your tricks won't work this time, witch," snarled Kelvris. "Drop your swords."

For a moment, she considered giving up and going with Kelvris back to Lorm. She would be imprisoned, or perhaps killed there. What did it matter now? Tolian was beyond her reach anyway. Perhaps death was the only answer. But as she removed the Moonsword from its scabbard to comply with Kelvris's order, she felt something. The sword sent a pulse of energy to her and within it a message. She heard its words inside her head: "Brythia, please don't give up on the Goddess. There is still hope."

That was all. In that instant, her mind was made up. She realized that no matter how dark things looked, she could never abandon her love. Somehow there would be a way to get to her. She could not go with Kelvris; that much was certain.

She let out a bloodcurdling scream and swung the Moonsword at the nearest Lormian warrior. The poor fellow, who she recognized (but couldn't recall his name), did not suspect an attack until too late. He slid dead from his horse, cleaved in two across his abdomen. Brythia felt the Moonsword now coming fully alive in her hands. It led the attack. Before she realized it, she had slain four more Lormians. Pandemonium raged now. Findelbres and Kiliordes joined in the fight.

Kelvris shouted, "Kill them all."

The odds were against them. The soldiers on horseback outnumbered them. Despite the power of the Moonsword in Brythia's hands, she knew if she could not determine a way to escape, the three of them did not have long to live. Findelbres was fighting valiantly, but Kiliordes was ill prepared to be involved in such a battle with the most skilled warriors in the world. He was already bleeding from a dozen wounds and probably would not be able to hold on much longer. Brythia fought her way to his side and deflected most of the sword thrusts directed at him. Findelbres fell in stride and together, back-to-back, they fought for their lives. Only a moment later Kiliordes fell. Brythia could not tell if he was alive or dead. She fought all the harder.

Brythia was now fighting off Kelvris's attack. She had never regarded him as much of a warrior before, but she had to admit he was capable of fighting with much skill and ferocity. He was able to parry every strike of the Moonsword. He was of the House of Hemris, she remembered, and the fighting blood was strong in him. With a move that was too fast for her to block with the lunar blade, Kelvris struck her in the hand. She cried out as the Moonsword fell from her grip.

Kelvris brought his sword to her throat, "This time witch, there will be no escape." Then came the eerie screams from the surrounding pines. The sandy woods suddenly glowed with mysterious bright lights moving above the tree line, and then went dark again. The rushing of large leathery wings filled the air. Kelvris looked straight up and a look of horror took hold of him. An instant later, he was snatched into the air and vanished into the darkness with a scream of raw terror.

All around Brythia, Lormians cried out in fear and pain as some unspeakable terror descended from the black sky and fell upon them. She knew what was happening, of course, and even she felt some measure of fear. It was the Pine Devils, though she could not be sure if they were coming to her rescue or were merely destroying trespassers. She bent down to pick up the Moonsword, and as she rose again, Kelvris's bloody and mangled body fell dead before her.

Screams rang out in the darkness. Torches fell and extinguished themselves, rendering the chaos less and less visible. The occasional inhuman shrieks of the Winged Satyrs added to the terror of the scene. She crouched down and put her arms over her head. Findelbres crouched over her, covering and protecting her. Around them the wild, frantic neighing of horses and shouts of the Lormian soldiers became more and more infrequent, until all was quiet. It was then that Findelbres stood, backing off from her. "It's all right," he said. "We're safe."

Brythia uncurled herself and stood slowly. Standing around her, she could just make out their inhuman shapes among the carnage of slaughtered men and horses. Their own steeds were unharmed, she noticed, though how on earth the Pine Devils could tell whose horses were whose was beyond her. She could tell there were a lot of them out there, but it was impossible to get a firm count. Some were no more than movements in the shadows.

The nearest stepped even closer and bowed. "Greetings again, Moon Goddess' wife," he said.

"Greetings," Brythia answered solemnly (for she was sorry about the fate of the Lormians). "Thank you for saving our lives."

"As I said before, it is our wish to help you if it is within our power. We saw an opportunity to assist you here. Come, I shall lead you to a suitable campsite for the evening."

"Wait," said Findelbres, "Kiliordes is still alive. Actually, most of his wounds appear to be superficial."

"Thank the stars," exclaimed Brythia. "Excuse me for a moment," she said to the Pine Devil.

Findelbres was exactly right, she quickly observed. Kiliordes would be fine. She addressed the Pine Devil who was waiting patiently, "Very well, let us help our friend, and we'll follow you."

"We shall tend your companion," said the Pine Devil. "Mount your horses and follow me."

Brythia looked at Findelbres, who shrugged with almost nihilistic indecisiveness. Clearly, he was as sorrowful as she. Their companions, the traitor Delorick and the noble Pagyrus slain, as well as far too many brave Lormian warriors. Tragic. Death had always weighed heavy on Findelbres. She could not but help but wonder if that were because as an immortal the loss seemed imbued with extra meaning and mystery. Did all faeries regard death so? Brythia did indeed feel a sense of loss, of sorrow, but as a druid, she understood the necessity of death. She felt no pain over Delorick's death, however. In fact, she spit upon his corpse as she passed it.

How strange everything was as they rode. The Moon was near full and as it rose it shown down its silver light over the Pine Barrens of Lorm. It cast its eerie glow on the scene, washing the pine needles in its uncanny light. There was no need for torches or lanterns. She could see perfectly well. She and

Findelbres rode, leading the other two horses. One of the Pine Devils easily flew, carrying Kiliordes just above the trail, and before them their guide bounded over the trail, springing lightly. It seemed so unreal.

The Pine Devils did not lead them far. Soon the sandy trail emptied into a circular area of sand and pine needles. Kiliordes was laid gently on the ground.

"Camp here this evening," the Pine Devil instructed them. "You are tired. You need your rest. We shall make you a fire and guard you as you sleep. May the Goddess' light bring peace to your worried minds."

It was amazing to Brythia how quickly the Pine Devils had a fine campfire burning. The warmth called to the part of her that was exhausted. She rolled her sleeping blanket out in a daze. Neither she nor Findelbres spoke to each other. Both watched to make sure the Pine Devils were taking proper care of their wounded friend, and then laid themselves down. She couldn't take her eyes off the Winged Satyr that casually removed Kiliordes' sleep gear from his horse and spread it out over the ground. How strange it seemed, watching this fantastic being do something she had done a thousand times before, but that should be so alien to its own routine. It did it expertly. Did it even realize that it had indeed used Kiliordes' own sleeping bag, or was it a coincidence? She had not finished pondering that question before she dozed off.

At some point, she started to dream. It had been several days since the last time she had dreamt. They were already on the Moon, or, at least, that was her immediate impression. The White Hart trotted down a road paved with silver. Along the sides of the road were lifeless and barren trees, thin, sickly, and twisted, huddled together tightly, but still seeming sparse. A light coating of snow skirted the bases of the strange trees. They were not a species of tree she was familiar with. Overhead the stars twinkled with perfect clarity. She was dazzled. As she leaned up to catch the celestial spectacle, she saw it. A sinking feeling came into her as she realized what it was. Directly above her, high in the starry heavens was a sphere, blue and cloudy, with patches of green and brown visible. A jewel in the fabric of space.

The White Hart must have sensed her discomfort at the sight, for it said, "Yes, Princess, it is your world. Few mortals have ever beheld it so. Fear not, you are safe. Naught shall befall you here. We shall be at the Goddess' Tower in moments. See it there, yonder?"

Brythia lowered her head and looked straight ahead in the direction the road led. A white tower stood before them. Tall, but no more so than the towers of the palace of Lorm. But this tower looked nothing like Lormian architecture. It seemed to be hewn out of a single piece of stone, for no seams were visible.

Though Brythia could not perceive how it would be so, the White Hart arrived at the foot of the tower so quickly it seemed as if it had happened in an instant. The animal halted just before the door. "Go in, princess. She is waiting for you," said the White Hart.

Brythia climbed off the beast's back and regarded the open doorway for a moment. "Thank you," she said softly in gratitude.

The White Hart bowed and smiled.

It was hard for her dreaming mind to focus on the details of the interior of the tower. A winding staircase called to her. Purple tapestries and silver candlesticks sporting flickering flames. It was difficult for her to concentrate on her surroundings. Nonetheless, a sense of familiarity permeated the place as she ascended the stairs.

A great throne room was located at the top of the stairs. Beyond anything in her experience. Silver and crystal everywhere. No mortal monarch could boast of such riches. Then her eyes fixed upon the figure on the throne. She ran towards her. The throne itself was cast in pure silver and was decorated with crescents. Upon it was seated a woman dressed in a white shimmering gown. Her hair was chestnut. It was Tolian. Brythia's heart leapt for joy, though even then, a little voice reminded her that it was just a dream. As she neared the figure that seemed to be Tolian, she noticed something strange. She was bound and secured to the throne by the coils of a black chain wrapped around her from her neck to her feet. A powerful radiance within her seemed held in check by the chain. How Brythia understood this, she was did not know. The druidess gasped to see her love so, and she fought hard to remember that it was just a dream. No, it was different from a dream.

"Greetings Brythia," said the woman who looked like Tolian. "Welcome to the Moon. I regret that I cannot greet you properly, my love."

So like Tolian, and yet so different. So lofty, so distant, so familiar.

"Tolian?" Brythia asked cautiously.

The woman smiled. "Yes, my love, it is I. It grieves me that you should see me in such a state. But I am Tolian and I am the Moon Goddess."

Brythia jumped up to the dais. "Here, my darling, let me get you out of those."

"You will not be able to release me," replied the Moon Goddess, "at least not here, for I am a reflection, of sorts. I am bound by the Dark Moon Metal that my earthly incarnation wears."

Dark Moon Metal? But that question did not linger long in her mind, before a more urgent one pushed it aside.

"So, you are not Tolian. Not really my Tolian, then?"

"I am and I am not. There is no difference between us, save that I exist outside time and 'your Tolian' is within its sway."

"I'm sorry," said Brythia, "I don't understand. How can that be?"

"I was born into your world as the infant Tolian, but I had always existed. I entered your world, yet part of me, the divine essence, if you will, is always present here. Tolian is the reality; I am the ideal. We are the same. I have experienced everything your wife has and will experience. There is no difference. I know you well, and I love you, my druidess."

The Moon Goddess was crying. Brythia could take it no longer. She wrapped her arms around the captive Moon Goddess and embraced her. She covered her mouth in soft, passionate kisses. Brythia lost herself in the kissing. A dream and not a dream. Tolian and not Tolian. The Moon Goddess seemed to relish it as much as she did, but disengaged herself from Brythia with a turn of her head (the only thing she could move).

"We do not have time for this now," she said.

"I thought you said we were outside time?" Brythia asked.

"You and Tolian have brought time here."

"But, I don't understand."

"You will eventually. But Tolian needs your help now."

Brythia's head was spinning. She was finally reunited with Tolian, except it wasn't really Tolian, but it was. Her mind struggled with concepts she could not grasp.

"You worry about that which you cannot possibly understand yet," the goddess admonished her. "Your time here is short. You will awake soon. You must listen to me."

"Yes, my love, my goddess," she replied obediently. "But, there is no way into Faerie. We have tried everything."

"There is another way. It has never been done before," said the lunar deity, "but your love shall guide you, as shall the Moonsword. It is the only chance we have."

"What way is this?" Brythia asked, bewildered and becoming a little panicked. "I do not know what you are talking about."

"Calm yourself, my love," said the Moon Goddess. "The answer will come to you presently. We must quickly address two more issues. Everything relies on you, sweet druidess. Everything. The Demon moves in both Faerie and in the mortal world. In one, his evil has polluted and perverted much of the realm. Beware, Faerie is now a place of evil nightmares come to life. In your world, I can feel his evil, but it is shrouded. He is biding his time, waiting for the right moment. Be wary."

"I shall," Brythia said, her hand resting on the Goddess' knee.

"If the Dark Moon Metal is the lock, then the Moonsword is the key," stated the Moon Goddess, cryptically.

Suddenly, everything was becoming even more vague. Brythia was almost unable to hold her vision still. The Goddess was speaking.

"If you free her, come back here. And, Brythia, you must then stay here until everything is settled. The love magick has made you my greatest weakness. Be strong, my love. Your presence here has brought new joy and hope to my heart."

Brythia planted a kiss on her lips, and then she was awake.

High above, seagulls called out. At first, it sounded as though they were shouting, "Get up, get up, get up."

There was not a moment to lose. She knew exactly what she had to do.

Chapter 38

Tolian was ready. For six days, she had prepared and planned. At first, she had no idea what to expect. She had experimented, slipping out furtively for a few moments here and there when neither Mesdor nor Gredalon were about. For those few moments, she felt powerful. Not physically strong, but inwardly powerful and capable of remarkable acts. She could not lift the table on the balcony, but she could make it levitate with her mind. Only a few feet, but that was only the second time she went out into the moonlight. Now, she could do much more than that. Unfortunately, the power did not last long once she went back inside. She had only a few moments to show Kreel the smallest demonstrations of her powers, before they left her.She had managed to break herself of the habit of smoking the faerie pipeweed, though it had not been easy. She wasn't hiding from her feelings anymore. The pain from her wound was much more noticeable, of course, especially when she stood for more than a few minutes. It wasn't unbearable—she could endure it. She also watched the tapestries again, both to face her guilt head on and to prepare herself for what she would find once she had escaped the tower. It was hard to watch the scenes of twisted horror the tapestries revealed. Faerie had been reformed in the chaotic and nightmarish image of the Demon's horrific imagination. Lush forest had become places of gray and gnarled vegetation filled with hideous monsters, creatures of unspeakable horror. Buildings even, took on more forbidding appearances. One castle, which had previously appeared a bustling, inviting household, was now a lonely place of malefic aspect. Drabness had infiltrated every stone and the once welcoming gateway now resembled a gaping, fanged mouth. Everything in Faerie had changed to some degree. The people had undergone the most drastic transformation. Most of formerly proud faeries were now bent and corrupted. They snarled and shuffled about She cried as she watched, for she knew all of it was her fault. She should have tried to escape sooner; she should have risked sacrificing

Brythia and herself. As hard as she was on herself, she knew that the love magick that bound them would have prevented her from doing anything that could result in Brythia's death. What she saw in the tapestries made her entertain thoughts of remaining safe in the tower. She quickly shrugged off such thoughts. That was fear talking. It was apparent that the Demon would soon no longer require her presence to hold full sway over Faerie. It was nearly all his already. No doubt he would have her killed, probably Dowbreth, too, for what use were they, once the Kingdom of the Fay was the Demon's own country? Every day she felt with greater certainty that day was quickly approaching.

Now was the time. She sneaked out to the balcony for what she knew would be the last time. The Full Moon was already in the sky. She felt its energy pouring into her. She opened herself to its silver rays, visualizing herself absorbing all the lunar power she could. She made certain to hold on to as much as possible. She did nothing that would cause her to discharge the energy. She could not test the power for she needed every ounce of it for her plan.

She breathed in deeply. The cool air was invigorating. She had considered trying to fly down from there. Several things dissuaded her from this plan. She would be unable to take Kreel, and there was no way she was going to leave her best friend at the mercy of Dowbreth. Never. In addition, such a dramatic escape would attract much more attention than she would like. On top of that, she had no way to know for sure she could, in fact, manage the vast distance safely. No, her plan was the best way, and she was ready. Now to put it to the test.

She went back inside and secured the door and curtains behind her. Kreel, dressed in a pink nightgown, was pacing nervously across the bedroom, holding her sword. It was clear that she was afraid. Tolian couldn't blame her. There was every chance that her plan would not work, that they would be caught and killed or, more likely, worse. She was frightened too, but for the first time since she found herself simply a woman without supernatural powers, she did not let her fear control her. She had found a place beyond fear. So what if she was essentially a mortal woman, not a powerful male warrior, or a goddess? Many women overcame nearly impossible obstacles. How else could they live their lives with the physical weaknesses of their gender, save by another strength, the strength of character? True strength in the face of real fear, pervasive fear men could not even imagine. That was the power of woman. It was extraordinary. To try anyway, despite everything.

"You look so frightened," she said to her faerie friend. "Repeat this quietly in your mind, it helps: I will hold no fear. Fear is defeat and the forerunner of defeat. Fear is for my enemy."

"I'll try that," Kreel said with an anxious chuckle.

"Good, let's get going. Mesdor will be back from the bathroom any minute," Tolian said. She smiled encouragingly.

Kreel smiled darkly. "You're certain this will work?" the faerie asked.

"Oh no, I'm not guaranteeing anything," Tolian said, leading her to the door.

They had about two more minutes before Delotti returned with their mulled wine and Mesdor trotted back in about a minute after that. Their ritual had not changed in more than a month. The obligatory warm wine to send her off to a dreamless slumber and Mesdor's eleven o'clock urination. Small occurrences, seemingly of no consequence, but they were chinks in Dowbreth's armor. For only for those few moments, when everyone thought that Tolian was finishing off her evening with some diversion with Kreel and preparing for bed, they were alone. Those were the only times, for Mesdor and Gredalon trusted Kreel less and less it seemed as they looked on her with resentment, no doubt for her beauty and her friendship with Tolian. This was the time. Gredalon was asleep, having spent most of the day keeping an eye on her, covering her with suspicious looks from her ruined visage. Now.

Tolian opened the door and walked as nonchalantly as she could down the corridor. Kreel followed, appearing far too agitated. No one would think twice to see them. They were doing nothing wrong. Uiyrlpi, one of the kitchen staff entered the hallway from the parlor. She curtsied and Tolian smiled and wished her a good night.

It took only a few moments to walk the distance from her room to the door to the garden. The closer they got to the door, the more nervous she became. Not panicked. No, she would not allow herself to get overwrought. She had resolve if not courage, and that would have to do. She took Kreel's hand in hers to lend her strength. She could hear the faerie whispering under her breath, "Fear is defeat and the forerunner of defeat. I will hold no fear."

Tolian did not need the mantra, for she had become it. Kreel squeezed her hand.

"This is the best way, right?" the faerie asked.

"Yes, no one will be out there at this time of night; it's the perfect place to sneak out," Tolian responded.

"Tolian, you've seen it. Faerie has gone mad. It's a nightmare out there," Kreel fretted. "I doubt the garden's going to be any better."

"Yeah, give me your sword." She took the faerie blade. She closed her fingers around the hilt. It felt good to grip a sword again. She had not touched a weapon in over two years. She looked down at her wrist and the black bracelet that adorned it. Kreel must have caught her look.

"Now, remember, you promised that you would only do that in case of extreme emergency. You promised," the faerie reminded her.

"I know," mumbled Tolian. She regarded the door for a moment. As she did so, something amusing flashed across her mind. She looked down at herself, her own white silky nightie shimmering in the lamplight of the hallway, Kreel looking positively cute in her own feminine sleepwear.

"What do you think," asked Tolian, "our old selves would think if they could see us now?"

"Hmmm," pondered the Elven maiden, "I don't think they would believe it was us."

"Probably not," Tolian agreed.

The door. A magick door. Of course, it didn't look like a magick door; it looked like a regular door of heavy wood and strong iron hinges. She held her hand up to the door and allowed her power to flow toward it. She imagined herself and Kreel walking through the door constructed, not of wood, but of the astral. The astral was under her sway and subject to her whim. She pushed her hand tentatively and gently through the door. Her hand seemed to end right at the wrist and that concerned her, though only slightly. She pulled her hand back and examined it Good. There's no damage, Tolian thought, determined to continue. My power is working.

"Okay," she said, walking through the door pulling Kreel behind her. "Let's go."

Chapter 39

Brythia jumped out of her sleeping gear. She was surprised to see Kiliordes sitting next to the fire while Findelbres cooked something on a skillet over the flames. The scent of sausages wafted to her nose. Her mouth started to water immediately. She looked around, but could see no sign of the Pine Devils.

"Good morning," she said. "How are you two? Kiliordes, are you feeling all right?"

"Aye," he said absently, "well enough I suppose. I think I'm still in shock. A lot happened last night."

"Good morn," said Findelbres. His eyes narrowed. "Wait, what's this, there's a gleam in your face, I haven't seen for some time. To what do we owe the pleasure of your smile? Is it the sausages? Have you come to accept the philosophy that life is only as bad as the sausages, or lack thereof?"

She laughed. It surprised her. But, there was no denying her mood had improved.

"Well, the sausages do smell wonderful, Findelbres, I'll give you that, but that's not the reason I'm in a good mood. I know how to get to Faerie." She watched the looks of surprise flash across their faces.

"How?" Findelbres asked.

"Simple," said the druidess, "the flying smoke."

"The flying smoke? Are you sure you—"

"That's madness," Kiliordes said. "It's suicide, or worse. You know this."

"I can do it," Brythia declared.

"I shall accompany you," Findelbres said.

"I'm afraid I won't allow it. It won't be safe for you. I'll have the pull of the love magick to guide me, and the Moonsword's power, but you—you would be lost forever."

"But—"

"No, Findelbres. That's final."

Kiliordes shook his head vigorously. "What makes you think that will be enough to get you there safely? People have tried in the past, to use divining rods and magickal items to guide them to other worlds using the flying smoke. No one has done it. What makes you so sure of yourself?"

"There is no other way, Kiliordes," she said steadfastly. "It is as simple as that. I have to make it."

Kiliordes sighed. He did not share her confidence. "I have to," she whispered, entreating him to trust her with her brilliant blue eyes. "I shall leave at once."

"Of course, you will," he replied at last with a gentle smile.

"What of you, Kiliordes?" Brythia asked. "What would you do now? Will you go back to Lorm? With Kelvris dead, there will be no one there to levy charges against you. You should be fine."

Kiliordes shook his head wistfully. "No, I intend to honor my promise to Pagyrus. I will go and join the Solar Pilgrimage Festival in Southern Surtiz. I will even become their leader if that is their wish. It is what Paygyrs wanted badly. He gave his life for me. I owe him my word."

"Well," suggested Findelbres, "let us eat one final breakfast together, before we take our separate paths. The sausages are done."

" I can't," she said. "I should probably have fasted more than I have, but there is no more time."

A Pine Devil dropped down from the sky and landed right before them.

"I have come to see if you require anything more of us," said the Winged Satyr. "If not, then we would say our farewells."

"Actually," said Brythia, "I have a favor to ask, first. I am going to try to use the Druidic Flying Smoke to get to Faerie. Can you take me somewhere secluded? I cannot be disturbed in the attempt."

"As you wish," replied the Pine Devil. "I can take you now, if you like."

"What about the horses?" she suddenly remembered. Findelbres answered, "You don't need to worry about the horses. Whisper will lead them back to the palace. They'll be fine."

"I'll take Pagyrus' horse and personal effects back to the Solar Pilgrimage Festival, so that will leave your horses and Delorick's to make the trek back to the palace," said Kiliordes.

"That will work," said Brythia.

She grabbed Kiliordes and embraced him (a little before the surprised fellow was expecting any such thing).

"You've proven yourself to be such a good friend to us," the druidess gushed. "I'm sorry for not seeing you for yourself when I looked at you before. I'm sorry for the way Tolian and I avoided you at the palace. Travel safely and reach your goal. The blessings of the Sun and Moon upon you. Thank you for everything."

And she kissed him on the cheek.

He was clearly embarrassed but he squeezed her in return and released her. He looked her square in the eye.

"Thank you, princess," he said. "You have taught me quite a bit first as Kilfire and, now, as Kiliordes. Go and find Tolian and bring her home. I'll bring the pilgrimage to Lorm and we'll celebrate our reunion."

"And you," said Findelbres, embracing Brythia. "You fly straight and true to her. My mind weighs heavily on your errand, my friend; it churns with doubts, but my heart knows that you can succeed. I can usually tell, when I'm seeing someone for the last time. We will meet again."

He kissed her forehead. She hugged him and then stepped back. They were both smiling at her.

"Now, your Pine Devil awaits," observed the former royal adviser.

A moment later, she was flying over the Pine Barrens, just above the trees. The Pine Devil grasped her securely by her shoulders and carried her forthwith the easy beating of his mighty wings. The cool air rushing in her face. The chill, the invigoration, the sense of hope. She remembered the last time she had flown on a cold winter's morning, on the back of a dragon over Keythion. As the Demon's prisoner. The image that had come to her in the library cavern flashed across her brain once again. Circling the city. The Demon split in two people—one with her, and one flying across the city with someone else. With the dark, bearded man. Yes, there was something familiar about the man. Where had she seen him? He was even more familiar now than he had been when this memory came to her at Hyge Bryth. Then, she knew. There was no doubt. The fellow looked remarkably like Pagyrus. It was as though a cloud had been removed from her mind. Pagyrus was the Demon's helper. Pagyrus. But he was dead now, too. Some questions still nagged her. What was his motivation in trying to get Kiliordes to join the Solar Pilgrimage Festival? What benefit could that provide to the Demon? She could think of nothing to be gained. Well, whatever his plan, it no longer mattered, did it? He was dead. She pondered these questions while staring below at the desolate, yet beautiful, tract of sandy pine and oak woods cut by trails and now and again a slender winding river of brown cedar water.

Finally, the Pine Devil brought her lightly to the ground. She was relieved to feel the hard earth under her feet once again. The Winged Satyr released his grip on her shoulders and rose once again into the air.

"Farewell, Moon Goddess' wife," he called down to her and then he was gone.

She was alone. The spot where the Pine Devil set her was a small grassy clearing set amidst fire-blackened pines. The grass was brown and dormant for the winter, but still soft enough to provide a comfortable cushion against the winter-hard earth. The burnt pines were coming back to life; the fire that wrought its havoc upon them had raged through there three or four years ago. She smiled at the forest's resiliency. It was hard to keep the forces of life down for long. She took that as a good omen. She wasted no time. She dropped into a cross-legged sitting position on the dry grass and fished out the pouch with the flying smoke and the ritual pipe from her bag. She tried to quiet her mind as she dipped the pipe into the pouch and filled its bowl with the flying smoke mixture. Her nervousness and excitement made this difficult, of course. Quiet refused to enter her consciousness. She chuckled morbidly. She had not fasted the required time, she could not still her mind, she had no image of the place she wished to go, and she was attempting to travel to a place no one had ever succeeded in getting to. None of that mattered.

Brythia pulled the Moonsword from her scabbard and laid it across her legs. Then she sparked a fire with her flint and set the flying smoke to blaze. She brought the pipe to her lips and drew the magickal fumes into her lungs.

The smoke tasted even worse than it tasted the last time.

She put one hand on the hilt of the Moonsword as she smoked. She had no location to visualize so she drew a vision of Tolian in her mind's eye and held it there. It was easy enough to picture her. The depth of her deep brown eyes, flecked with purple. The sun brought out the copper, red, and gold highlights in her chestnut hair. Brythia knew every curve of her body. As she built this image, her thoughts became calmer, clearer. The ever-present longing for Tolian surged within Brythia as she focused on her.

She felt the effects of the mixture with her second puff. The ground around her quivered slightly as a sudden, extreme tiredness took hold of her being. Another puff and everything started to spin and the thunderous rushing sound raged in her ears. She took one more puff and, as carefully as she could, stuffed the pipe and pouch back in her bag and made certain her hold on the Moonsword.

All at once, the universe bent, swayed violently, and then twisted. Trees, grass, and sky swirled together and flowed by her as a river. The sensation of flying passed through her in waves. She kept her thoughts focused on Tolian. "Tolian," she screamed psychically. "Tolian. Tolian. Tolian. Tolian. Tolian. Tolian. Tolian." She repeated her name as a mantra.

Once again, she became aware of the presence of the spirit of the flying smoke. She could not even tell how she sensed it, or what faculty she employed to do so. A vague presence. Angry and curious. Brythia heard its question clearly.

"Why have you come again to my realm? You seek to travel where none may travel. Your soul is forfeit."

The impressions the druidess was receiving became more intensely realized. The spirit radiated an impossible vastness. Its outrage was palpable. It had placed itself directly in her path. She had stopped moving. Stalled in the realm of the flying smoke. Not good. She tightened her grip on the Moonsword and projected a message of her own. "Get the hell out of my way. I'm going to Faerie and you are not going to stop me."

Chapter 40

Moonlight flooded the garden. Tolian felt the lunar energy flowing into her. She pulled Kreel along behind her by the hand. The place was overgrown with unruly plants of the least desirable kind. The Demon's power had twisted the park from one of singular beauty into a neglected collection of ugly and malefic weeds. Everything looked foul. The flowerbed of sunflowers by the door had turned black. The flowers themselves possessed fanged mouths and were moving, stretching over the nearby pavement searching for food. Tolian led Kreel well around that. What other horrors would be lurking there, Tolian wondered. She gripped Kreel's sword tightly in her other hand. At least the place was deserted.

"Which way?" Tolian asked her faerie friend.

"Uh, I think the quickest way is straight ahead and out the back gate. That should get us close to the nearest portal back to your world, if you can open it. If we're not disturbed, we can make it in about three hours, but about half of that time will be outside the garden." Kreel paused and gulped. "I'm not looking forward to that."

"Oh, you won't get that far," said a voice from above them. It was Mesdor flying overhead. Before Tolian was aware of what was happening, the harpy-like faerie came crashing down upon them and sent Kreel sprawling across the pavement with the force of her talon-like feet. The faerie cried out briefly then fell silent and still. Mesdor landed a few feet from Tolian and regarded the escaped prisoner with deep contempt.

"You are going to pay for that," Tolian said bravely.

"Oh, not as much as you will," growled Mesdor, "once Dowbreth gets here. Gredalon is fetching him right now. Your betrothed will be angry with you. Very angry. Now come along, like a good little Moon Goddess, and take your punishment."

"I actually liked you, at first," Tolian commented, looking now with horror at the deformed and birdlike creature before her.

She looked up at the Moon and then at the sword in her

hand.

"This is for Kreel," she said quietly.

She let go of the sword. It hung in the air for a moment and then with lightning speed it closed the distance between them and plunged directly into the harpy's chest.

"Surprise," she said as Mesdor fell dead. She rushed over to Kreel. She had a nasty gash in her shoulder, and she was unconscious. Tolian tried to pick her up. She just managed to lift her. She could not travel far or fast with the faerie, however. An idea came to her. She released the girl, and with a slight effort of her mind, levitated her in the air before her. She was able to travel much quicker with Kreel hovering just in front of her as she walked. Unfortunately, she did not know the way. Kreel had said that they needed to go straight back. Tolian could do that much, being careful to stay safely in the middle of the pavement, away from any plants, all of which sensed their presence and reached out for them. Tolian hoped Kreel would regain consciousness before they left the garden. Suddenly, she froze as she heard a voice calling from the base of the tower. It was Dowbreth.

"My betrothed has broken her promise. I shall see to it that your lover and your friend both die horrible deaths for this. You know that, don't you?"

Tolian shuddered. Her fear came pouring back into her. She was almost paralyzed by her trepidation. Yet, somehow, deep inside herself, a certainty came into her. Brythia was beyond Dowbreth's power now. She could feel it. Unfortunately, Tolian and Kreel were not. She hurried deeper into the garden.

"I am coming for you my betrothed," he bellowed violently. "I shall find you."

Chapter 41

The spirit of the flying smoke was clearly not happy with Brythia's defiance. Though none of her senses provided her with input in the normal manner, she became aware that the spirit was wrapping around her, engulfing her essence. It was trying to consume her. She felt her consciousness receding as the life force was drained from her. Psychic suffocation.

"No," she shouted mentally. "Tolian needs me. I can't die now. I can't."

A splash of purple light shot out of the Moonsword and flashed throughout Brythia's being. As if in response, six rays of light, each coming from a different direction and each a different color, converged upon her and the spirit. The rays were charged with tremendous power and each seemed to possess a unique energy. Red. Orange. Yellow. Green. Blue. And indigo. Combined with the purple light the Moonsword was generating, the colors formed a spectrum. Raw energy flooded the realm of the flying smoke, and the rainbow of power poured like a waterfall upon the druidess and the spirit.

The spirit of the flying smoke screamed in pain as the lights pierced his being.

The rainbow beam spoke, each light with its own voice, but in unison. Divine voices, thought Brythia. Only the violet-purple ray was silent.

"She is not for you. You cannot have her. She is on an errand of the gods. None may interfere. Let her pass, for if she fails, all is lost."

The voices passed right through her, charging her with a sense of calmness.

Brythia felt the spirit release her immediately. Divine love surrounded her. She knew what the rays were. The energy of the gods of the spheres. The Moonsword had sent a distress signal and the gods themselves had answered.

Now the voices addressed her. "Go, child of the Earth. Go, and seek your lady. Only you can help her; we cannot directly interfere in the workings of your realm or in Faerie. The future of the created universe rests now with you, and then with her. Travel forth, with the blessing of the gods and of the highest."

Then the lights and the Spirit of the Flying Smoke were gone and Brythia once again became aware of movement. She felt hard stone beneath her feet. A cool evening breeze caressed her cheek (though it was much warmer than the winter's bite she had just left). Strange, indescribable scents accosted her. The rustle of vegetation in the light wind caught her ears. Though her senses were encountering unknown stimuli, they were all working, save one. Her eyes were open, but the images she saw made no sense. There was darkness and shadow, but also strange colors that had no correspondence in the mortal world. A jumble of images, shadowy but bright. Out of focus. She rubbed her eyes, but to no avail. She could make no clear sense of the world around her. She must be in Faerie then, though she had not expected to be without her vision there. Wonderful, she thought.

She gripped the Moonsword in both hands before her. She closed her eyes to shut out the distracting and useless visual input, and stepped forward moving the lunar blade before her.

"Take me to Tolian," she whispered. "Guide me truly and carefully, my friend, for I can't see here."

In response, the Moonsword pulled her gently forward. She followed with slow cautious steps. She had been trained to travel without her sight, as the druidic discipline had required a series of exercises that tested neophytes' abilities without each of their senses. Of course, the sensory input she was experiencing now from her other faculties was nearly overwhelming.

She had only traveled a short distance when she heard a voice with savage inflection cry out in the darkness, "You cannot hide from me. I shall find you."

She had only heard the voice once before, but she knew who it belonged to. Dowbreth. And she knew at once he was looking for Tolian, too.

Chapter 42

Tolian ran now, yet all the while making sure to maintain Kreel's stable transport via her newfound telekinesis. The garden was huge, with acres upon acres of corrupted vegetation reaching out for her, trying desperately to capture her in its slimy tendrils and vines. She moved between terror and rationality. Of course, she was afraid of Dowbreth, and she did not wish to test her power against him if she did not have to. Escape still seemed like the best plan. She stopped for just an instant to listen for him. Nothing. She stayed frozen. No sounds. He could be anywhere. She peered around the moonlit garden. Only the rustle of plants swaying in the breeze, searching for her. It felt like everything in the garden was trying to find her. As if everything were an extension of the Demon. Everything moved with his will. Wait—there was the sound of a footfall twenty or thirty yards to her right. She mentally set Kreel down on the ground for a moment and made secure her grip on her sword. She leaned forward to looked past the hedge hiding her view. She waited, holding her breath.

Then she felt his hand take hold of her from behind and in one motion dislodge her grip on her sword and send her crashing across the pavement stones in the opposite direction. She caught just a glimpse of his fiery red eyes in the moonlight. *Damn*, she thought, feeling her wrist break on impact as she tried to slow her tumble. She hadn't even heard him sneak up on her.

She turned to face Dowbreth who loomed over her with great menace. She held his gaze.

"I am not afraid of you," she declared defiantly. She stretched out her hand, palm outward in his direction, and shot a bolt of energy at him. He fell roughly backwards into a stone wall. Tolian could clearly hear the sound of the impact.

Nevertheless, Dowbreth quickly gained his feet. "You forget," hissed the faerie warlord, "that I have magick of my own." He reached down, pulled the Demon's head out of the sack on his belt, and held it up high. It cackled insanely as he did so.

"You think you truly control the substance of Faerie?" the Demon's head squealed in maniacal fury. "I am the Power of Faerie. It is mine."

And a shadow passed over the Moon and its light was instantly diminished. Tolian felt the mystical energies of the silver sphere that had charged her being ebb all at once. And she knew that her powers were gone. It was just Tolian against her enemies. She looked over hastily at Kreel's sword lying a dozen feet away, barely visible in the darkness.

"Oh, you wish to battle Dowbreth and destroy me," croaked the foul, rotting head. "You are a puny woman, how could you hope to overthrow my power? Take the sword, if it will make you feel better. Dowbreth, set me down over there and battle her. Take your time, cut off her breasts one by one as you do so."

"As you command, my Lord," replied Dowbreth.

There was no fear in her now, only rage. Rage against the evil that she had allowed to go on for too long. She would end it now, somehow. Without the Moon's light, it was difficult to see far in the deepening shadows. She walked the few steps to fetch Kreel's weapon from the pavement. As she reached down to pick it up, she was distracted. A cloaked figure stepped forward from the darkness; she held something in her hands.

"Try this sword, my Lady," said the voice, in a soft whisper.

Tolian's heart leapt. It was Brythia. Tolian just captured a glimpse of her smile under the hood of the cloak. The flash of recognition left her stunned. How was it possible?

"Later," Brythia said in a hushed tone, reading her mind.

The druidess grabbed her wife's arm and whispered, "If the Dark Moon Metal is the lock, then the Moonsword is the key."

The nature-priestess touched the lunar blade to the bracelet and it popped open and fell from Tolian's wrist. Tolian's head was spinning. She took the Moonsword from Brythia's hand, kissed her quickly on the cheek, and turned to face Dowbreth. The faerie was straining to peer into the darkness. He was aware something strange and unexpected had happened, but he obviously had no idea what exactly it was.

As soon the bracelet ceased contact with her skin, Tolian felt all of her power return—not just the telekinesis, but the strength, too. She felt as though she was filled with the purple flame of the Moon. Energy surged from deep within her and she felt as if her soul was on fire.

"Dowbreth," she said, "are you ready to die?"

He snickered. "Woman, will you never learn your place?"

"You know what? I want to see you die more clearly than this." She waved her left arm in the air (her wrist was no longer broken) and the Moon shone forth brightly again. The silver light cascaded upon her. She felt herself glowing with a white brilliance. Pure energy flooded every fiber of her being, moving through her with healing and strength. She leveled her gaze at the giant.

He was afraid. It was that simple. The snicker faded into a fearful frown. His icy pale skin paled even further. Already she felt avenged. In that moment, she taught the giant fear, though he would have little time to indulge that new sensation. He was shaking.

"You have earned the wrath of the Moon Goddess," she said with much drama. "You will die now."

Her movements were too swift for any eye, faerie, mortal, or demonic to perceive. She operated outside, even her own awareness, yet some part of her knew exactly what she was doing. As always, there was a flash of whiteness, of the silver light, and it was done. Dowbreth's corpse lay dead and bloodied at her feet.

Brythia walked slowly up to her and threw herself into Tolian's arms. She buried her head in her bosom. Tolian wrapped her arms around her. It was almost impossible to believe. She felt complete once again. She wanted to hold her beloved in that embrace for all time. Unfortunately, there was still other business at hand. Letting go of Brythia was the last thing she wanted to do at that moment. Tolian did not even know if she would be able to disengage. She smothered the druidess in kisses, and gently broke away from her.

"I'll be right back," she explained, then turned her attention to the Demon's head. She made her way around the giant's sizable cadaver and stared down at the sinister remains of Hertrid's head. The Demon's head. It was chuckling softy. Tolian kicked it over on its side.

"What do you laugh about, fiend? It is over, you have lost," the goddess pointed out to the Demon.

"Oh no, my adversary, it is far from over. Yes, of course, you will destroy this vessel. It is of no consequence; it has served its purpose. In a few moments, this garden will be flooded with all the evil I have wrought here. I have called it here to destroy you. Then, my plans for your world will be unchallenged. You do not yet know how to control your powers enough to survive this. Farewell, Moon Go—"

With a few sword strokes, Tolian rendered the thing an unrecognizable mass of blood. Then she had Brythia in her arms, and their lips pressed together. Their hearts abounded in love. They clutched each other tighter and tighter; tears of happiness streamed down their checks. They were finally together against all hope, against all adversity. Holding Brythia erased the hurt, the loneliness. They didn't need to say anything; words did not matter. They understood each other. Their deepest wishes had come true. Finally, together. Both of them would have given anything to share this moment. But it was only a moment.

"I love you," Tolian finally declared.

"I love you, too."

But before they could savor their reunion, the air filled with the shouts, screams, and cries of foul things. Growing louder. Getting nearer. The Demon had unleashed the twisted hell he had promised—fashioned to annihilate them. And it would be there any moment. Tolian knew she would probably be able to fight them off for quite a while, but even she could not hope to survive against all of Faerie gone mad. It was ironic, Tolian thought, her Moonsword humming with glee in her hand. Here was Brythia, finally in her arms, her powers were restored, she once again possessed her trusty Moonsword, and now they were going to be killed any minute.

"Not much time together," mused Brythia, again reading her mind.

"Well, at least we'll die together," said Tolian.

"It sounds as if they'll be here any—".

"Wait," said Tolian, "what's that?"

"I don't know," Brythia said, sounding as if she were on the verge of laughing in spite of their situation.

She's frightened, Tolian thought. She must be.

"I can't see anything," Brythia said.

"Oh yes," recalled Tolian, "I remember; I had that problem here at first, too. Well, it's like the air around us is boiling, though it's not hot or anything, but that's what it looks like."

That's exactly what it looked like to Tolian. As if the air was churning in a raging boil. Then, suddenly, it became still again, but now an army of Pine Devils appeared, and, unless she was mistaken, Findelbres, wearing his wings, was leading them. Tolian kissed Brythia once again.

Chapter 43

They had all settled in well to life on the Moon, Brythia thought. The tower, their tower, had become so much more vivid and lively a place since she had visited it in her dream. It wasn't an insubstantial, vague backdrop any more. It was real and solid. It felt like home now, though they couldn't have been there more than two weeks. The girls from Tolian's staff in Faerie were all fitting in nicely, and seemed to have quite the hang of the place. Tolian had refused to leave the ruined realm without them, and Findelbres and the Pine Devils had to rescue them as well. Brythia did not allow herself to dwell on the chaotic madness that had all but consumed that enchanted land. Still, the faeries in their company held out hope that one day it could be restored to its former state. Brythia sighed.

She looked out their window. The winged cat, Pilt, who darted past playfully chasing a Will-o-the-Wisp, startled her. In the courtyard below rainbow-colored flowers surrounded gorgeous marble fountains. A small contingent of Pine Devils meandered there, and over by the pond, Kreel and Findelbres were walking. Brythia smiled to herself as she noticed they were holding hands. She looked up in the sky. The Sun was low, but high above, the Earth glowed blue. She turned back to Tolian, who lay naked in their bed.

"I like it here," the Moon Goddess' wife said.

"Me, too," agreed the goddess, "but I'm going to have to go back there sooner or later."

"Well, not today," laughed Brythia. She jumped back in bed and wrapped her arms around Tolian.

Chapter 44

The Solar Pilgrims gave Kiliordes Krin-Gul's old tent. He had protested, but it was to no avail. Krin-Gul had wanted Kiliordes to take over the mantle of chief Solar Pilgrim, and that was exactly what the rest of the pilgrims demanded. They would accept none of Kiliordes' protestations of unworthiness. They had placed all his things in the tent and that was that. He had only gotten there a few hours ago. His journey went smoothly from Lorm, through the foothills of the Haunted Mountains into the kingdom of Surtiz. Though it was only the journey of a few weeks on horseback, it seemed warmer in southern Surtiz. Hints of spring in the breeze whispered soft promises to the winter-weary traveler. Joy seemed to increase with every minute he spent among the jolly pilgrims. He had missed this life, though he had not been able to enjoy it when he had been with them before. He had traveled with the pilgrims as they traveled, moving their brightly colored tents and carrying their constantly roaming party from the estate of one benefactor to another. Always they spread the joy of the Sun. He felt it immediately. They sang hymns and carols to the Daystar almost constantly. Their joy was infectious, even to him this time. He found himself humming a catchy little carol under his breath as he put his things away. Wait, this belonged to Pagyrus, he thought. They've gotten our belongings mixed together.

"Huh," he said. "I wonder what's in this bag." He carefully opened the sack, and rolled the contents onto the table. It was a head—Perelisk's head.

The head's eyes opened and their black orbs fixed upon him. "Hello, Kiliordes, remember me?" it hissed.